VIOLET

SACRAMENTO PUBLIC LIBRARY
828 "I" Street
Sacramento, CA 95814
10/19

D0030757

SCOTT THOMAS

This is a work of fiction. Names, characters, organizations, places, events, and incidents are either products of the author's imagination or are used fictitiously.

Copyright © 2019 Scott Thomas
All rights reserved.

No part of this book may be reproduced, or stored in a retrieval system, or transmitted in any form or by any means, electronic, mechanical, photocopying, recording, or otherwise, without express written permission of the publisher.

Published by Inkshares, Inc., San Francisco, California
www.inkshares.com

Cover design by Lauren Harms
Edited by Adam Gomolin
Interior design by Kevin G. Summers

ISBN: 9781947848368
e-ISBN: 9781947848375
LCCN: 2018943991

First edition

Printed in the United States of America

For Kim
For Aubrey and Cleo
And for my dad

WITHDRAWN FROM
CIRCULATION

PRAISE FOR KILL CREEK

"A menacing and cinematic story that starts off merely creepy but evolves into a bloody, action-driven terrorfest [and] a thought-provoking and enjoyable look at the genre itself, as the characters discuss horror, its history, and its tropes at length. A match for readers who enjoyed Shirley Jackson's *The Haunting of Hill House*."
—*Booklist* (**starred review**)

"Intensely realized and beautifully orchestrated Gothic horror."
—**Joyce Carol Oates**

"Not since I read *The Shining* in eighth grade has a book scared the crap out of me as much as *Kill Creek*. The combo of a great premise and an exquisite ability to conjure dread and terror make Scott Thomas's debut the perfect Halloween treat."
—**Andy Lewis,** *Hollywood Reporter*

"*Kill Creek* is the horror debut of 2017. . . . An intimate, twisted gothic testament to horror as a genre . . . *Kill Creek* is a book from a horror fan to horror fans—creepy, atmospheric, and messed up in all the best ways . . . a must-read for anyone who likes it when their fiction goes to dark places." —**Barnes & Noble Sci-Fi & Fantasy Blog**

"Scott Thomas splendidly creates a fascinating co-dependency between the spooky edifice and the folk that perpetuate (and amplify) its morbid history. Thomas does a fine job with his characters, and the atmosphere is chock-full of delightfully unsettling images. Horror aficionados will welcome it with open arms." —*Scream* **magazine**

"Suspenseful, foreboding, and macabre, *Kill Creek* is high-grade horror, successfully bringing together old-world classics like *The Haunting of Hill House* by Shirley Jackson, elements of the highly stylized Japanese scare movies like *The Ring*, and a bit of *The Amityville Horror* to give readers original twists and deathly scares."
—**Fantasy-Faction**

"There'll be no admonitions to read this one with the lights on or alone at night. That's a given. Alone or with friends, lights blazing, or a single reading lamp casting shadows over the page, it won't matter. The result will be the same: shivers for many nights afterward. *Kill Creek* is the perfect novel to read on Halloween."
—**New York Journal of Books**

"*Kill Creek* is a slow-burn, skin-crawling haunted house novel with a terrifying premise and a shockingly brutal gut-punch of a conclusion. This debut establishes Scott Thomas as a force to be reckoned with on the horror scene. His remarkable ability to build tension and suspense had me on the edge of my seat until the last page."
—**Shane D. Keene,** *HorrorTalk*

"*Kill Creek* delivers the cinematic scares of *The Conjuring* without losing a literary feel. This is the kind of book that reminds you binge-reading came way before binge-watching." —**Kailey Marsh, BloodList**

"Gives us just the right kinds of Halloween-spirit thrills while throwing in some new twists, and great characters." —*Horrible Imaginings* **podcast**

"I thought there were no more good haunted house stories to tell until I read *Kill Creek*. Scott Thomas uses a foundation of the expected tropes to build a story with not just a classic horror ambiance but also a unique architecture of tension." —**J-F. Dubeau, author of *A God in the Shed***

"An exquisite horror tale . . . The story's unique blend of literary horror and psychological thriller made it an addictive read."
—**BiblioSanctum**

A group of best-selling horror writers team up for a publicity stunt at an infamous abandoned haunted house in the Kansas countryside, and guess what happens? Shit gets real!!! They end up awakening an entity that comes after them. That is creepy and crazy and it has a vibe like, hey, guys, you kind of had it coming. Oh, and it all goes down ON Halloween night. Yeah, *this* is an obvious All Hallows Read selection." —**Geeks of Doom**

Friendship is one mind in two bodies.

—Mencius

Sorrow's child sits by the water
Sorrow's child your arms enfold her
Sorrow's child you're loathe to befriend her
Sorrow's child but in sorrow surrender
And just when it seems as though
All your tears were at an end
Sorrow's child lifts up her hand
And she brings it down again

—Nick Cave & the Bad Seeds, "Sorrow's Child"

PROLOGUE

UNDER THE RIVER

SHE KNEW ALMOST nothing about the history of the town.

She did not know that once upon a time, the town was not a town at all but a wound in the gypsum hills overrun by Johnsongrass, musk thistle, and milkweed. In those days, the Verdigris River slithered like a brown, muddy snake through the lowlands, the curve of its back brushing up against the towering stalks of thick weeds. The Kiowa called this place *p'oiye tsape t'on,* meaning "hidden water," because not a glint of sunlight on the surface of the river could be seen from the steep ridges overlooking the area. There was no reason to go down into the impenetrable brush. There were no animals worth hunting there, no vegetation worth picking.

The town itself seemed to appear out of nowhere, a collection of small, one-room structures along a dirt road etched into the wild countryside. At one end of the basin, the gypsum hills parted like stone curtains, just enough to allow the road to enter. At the other end, the dirt path hugged closer to the river, following its curve around the bluffs. And then, suddenly, the path shot straight north as if startled out of the odd valleys, back into the vast Kansas prairie.

She did not know that the town's name, Pacington, was nothing more than a bastardization of the original words. But many had forgotten its origin. By the time the first shop owners opened their doors along Center Street, the Native Americans living in Southeast Kansas had long ago been "relocated" to Oklahoma. As more and more white settlers found their way between the river basin, fewer bothered to consider the people who had lived there before them. The untamed tangles of brush and vine along this section of the Verdigris belonged to the town of Pacington.

She vaguely remembered the stories her father told her about the day the Army Corps of Engineers began construction on a reservoir just outside of town. Their intention was to control flooding to the farmland along the river, but on the second day, workers broke through into a chasm hidden beneath the river floor, unleashing a body of water buried eons ago by the shifting earth. It swirled up through the lazy current of the Verdigris and pushed its edges deep into the surrounding forest. In a matter of minutes, the river became a lake, the fleeing water moving too quickly for man or machine to escape. Two workers lost their lives that day. They were swept down into an ancient abyss, the depth of which easily swallowed fifty feet of a toppled crane. The equipment was recovered, but the bodies were not. Some said they just kept drifting down, down, deeper into the dark, endless waters of that underground lake, forever falling into the earth.

Those unlucky enough to own property along Lower Basin Road were paid a reasonable sum by the government. The peak of one roof breaking the water's surface was all that was left to remind them of what they had lost. A new site farther south, near the town of Oologah, Oklahoma, was chosen for the intended reservoir, and so the Army Corps of Engineers left behind an accidental body of water and more than a little of their pride.

In a single day, Pacington was transformed from a river town to a lake town. For a while, the government's blunder appeared to be a blessing in disguise. The water in what became known as "Lost Lake" was remarkably clear, a sliver of glass nestled between the red gypsum hills. The cool blue oasis was a summer destination for locals desperate to escape the sweltering heat of Southeast Kansas and Northeast Oklahoma. Pacington was a refuge.

The contrast between the pristine appearance of the lake and the brownish-green waters of the Verdigris River that fed into and from it were striking. The explanation was fairly mundane: the floor of the lake was essentially a crater in the earth, composed of the lighter solid granite than existed beneath the muddy bed of the rest of the Verdigris. That did not stop some from viewing Lost Lake as a natural—or in some cases, supernatural—wonder.

She had first glimpsed the sparkling ripples playing across the lake's surface when she was four years old. That was in 1982, and the town had been a quaint lakeside resort for over two decades. That was the Pacington she remembered. That was the place where mornings were for sleeping in late, where afternoons were filled with hiking and fishing and rowing, where evenings were painted pink by brilliant sunsets above the hills as her father grilled largemouth bass over a smoldering mound of charcoal. She could smell the life of the forest on the air and stare into an infinite field of diamond-like stars at night. She could imagine anything in the Pacington of her memories, for it was a land where lakes could spring from the ground without warning. It was a place of creation.

Yet there was much she did not know. She did not know that, in this place of beauty, something dark and malicious was mutating beneath her mother's sun-kissed skin. She did not know that her parents had been aware of it since she was three, or that it was the reason her father had bought the summerhouse on the shore of Lost Lake. She did not know that every summer, her mother was getting sicker, that every day they spent was not the beginning of their life together but the end. She did not know that, after she went to bed, her parents cried and held each other, that they tiptoed out of the lake house one night to make love on the shore.

She did not know of the unspeakable things that came after she left—the shadow that fell over Pacington, the pain and fear that twisted through the town like a barbed, poisonous vine.

Perhaps it was for the best. Sometimes it is easier to not know. Life is happier lived in ignorance.

But that does not mean the unspeakable things are not there. They are simply hidden, like water beneath the ground, searching for a way to flow into the light.

PART ONE

THERE IS A LIGHT THAT NEVER GOES OUT

CHAPTER ONE

THE ROAD SLICED a gray line through the black night. Beyond the beams of her headlights, the land was at the mercy of the moonlight. She imagined the road ending without warning, driving over the edge, plummeting into an infinite nothingness, until her screams became a song for the darkness.

It was silly to think such things, but the threads of her life, the loose pieces she had tried for so long to keep in place, had finally unraveled. And so she drove, her eyes on the farthest edge of the headlights' reach, staring at that line where vision failed and the world became shadow.

Kris Barlow glanced at herself in the rearview mirror and saw a stranger staring back at her. The soft glow of the dashboard deepened the hint of crow's feet that stretched from the corners of her eyes. Her porcelain skin attempted to peek through large clusters of freckles. She wished her mother had forced her to wear sunscreen when she was little, as Kris did religiously with her own daughter. But that was a different time, before words like "SPF" and "reapply" were drilled into the vocabulary of children. She recalled the odd satisfaction of slowly peeling away thin layers of dead, translucent skin, trying to keep a large section intact. Once, she managed to remove a patch as large as the palm of her hand. She placed it carefully over her right cheek and admired herself in the bathroom mirror, feeling like a lizard as the edges of the old pulled back to reveal the new.

Kris stared at her face in the rearview mirror. When had she become this person? If the measure of her lifespan were her father, who passed away at eighty-two, then she had officially reached the midpoint. If it were her mother, Kris was knock-knock-knockin' on heaven's door.

In the back seat, something shifted.

Kris adjusted the rearview mirror until she could see the pale form of Sadie leaning against the side window. The seat belt held her upright, her head hanging limply, chin against her chest. Spirals of red hair twisted down around her sleeping eyes. An iPad and a notebook lay on the seat next to her, both untouched since they'd hit the road.

That was me, a thousand years ago. Kris could still picture her father driving, his hands obediently at ten and two, and her mother reading by the soft glow of a penlight.

Back then, they'd always waited until her father was done with work before hitting the road. It was less than a two-hour drive, so leaving their home in Blantonville at seven or eight in the evening did not seem like such a big deal. They would hear his key in the lock, and Krissy would leap up from the beanbag chair in front of the living room television and race to throw her arms around his waist. It was Daddy, still in his work clothes, the perfect pleats of his slacks, the smooth brown leather of his belt, the stiff, starched shirt and wide, striped tie. As a child, Kris grappled to understand exactly what her father did for a living.

"I sell insurance," he had told her on more than one occasion. "It's like the promise that someone will be there if things go wrong."

Now she knew the truth. Insurance meant hours of phone calls and stacks of paperwork. It meant dealing with a company that searched for any conceivable loophole to get out of paying what they had promised. It meant waiting months, sometimes even years, before the check arrived, if it ever did.

Kris knew the people who were there in an instant when things went wrong, and the insurance company was not one of them.

Not that she had wanted anyone there. Not the neighbors who arrived on her doorstep with still-warm casserole dishes in their hands, as if potatoes covered in cheese and corn flakes could resurrect a loved one. Not the parents from Sadie's school, who secretly hoped for the destruction of others' happiness to prove that their own miserable existences were not as bad as they feared. Not the relatives who'd never thought she was good enough in the first place, the ones who'd placed him on that pedestal and convinced her that she had to rise up to his level.

They had not seen what she had seen. None of them were there when the police called in the middle of the night. They did not know the ice-cold panic of realizing your entire life had just been shattered into a million jagged pieces by the ring of a cell phone.

She knew. She knew the uncanny artificiality as she arrived at the Lake County Coroner's Office in downtown Black Ridge, Colorado. The reception area could have been the front desk of any small-town motel. A fake plastic plant, its warped green leaves covered in dust, stood in the corner beside an oddly placed wooden chair, white stuffing peeking out at the seat cushion's edge. A random collection of fashion and outdoor magazines lay spread across a glass coffee table, as if anyone there to identify a body would want to first flip through a six-month-old issue of *Guns & Ammo*. The beige walls of the room did not appear to have been painted that color; rather, the original white had curdled over the years, aged by the medicinal stench of embalming chemicals and the dread of those who walked through the front door.

This is a waiting room, she thought. *This is purgatory.*

No one had been there to greet her. Not the officer who had woken her at three in the morning, when Jonah should have been home, snoring beside her. Not whoever had left the front door unlocked in anticipation of her arrival. She was welcomed only by the soft rattle of a loose air-conditioning vent and the noxious aroma of chemicals and raw meat seeping in from another room.

Kris blinked, and the highway was once again before her.

She could hear the steady hum of tires skimming across asphalt, hundreds of miles of rough, uneven surface peeling tiny bits of rubber away like sunburned skin.

She knew there was no use searching the radio for music. On the open prairie, closer to dawn than dusk, she would find only static and the rabid shouts of a fire-and-brimstone preacher.

Reaching to the center console, she felt for the charging cord leading to her cell phone. For a moment, her thumb traced the edges of the home button as she considered opening Spotify or Audible, anything to fill the silence.

Behind her, Sadie whimpered softly.

Kris took her eyes off the road just long enough to glance over her shoulder. Sadie had shifted, but her eyes were still closed, head slumped, her curly red hair draped over her face.

Kris let the phone slip from her hand.

Don't wake her. Let her sleep. We'll be there in a few hours.

Far off in the distance, she could barely see the headlights of an approaching car, two pinpricks hovering like the eyes of an animal stalking through the night.

A raccoon.

Or a fox.

Fox.

That had been his name.

Howard Fox.

She had seen the name before she saw the man. It was printed in a large, sweeping script at the center of a very official-looking certificate adorned with a gold-leaf stamp and a thick, shimmery blue border:

**THE COLORADO CORONER-MEDICAL EXAMINER ASSOCIATION
HEREBY CERTIFIES THAT
HOWARD FOX
HAS COMPLETED THE REQUIRED CURRICULUM FOR
DEATH INVESTIGATION**

The term had plucked a sour chord from her already frayed nerves. "Death Investigation."

The sudden opening of a door had startled her, and she had felt her entire body stiffen.

Like the bodies that were growing ever more rigid in the back room.

Like Jonah's body.

A plain, slightly doughy man wearing round, wire-rimmed glasses was standing in the doorway. His mouth was frozen in the habitual hint of a compassionate smile, the exact same expression he offered every confused, distraught visitor who stumbled through the front entrance.

"I'm so sorry," Howard Fox said. His voice had a strange, thin quality to it, as if he were constantly fighting a sneeze. "I didn't expect you so quickly. I thought you were coming from farther away or I would have been here to greet you."

"I live—" Kris's words caught in her throat. She swallowed and tried again. "I live in town. I've seen this place before, but I've never been inside . . ."

"No reason for you to," Howard replied, his brow furrowing in a robotic attempt to convey sympathy. "Please, follow me. If you're ready."

He did not wait for confirmation before turning and disappearing through the open doorway. Perhaps he knew that if he left the decision to Kris, she would freeze in place, her muscles refusing every command to keep her from entering that room.

From seeing Jonah.

No, not Jonah. The thing that had been Jonah. The mangled shell he had left behind.

Instead, she took a step without realizing it. And then another. And another.

A waft of frigid air greeted her, and she shivered, her entire body prickling with gooseflesh.

Howard waited off to her left until Kris was well into the room, then he swung the door shut behind her. The door latched into place with a dull thud that echoed softly off the surfaces of the hard, cold room. This place was not for the living. It was a place of dissection, of splitting rib cages and weighing organs like lettuce at the supermarket.

Metal shelves were crowded with plastic bottles full of instruments soaking in neon blue and yellow liquids. Several cabinets made from sleek stainless steel lined the other walls. A massive LED spotlight stretched down from the ceiling on a hinged arm like the staring, cyclopean eye of an alien creature, projecting a cone of bright, pristine light onto the black plastic sheet that rose into a vaguely human shape.

"I know this is a very difficult thing to do," Howard said from just over her shoulder.

Kris flinched. She had forgotten he was in the room with her.

"Take all the time you need—"

"I want to see him," Kris said, cutting him off.

"Are you sure?"

"I don't want to think about it. I just want to do it."

Howard nodded. "Right. Of course."

The rubber soles of Howard's bright white Nike sneakers squeaked on the equally pristine tile floor as he crossed to the gurney. He grasped the top of the plastic sheet with both hands. Kris could see the hairs on his knuckles blowing like cattails in an invisible breeze from the overhead AC vent. Nearby, an exhaust van whirred as it sucked the air from the room and into what must have been the brightening purple sky of approaching dawn.

But Kris had no way of knowing anything about the outside world, about anything outside of that cold, sterile room.

Howard pulled back the sheet. He took a wide step to the side and clasped his hands in front of him.

"Whenever you're ready," he said.

Kris's mind tried to stop her. *Wait—*

But she was already moving, her legs propelling her forward before her brain could override them. Her hip bumped the edge of the gurney. She was there.

At first her mind could not make sense of the shape before her. There were no familiar landmarks to convince her that what she was seeing was a face. Where the cheekbones normally would have protruded, there was a deep valley that ran horizontally over the tip of what should have been his nose. Something had smashed it all in.

The steering wheel.

"The airbag never deployed," Howard said, as if reading her mind. "Could probably sue the automobile company, you know, if you . . ." He let his words drift off, perhaps realizing that it was not the time to speak of litigation.

Below the mashed, indented thing that had once been his nose, Jonah's lips were closed, and yet Kris could see the top row of his teeth. Her brain stuttered, bare wires crossing, the contradictory images causing a split-second glitch in the system.

And then she realized what she was seeing: the impact had folded Jonah's top teeth up so that they pointed straight out from his face, and the edges of his incisors had been forced through the skin above his upper lip. He looked as though he were eating his own mouth.

Dark, thick blood traced a line between the side of his face and the surface of the metal gurney. Kris followed this like the red line of a river on a state map—up past a chewed piece of flesh that could be pieced together, with some imagination, to resemble an ear—to the source of the blood: a wet, matted clump of long, brown hair just above his temple.

There were diamonds in his hair, nestled like stones in seaweed. They glistened in the fluorescent light.

No, not diamonds, she knew. *Glass.*

Shattered pebbles of tempered glass, embedded in his scalp.

The entire right side of his head was completely flat, like a cartoon character hit with a frying pan. The once-sturdy skull was nothing but a patch of bloody sludge. She could press her fingers into that red mud if she wanted to, digging her fingertips all the way into the spongy gray center of his brain.

Jonah had been starting to show his age—his toned body beginning to sag in places, his face puffy from drinking, silver peppering his brown stubble whenever he put off shaving for a week—but she had always been able to look at him and see the man she had fallen in love with all those years ago.

Had loved, Kris thought.

Still loved, another voice insisted. This was hopeful Kris. Naïve Kris.

Hated, a third Kris chimed in. The voice echoed up from the blackest depths of her mind.

She looked down at the swollen, battered face of her dead husband, one eye bashed to a deep purple, sealed shut like a heavyweight boxer in the twelfth round, the other open, staring upward at some profound knowledge revealed only to the dying. Was it love that kept her from instantly glancing away in disgust? Or had her heart flipped a switch to survival mode, the same sensation one feels when slowing down to gawk at a terrible accident on the highway, that sense of morbid relief that washes over as one realizes, *Not my time. Not yet. Not yet.*

With clenched teeth, Kris leaned closer to Jonah's tortured corpse. Her right hand began to tremble, and she quickly clamped her left hand around her wrist to steady it, but the sensation was loose, working its way up her arm and across her shoulders. Her entire body shook, each breath a series of sharp, staccato thumps, like a car driving over a bad stretch of road. She forced her lips within inches of that torn, dangling flap of shredded flesh that had been Jonah's ear.

"You asshole," she whispered as fresh tears slipped down her cheeks. "You dumb, selfish son of a bitch. I'll never forgive you for this. Never."

The sound of an explosion, like a shotgun blast, thrust Kris brutally back into the present.

The Jeep was veering sharply to the left, into the other lane.

Sadie was instantly awake, crying out in desperate confusion, not with words—she hadn't spoken more than a handful since her daddy died—but with an animalistic howl. The fear in that sound sent a sheet of ice grazing across Kris's skin.

Instinctively, Kris clamped both hands down on the steering wheel, the toe of her right boot mashing the brake pedal.

The back of the Jeep began to skid.

Sadie's high-pitched screams mixed with another shriek that, for a second, Kris could not place.

Tires. The shriek of rubber tires trying to grip the asphalt.

She jerked the wheel to the right. The Jeep reentered her lane, but Kris realized immediately that she had overcorrected. The car careened across the lane at a dangerously sharp angle. Beyond the dirt shoulder was a barbed-wire fence marking the border of someone's farmland.

She was instantly aware of two things—the pale orb of the moon reflected in the glass of the windshield, and the sensation that the Jeep was leaning to the left, that half of the vehicle was struggling to keep up, an animal with a lame leg.

"Hold on!" she heard herself yell back to her daughter. Kris turned the wheel to the left, just enough to keep the car from leaving the shoulder and entering the shallow ravine that cut through the weeds beside the fence. At the same time, she let off of the brake, waiting until the Jeep was under control before returning her foot to the pedal.

Brake. Release. Brake. Release. Brake.

They were slowing.

Now there was a new sound, the unmistakable *thwump-thwump-thwump* of a flat tire trudging over the dry ground.

Kris pressed her boot down hard onto the pedal and the Jeep skidded to a stop. Dust billowed around them. She watched as it wafted into the headlight beams, twin souls escaping into the night.

She glanced over her shoulder at her daughter. Sadie's eyes were wide in frozen panic. But she was quiet. She did not cry.

She's trying to be strong. For you.

"It's just a flat tire. Everything's okay," Kris assured her "There's a spare in the back. I'll change the tire. It's fine, Sadie. We're fine. I promise."

Kris reached for the door handle. She felt something tug on the back of her shirt.

Sadie was leaning forward in her seat, an arm stretched out to stop her mother.

"It's okay. It won't take long. I'll be right outside."

Sadie's fingers loosened, just enough for Kris to pull the fabric of the shirt from her grasp.

Kris opened the door and stepped out.

A cool wind whipped over the prairie and curled around her body. Kris pulled stray auburn locks from her face and tucked them behind her ear. She looked down at the front tire. The metal rim rested on deflated rubber. A flap of black tread dangled from an open wound near the top of the tire.

Like Jonah's ear, dangling from the side of his head.

Her legs began to tremble. The tremors worked their way up her torso and into her shoulders. Her body quaked.

She closed her eyes and breathed in deeply through her nose. She could smell the Kansas countryside: the ripe green wheat; the powdery earth of the dirt shoulder; the harsh bite of burned rubber still lingering in the air.

It's just a flat tire, she reminded herself.

Her body calmed. She opened her eyes again.

The moon had disappeared behind a thick layer of clouds. Even the stars seemed to have retreated into the black sky. The ground below her was gone. She was floating in an abyss.

Kris Barlow stared at the point where the headlights lost their battle with the dark and the night consumed them. She had to believe there was a road in that void beyond the headlight beams. She needed the road to be there.

Because she could not go back.

Not yet.

Not yet.

CHAPTER TWO

THE SOUND OF the car had changed. The chorus of tires now had a soprano, as the spare tire—a compact donut whose tread was half the width of the others—worked double time in its frantic effort to keep up.

Kris glanced down at the speedometer. A sticker affixed to the sidewall of the donut had warned not to push it past fifty miles per hour, but only when the needle was edging closer to seventy did she ease up on the accelerator.

She could feel her destination drawing her forward into the darkness like a magnet.

In her chest, something fluttered, like the tickle of feathers. It was as if the Jeep had suddenly dropped down a steep hill, even though the road before her was as straight and level as the last hundred miles.

It was the same sensation she had felt when she woke two nights before, her body slick with cold sweat.

Filling her mind had been a perfect image of the house. It could not have been more clear if someone had held a photograph before her eyes. Eventually the house faded, her eyelids drooped, and Kris fell back asleep. But even in the morning, she could not shake the residual image, burned like a nuclear shadow into her brain.

The house. Surrounded on both sides by trees. The blue sky reflected in its windows. The shimmer of sunlight on the lake just down the steep slope of the backyard.

It had been a week since they lowered Jonah into the ground. In that week, Sadie had not cried. She had remained silent, choosing instead to communicate through simple nods and shakes of her head.

Kris had cried, alone in her bed at night. She had clamped her hands over her mouth, trying to muffle the sounds, hoping Sadie was fast asleep. First she had cried out of sadness, then anger, then loneliness as she realized this was the rest of her life.

When she had slept, she dreamed of a deep black hole in the earth, of staring into that darkness as if waiting for something to emerge. She knew something was down there. She did not want to be near when it came roaring out of the blackness, and yet she could not look away. She stared into the impenetrable depths, fully aware that the thing down there in the shadows was staring back with wide, unblinking eyes, its lips curled over slick, wet teeth. And then the image of the house had reappeared, and Kris no longer felt like crying. She no longer worried about the thing in the hole in the earth.

The next morning, she had dragged the large, black trash barrel in from the garage and began clearing the refrigerator of the leftovers from Jonah's wake—trays of hardening cheeses and drying meats, aluminum pans of gelatinous pasta, drawers of wilted lettuce and shriveled carrot and cucumber slices.

She remembered their faces, the family and friends who had stopped by to offer condolences. The pity didn't bother her; she had expected that. Nor did the morbid curiosity of those who came simply to see how a middle-aged woman dealt with the death of her husband. No, the one thing she had not prepared herself for was the hint of accusation in some of their eyes. She had not thought they would choose sides. And yet a few of them—not many, but enough to convince her it was not coincidence—smiled with narrowed eyes that said, *You brought this on yourself.* They thought they had accomplished something by judging her, by gloating in the face of her pain.

But they no longer mattered. There was the house, and the house called for her to return. It was an opportunity to heal. It was hope.

School was over by then, and Sadie had missed the last few days of her second-grade year. So when Kris announced that they would be going away for a couple months, her silent little girl simply shrugged. Then Sadie returned to her bedroom, where she buried her face in her pillow, as if hoping that when she opened her eyes, the illusion of happiness she had known since birth would be restored.

This is a good idea, Kris had told herself. *The house is exactly what we need.*

She waited for the second voice to speak. It always did, especially when she felt conviction. It spoke in that irritatingly unsure tone, as if it felt a sense of purpose in casting doubt. It was only a fleeting moment, and then, just as she had expected, Timid Kris worked a fissure into the peace like water in a stone, splitting it with her favorite word: *But.*

But . . . this is her home. She might be better off here, with her friends.

They'll only remind her. They won't let her move on, Kris shot back.

In the pitch black, far in the recesses of her mind, something squeaked: a tiny door creaking open, just a crack, enough to let that taunting third voice through. Her shadow voice. From behind that door, Shadow Kris purred, *It doesn't matter where you go. Her daddy's dead. And what if, God-forbid, something happens to you? What then? Sadie will be alone. All alone. All alone . . .*

Kris squinted as she imagined forcing that little door shut. Even then, she could still hear the soft scratching of nails against its far side and the muffled whisper of the truths she wished were lies.

We're going, Kris had thought. *We* have *to go.*

No sooner had she made this mental declaration than she was overcome by a sense of dread. The house might not be available.

Not long after her mother's death, Kris's father had made it available for rent. They had become a family of two, and a trip to the lake for summer vacation no longer held a sense of release. Besides, Dad was spending more and more time in his woodworking shop behind the garage, and Kris was often out with her friends, riding bikes along Sycamore Creek or hanging out in the empty bleachers at the middle-school football field. When she pedaled into the garage each evening, she could still smell the earthy odor of sawdust and whiskey in the air.

A real estate agent in Pacington had handled the day-to-day—drawing up the contracts, supplying keys to renters, hiring the cleaning crew. And so it went, as far as Kris knew, the modest two-story house on the rocky slope overlooking Lost Lake's crystal-clear waters abandoned to a revolving door of strangers.

When her father finally passed away from cirrhosis a year ago, it had occurred to Kris that she should phone the agent, if for no other reason than to make sure the rent money wasn't going straight into his pocket. But she never made that call.

Now the idea of spending the summer at the lake house had taken root in her mind, and she knew she could no longer ignore it.

According to Google, there was only one real estate company in Pacington: Mid-Nation Realty. Clicking on the link took her to Mid-Nation's homepage, where buttons in the lower right corner offered two options: "buy" or "rent." She had clicked "rent" and mentally crossed her fingers.

She could not recall the exact address, although the words "River Road" materialized from the roiling black fog on her distant memories. It was the antiquated nature of the name that allowed it to survive the erosion of time: the "River" the road had once chased had been swallowed by the lake decades ago.

She had typed these words into the search window, tapped the return key, and watched as a new page loaded. She had felt her chest hitch and a cool breath suck quickly between her barely parted lips.

The thumbnail image was barely one inch by one inch, but she recognized the house instantly. After all, it had been appearing in her mind practically every hour on the hour. She slid her finger over the trackpad and clicked.

In a bold sans serif font, the listing christened this property a "Charming Summer Home on the Shores of Breathtaking Lost Lake!" There was a gallery of nearly twenty pictures, and as she scrolled through them, she felt as though she were seeing through a tear in the fabric of time. In a way, she was. The soft focus and faded colors instantly told her she was looking not at the multiple-megapixel snapshots of a modern digital camera but at photos taken on actual film. The glowing orange date stamp in the corner of each photo confirmed this: 4/23/98.

At the bottom of the screen, a rectangular box contained the words: "Check for Availability." For the second time, Kris had drawn in a nervous breath as she forced her finger down on the trackpad.

All of June was wide open, as was July and August and September. Unless there was a problem with the site, the lake house at 106 River Road was free and clear through the end of December.

Kris had sat back from the iMac that was wedged into a too-small shelf in the mudroom, and she realized she was smiling.

Okay. This could work. This could actually work.

She clicked the contact us tab, and a fresh email opened in a new window. There was no way she was paying the listed rate of $105 a day for a house her family had owned since she was five. Her fingertips flew over the keys, the driving rhythm of her typing growing faster and faster until her eyes could barely keep up with the words as they scrolled across the screen. She hit send without looking back through what she had written. And then she waited.

Thirty minutes later, a *ding* announced the arrival of an email from Mid-Nation's one and only agent, Darryl Hargrove. His response began with the expected pleasantries. He knew Kris's father well and had been saddened to hear of his passing. He had been a "good man" who was "always pleasant" and "very proud of his family." How the hell Darryl Hargrove knew that her father was proud of his family was anyone's guess. The next few lines proved to be less helpful. Yes, Hargrove admitted, their lake house was available, but it hadn't been rented in some time and probably needed some "sprucing up." He could offer Kris any number of other summer homes around Lost Lake or, better yet, a house in town just off Center Street, "a block away from Pacington's best shops and restaurants." Free of charge, of course.

A house off Center Street hasn't been stuck in my goddamn head like the catchiest pop song ever written, Kris thought. What she wrote in her reply was considerably more polite. A little dust didn't scare her. She wanted their house, please and thank you.

"This is going to be good," she had whispered to herself as she waited for those other voices in her head to announce their protest. But they remained strangely, suspiciously silent.

Kris had packed their things in a single afternoon. Duffel bags full of clothes. Cardboard boxes of items she knew Sadie would miss—stuffed animals, blankets, chapter books, and, of course, art supplies. The girl had never picked up a sketchpad or notebook that she didn't desperately need. Before the accident, back when Sadie had a shimmering light behind her eyes, she would sit for hours filling blank pages with her drawings. Sometimes they were landscapes crawling with colorful insects and exotic beasts. Other times they were intricate designs and patterns of her own invention.

But in the days since Jonah's death, not a single notebook was opened, not a single crayon was picked up. Kris packed them anyway. She longed to see that light again. She could not allow herself to believe that it had been snuffed out.

Two days after waking to the impossibly real image of the lake house in her mind, Kris and Sadie were on the road. They drove out of Black Ridge as the sun broke over Mount Ash, the shadow of its jagged peak like a broken tooth. In her rearview mirror, the mountains of Colorado sank down below the horizon, and the shimmering waves of the Great Plains stretched out before her, beckoning them like the mirage of a waterless sea.

Gold fire burned a line across the horizon, melting away the night. Soon the deep blue would fade like a bruise, and the sky would become a robin's egg, its color swept away in places by wisps of white cloud.

They were headed straight for the house. Despite the fact that there was still over eighty miles to drive, Kris could feel it there, just past the edge of the world. She was on the descent, like a rocket being drawn back to Earth by the pull of gravity. This arc in the highway would deliver them straight to its door.

It was waiting for them.

Empty.

Eager for their arrival.

In the back seat, Sadie shifted uncomfortably. She said nothing, but Kris knew what this sound meant, the refrain of every child, dead father or not: *Are we there yet?*

"Not much longer," Kris assured her.

Tell me about the house, she imagined Sadie asking. Kris rarely heard her daughter's voice these days. When Sadie did speak, her words were flat and emotionless. They no longer danced on the sweet, lilting breeze of her childish voice. They bore a cautious skepticism no eight-year-old should know.

"The house . . ." Kris began. She could see it again, right in front of her. She forced herself to look through it, to keep her eyes safely on the road ahead.

"The first thing you'll notice, when we get close, is the lake through the trees."

She remembered being a little girl, sitting up in her seat to peer out the side window of her father's station wagon. Through the trees, she glimpsed it—light on the water—and a shiver of excitement stirred in her chest. It was as if the branches had parted just enough to let her, and only her, see through, as if she were getting a peek at a magical place.

But the house . . . the house was the true gift. The same thought occurred to her each time they rumbled slowly through the open gate and down the smooth concrete drive: the forest had given this house to them. A thousand years ago, the forest had opened up and there it was, built from the wood of the trees, from the stones of the earth.

Unbuckling her seat belt, little Krissy would slip to the edge of the vinyl seat and peer over her mother's shoulder as, through the windshield, a fairy-tale illustration came to life before her eyes.

A simple brick path leading to the house cut a passageway between bushes thick with wildflowers. Honey bees clung to the petals, their legs fat with pollen. To one side, ringed at its base by patches of orange butterfly milkweed blooms, was a ceramic birdbath. The statuettes of two bluebirds perched, motionless, on either side of the basin. Birds of all sizes and colors—cardinals, blue jays, finches, sparrows—flocked to this shallow pool, its water warmed by the summer sun, just as people in neighboring towns flocked to Lost Lake. The front yard was alive with the buzz of insects and the cheerful whistles of songbirds.

At the end of the path, three steps rose up to the porch. Four columns of stacked river rock, held in place by gray mortar, rose three feet from the wooden floor, and then thick pine trunks sprouted from the top of each one, as if the trees had forced their way up through the stone to be part of the house.

The outside of the house was painted a pristine white, and it glowed in the sunlight as if it had been sprinkled with fairy dust. Around each window was a cherry-red frame that popped against the white clapboards like lipstick on a shirt collar.

There were two things in particular that filled young Krissy with the sensation of being a princess spirited away to a secret retreat in the woods. The first was the thick-cut western cedar roof, gray and weathered nearly to the point of petrification. The humid summers had warped the shingles into their own unique shapes. Wedged into the wide spaces between the shingles were dried leaves from autumns past. Patches of bright green moss dotted the roof. This was the roof of a princess's hideaway, like the fairies' cottage where Princess Aurora was taken as a baby in hopes that her delicate fingers would never feel the cursed prick of a needle.

The other was the oval window on the right side of the second story. It, too, was trimmed in a brilliant red, but its shape, when coupled with the sunlight glinting off its textured glass, gave it the appearance of a coin at the bottom of a fountain. When the shade was pulled halfway down, it looked like the house was winking—

"Winking?" Sadie whispered in disbelief.

The sound of Sadie's voice jolted Kris. She hadn't realized she'd actually been speaking aloud. She rose up in her seat to get a better look into the rearview mirror. Sadie was staring out the window, watching the countryside flash by, her face slack, expressionless.

"Yeah. That's right, sweetie."

Flicking on her blinker, Kris steered the Jeep over to the next exit ramp and onto Highway 75. A mere ten miles more and they would leave the highway altogether, exiting to a narrower two-lane road that dipped low between hills much rockier than the lush green mounds of the Flint Hills through which they had just passed.

"I can even remember the way the place smelled," Kris told her daughter. "Right when you walk in, it's like the wood in the walls is still alive. At the back of the house, it's all windows, the whole wall. They look like they stretch up to the sky. You can see the lake from there, behind the house. Sadie, you've never seen water as clear as this. It's like liquid glass. And behind, that's the red hills, redder than the windows on the house, and you have to wonder if this is just . . ."

She didn't say it. She couldn't. Not aloud.

So her mind finished it for her: . . . *make believe.*

The highway, as straight and narrow as every other road they had driven on since entering the Sunflower State, began to dip into the basin of Southeast Kansas. Without warning, the road sloped sharply down as it prepared to pass beneath a rusty, vine-covered railroad bridge. Tendrils hung down like dangling arms, leafy fingers attempting to caress the top of their car as they passed.

The Jeep shot through the shadow cast by the bridge. The vines swung in their wake like a hangman's ropes. Kris forced these dark thoughts away. She focused on the house. *Their* house. The reason they had traveled all night to this place.

For Sadie. Because this place could make things a little better. Just as it had for Kris.

"Behind the house, there's a dock, and a rowboat we can take out on the lake. What do you think of that?" She didn't bother waiting for the reply she knew would never come. "It's going to be good, Sadie. You'll have your own room. And upstairs there's a playroom—"

"What's that writing?" Sadie asked. Her soft voice seemed so fragile, the fluffy white mound of a dandelion head, destroyed by the slightest breeze.

Kris glanced up at the reflection of her daughter in the mirror.

"Writing on what?"

Sadie was craning her neck to try to get one last look at something behind them.

"On the bridge?" And then Kris gave a nod, realizing, "You mean graffiti? Was it graffiti?"

Sadie scrunched her eyes, clearly not understanding.

"It's when people spray-paint things like their names on stuff," Kris explained.

Sadie's face relaxed. She nodded. "It was names," she said, the confirmation not for her mother but for herself.

For a long, silent moment, Kris stared at her daughter's reflection in the mirror, at the deep red curls twisting down around her face like tentacles, at the porcelain skin that rose to the faintest hint of pink on the tops of her cheeks, at those eyes that glimmered like polished emeralds behind long, curving lashes.

God, she's so perfect, Kris thought. But she knew this was not true. Sadie had been born perfect, just as every child was until they opened their eyes and realized they were no longer alone. The flaws of their new world destroyed them—not instantly but little by little, over years, chipping at their souls until they no longer remembered what it was like to float in wonderful, absolute silence.

Kris knew that the first thing Sadie had seen when she blinked open her eyes was the sweaty, beaming face of her mother, exhausted from nearly twelve hours of labor yet filled with the exultation of meeting the life she had grown inside her. That moment was perfect. That was safe. It was the next glimpse that worried Kris—the way Jonah's expression had, for a brief moment, become frozen in a half smile, as if something inside had cautioned him about feeling true joy, like a voice, his own shadow voice, that whispered, *Are you sure?*

Kris told herself that a baby could not have read such subtlety in an expression. But Kris had. She had felt a sliver of ice slip like a thin blade into her heart. Had the same happened to Sadie? Was it possible that even though they no longer shared a body, this flawless baby girl had felt her mother's heartbeat stutter? Kris could still picture her child's dark, wandering eyes as they slowly turned to the man standing over her, and Kris imagined Sadie's voice—the sweet, tentative voice of her now, at eight years old—speaking in Kris's mind, asking, *Is it okay if I love him?* And Kris responding in her calm, even tone, *Yes, Sadie. He's your daddy. He won't hurt you.*

You lied to her, Kris told herself, her grip on the steering wheel tightening. The edges of the aged, cracked leather bit into her fingertips. *You were supposed to protect her. And you lied.*

On the ridges above them were the swaying green tops of untamed fields. They were below the earth now, where the highway carved a narrow canyon through jagged slopes of red gypsum, pale limestone, and deep brown clay. The mineral glowed like the brick walls of a fireplace in the afternoon sunlight. The sides of the hills became rockier the farther down they went, the road plunging at such a steep angle that Kris felt the ground would open at any moment and swallow them whole.

Kris heard Sadie give a soft gasp and knew what her daughter was thinking: *It's going to smash us, and there will be nothing left but bone and blood and metal.* The pass was growing too narrow. They could not make it through.

As a little girl, riding alone on the bench seat behind her mother and father, Kris had felt the same sense of growing unease, tempered only by the understanding that her parents would not purposely put her in danger.

But the fear was only the first half of the experience, because she now knew what came next.

Kris gently pressed her foot down harder on the accelerator, just as her father had done back in the day, the speedometer inching upward as the Jeep rocketed toward the frighteningly narrow gap. A metal sign mounted on a splintered wooden post and peppered with rusty bullet holes flashed by—

Welcome Home to Pacington!

Pop. 1,007

—and then the road suddenly shot out into an open valley. The crumbling asphalt of the old highway was replaced by fresh black tar, laid no more than a year before.

From the back seat, Kris heard Sadie exhale a breath of relief and exhilaration as the danger of the chasm instantly fell away and the world opened like a book.

Almost immediately the road split, a well-maintained street sign proclaiming "Center Street" as dead ahead and the equally literal "River Road" as the dirt track veering off to their right.

She remembered this. The slight curve felt natural, like muscle memory taking over, guiding her back to a place she was meant to be. Something long dormant stirred inside her, a tickle that started in her shoulders and ran up the back of her neck to the base of her scalp. She heard the easy whir of smooth asphalt swiftly transition into the crunchy chug of dirt under the bouncing tires, and it was like an old country song that spoke to her soul despite being written well before her time.

Shadows played across the dull paint of the Jeep as they entered a heavily wooded area thick with sycamores, white poplars, and silver maples. The car's wheels fell into well-worn ruts, billowing dust in their wake. Kris looked at Sadie's reflection in the rearview mirror. She was leaning against the door, her chin on her crossed arms. Dappled sunlight played across her face. Perhaps it was Kris's imagination, but the corners of Sadie's lips appeared to curve upward into the hint of a smile.

She feels it, too, Kris thought, the tingle of excitement growing stronger. *This is good. This is exactly what we need.*

She glanced over at the blur of trees flashing by, and there it was, glimpsed every now and again through the thick foliage: the sparkle of sunlight on water.

A breath caught in Kris's throat.

"Do you see it?" she asked over her shoulder. "That's the lake. That's Lost Lake. That's where we're going."

Sadie whispered something, her voice too soft to make out.

"What, honey?"

The little girl tapped a finger against the glass of the window. "Snow," she said.

Kris looked. Fluffy, white flakes were beginning to drift through the shafts of sunlight cutting through the trees. They whipped around the Jeep as it cut a path through the air, sending them swirling wildly in its wake.

"No, it's not snow," Kris explained. "It's from the cottonwood trees. They bloom in the summer and the wind blows the seeds off the branches."

Up ahead, the wind shook the tree branches, sending a cloud of puffy white clumps swirling into the middle of the road. Kris eased her foot off the accelerator and let the Jeep coast through, parting the mass of seed pods like a white curtain.

She guided the car gently to the right, where the dirt shoulder began to rise into an embankment of sunbaked clay and loose stones. Her eyes scanned ahead, searching for the wooden gate that marked the entrance to the dirt path leading up to the house. She remembered how her father would stop the car, the engine idling as he climbed out to open the gate. As a child, Kris knew that the last day of school wasn't truly the beginning of summer; it was this moment when the station wagon slipped through the narrow gap carved into the embankment. Everything leading up to their arrival at the lake house was merely a prelude.

The wistful smile playing at Kris's lips vanished as her face went slack. Something was wrong.

The wooden gate lay on the ground at the edge of the road, a few feet from the metal post on which it had once hung. Vines had snaked their way across its weathered body, tethering it to the ground as if to let all who passed know that nature had claimed it. Kris steered the Jeep around the gate, careful not to let the tires clip its wooden edges. On either side, the embankment allowed only a few inches for the Jeep to pass through. Beyond this, the dirt path had all but vanished, overtaken by switchgrass and thick clusters of goldenrod.

She listened for the easy hum of the tires finding the concrete drive that would take them the rest of the way to the house, but she only heard the scrape of thick weeds digging at the skid plate beneath the nose of the Jeep. Then the crunching of uneven rocks shifting under the car's enormous weight. It took a moment before she realized she *was* on the driveway, or what had once been the driveway. The concrete had been fractured by countless fault lines, splitting its smooth surface into a path of uneven rubble. Stalks of tallgrass had found these gaps and made them their homes.

She let the Jeep coast for a few more feet before bringing it to a stop with a faint squeal of brakes.

There, perched on the edge of a bluff overlooking the water, was the lake house.

Kris stared silently at the structure. Behind her, she heard a click as Sadie unfastened her seat belt. She could feel the little girl's eyes peering over her shoulder, staring out, just as Kris was, through the windshield.

For a long moment, neither spoke.

It was Sadie who broke the silence. Her willingness to speak should have thrilled Kris. But Sadie's voice was hesitant, slightly squeaky, like a door being cautiously opened.

"Mommy . . . is that . . . Is that where we're staying?"

Before them was the decaying wood and stone corpse of the house that had called to Kris over hundreds of miles with what must have been its dying breath.

CHAPTER THREE

KRIS OPENED THE driver's-side door and stepped out.

The air was warm and smelled of earth, as if each invisible breath left a thin coating of dirt on everything it touched. It made Kris feel immediately unclean. She rubbed a hand across the back of her neck and felt minute granules of dirt mixed with the moist warmth of sweat.

This is not our house, her mind insisted.

But it was. It was not the way it existed in her idyllic childhood memories, but it was without a doubt the lake house her father had bought when Kris was a pale green-eyed child and her mother was healthy and happy. Yet unlike her memories, the house had not been preserved by fondness and nostalgia. Time had stripped the flesh from its bones like a vulture tearing at the fetid meat of carrion on some forgotten back road.

The area in front of the house, once separated from the rest of the clearing by its subtle landscaping, was a twisted jumble of countless plants, like the matted mess of a child's unwashed hair. A thick layer of dirt and dead leaves filled the birdbath's bowl. The stone bluebirds on its lip no longer appeared to be the friendly harbingers of summer joy that had greeted little Krissy and her parents each June. The larger of the birds still had its beak wide open in what had once appeared to be an exultation of carefree joy. But now the bird seemed to be shrieking in terror as the invasive vines reached hungrily for its plump body. The second bluebird was missing its head entirely.

The vines and weeds had worked their dark magic on the brick path as well, pushing them up from their beds so that the straight shot to the porch became an obstacle course of uneven rectangles. In several places, the bushes had become so overgrown, they left only a few empty inches for passage.

Along the foundation of the house, the mortar between the stacked stones had turned to powder. Several of the fieldstones sat loose enough to pull free. A few flakes of white paint still clung to the wooden sides of the house, but the majority of it had peeled away after decades of scorching summers and frigid winters. The clapboard siding was now a sickly grayish-brown, the wood splintered and rough. Cracked red paint trimmed the windows like smears of drying blood.

The house looked like a crumbling headstone on a forgotten grave.

A door hinge creaked behind Kris.

Sadie was out of her booster and standing in the open doorway of the back seat. She stared out at the lake house with wide, unblinking eyes.

"It's fine," Kris said, answering a question her daughter had not asked. Glancing back at the house, she tried to conjure up an explanation. "I guess not that many people have rented it or else someone would have . . ." She let her words drift away, suddenly afraid of the logic trail down which she found herself traveling: *or else someone would have maintained the house. But no one comes here anymore. This is a forgotten place.*

She turned to Sadie. For one brief moment, Kris had the odd sensation that she was staring back at herself as a child. There she was, a little girl again, her bright, fiery hair curling down around freckled cheeks, the green irises of her eyes igniting into yellow sunbursts just before they reached the all-consuming blackness of her pupils.

Kris held out an open hand.

"Come on," she said. "Let's see what it's like on the inside."

Sadie paused, unsure, and then she slipped her delicate fingers into her mother's palm and allowed her feet to drop to the ground.

Kris led Sadie through the overgrowth. Grasshoppers buzzed by on wings of ancient papyrus. With her free hand, Kris parted a cluster of waist-high weeds, sending leafhoppers, no bigger than the heads of pins, scattering in all directions. Suddenly the ground wobbled beneath their weight, and Kris realized they were on the pathway leading to the porch. It was a world without humans, one reclaimed by the countryside.

"Watch your step," Kris warned her daughter.

Slowly, carefully, she made her way down the path, Sadie just a step behind her. Thorny branches reached out from a shrub that seemed to have exploded from the earth. Kris could feel the tips of bushes and weeds tugging at her clothes. And then the untamed plants fell away, and they were moving up the brittle planks of the front steps.

Like everything around them, the years and the elements had taken their toll on the porch. The trunks rising up from the stone columns were ringed with zigzagging canals where termites had gnawed passage through the wood. Overhead, long, sticky lines of spiderweb wound through the rafter beams, thickening into clumps dotted with the dried corpses of dead bugs.

Sadie's grip tightened on Kris's hand. Kris glanced back. The unease in her daughter's expression had evolved into fear. She glanced slowly around as if she expected something to leap out of the shadows at any moment.

Kris forced a smile and offered in a reassuring tone, "We'll get some bug spray later when we go into town. I'm sure these spiders are harmless but, you know, just in case."

Sadie did not appear to register her mother's words. Her eyes remained on the darkest corners of the porch and the things she imagined crawling there, staring with black, bulbous eyes.

The front door looked as if it had been sliced from the center of a massive tree. Kris ran a finger down its smooth surface and was relieved to find that its varnish had held, preserving it while the rest of the house fell into ruin.

She grasped the tarnished brass doorknob. Its sides were decorated with wavy grooves meant to simulate rays of sunlight bursting from a comically surprised face on the front of the knob. She twisted it. The knob turned an inch and then stopped. Locked.

"Mr. Hargrove said he would leave a key under a pot . . ."

There were several ceramic planters of various sizes, each containing a withered brown plant drooping above bone-dry soil. The first two pots that she tipped over revealed only a few scurrying bugs—earwigs and millipedes and slower, clumsy roly-polies.

A breath caught in her throat. Hargrove had forgotten. Or, worse, he had refused to leave the key. For whatever reason, he had seemed hesitant to let her stay at this house, despite the fact that it was hers. He was going to force her to drive into town, storm into his office, and demand that he open up the house. He had no right. He—

There it was, under the third pot, a shiny silver key on a simple steel loop.

Kris let out a breath.

She slipped the key into the silver lock just above that ridiculous grinning doorknob and turned it. The dead bolt retracted.

Kris twisted the knob and pushed. The summer heat had caused the wooden door to swell in its frame, and at first the door did not budge.

"Shit," she cursed softly, hoping Sadie did not hear.

She twisted the knob again and this time put her full weight into the attempt.

There was just enough time for that timid voice in her mind to offer hopefully, *It'll be better on the inside*, and the dark voice, Shadow Kris, to purr, *It's rotten, even there, you'll see . . .*

There was the faint screech of wood on wood, and then the door swung open.

The smell was like something decaying beneath wet leaves. It was not overwhelming, but it was there at the end of every inhalation.

Kris glanced down at her daughter. Sadie gave no indication of noticing the foul odor. She appeared to have retreated to the place she had been for the past two weeks, her eyes staring but not seeing, always looking inward, always trying to make sense of the impossible.

Kris stepped into air heavy with dust. She was standing in a tight entryway. To her right was a mirror clouded with smudges and grime. To her left, a row of small antlers mounted on the wall provided hooks for hanging hats and coats. The soles of her boots brushed across something coarse, like horsehair, and she looked down to find an old door-mat beneath her feet. Kris instantly recognized it. Two arrows pointed back toward the threshold. Between these were words in a stenciled font: "Please Leave Problems at Door." Her father had bought this doormat the year before their last summer together, one last defiant laugh to share with his wife.

"I'll try, Dad," Kris whispered to the ground.

She brushed the rubber soles of her boots across the top of the doormat and went to take another step, but Sadie remained in place like an anchor behind her. The little girl's eyes glistened in the dim light. Her eyebrows were arched to a point, questioning.

"Come on," Kris said. She tried to sound reassuring.

For a moment, Sadie did not move. And then she allowed her mother's hand to pull her forward, into the lake house.

The entryway led to a very simple—and very dated—kitchen. The height of style when the house was built in the late 1950s, the kitchen now looked like an old photograph fading away in a family album. The once vibrant yellow tile countertops had dulled to the color of dried mustard. The cherry cabinets had long ago lost their rich gleam. The cabinet doors, both above and below the countertop, were all slightly askew, giving the appearance of a grinning mouth full of crooked teeth. An aged white refrigerator sat in the corner. It emitted a soft, irregular buzz as if filled with hundreds of thousands of confused bees.

Next to the white ceramic sink, several empty beer cans sat with their sides dented in. A layer of dust had settled on these, just as it had settled on everything in the lake house.

Kris slowly drew a breath in through her nose, desperate for scents she knew could no longer be there—the buttery sweetness of banana pancakes bubbling on a skillet, the savory bite of a ham-and-cheese omelet browning in a pan as her mother and father worked in tandem to whip up breakfast. But there was only the foul odor of dust and decay.

Kris felt Sadie press up close to her side.

"It kind of stinks in here, doesn't it?" Kris asked.

Sadie did not reply.

Hargrove didn't even bother coming in, Kris realized. *If he had, he would have noticed this stench. He left the key beneath the planter and drove the hell away. He hasn't been inside this place in months. Maybe years.*

At the far end of the kitchen, just past a small breakfast nook nestled under a long row of narrow windows, a rectangular archway opened into the great room. The plaster ceiling of the kitchen abruptly vanished, replaced by a cathedral ceiling ribbed with walnut beams that spanned the width of the room and disappeared into shadowed corners. Spiderwebs hovered there, thick as spun sugar, like pale ghosts in the darkness.

Kris held out a flattened palm to Sadie. "Stay here."

True to its name, the great room was as massive as the front entryway was constricting. A brown leather couch—its cushions sinking, its hide cracked—faced a fireplace constructed from the same fieldstones that made up the house's crumbling foundation. The firebox was wide and deep and stained black from decades of soot. Above a mantel made from a halved cedar trunk, the chimney rose like a guard standing at attention, its stone face disappearing through the exposed planks of the ceiling high above.

Flanking the leather couch were two chairs, one a bare-bones mission-style glider fashioned from solid oak where young Krissy had spent many summer evenings cuddled up to her mother's chest, the other an armchair with cushions upholstered in a busy print featuring fishermen pulling bass the size of Atlantic salmon into a steel canoe. This chair had been her father's favorite, and Kris could still see him sitting there with his morning coffee, steam curling up around the rough patch of stubble he called his "summer beard."

Mounted over the fireplace mantel was an antique hickory fishing rod complete with a Western's winding casting reel. Kris reached up and tapped the handle hard enough that it spun one full rotation, pulling in a length of invisible line.

The far end of the room was all glass, composed entirely of four narrow windows stretching from floor to ceiling. They narrowed at the top, following the upward slant of the roof until they met at the peak. The panes glowed a warm yellow, but the light did not appear to penetrate any farther. It was held back by layers of dirt.

Kris stared up at the illuminated monoliths towering over her.

You've been here before.

Of course, she had. Her father had brought her and her mother to the lake house every summer until that last summer when her mother—

Not here, Kris realized. *Not these windows, but ones just like them.*

A church.

Holy Cross Catholic Church in Blantonville, Kansas. The sanctuary hot and musty. The priest in his violet vestment. The sound of sniffling and choked voices echoing from the ornate Gothic ceiling high above.

The cathedral ceiling.

There was Krissy, ten years old, sitting beside her father in the first pew, his body rigid and straight, his sweaty hands clasped so tightly that the tips of his fingers were bloodless and white. She kept her head bowed, not wanting to make eye contact with anyone for fear they would feel compelled to speak to her, to say those things that meant little and changed nothing: *I'm so sorry, it's going to get better, God has a plan for us all, she is at peace now, she is in heaven, God has called her home.*

Called her home.

And she went, little Krissy Barlow thought bitterly. *He called and she left us.*

She remembered the casket at the front of the sanctuary. Its black, glossy surface glistened like the curved back of a beetle. In there was the fleshy shell that had once contained her mother. Now it was empty. The mortician had done his best to preserve it, applying too much makeup to the withered, sunken face in an effort to make the cheeks look less like shadowed valleys between bone, the eyes less like sinkholes, the lips less like dried, cracked strips of meat. But even at her young age, Krissy had known the thing in the coffin was a husk.

She was called home, and the rest of them were left behind to bear the weight of her absence.

The smell was worse in the hallway.

Kris stood at the edge of the entryway and stared down the dim corridor. There were no windows. The first two doors—one to her left and another a little farther down on her right—were closed tight. At the far end, a third door was open just an inch or two, and except for the soft glow of light from within this room and a slanted shaft of sunshine drifting down from an unseen staircase across from it, the hall was dark.

She stepped into the gloom, scanning the wall as she went. There had to be a light switch somewhere. The shadows grew thicker around her, as did that odor of rot and decay. Whatever was causing the nauseating scent was in the hallway with her. It was too dim to see, but it was there, she knew it, just as she knew the light switch was there. She imagined kneeling down and reaching into the deepest shadows that swirled like black mist at the base of the wall, her fingers grazing matted fur, her fingertips sinking in to touch damp, spongy flesh writhing with ravenous maggots.

And then the shadows were peeling away, stripped from her and the hall around her by the yellowish-white glow of sunlight. She had reached the third door. She shoved it lightly, and it swung open a few more inches on angry hinges. As it did, the swath of light in the hall expanded, forcing the shadows farther into retreat.

Slowly, Kris turned. Across from her, the hall cut a sharp right angle, continuing for another fifteen feet before coming to a dead end. To the right, a steep staircase sliced the hallway in half. The steps rose up to a landing lit by golden sunshine from a small, square window.

Kris drew a short breath in through her nose. The stench was down here with her. There was no mistaking it.

She guided herself into that narrow passageway to the left of the stairs. The underside of the staircase was completely exposed, each step mirrored in a strange upside-down ascension.

Something was piled in a heap in the corner, something black and jagged, as if the shadows beneath the stairs had shattered into pieces like glass. This was the source of the smell. Whatever that thing was, it was rotting into the floorboards like a fly dissolving in the gullet of a pitcher plant.

Kris pulled up the neck of her T-shirt to cover her mouth and nose as she stepped closer to the object in the corner. Bits of it were scattered about like fallen leaves, the pieces long and slender with bristled edges.

Feathers, she realized.

She glanced to the thing in the corner. It was splayed out like a poorly drawn star. For a moment, she stared at it, trying to make sense of its odd dimensions.

A wing. Frozen in full extension. Talons curled as if around an invisible branch. Another wing folded unnaturally in half. A black pupil set against a yellow eye like a moon dwarfed by the enormity of its sun.

A bird.

She could not be sure of the species. It was smaller than a crow. A grackle perhaps. In this light—or lack of it—it was impossible to determine if the creature had a grackle's trademark purple hood.

Does it matter? Kris asked herself. *It's a dead bird, and it's stinking up the house.*

But was that possible? The stench had been revolting from the moment she opened the front door. Could this small, pathetic beast be the cause of that?

Maybe there are more, the voice from the back of her mind—the voice of Shadow Kris—whispered. *Or maybe there are other dead things here. Hiding. Waiting to be found.*

Kris clenched her teeth and forced this voice away.

Gripping the tips of its toes between her fingers, she lifted the bird. There was a soft ripping sound, like packaging tape being pulled free, as its remaining feathers released their hold on the wood floor. Its body dangled limply, that one wing still outstretched in a mockery of flight.

Now what?

She wasn't entirely sure. She had to find a way of disposing of the body without Sadie seeing it.

The window. At the top of the stairs.

Kris had learned long ago not to trust in the power of prayer, but in that moment, she allowed herself the futility of hoping that the window still opened after all these years.

Loose feathers billowed from the floor as she moved quickly out from under the stairs. If there wasn't one in the house already, she would have to get a broom to sweep up this mess. For now, disposing of the bird was enough.

She swung around the newel post and moved lightly up the stairs. The bird swung beneath her fingertips like the pendulum of an obscene clock.

The latch on the square window at the top of the stairs was stubborn, but with a little force, it twisted. With her free hand, Kris slid the window open. A gust of summer air puffed in her face like hot breath. After the stale stench of decomposing flesh, she was thankful for the reprieve. She could smell the world on that air—the sweetness of honeysuckle, the perfume of lavender, the green bitterness of leaves, all of these scents riding on the crisp breeze blowing over the crystal waters of Lost Lake.

She closed her eyes and took another few seconds to enjoy the moment, and then she lifted the dead bird by its feet up to the window. She meant to swing it back for momentum and then heave it away, hopefully over the edge of the porch roof and into the thick of a bush where it would remain hidden until insects and small creatures had time to break it down into bone.

But something made her pause.

She was staring directly across the bird's beak and into its yellow eyes, even though its back and the curve of its tail also faced her.

Its neck was broken.

Trying to get out, she told herself. *Hitting the underside of the stairs. That's why all the feathers were on the floor. It panicked. It broke its neck trying to find a way out.*

It would have made sense had it not been for one thing.

As she gently swung the bird's body beneath her fingers, she noticed the rips in its neck, the places where ligaments stretched between tufts of feathers.

The bird's head had been twisted around so many times, it would have already fallen off had it not been for those last few lengths of desperate sinew.

In one fluid motion, Kris flung the bird's body outside and slammed the window shut. She did not bother to watch where it landed.

Sadie was no longer in the kitchen.

Kris stood in the great room, her back to the hallway, and stared at the spot where she had left her daughter waiting. She was nowhere to be found by the dated appliances or at the island that created an artificial border between the kitchen and the dining area. Nor was she at the breakfast nook. The two chairs on either side of the table and the bench along the wall were empty. Shafts of dusty sunshine fell in from the windows above the bench, laying squares of light across the table like golden place settings.

A soft knocking got her attention.

The French doors were wide open, cutting a rectangle into the center of the four towering windows along the south wall. One of doors swayed slightly in the breeze. Its white frame bumped against the rusted arm of a wrought-iron porch chair every time the wind drew it back.

Sadie was there, standing at the edge of the deck and staring out at the sparkling waters of Lost Lake. The breeze lifted her scarlet locks into the air and then set them gently back onto her shoulders.

Kris stepped through the open doorway and onto the deck. Redwood slats ran at a forty-five-degree angle away from the house and toward a steel railing around the perimeter. Even from here, Kris could tell that the railing was loose. It tilted slightly toward the backyard and the slope leading down to the water. Orange flakes of rust peeled up from the twisted steel balusters and along the top of the handrail like burned skin.

She felt the planks sag just a bit under her weight as she crossed the deck. The wood was weathered—it was a safe bet that it had been decades since it was last sealed—but with the exception of the loose rail, the structure seemed safe.

She slipped a hand across Sadie's back and around the curve of her arm.

"I didn't know you were out here."

Sadie did not respond. She was, Kris assumed, still trying to make sense of their accommodations.

Say something, Kris thought, attempting to will her words into her daughter's mind. *Say you hate it. Say you can't stay here. Yell at me for bringing you here. Anything.*

Sadie showed no reaction, her back to her mother, her eyes trained straight ahead over the deck railing.

Any hope that the backyard was in better shape than the front was dashed as Kris glanced around the lot. The weeds and wildflowers had invaded, turning what had once been a trimmed patch of wild grass behind the deck into another waving stretch of Kansas prairie.

Just past the deck, which ran along three quarters of the house, the yard opened up even wider to make room for a small garden. Chunky railroad ties bordered it, but any other evidence of the garden was long gone. Years ago, it had been home to her mother's carefully pruned tomato plants; now it was nothing more than random weeds and a thick patch of sunflowers. Their blank, brown faces peered out dumbly in all directions.

Kris could still see her mother there in her old blue jeans, a T-shirt, and a ridiculous wide-brimmed hat, a red-and-black plaid bandana tied around her neck, the damp dirt staining her knees as she pulled up the weeds that had sprouted up over the spring. But her mother was no longer there to tend to her garden, and the man in town had decided, for whatever piss-poor fucking reason, to let nature reclaim it all.

Because he's lazy. Because this place means nothing to him. Not when Dad was alive and definitely not now that Dad is dead.

But they were all dead, weren't they? The two people who gave them life, and the one whose passing drove them back to this place.

Everyone Kris had ever allowed into her heart was dead.

Not Sadie, that timid yet infinitely hopeful voice spoke up in her mind. *Not your baby girl.*

And not you, Kris reminded herself. She was alive, and so was her daughter, the other half of her soul. She could fix this place. She *had* to fix it. Coming here had been her idea. And it had been a good idea, she was sure of it. At home, there was no way to escape the constant reminders of Jonah's death. The framed photographs displayed all around their house. The pity on the faces of friends and co-workers. For Sadie, her friends were off to camp. But there would be no camp for Sadie this summer. Kris could not bear the thought of sending her daughter to a place where every look from every boy or girl would say, "Sorry about your daddy."

The lake house had helped Kris get through one of the most awful summers of her life. It could do the same for Sadie. But not like this. It had to be the place she had promised Sadie. They needed the fairy tale, just until August, and then they would return to whatever reality awaited them back home.

Kris drew in a breath and pushed her shoulders back so that she stood straight and tall. She let her eyes drift away from the old garden, which surely only needed a good pruning and some fresh plants. She scanned the yard until her gaze fell upon the crooked skeleton of a long-abandoned swing set. The ends of its metal frame slanted like poorly drawn A's. Vines twisted up from clusters of grass to curl around its legs. The splintered wooden seats of two swings hung from chains caked with rust and dirt. One of the swings, the one hanging slightly lower than the other, was cocked at an irritatingly uneven angle, each of its chains set to a different link.

Kris nodded, accepting the challenge. A few new bolts, nice and tight. A good sanding for the seats. An overnight vinegar bath for the rusty chains.

What else you got?

Behind the deck, tallgrass rippled like the tails of irritated cats.

A weed whacker. Yes, she thought, imagining the catharsis she would feel slicing through the tallgrass like the grim reaper.

She imagined it all cut down, and in her mind, the backyard revealed itself. At the bottom of the back steps, a line of stones wove a crooked path away from the house and through the overgrowth until they disappeared over the slope's edge. The stones became stairs, carved into the side of the slope, making for an easy descent down to the shore. The white sliver of a wood dock stretched out over the water. She remembered sitting on the shore as a child and watching her father, shirtless in ripped jean shorts, as he sank the first piling.

And then it became more than a memory. She could see it. The place beyond the weeds. An expanse of sun-kissed water.

The lake.

Or at least their section of it. Their lake house was perched on a bluff overlooking one of several coves pressed like thumbprints into the earth around the outer edge of Lost Lake. It was easy to think this was the entirety of the lake; this cove alone was nearly a quarter of a mile across and twice that in length. But a glance to the far end of the cove revealed an even greater body of water stretching out for what seemed like forever. The tiny gray dots of fishing boats bobbed out there, disturbed periodically by an arrogant speedboat pulling a water-skier behind it.

"We should go into town," she realized suddenly. "We need groceries." She nodded toward an ancient charcoal grill in one corner of the deck. Silky strands of spiderweb zigzagged between its grimy legs. "We can get some things to grill."

Sadie shot a look at the grill.

Kris smiled and gave Sadie's shoulder a gentle pinch. "We'll clean it first. We'll clean everything."

CHAPTER FOUR

A LITTLE OVER a mile after the intersection of River Road and Center Street, the first building appeared: Hope Church, a simple square chapel with white wood siding, pale blue shutters, and a small bell tower atop its steeply pitched roof.

Soon after was a house, then another, and another, until Center Street—technically Kansas Highway 44—became an official part of the town, lined on both sides by well-maintained one-story homes and lush trees shading redbrick sidewalks. In more than one yard, American flags flapped gently atop metal poles, their colors faded by the sun, their edges frayed by the wind.

Cross streets began to intersect the main road, all named after local trees. Elm Street. Oak Street. Walnut Street. Surprisingly, Pacington seemed to have avoided the economic hardships that plagued nearby communities. There was not a brick out of place on the sidewalk, not a single overgrown lawn, not the slightest hint of a pothole along Center Street. Here in the river basin between the gypsum hills, Pacington was untouched by the outside world. Kris loosened her grip on the steering wheel and sank back slightly in her seat. She breathed in a lungful of artificially cooled air and slowly exhaled, feeling her tense muscles relax, just a bit. The condition of the lake house may have been a shock to her system, but at least the town was as she remembered it. Maybe there was hope after all.

They needed cleaning supplies. There was no way she was going to move her daughter into that house until they had at least removed the grime from the kitchen, swept the spiderwebs from the rafters, and wiped the dust from every reachable surface. Only then would she begin to unpack the things they had brought with them from Black Ridge.

But there was something more pressing, as their growling stomachs had abruptly reminded them: they needed food. They hadn't enjoyed a real sit-down meal since stopping for dinner at an Applebee's outside Pueblo the night before. Sadie wasn't eating much these days, but Kris hoped the change of scenery would at least inspire her to pick at a short stack of pancakes or nibble on a few strips of bacon. Regardless, Kris required coffee—a lot of coffee—if she hoped to get through an afternoon of scrubbing floors and counters.

At Sycamore Street, the residential neighborhoods abruptly ended, giving way to, as the ornate sign at the corner of Sycamore and Center proclaimed: "Historic Downtown Pacington." It was true, the history of the town was on full display—three and a half blocks of buildings constructed in the late 1800s, each a different shade of brick and stone, each with its own unique cornice above rows of tall, narrow windows. Streetlights designed to look like nineteenth-century gas lamps rose elegantly over the sidewalks. Even the names of the businesses—Patty's Plate, the Daily Grind, You Old Sew and Sew, the Dairy Godmother, the Book Nook—harkened back to a simpler time.

Kris pulled into an open parking spot in front of Patty's, with its yellow painted brick and forest-green window frames, sliding the Jeep between two dented and rusted pickup trucks. Both trucks had a gun rack in the back windows, one displaying a modern pump-action shotgun with a faux wood stock and the other a tarnished rifle that looked like it would have been more at home in Wyatt Earp's saddlebag. Inside the first truck, a rosary hung from the rearview mirror.

She reached for the door handle of the restaurant, and then paused, looking back over her shoulder. Sadie had not moved.

"We'll get breakfast, stop by the market, and then you can help me clean the house. That sounds fun, doesn't it? Helping Mommy clean?"

Kris offered a playful smile, but Sadie's expression remained unchanged—furrowed brow, downcast eyes, pursed lips. Without a word, she unbuckled her seat belt, slid out of her booster seat, and opened the rear passenger-side door. Kris watched as her daughter stopped in the middle of the sidewalk, waiting to be led wherever her mother wanted to go.

Because you dragged her here, that echoing voice taunted from her mind's abyss.

For her own good, Kris told herself.

Against her will, the voice insisted.

She's eight, Kris responded coldly. *I am her will.*

There was no reply. Shadow Kris had retreated to a darker corner.

Kris sighed, suddenly feeling as though the gravity holding her firmly to the ground had doubled. It was pulling her down, as if invisible vines had wrapped around her wrists, her biceps, her ankles. She was bombarded by the realization that she had not slept in over twenty-four hours and probably wouldn't sleep for at least another twelve thanks to the decrepit state of the house.

"Shake it off," she whispered to herself. She did exactly this, giving her arms and legs a small shake to free them from the phantom bindings. She made a deal with herself: push through the rest of the day, get a good night's sleep, and tomorrow she could relax. She knew this was bullshit, but for the moment it worked its magic, the vines loosening, the force pulling her down easing.

Okay, she thought. *Okay. One step at a time.*

She crossed around the hood of the Jeep to where Sadie stood. She took her daughter's hand, and together they moved forward.

The moment they entered Patty's, Kris was yanked off her feet and whisked back to her childhood: the smell of salty bacon and sweet, syrupy waffles; the rustic country décor featuring nursery rhyme scenes hand-painted on crosscut slices of pine; the mismatched tables and chairs; the checkered plastic tablecloths, quickly wiped down with tattered rags by waitresses as old and comforting as the furniture.

Just inside the front door was a hand-painted sign featuring a rooster crowing, "Sit Anywhere Ya Like!" Kris and Sadie chose a table in the front window. Red-and-white striped cloth curtains flanked the panes, pulled back with thick gold rope. Kris quickly scanned a one-page laminated menu whose most extravagant offerings were a Denver omelet and a three-egg hash brown scramble.

"How hungry are you?" she asked.

There was no answer.

She glanced over the top of the menu. Sadie was staring out the window at a scraggly greenfinch perched atop a blue mailbox. Clumps of its grayish-brown feathers had fallen out in several places, leaving patches of bare, prickled skin. It stood on one leg, its other leg missing. Kris noticed several raw, blistering sores at the base of the finch's beak. Most likely trichomoniasis. She had treated several cases over the years at her clinic in Black Ridge. The worst had been when Dorothy Atwood took in an injured pigeon and chose to allow the poor creature to share a cage with her darling cockatiel and a blue budgie. By the time Dorothy brought them in, all three birds were infected with the parasite. The pigeon was dead in a day. The cockatiel and budgie flew off into the great beyond two days later. Kris assumed this greenfinch wouldn't make it to see the weekend.

"Sadie," she said, trying to draw her daughter's attention away from the window. "You want eggs? Or pancakes?"

"Eggs, I guess."

"And bacon?"

Sadie shrugged, never taking her eyes off the mangy bird.

There was the sound of rubber soles shuffling along the tile floor, and one of the waitresses, an alarmingly thin woman in her seventies, sidled up to their table. Her brittle hair was a dull gray and long—so long that Kris feared it could snap at any moment like a bundle of dry twigs. Canyons of wrinkles lined her sun-damaged face. On the breast of her light green blouse was a plastic nametag in the shape of a saucer. Printed in bold black letters was her name: Doris.

"Mornin'," Doris said, her lips, shellacked with layer upon layer of thick red lipstick, stretching into a tight smile.

Kris did her best to return the smile. "Good morning."

Doris held up a small spiral notepad, the tip of her ballpoint pen hovering in anticipation. "What can I get 'cha?"

Kris motioned toward Sadie. "She'll have eggs, scrambled, with a side of bacon. And can you melt a little cheddar cheese on the eggs please?"

"Cheddar cheese, yep, you got it." Doris scribbled the order in chicken scratch across the lined page. "And for you?"

"A short stack of buttermilk pancakes. And coffee. Black."

"Hash browns or country fries?"

"Um, hash browns, I guess."

"White or wheat toast?"

"Wheat."

"Buttered or dry?"

"Dry is fine."

Doris frowned slightly as if she disapproved of this answer, her deep wrinkles splintering at the edges into tinier hair-thin fractures. "You wanna add a side of biscuits and gravy?"

Kris noticed there were words printed across the side of Doris's pen, an advertisement for a cholesterol medication. The sharp ripple of a chuckle tried to fight its way up from Kris's chest, but she caught it before it could escape her lips, and she pretended to cough. "No, I think I'm good."

Doris jotted down the rest of the order. She began to step away, then paused. She was staring at Sadie. Her red, razor-thin smile sliced farther into her ancient cheeks. "Why, you're pretty, just like your mama. You got the most beautiful hair, ya know that, sweetheart?"

Sadie glanced nervously to her mother. The morning sunshine fell softly across the back of the girl's head, and the light seemed to ignite her curls.

"Thank you," Kris answered for her. "It's just like mine, when I was her age."

Raising a bony hand to her face, Doris slowly ran her fingers back and forth over a cheek covered in skin as thin as tissue paper. It was an odd gesture of which she barely seemed aware. It was as if she were pretending it was someone else's hand, attempting to soothe her.

"I bet you're smart, too," she said, her gaze never leaving Sadie. "Bet you do real good in school. Polite. Listen to your teachers."

Her hand stopped, her palm under her chin, fingers cradling her face.

"Such a sweet girl. Such a sweet, sweet girl."

For a brief moment, Doris fell silent, her thoughts pulled to a sad, faraway place. Then she cleared her throat, as if the sight of Sadie had caused a breath to lodge painfully there. "Well," she said, her voice small and weak, "welcome to Patty's. Food'll be up shortly."

"Thanks," Kris said again, but Doris was already shuffling off toward the kitchen. She did not look back.

Kris turned to Sadie with the intention of offering an apologetic smile, something that acknowledged the awkwardness of the interaction. But suddenly a strange sensation gripped her, like a memory surfacing from beneath dark waters. There was something off about it. It was as if she were experiencing the memory from someone else's point of view—not an out-of-body experience but what she could only think to call *other* body. It was the uncanny feeling she got when she stared at her own reflection in a mirror for too long. She began to feel as though her reflection were a separate entity, no longer bound to her movement. At any moment, it could grin and wink to let her know it was free.

And then she realized what had caused that odd sense of dislocation: Sadie was now Krissy, the little girl with untamed red hair, and Kris was the mother who could only gaze upon her daughter and try to recall what it felt like to be so carefree.

Except she isn't. She knows pain, more than any child should.

"If you catch an animal, can it be your pet?" Sadie asked suddenly.

For the second time since entering Patty's, Kris felt herself yanked, without warning, through time.

Sadie was looking out the window again. The greenfinch's head was twisted backward, its beak digging desperately into its raggedy feathers to snap at whatever microscopic creatures were burrowing into its flesh.

"What?" Kris asked, her mind foggy, as if she had been startled out of a dream.

Sadie did not repeat her question. She set her chin down on her folded hands and stared out the window as if she had never spoken.

Out on the mailbox, the diseased finch fluttered its itchy wings.

The faintest hint of a smile played at the corners of Sadie's lips.

It was close to noon when Kris pushed open the front door of Patty's Plate, and she and Sadie stepped out into a far gloomier day than the one they had left less than an hour before. Large white clouds dotted the blue sky like puffs of smoke from a cartoon train, moving lackadaisically past the sun to plunge the town into momentary shadow. The air had warmed to a moderate eighty-four degrees and would probably only rise a few degrees more before evening.

At breakfast, Sadie had taken tiny, hesitant bites of the gooey orange eggs on her plate, but by the time the check had come, she had managed to eat enough to satisfy Kris. The food seemed to have done them some good, their steps lighter and their strides longer as they crossed to the Jeep parked at the curb.

"It won't take long, I promise," Kris said.

Across the street and one block down, the gentle rise and fall of downtown's brick buildings, all built in the same Western false front style, came to an abrupt end to make way for the large parking lot of a Safeway. There was no way for anyone but the oldest residents of Pacington to know that six original structures dating back to the town's incorporation—including the four-story limestone Riverfront Hotel, with its grand rounded arch over the entrance—had been demolished in the mid-sixties to make way for the supermarket, all in the name of keeping up with larger towns in Southern Kansas and Northern Oklahoma.

Stacks of water-filled tubs full of fresh-cut sunflowers and prairie asters perfumed the air as they passed through the store's automatic doors. Kris pulled a shopping cart from a line of interlocking metal baskets and immediately cursed her luck. The right front wheel veered at a forty-five degree angle, rattling loudly as it shook in its casing. Sadie followed closely behind, eyes on the floor, hands in the pockets of her light blue shorts. The soles of her Chuck Taylor high-tops squeaked against the waxed floor with each step.

Kris had brought some food from their house in Colorado, mostly bags of chips, sleeves of crackers, canned goods, things that would keep. Here, she loaded the cart with perishable items—fresh fruit, vegetables, mayonnaise, mustard, a loaf of bread, hot dog and hamburger buns, an assortment of meats and cheeses. It hadn't occurred to her to test the faucets in the lake house, and the thought of putrid brown water spurting violently into the kitchen sink called for a stop in the beverage aisle for bottled water and a case of diet soda, as well as two cartons of milk and a jug each of apple and orange juice.

"You wanna push the cart for a while?" Kris asked.

Sadie shrugged and wrapped her small hands around the cart's handle. Kris walked in front, a hand on the end of the cart's wire basket, both to keep the damaged wheel from taking them off course and to give Sadie a little secret assistance.

They worked their way from one end of the store to the other, zigzagging up and down the aisles. The brand names had changed since Kris was last there in the late 1980s, but little else had. Kris glanced over her shoulder and, for the second time, she had the sensation of witnessing someone else's memory. Her mother had let her push the cart just as Sadie was now. Her mother would fill the basket, and yet no matter how many items she threw in, the cart never got too heavy to push. Kris looked down at her fingers, slyly tugging the cart forward and realized she was instinctively pulling the same trick.

Kris felt her skin break out into goose bumps as cool air wafted down from the wall of vacuum-sealed meat. Sadie moved the cart down the frigid shelves as Kris picked up a few things she knew would fit in the refrigerator's small freezer: packages of hot dogs, ground beef, and chicken breasts.

A sign at the end of the meat section announced: "BBQ Essentials!" Beside it was a display of grilling utensils, marinades, dry rubs, and stacked bags of charcoal. Kris grabbed a ten-pound bag of E-Z-Lite briquettes and slid it onto the rack beneath the cart's basket. She threw in a box of wooden matches just in case there were none at the house.

Their last stop was the least exciting but the most necessary: cleaning supplies. Sadie maintained her place at the head of the cart while Kris piled it high with the necessary powders, liquids, and utensils. She snatched a pair of rubber gloves from a metal display and tossed them on top of the heap, then grabbed a second, extra-small pair for Sadie. At the lake house, cleaning would be a family affair.

Unlike the ancient staff at Patty's, the Safeway employees appeared to be children barely out of middle school. A teenaged checkout girl with a nose ring and a purple streak dyed into one side of her jet-black hair rang up the items in silence. A shockingly tall boy, his face covered in painful-looking whiteheads, shoved the items into plastic bags.

Kris nodded toward the racks of candy bars and celebrity tabloids that lined the checkout lane. "You wanna pick a treat to take with you?"

Sadie glanced over the selections, hesitant at first, then quickly snatched up a Hershey's with almonds.

Kris smiled. "Solid choice."

The pimple-faced boy stacked the last of the bags in the cart, and Kris and Sadie were on their way. Kris took over control of the cart, pushing it faster, despite the angry rattle of the lame wheel.

They were almost out of the store when a man's voice called out from behind them, "Mrs. Barlow?"

Kris swiveled awkwardly around, her hands still clutching the cart's handle. A short, balding man was striding toward her. He wore an ill-fitting brown suit over a sickly yellow dress shirt that made his tanned skin appear orange and artificial.

"Mrs. Barlow?" he asked again.

"Yes," Kris said, confused.

The man thrust out a stubby-fingered hand. Kris shook it, still not understanding what was happening. The man's palm was warm and slick with perspiration.

"I thought that might be you. Not a lot of new faces in this town. I'm Darryl," he said, as if the name should mean something to Kris. When she did not immediately respond, he added, "Hargrove? The real estate agent? I've been taking care of your daddy's house for ya?"

Kris gave an embarrassed laugh. "Right! Mr. Hargrove, I'm so sorry. My mind is just . . ." She did not bother finishing the sentence, instead swirling a finger in the air to demonstrate her mental state.

Mr. Hargrove gave a loud, hearty laugh, his shoulders bouncing up around his thick neck. "No worries! I wouldn't expect ya to recognize me. I knew your daddy, but I can't say I ever met you, except over email, of course."

"I haven't been back here in a long time."

"Uh-huh." He nodded. "Right." He fell silent for a moment as if he had completely forgotten why he had stopped her in the first place. He cocked his head, thinking, and Kris saw that the collar of his shirt was stained brown from sweat. "Well, listen, I won't keep ya. Just wanted to make sure you got in the house okay. Key was there, right where I said it'd be?"

"Yeah."

"And the place was . . ." Hargrove searched for the appropriate word. "Satisfactory?"

Kris thought of the rancid stench when she had opened the front door, of the corners thick with spiderwebs, of the dead bird with its twisted neck. She wanted to back this grinning bastard up and ask him why the hell he hadn't bothered to fix the front gate or trim the weeds or at least go inside the house to make sure it was habitable before sending her and her daughter in for a three-month stay.

Hargrove swallowed hard, reading the displeasure on her face. "Is something wrong?" he asked nervously.

Kris forced herself to tamp down her rage. "When's the last time you rented the place?" she asked.

Hargrove fumbled for an easy smile. "Well, I would have to check my records—"

"Because," Kris interrupted, "it looks like no one's been out there in months. Maybe years. Don't you have a cleaning crew or a gardener or somebody who maintains these places?"

"Yes, but—"

Kris could feel the bile rising once again. The skin on her neck flushed hot, the heat working its way up the back of her scalp.

"Is this the way you handle all of your rental properties? Or just the ones whose owners have died."

"Mrs. Barlow, I assure you, your father's house—"

"My house. It's my house now."

Offering a smug smile, Hargrove corrected himself. "*Your* house, 'River's End,' as it's come to be known 'round here, it's . . . well . . . it's a unique situation. You see, I was instructed to cancel all upkeep. It wasn't my choice. Trust me, I would prefer to maintain it with the same professionalism and care that I afford all of my rental homes."

But Kris was no longer listening. She stared at him, confused, her brow furrowed. "Cancel . . .? Who told you to do that?"

Any trace of a smile faded from Hargrove's face. "Actually, it was your father. About a few years before he . . . before he passed. He called me, completely out of the blue, and he said he was no longer willing to pay for cleaning and maintenance. I told him, Mrs. Barlow, I told him that that was not a wise decision. As you well know, the summers in these parts can be brutal, and the winters aren't always a picnic either. I mean, one bad hailstorm and everyone in town is calling State Farm for a new roof. Quite frankly, it's dumb luck the house isn't in worse condition. But your daddy was being damn stubborn, if you'll excuse my language. I even offered to cover the costs myself. I figured I could up the rental price a bit to balance things out. But he said it wasn't about the money. He . . ."

Kris waited, but Hargrove clearly had no intention of continuing. "He what?" she asked finally.

"I got the feeling he knew he didn't have much longer on this earth." It was more an excuse than an explanation. "His health must have been fairly bad, even then. Maybe he wasn't thinking straight."

"What did he say?"

A bead of sweat rolled down from what was left of Hargrove's hairline, and he swiped at it as if shooing away a fly.

"He wanted it to rot. He said he hoped the place would rot. He said he wanted to die knowing that no one would ever live in that house again."

For a moment, Kris's brain refused to make sense of these words. They were only sounds coming from Hargrove's lips, with no connection to anything in the known world. And then an image of the dilapidated lake house flashed across her mind, and the image became the meaning of that word.

"Rot," Kris said under her breath. She immediately regretted it. Speaking it aloud felt like she was giving it power, like she was making it real.

"I only put it back up to rent after your father died," Hargrove continued. "I thought I'd honored his wish, and . . . I guess I pitied the house. Not that it mattered one way or the other. Hasn't been a single inquiry, not before yours, I mean." He lowered his voice to a whisper as if he were sharing a secret. "Things 'round here aren't the way they used to be. The town's, well, it's not exactly a destination anymore . . ." Hargrove's words trailed off

She glanced at him. His face had gone slack. He was looking at something just past Kris.

Sadie had stepped out from behind her mother. Until then, she had been out of Mr. Hargrove's line of sight.

Kris blinked and tried to shake off the fog of confusion. "I'm sorry. This is . . . this is my daughter, Sadie."

"Hello," Mr. Hargrove said, his voice strangely flat. His eyes darted quickly between Sadie and Kris. "Um, listen, Mrs. Barlow, I feel terrible about, you know, not telling you about the state of the house. Don't even think the place has internet. I know kids. You're gonna need Wi-Fi for all your girl's gadgets. Plus the action on the lake can get wild this time of year, what with all the boaters and people fishin' and whatnot. What do you say I put you two closer to town? Something more modern. I have several rental properties just sittin' empty for the whole summer. I'd be happy to—"

"We're fine," Kris said sharply. The anger was back, simmering low in her gut.

Hargrove clacked his tongue as if his mouth had suddenly gone dry. "It's just . . . River's End is so far out. You and your daughter might enjoy being able to walk to downtown. Never have to get in the car all summer."

Kris felt Sadie's fingers tug the back of her pant leg. She bent down so Sadie could whisper straight into her ear.

"I want a different house," she said, too faintly for Hargrove to hear.

"What do you mean?" Kris asked. She could feel Hargrove watching them as he attempted to decipher their hushed words.

Sadie's lips pressed even closer. "It's gross. And creepy."

"Mrs. Barlow . . ."

Kris ignored Hargrove. She cupped a hand over her mouth to hide her lips as she said to Sadie, "We'll make it better. I promise. You're going to love it."

She has to or else this was all a mistake. The thought struck a sour chord within Kris like a child pounding the keys of a piano.

Straightening up, Kris said loudly for Hargrove to hear, "It's okay, sweetie, we're going."

Hargrove held out a hand, a plea for one more minute of her time. "I can show you some photos of the places, if you'd like to stop by my office. It's just a couple blocks down."

"The lake house is why we came here, Mr. Hargrove." She put extra emphasis on his name, as if it were meant as an insult. "It's my family's house, and we're going to show it the love it needs."

"Sure," he replied, the word sticking in the back of his throat. Then, without warning, he gave an unprovoked guffaw, his body bouncing. "Sure! It's a great location, that house. Beautiful view of the lake. Great hiking and fishing and . . ." He had come to the end of everything he could possibly say.

"I'll call if I need anything," Kris assured him.

"Anything," he repeated as if he had forgotten what the word meant.

Kris turned back to the main doors, and Sadie turned with her, one hand still clinging to the seam of Kris's jeans. Fresh worry creased her young face.

"You wanna carry the mop for me?"

Sadie glanced at the mop sticking awkwardly out of the cart. She nodded, and Kris withdrew it from where the pimply-faced boy had wedged it. Sadie gripped the handle with both hands, just above the dangling white strings of the mop head.

They had stepped outside into the warm summer air, into the sickeningly sweet aroma of cut wildflowers, when Hargrove called after them, "You be careful out there." Then the automatic doors whooshed shut, and Mr. Hargrove was gone.

She decided to take the long way home.

From downtown, Center Street curved to hug the north edge of Jefferson Park, which sloped down in a treeless stretch of thick green fescue to the shore of the lake. At the entrance to the park, Center Street officially ceased to be, splitting to the left into Willow Street and curving off in a soft right to become what the locals called "New River Road," although the street sign officially gave it the painfully clinical name of CR-134. This is where the buckled asphalt ended and the road became a powdery blend of brown dirt and gray gravel.

Glancing in her side mirror, Kris caught one last look at the flat roofs and painted brick of the downtown buildings, and then the trees swallowed them, their branches folding in to block her view.

Take her back, the timid voice said suddenly in her mind. Kris knew it was not referring to the modest shopping area behind them. *Take Sadie back to Black Ridge and get her the help she needs. Take her to see someone—*

She doesn't need a shrink, Kris shot back. *She needs time away. With her mom. I can help her.*

To their left, dense forest stretched into impenetrable shadow, the thick cover of leaves refusing all but the narrowest rays of sunlight. It was an uncanny sensation. She knew that the south end of Jefferson Park merged with the shoreline, yet this road had somehow avoided the park, even as she drove in a direction that had to take her through it. The forest had inexplicably engulfed them. Both the park and the lake were nowhere to be found.

She's right, her shadow voice purred. *You can't do this alone.*

Kris picked up speed, anxious to escape the darkness.

In the distance, she saw a growing light, like a brightening star. She knew this marked the merging of CR-134 with the original River Road. Years ago, she had ridden in the back seat of their station wagon while her parents drove this same stretch. But the fear did not subside. She could not shake the feeling that when she reached that light, she would be somewhere else with no idea of how to get back.

She pressed the toe of her boot harder onto the accelerator, pushing the Jeep faster. Up ahead, the light expanded, growing larger and brighter as her speedometer arced higher.

And then she was out of the tunnel. Sunlight engulfed her in its warm embrace. Her eyes flicked up to the rearview mirror, and in the sliver of empty space between the mound of luggage and groceries and the ceiling, she saw where they had been. It was not a tear in the fabric of time and space, but a strip of forest that cut through a shallow valley at the far end of Jefferson Park.

Kris let out a slow breath. Woods still surrounded the road on both sides, but the coverage was thinner. Dappled sunshine played across the windshield.

Leaning up slightly in her seat, Kris realized Sadie could see her reflection in the mirror.

"It's okay," Kris told her. "Everything's fine."

Sadie did not look away. She stared at her mother's reflection with the expression of someone who knew they were being told a lie.

CHAPTER FIVE

IT WAS JUST after one in the afternoon when the Jeep pulled into the front drive, flattening the weeds that grew up through the two inches of dirty white gravel.

Kris brought the car to a stop, shifting it into park and killing the engine, but she did not move. One hand remained on the gearshift, the other with a finger resting against the ignition button. She stared through the windshield just as a shadow fell over the lake house. Without the golden glow of the sun to give it life, the house looked like a corpse tossed into a weed-filled ditch to—

Rot.

The word made even less sense to her now. After all these years, why would her father want to abandon this place? He knew that when his drinking finally finished toying with his liver and decided to off it once and for all, the lake house would go to his only child, just like his home in Blantonville and the meager retirement funds that made up his "estate." So why let it fall into ruin knowing that—to use it or to sell it—Kris would have to fix everything Hargrove could have easily maintained?

Unless he thought I wouldn't come back here.

It was true she hadn't even asked about the lake house since their last summer here. But if he suspected she would never use the place herself, that left only two options: let Hargrove try to sell it or . . .

Let it rot.

No. Her father had always been a practical man. Buying a summer home, even one as modest as this, had been the one extravagance he ever allowed himself. Plus, there were too many memories associated with the house. Good memories of fun and love and family.

The door at the back of her mind creaked open.

Not all good, the dark voice sang.

In the back seat, Sadie's seat belt clicked as she unbuckled it. There was a soft zipping sound as it retracted into the plastic wall.

"Hand me that iPad, would ya?" Kris asked.

Sadie looked down at the device beside her on the seat. She stared at it as if she had forgotten what it was, and then she held it out for her mother to take.

Kris made sure it was powered down. She slid the iPad into the glove compartment and slammed it shut. "Sorry, kid, no Wi-Fi means no iPad. We're unplugged. Think you can handle that for the summer?"

Sadie said nothing. Before the accident, losing her device privileges would have resulted in, at the very least, a pouty "No fair!" But now it seemed she couldn't care less.

Kris gave a sharp sigh and climbed out of the car. As she had done a thousand times before, she opened the rear side door and waited as Sadie slipped down from her booster seat. Gravel crunched as Sadie landed on her dingy white Converse.

Kris slammed the door and crouched down so that her eyes were level with Sadie's.

"Help me carry in the groceries?"

Sadie nodded obediently.

For a moment, neither of them moved.

Kris bit her bottom lip between her front teeth. "The house *is* kind of gross, isn't it?"

Another pause, and then Sadie gave her head a small nod, her curls bouncing like weak springs.

"Well," Kris said, "we're going to fix that. Together. Okay?"

An equally timid nod of the head, quicker this time.

"Okay. Good."

Kris took the tips of Sadie's tiny fingers in her own, running the pad of her thumb over the shiny surface of Sadie's nails. She remembered holding Sadie's hand just after she was born, the digits impossibly small, her entire hand curling around Kris's index finger and squeezing as if asking, out of some preternatural instinct, if she were safe.

Kris gazed up at the dilapidated lake house. Sound in his mind or not, her father had let it fall to ruin. But she would restore it. She would bring the house known as "River's End" back to life.

The metal bucket clanked loudly as it was set into the sink basin, and a plastic bottle went *glug-glug-glug* as a healthy dose of Pine-Sol spread across its bottom. Kris turned on the faucet, and the bucket instantly filled with suds.

"Go wild," she said as she held the mop out to Sadie.

Her daughter stared up at her skeptically.

"Seriously," Kris told her. "The entire floor is your canvas and this mop is your paintbrush. Get to work, Picasso."

Sadie's lips spread into a smile.

Kris felt her heart flutter in her chest.

A smile!

An actual smile!

How long had it been?

Kris did not want to entertain the question. The equation was too easily solved.

The top of the handle towered a good twelve inches over Sadie's head as she carefully dropped the mop into the sudsy water. The bucket jiggled in place, threatening to fall over. Sadie shot a concerned look to her mother.

Kris smiled. "For real, you can dump the whole damn thing. It'll just make the floor cleaner than it already is."

Sadie's furrowed brow, seemingly chiseled into stone up to that point, relaxed, her eyes widening with the look of a child who had just realized there were no consequences to her actions. She pulled the mop head from the bucket and slapped it down onto the kitchen floor with a wet smack. Kris watched as Sadie slopped the mop's wet cloth fingers across the large cracked tiles, and she felt a tingling warmth rise into her chest like embers kicked into the air by a fire that refused to die.

Outside, the wind picked up, gliding up from the lake and over the rooftop. It moaned low into the shingles, and its voice echoed down through the chimney's open flue and into the great room. The walls and ceiling creaked loudly against the force of the wind, but the structure was sound. It was not ready to let the elements win.

And they won't, Kris told herself.

First, the countertops. She soaked a sponge under the sink faucet and gave it a squeeze. She picked up one of the spray bottles from her collection, twisted the nozzle to on, and pulled the trigger. A thick mist of cleaner settled onto the grimy tiles, the scent of lemon filling the air. It was artificial, a man-made approximation of citrus, but Kris breathed it in deeply, enjoying the illusion of what it wanted to be. Fresh. Clean.

She leaned down hard on the sponge and worked it across the dull yellow tiles in short, forceful strokes. She made her way from the end closest to the foyer, over the grease-specked surface of the 1960s-era GE electric range and down toward the sink where the collection of old beer cans still stood like a redneck Stonehenge. Kris snatched up the cans and tossed them into an empty Safeway bag, then scrubbed at a beer stain that darkened the tiles like an irregular mole until every trace of it was gone.

It took about half an hour for Kris to make her way to the end of the counter, across the dusty shell and filthy top of the fridge (where an entire army of crickets had met their demise) and over the island's butcher block surface with its countless knife wounds. Another twenty minutes, and she had given each of the upper cabinets a quick cleaning, not exactly thorough but "good enough for jazz" as her father used to say. Most of the hinges on the cabinet doors needed to be tightened and a few would have to be replaced, but that could wait.

Tossing the now-blackened sponge into the sink, Kris stepped back and allowed herself a moment to admire her work. The yellow-tiled countertops sparkled with a cheerful retro charm. The dampness from the sponge brought a richness to the cherry cabinets. Sunlight filtering in through trees outside the breakfast nook windows cast leaf-shaped shadows across the entire room. They swam over the island like lazy tadpoles.

She could see the faint image of herself there, not much older than Sadie, standing beside the island while her mother, wearing her favorite Heart T-shirt (from the actual concert, not the bullshit recycled shirts twenty-somethings wore these days) and jean shorts, cooked grilled cheese sandwiches dripping with gooey Velveeta in a cast-iron skillet.

Kris took a deep breath and slowly exhaled. The stress of the day loosened a bit in her chest and shoulders. A warmth shimmered through her tight muscles.

Behind her, a small figure moved by in a strange swaying dance. Kris turned.

There on a stage streaked with irregular lines of soapy water, back-lit by the golden pillars of the towering windows, stood the silhouette of a small girl. She grasped a tall wooden handle at its center and clumsily yet methodically dragged its end back and forth over the floor.

Another ripple of warmth shifted through the twisted ropes of muscle at the base of Kris's neck.

She's been at it this whole time. Helping her mama.

"Sadie," Kris called out.

The sound startled the little girl, the mop handle slipping from her hands and tipping like a felled tree. It hit the floor with a sharp crack.

"I'm sorry," Sadie said in her soft, timid voice. "I didn't mean to . . ."

"Oh God, no, it's okay, sweetie."

Kris carefully crossed the wet floor and lifted up the mop, leaning the handle against the side of the couch. She crouched down as she always did when she wanted to speak to Sadie on her level.

"Do you want to take a break?" Kris asked.

Sadie considered the question for a moment, and then she shook her head.

Kris smiled. "Okay, well . . ."

She looked around the massive room. Shadows clung to every corner. It was so strangely dim for such a sunny day. At first Kris assumed another cloud had momentarily covered the sun, but the windows still glowed with golden fire. It was as if the light stopped there, the grime covering the glass refusing to let it pass through.

The windows, Kris thought.

It was time to let the light in.

"I have an idea," Kris told her daughter.

She crossed back into the kitchen and dug into one of the Safeway bags, fishing around until she found two fresh rags. She snatched the bottle of Windex from the breakfast nook table as she passed back through the archway, into the great room. She held one of the rags out to Sadie.

"Let's see who can clean the windows the fastest. What do ya say?"

Sadie did not move.

Kris held the rag up higher, just to the side of Sadie's face. "You take the left, I'll take the right. First one to finish gets to eat that Hershey's bar."

For the second time that day, a smile succeeded in lifting Sadie's cheeks. In a flash, she reached out and snatched the rag from Kris's hand.

"On your mark . . ." Kris set the toes of her boots against the floor as if she meant to launch into a sprint. "Get set . . ."

She won't go for it, Kris's mind told her. *She's in mourning. She doesn't want to play games. She's only helping you clean because it takes her mind off of the awful fucking situation you and Jonah have put her in.*

Jonah put her in, Kris corrected herself.

But a child did not think such things. A child looked to both of her parents equally, expecting them to do everything possible to protect her from pain and sorrow. And in that sense, both Jonah and Kris had failed. They had allowed Sadie to know the harshest truth that life has to offer: happiness is not guaranteed. It is not a God-given right. It is not forever earned. We are all children with our hands in the cookie jar, and our happiness can be snatched away at any moment and held cruelly out of our reach.

"Go!" Kris heard herself cry.

But Sadie did go for it.

Without warning, she snatched up the bottle of Windex sitting by Kris's foot and raced to her section of windows.

"Hey!" Kris yelled playfully.

Sadie giggled—*Giggled! Sweet baby fucking Jesus she's laughing!*—and with both hands, the rag still clutched tightly in the palm of one, she squeezed the trigger and sprayed a thick mist of cleaner across the smeared, filthy glass.

Kris rocked back on one foot, a hand to her lips, and watched as her daughter frantically swiped through the dirty lines of cleaning fluid quickly running down to the base of the window. The other side of the pane would need to be cleaned as well, but even with this simple action, streams of sunlight burst through the clear sections of glass, brightening the room.

One room at a time. We will bring this place back to life.

Sadie had just sprayed another healthy dose of cleaner across a dingy section of the window when Kris walked briskly by and snatched the plastic Windex bottle from her hand.

Sadie cried out in exaggerated protest.

"It's a race," Kris told her with a wry smile. "You gotta do what it takes to win."

She gave the squirt bottle's trigger a few quick squeezes, covering a large section of the right windows with bubbling solution.

Kris brought her own rag up to begin sweeping away the running lines of liquid, but her hand froze inches from the glass. The Windex bottle dangled from the fingertips of her other hand, suddenly forgotten.

She frowned.

It was not dirt that was caking the glass, that was keeping the sunshine from fully penetrating. It was countless smudges, the same odd shape stacked one upon the other.

For a moment, Kris stared dumbly at the window, unable to separate the layers to create a single, concrete image.

A flat center, about the size of a silver dollar. Thin lines stretching out from this. Four on top. A smaller one off to the side.

Fingers, she realized. And the silver dollars were the flat smudges of palms.

They were handprints. Countless little handprints.

Without realizing exactly what she was doing, Kris reached up and wiped the rag across the glass. It cut through the smudges and streaks of cleaning liquid slipping quickly down to the base of the window.

They were on the inside. Tens. Hundreds. Thousands of handprints. Small, like a child's.

They covered each column of the rear windows from the bottom frame to a spot about five feet up where the finger marks became impossibly long, streaking down to the flat of the palm, as if something—*someone*—had leapt up and let their hands slide down the pane until their feet were firmly on the ground again.

Someone had been in the house. A child.

Pressing their hands against the windows as they looked out. Jumping up to bang on the glass in a desperate attempt to get someone's attention.

Kris stared at the layers of little handprints covering the glass, and the skin on the back of her neck prickled.

It was just a kid playing, a kid pounding on the window, something a parent should have stopped. Just a rowdy game. That's all it was.

Yet she was filled with the unbearable need to quickly wipe them all away, to scrub the window until every last fingerprint was gone and the window sparkled, clean and clear.

CHAPTER SIX

SADIE WEDGED HER lithe body into a narrow space between the end of the fireplace hearth and the perpendicular wall that led to the kitchen entryway. Tucked back there, out of sight, were three levels of built-in cabinets. Their doors were the same color and width as the pine panels lining the rest of the walls. Had it not been for their hammered metal handles, the cabinets would have gone unnoticed.

"Mommy?" she called out in a voice as sweet and light as a flurry of fairy wings.

Kris stepped down to the floor. She had pulled a kitchen chair over to the back windows so that she could reach the smudges above her five foot, six inches. She glanced around the room, now illuminated with a swath of warm sunlight.

From the side of the fireplace, a poof of red hair popped out, and below it the gleaming eyes of a child who had found treasure.

"Look."

Sadie reached into the cabinet and pulled out a rectangular metal object, gripping its sides with both of her hands to make sure she did not drop it. Its face was covered in buttons and knobs with a clear plastic window like a wide-open mouth at its center. Two large black speakers covered in metal mesh peered out at her like eyes from either end. A swiveling handle protruded from its top. Kris's mother and father had called it "the stereo," but ten-year-old Krissy had known it by its trendier name.

"Mom's boombox," she whispered, the words pulled out of her mouth as if by a string.

Just like that, the ghosts were back. Her father sat in the sagging leather recliner. He was the same age that Kris was now, a year over the hill, and the subtle paunch of a beer belly was threatening the snap buttons of his plaid Western shirt. He was just starting to grow his summer beard. His jawline and cheeks were covered in creeping black stubble. He was smiling at her mother, who sat on the cool stones of the fireplace hearth. She was not a redhead like Kris and the granddaughter she never knew; her hair was straight and brown and fell like smoke across her shoulders. But her eyes were hazel, sometimes taking on the brown tones of Kris's father, other times exploding in the green that enveloped Kris's pupils. Her mother was there for both of them equally, and they loved her for that. Kris could see her mother holding up a cassette tape and her lips moving joyfully, saying words that looked like, "This one will change your life." And then the ghosts were gone.

"There should be . . ." Kris began, letting her words trail away. She pointed in the direction from where Sadie had come. "Is there anything else back there?"

Why don't you check? Shadow Kris was smirking. She could feel it. *Why make the little girl look?*

But Kris said nothing as Sadie leaned down to explore the depths of the cabinets. Kris's mind conjured up all of the things that could be awaiting her daughter's tender fingertips: the bared fangs of a black widow, the necrotic bite of a brown recluse, the quivering stinger at the end of a bark scorpion's tail.

"Mommy!"

Sadie was waving her hand in the air. She held something that caught the sunlight and sent rainbow shafts flickering across the walls. She rushed over and handed it to her mother. It was a dingy plastic case. Kris folded it into the bottom of her shirt and gave it a good wipe. She turned it over. Through the back, she could see words written in blue ballpoint pen. They were the names of songs followed by a dash and then the name of the band that performed them.

Sadie crouched down next to Kris. She could almost feel the little girl's confusion as she studied the foreign object in her mother's hand. "What is it?" Sadie asked.

"A tape. A cassette tape. It's how we used to listen to music when I was a kid. These were my mother's all-time favorites. We had other tapes we would play, ones I brought with me or that we kept in the car, but this one . . . this was a mix she made of the songs she could listen to over and over and over."

Kris quickly scanned the titles, each on its own line, printed in her mother's precise script. Most were from the 1970s and 1980s with a few choice cuts from the late 1960s. The Rolling Stones. Journey. The Cars. The Jesus and Mary Chain. Joy Division. Nick Cave and the Bad Seeds. Several songs had been singled out by her mother with personal expressions of excitement: a heart next to "Cosmic Dancer" by T. Rex; an exclamation point next to "Perfect Circle" by R.E.M.; two exclamations points for "Gypsy" by Fleetwood Mac; three for Prince's "Purple Rain."

She needed to play this tape.

Kris pushed the power button and waited for the slender green light beside it to glow with life. It did not.

She turned the boombox over and set it facedown on the floor. Near the bottom was an oblong compartment door featuring the raised outline of three D-size batteries. Even before she opened it, she could see the white crystals of sulfuric acid creeping out from between the edges of the door.

Her heart sank.

Slipping her thumb under the tab, she squeezed it against the side of the plastic door and popped the compartment open.

It was just as she had suspected. The copper and black bodies of three Energizer batteries were caked in flakey white powder. The metal prongs and springs at either side of the compartment had rusted and eroded. There was no salvaging it.

"Damn," she said softly, knowing that the word did not even come remotely close to conveying the level of disappointment she felt.

You got your hopes up, her mind scolded. *You know better than—*

On the side of the boombox, her fingers grazed the hinges of another compartment. Two letters adorned its door: AC. She opened the compartment door, and the thin black body of a power cord sprang out like a snake.

She glanced around the room.

There was an outlet next to the fireplace. Its cover was wrapped in faux wood, a pathetic attempt to match the richness of the wall.

Kris set the boombox on the edge of the stone hearth, plugged the power cord into the outlet, and once again pushed the power button. Slowly, the green light began to glow brighter and brighter.

She slid the cassette from its case and dropped it into a small compartment on the front of the boombox. Her index finger stroked the Play button with indescribable anticipation. Finally she pushed it down.

Inside the compartment, the spools began to turn.

At first there was only the soft hiss of white noise at the head of the tape. They waited in silence, Kris eagerly preparing herself for the first notes of the first song, Sadie unsure as to what exactly she was about to hear.

They waited for what felt like an eternity.

And then the speakers vibrated with the sharp snap of a snare drum and the strum of an electric guitar, its sound as cool and delicate as wind chimes knocked about by a winter breeze. A man began to sing in a calculated, sweeping lilt that somehow felt both self-conscious and painfully bare.

"Take me out tonight . . . where there's music and there's people and they're young and alive . . ."

It washed over Kris and a sob, equal parts joy and sadness, choked in her throat. "This is the Smiths, baby. And, man, did your grandma love them."

"Driving in your car . . . I never, never want to go home . . . because I haven't got one anymore . . ."

They sat side by side at the base of the great stone fireplace, listening as Morrissey's melancholy voice wafted around the room until finally it spiraled up to the cathedral ceiling.

They moved into the hallway, the music echoing ahead of them to drift around the corner at the end of the corridor.

Kris reached out and touched the wood-paneled wall as they walked, lightly dragging her fingers over its once-smooth surface, the grain now raised and jagged, the protective layer of varnish long gone. Her fingertips hit the edge of the paneling around the first doorframe.

She cocked her head to the side. Sadie was there at the edge of her vision, a small pale blur topped with an explosion of red.

"This was my bedroom," Kris said. "The one I stayed in during the summer."

She grasped the tarnished brass knob and turned it. The door swung open before them.

The room was much more basic than she recalled. It was a simple square, empty except for a chunky oak dresser slathered with a thick coat of pink paint and a full mattress and box spring in a vintage wrought-iron frame. Five metal bows were welded to the top bar of the footboard. She could still remember lying in bed at night and pretending that each of those bows had belonged to a princess who had once slept in this room. Once she had even used a length of red ribbon to tie her own bow alongside the others in hopes that when she woke in the morning, it would have hardened to metal.

Along the wall to their right, sliding mirrored doors opened to a shallow closet, just big enough to hold a summer's worth of clothes. Above the dresser was the room's only window, over which sheer drapes hung from a slightly bent rod. The years had aged the drapes from their original fresh cream to a jaundiced yellow. Sunlight filtered in through this, giving the entire space the dull brownish-orange glow of a sepia photograph.

A hiss filled the great room as the Smiths were followed by two seconds of silence. And then the next song began: the easy, simple strumming of an acoustic guitar called out, inviting in an electric twang that gave the easy groove a country and western feel. The chords cruised like a pickup truck down a dusty back road, and behind the wheel was Mick Jagger with his laid-back vocals, one hand on the wheel, the other out the open window to feel the summer breeze slipping through his fingers.

"Childhood living . . . is easy to do . . . the things you wanted . . . I bought them for you . . ."

Kris felt Sadie's small body wedge against hers in the bedroom doorway. She slipped her fingers into her daughter's twisted locks and gently massaged her scalp.

"You don't have to keep helping if you don't want to."

Sadie leaned in and eyed the room from the mirrored closet doors to the bed's headboard. "It won't take us long."

There was a trace of enthusiasm in her voice, just a hint, but enough to make Kris smile.

"Okay. Then go refill the mop bucket, soldier. Unless you can't handle it."

"I can handle it," Sadie replied with a playful smirk, and she hurried back into the great room. Perhaps it was wishful thinking, but Kris could have sworn she had a spring in her step.

She's coming back. The thought both thrilled and saddened Kris, because if it were true, it proved that Sadie had been gone, trapped in a dark place, away from her mother.

Mick Jagger's voice rose as the music swelled around him.

"Wild horses . . . couldn't drag me away . . ."

Kris inched her way into the bedroom. Something warned her not to move too quickly, as if she might startle the image before her and it would flash away, like a forgotten memory.

Carefully, she reached up and parted the drapes. They had lost their softness long ago and were stiff, like the parchment of an old manuscript. But with them open, the light could shine in unimpeded. It drove the shadows farther into the corners and under the bed. It played across the plaster walls, causing them to blush as it revealed a top coat of pink paint.

There was a texture to the plaster, a pattern, a single design duplicated over and over, rolled into the plaster when it was still wet. With her finger, Kris traced one of the lines, following it as it swung in small arcs, inward and outward, coming to a point each time before repeating the process. The series of arcs carried her fingertip around five distinct points, like a hand smashed flat.

A leaf, she realized suddenly.

A maple leaf.

Yes. When the plaster had first been spread, it had been imprinted with the shapes of maple leaves, each one about five inches in diameter. The rudimentary process gave each leaf its own unique imperfections— a soft side here, a crooked edge there.

There are pictures on the wall. The thought was less a revelation than a reminder of something forgotten long ago. When she was little, she would look at these shapes until . . .

Kris stepped back so she could see the entire design spread out over one wall. She stared at the irregular shapes until the negative space between each line turned the leaves into a gallery of crudely drawn sketches. Here was a bird with its wing raised as if it were waving hello.

There was an airplane flying straight up toward the ceiling. And down on a section of wall between the dresser and bed was a face, grinning a Cheshire cat grin so wide that its cheeks poked at the sides.

Kris returned the smile as the warmth of nostalgia enveloped her. Much had changed about the lake house, most of it for the worse, but here in her old pink bedroom, the pictures on the walls remained. They just needed her to see them.

In the doorway, Sadie returned, the handle of the metal bucket clutched in both hands as she struggled to keep the sudsy water from sloshing over the side. The mop handle was pinched under her arm, and the still-damp mop head dragged behind her, leaving wavering wet lines in its wake.

"Sweetie," Kris laughed, reaching for the handle. "Let me help you."

They set to work, Kris taking over with mopping duties, Sadie meticulously misting every other surface with a burst of Pledge and wiping it all down with a clean rag. Their chores did not take long. By the time they were stripping the old sheets from the mattress, only one other song—"Cosmic Dancer" by T. Rex—had followed the Stones.

Kris dropped the fitted sheet on top of the others in a pile at the foot of the bed. Later, she would unload their luggage from the car and find the clean sheets she had brought from home.

"This is your room now," she told Sadie. She hoped her smile didn't look as bittersweet as it felt.

Sadie said nothing. She did not even nod to acknowledge her mother's words. She stared at the bedroom in the same way she greeted her new classroom each year at school.

Across the hall from Sadie's room was the second closed door, slightly narrower than the others. Unlike the tarnished brass handles on all of the other doors, this one had an intricately cut crystal knob. Sadie admired its many edges as she slipped her hand around it.

"The bathroom," Kris told her.

Sadie gave the knob a twist.

There were no windows in this room. What little light fell in from the hall revealed a floor of black and white diamond tiles.

Kris reached over Sadie's shoulder, and her hand disappeared into the blackness. She slid it blindly across the wall, feeling the loose ends of wallpaper that lapped at her fingers like dry tongues. Finally her hand slid across the slick, glazed ceramic of a light switch cover. She flicked the switch up.

Overhead, a fluorescent light buzzed and gave a few strobe-like flickers as it attempted to come alive. Kris and Sadie stared into that flashing light, the glimpses of the room appearing and disappearing too quickly for their eyes to get a solid grasp on any details.

There was something in there, pale and rippled, seemingly suspended in midair.

Kris tried to force her brain to capture the image like a photograph, but just as she felt close to understanding what she was seeing, the space before her was swallowed by the dark.

She took a step closer. An inexplicable thought slithered into her mind: *Whatever it was, it will be closer this time. It will be right in front of you.*

The thought made her brow furrow, her eyes narrow, and she took a slight step backward just as the light clicked and the room became illuminated beneath a radiant white dome.

There was no furious specter waiting for them. The pale thing Kris had seen was an old shower curtain hanging from a curved metal rod. Beneath it, she glimpsed the lionlike paws of a claw-foot tub.

But she was wrong. Something *was* there. It was a little girl, staring back at them with wide green eyes, as green as Sadie's, as green as Kris's had been all those years ago, before life and pain and disappointment dulled their sheen.

Kris gasped, her heart suddenly pounding against the inside of her rib cage.

It looks like Sadie because it is Sadie, her mind reasoned.

She let out a slow breath.

The entire moment had taken no more than three seconds: one second of confusion, one of fear, and a final second of relief as she realized the voice in her mind was right.

She was staring into an oval mirror in a silver frame mounted over a dingy white sink with separate hot and cold faucets stained by age. It was an odd sensation to stare into those eyes, her daughter's eyes, once her own eyes, and for a brief moment to believe that the redheaded girl in the gray-and-black checkered shirt and light blue shorts was a stranger.

Sadie must have experienced a similar sensation, for she raised her right hand and her tense body relaxed as the girl in the mirror did the same.

It was a reflection. Of course it was. What else would it be?

Without a word, they began their job, experts after only three rooms.

CHAPTER SEVEN

THE BATHROOM TOOK a bit longer to clean than Sadie's room, mostly due to the bathtub. After three decades and who knows how many renters since Kris's last stay at the lake house, it appeared no one had bothered to give the inside of the tub a single scrubbing. Dirt ringed the floor and walls, and a grayish-black mildew crept up the sides and over the lip like a fossilized plant.

At least their chores had a soundtrack.

Mom's jams, Kris thought, and she found herself smiling as she continued the painfully mundane task.

The eerie, jangly chords of "I Let Love In," accompanied by the off-key croon of Nick Cave, drifted in from the great room like a wandering spirit as Kris worked her way out from the doorway with the mop.

"Despair and deception, love's ugly little twins . . . came a-knocking on my door . . . I let them in . . ."

It took two passes, half a can of abrasive Comet, and a sponge left in tatters before all of the muck was loosened from the sides of the tub. Kris twisted the stainless-steel cross handle marked Hot. Water swirled around the tub and spiraled down the drain. Once the porcelain was white and pristine, Kris twisted the handle back, shutting off the water. She wiped fresh sweat from her face and sat down on the side of the tub.

Sadie had crawled under the sink and was meticulously cleaning the curve of the trap.

She's such a good kid, Kris thought. And she was right. Sadie was a good kid. Despite everything she had been through recently, there she was, helping her mother clean room after room in an abandoned lake house to which she had never asked to come.

"You getting tired of this?" Kris asked.

Sadie looked over, and for a moment, her eyes said, *Yes, I was tired of this halfway through the kitchen.* But instead she shook her head and mumbled a halfhearted, "No, I'm fine. I like helping you."

And she does. She does like helping you. That's the problem. She's eight and you're forty-one and you should be helping her, not the other way around.

Kris set the sponge on the edge of the tub and twisted her hair into a tight ponytail.

"Why don't you go play?" she said.

Sadie remained crouching, frozen, as if it were a test.

"Come on, seriously. You've helped so much. Do you want to stop?"

Nothing. And then Sadie gave a small, sharp nod, her curls bobbing around her downturned face.

"Come here," Kris said.

Leaving her sponge on the tiles, Sadie carefully scooted out from under the sink and crossed the damp tiles until she was close enough to fall into her mother's arms. Kris held her tight, burying her face in Sadie's hair and breathing in a scent that still held the faintest hint of the bald pink scalp she had smelled that first day, when a nurse laid a newborn baby girl into her arms.

"I love you," Kris whispered, her lips brushing the inside curve of Sadie's ear.

In the great room, the fuzzy, dreamy sound of the Jesus and Mary Chain launched into "Just Like Honey."

For a long moment they sat in silence. Kris leaned against the tub, and Sadie leaned against her. Kris listened to the soft, steady breaths drifting in and out of her daughter's slightly parted lips. She closed her eyes, and the sound became the slow roll of the tide stretching lazily across sparkling white sand before folding back into the hush of pristine waters.

"We're done cleaning for today," Kris said finally. "Cool?"

Sadie nodded, her wild hair tickling Kris's cheek.

Kris stood up from the side of the tub, forcing Sadie to stand with her.

"What are we doing?" Sadie asked, confused.

Kris grasped Sadie's hand in hers. Both of their fingers were beginning to prune from the wet sponges.

"I think we deserve to have some fun," Kris said.

She gave a wink, and then she was pulling Sadie out of the bathroom, their feet nearly slipping out from beneath them on the wet tile.

She led the little girl quickly across the great room and over to the French doors.

"Mommy, what are we doing?" There was growing concern in Sadie's voice.

Kris did not reply. She crouched down to a squat, her back to Sadie. "Hop on."

Sadie did not move.

"Come on, girl, train's about to leave the station!"

Hesitantly, Sadie climbed onto her mother's back.

Sadie gave a startled yelp and tightened her grip as Kris threw open the French doors. Warm summer air rushed around them like an exhaled breath. Kris hopped across the rough wooden deck in her bare feet like a panicking firewalker, chanting two words over and over— "No splinters no splinters no splinters"—until she was safely down on the flat stone path that cut across the backyard. She leapt from stone to stone as Sadie flailed on her back, giggling with fear and exhilaration.

They reached the edge of the bluff. The waters of Lost Lake stretched below. A cluster of clouds, painted with the golden light of late afternoon, hung over the distant gypsum hills, but otherwise the sky was clear and blue. There was no wind, not even the hint of a breeze, and the surface of the lake was as still as glass.

"Okay, you're getting heavy," Kris announced with a tired chuckle. She bent down so Sadie could hop off her back. They both stood on the very last stone before the path descended down the other side of the slope, toward the dock.

Sadie looked up at her mother, and her eyes sparkled in the sunlight like polished jewels.

"What are we doing?" she demanded.

"We're going swimming."

"In our clothes?!" It seemed to be the craziest thing Sadie had ever heard.

Kris shrugged. "Well, we can't go naked, unless you want to get arrested."

Sadie looked from her fully clothed body to the cool water lapping the rocky shore.

"Can we do that?" she asked.

Kris delicately ran a finger under Sadie's chin, lifting her face until their eyes met.

"We can do anything we want. It's our summer."

An excited smile spread across Sadie's face.

They were down the slope in seconds, bounding from step to step as if being chased. When they reached the edge of the wooden dock, they both chanted Kris's mantra in perfect unison: "No splinters no splinters no splinters!"

Kris expected Sadie to slow as they neared the end, but the girl needed no prompting. She tightened her grip on her mother's hand and gave a squeal of pure, unbridled giddiness.

"Jump!" Kris cried.

And they jumped. Together. Hand in hand.

They screamed as they fell, a sound that vibrated like laughter. It bounced off the gypsum hills and returned to them, enveloping them in their own joy.

Kris had long enough to glance over and see her eight-year-old daughter, eyes wide, mouth wide open in a shriek of exhilaration. Then they were splashing down into the water, puffing their cheeks full of air as they plunged beneath the surface.

A thought flitted through her mind: *They were right. It's bottomless. It just goes on and on forever and ever.*

But there *was* a bottom, and she felt the tips of her toes dig into it, disappearing into slimy mud until they touched the layer of rock beneath. Even with her eyes shut tight, she could sense the shimmering sunlight cutting through the clear water. She pushed up toward the sunlight, her arms stretched out above her, her left hand still clutching the small hand of a child floating above her.

Kris broke the surface and sucked air desperately into her lungs.

Beside her, Sadie was treading water, her little legs kicking madly to keep her head from going under again.

"It's cold!" she cried out with a shivering laugh.

"It always is, even on the hottest days," Kris explained.

She gave Sadie's hand a light tug, and the little girl's body floated over and into her arms. She felt Sadie's legs stop kicking as she relaxed in her mother's embrace.

"I got you," Kris said softly. "It's okay, I got you."

Sadie rested her head on Kris's shoulder, her breaths warm and steady against Kris's neck.

"I got you," Kris said once more.

They fell silent, the water rippling around them as Kris gently sliced her legs like scissors to keep them both afloat.

On the bluff above them, the lake house stood, quiet and empty, awaiting their return.

CHAPTER EIGHT

SADIE'S BAG WAS the smallest piece of luggage, a purple duffel with cream-colored handles and a shoulder strap embroidered with orange-and-yellow daisies. Hand-sewn between two of the flowers was a square black patch featuring a red Anarchy sign, a personal touch from Kris. She just couldn't resist the need to break up the earnest childishness of the bag. Life was not all blooms and sunshine. Sometimes life threw you a curveball. Sometimes it beaned you at a hundred miles per hour.

Sadie had crammed so many possessions into the bag that the zipper's clamped teeth seemed to be clenching to keep from popping open.

"What did you pack in here?" Kris asked, pretending to strain under its weight.

Sadie shrugged. "Just . . . stuff."

After their swim, they had climbed up onto the dock where they lay side by side on the flaking white planks, allowing their clothes and hair to dry in the sun. There had been no reason to rush. Even at four in the afternoon, they still had over three hours of light before the sun sank below the rocky hills that curled around the west side of the lake like an alligator's tail.

It was close to six o'clock, and Sadie's freckled cheeks were still rosy from her time outdoors. Even though their clothes were slightly damp, neither of them had any intention of changing. Changing would mean officially closing the book on their afternoon together. They wanted to hang onto it for just a little while longer, to feel the cool fabric of their wet clothes sticking to their skin, to smell the mineral-rich odor of lake water on their frizzy hair.

Kris pushed open the door to Sadie's bedroom, and the hinges gave a slight squeak, like a startled mouse. The scent of lemon cleaner still hung in the air.

She set the bag down with a faint thump beside the bed and stepped back to allow Sadie to carefully pull the zipper across its bulging top.

"How about you unpack while I get dinner ready?" Kris suggested.

Sadie nodded and quietly began removing the items from her bag. She organized them into neat piles—socks, underwear, pants, shirts—until they formed a half circle around her. The stuffed animals she lined up in a row along the base of the dresser. Her favorite, a purple frog with crooked eyes, stood guard at the head of the plush menagerie. Its head sagged low on a neck in need of stuffing.

The sight of the frog sent a pang of sadness ringing in Kris's heart like a church bell.

Her daddy gave her that.

Kris backed away, out into the hall. She was turning toward the great room when something caught her attention, a dark shape at the corner of her eye.

She glanced back over her shoulder.

At the end of the hall, the third door stood half open, just as she had left it after disposing of the blackbird's corpse. The sunlight in that room had been bright then. But the sun had shifted as evening fell. Black lines ran like oil streaks down what little wall she could see. The longer she stared, the more it seemed like one of those shadows was closer than the others, as if it had taken a step away from the wall. It peered at her.

Bullshit. Shadows don't peer at you. You stare at anything long enough in this house, and you see shadow people behind doors and grinning faces in the walls.

Still, she could not look away. She stared at the shadow behind the door, and the shadow stared back, each waiting for the other to move.

An ear-piercing shriek sent an electric jolt down Kris's back.

She spun around.

In the pink bedroom, Sadie was crouched down in front of the dresser, her hands still on the round wooden knobs of the bottom drawer.

She winced. "Sorry."

Kris let out a relieved breath.

Slowly, Sadie pulled the stubborn drawer the rest of the way out. Its warped sides continued to make that god-awful sound, although in a lower register, like a recording of a scream played at the wrong speed.

Kris shook off the shock and started to walk away. But as she reached the entryway to the great room, she paused.

Look back.

She fought the urge, but the voice in her mind purred, savoring the words:

Look. Back.

She allowed herself one quick glance, just to satisfy her curiosity.

The sun outside must have shifted, because the shadow behind the door was gone.

In a storage space under the kitchen island, among baking sheets and pans burned black from years of abuse, was a cast-iron skillet. She rinsed it out in the sink, set it down on the largest burner of the electric range, and turned the corresponding knob to Medium. Beneath the skillet, the heating coil slowly came to life, transforming from gunmetal gray to a glowing red.

By the time Kris had buttered two pieces of bread and sandwiched a thick slice of Velveeta between them, Sadie had returned from her bedroom. She leaned her elbows on the island's butcher-block top and rested her chin in her hands, watching as her mother dropped the sandwich onto the hot skillet. The bottom layer of bread hissed angrily as it began to brown.

Kris had forgotten to take up the dusty cushions from the breakfast nook booth, and the thought of any dead roaches and crickets decaying underneath forced them to stand and eat their sandwiches at the kitchen island. They munched quietly as the gooey goodness of artificial cheese oozed out from between slices, pausing every now and then to dig into a bag of barbecue chips laying open beside them. It wasn't the fanciest dinner, but it just felt right.

It was close to seven now. The shadows in the great room had grown long and narrow across the freshly cleaned wood floor. The four grand windows at the far end of the house sparkled with golden sunshine, as did the surface of the lake beyond them. On the opposite shore, leaves shimmered in the breeze like schools of silver-skinned fish. The trees stretched for another quarter mile, and the red hills rose up from the forest. The ridge of the hills was a line of fire.

Kris checked the kitchen drawers until she found a corkscrew, which she twisted through the foil top of a bottle of wine and into the soft flesh of a cork. The cork gave a feeble screech as it was ripped from the bottle's neck. She found a 1970s-era amber glass tumbler in another cabinet, gave it a quick rinse with soap and water, and filled it halfway with the cabernet she had brought from Black Ridge. She had a few more bottles leftover from Jonah's wake that were still packed in a box in the Jeep. After that, she would have to find a liquor store.

The balcony called to her, and she opened the French doors, Sadie following her outside.

At one end of the deck was an old metal bistro table. On its surface was a mosaic sunburst that would have exploded in bright orange and yellow and red had it not been for the thick layer of dirt covering it. A spiderweb hung underneath the table. It stretched between the legs in an elegant circular pattern. This was not the random madness of a black widow's web. Kris knew whatever spider lived there would be harmless.

On either side of the table were two barstools. Their bare metal seats were in need of cushions and a few streaks of white bird droppings were crusted on their backs, but otherwise they were still in decent shape.

Kris pulled the stools away from the table, flicked away the bulk of the bird shit with her fingernail, and positioned them side by side before the deck's front railing. With her free hand, she tapped the seat of the chair closest to Sadie as if to say, *Hop up.*

Sadie placed a bare foot on the thin metal bar running low around the chair legs and hoisted herself up onto the seat. A blackish-orange line of rust and dirt was left on the bottom of Sadie's foot.

She'll take a shower later, Kris told herself. Then she shrugged. *Or she won't. She can go to bed with a dirty foot. Whatever she wants, as long as she's happy.*

She waited for the shadow voice deep in her mind to mock this, to tell her that Sadie would never be happy, never again. But there was only silence.

Kris slipped an arm around Sadie's back, and the little girl snuggled into her side. Neither said a word as they watched night gently descend on Lost Lake.

The flames behind the hills died down until only a sliver of pink separated the ridge from the darkening sky. The first star faded into view, and then another and another, and each one birthed a twin in the lake's mirrorlike waters. Soon a trail of stars stretched out infinitely into the blackness.

Just as the stars had appeared, faint lights began to flicker in the darkness around the shoreline of their cove. Other lake houses. Other people looking out their windows or sitting on their decks to witness the fantastic transformation of day to night, each one in awe as if they were seeing it for the first time.

From somewhere within the dark clusters of cattails that dotted the shore, bullfrogs began to croak. They sang from deep in their throat, a guttural song that crouched low to the rocky ground as it drifted up the slope to the house. In the weeds, the crickets responded with their own night music. Their higher pitch and faster rhythm should have clashed with the slow, steady bass of the frogs, yet somehow the two disparate tunes melded into something new and implausibly perfect.

Over by the swing set, its metal skeleton cloaked in shadow, a firefly blinked. Soon the entire bluff overlooking the lake was alight with the insects, their tails flashing in the darkness like silent fireworks.

Kris nuzzled closer to Sadie and whispered in her ear, "If we can find a jar, we could catch them. You could keep them in your room."

For a moment, Sadie considered this, and then she said, "But won't they die if we try to keep them?"

Fuck. Don't ruin this. Don't ruin this moment, Kris scolded herself.

"Yeah, you're right. Better to let them fly around free out here. They're pretty, aren't they?"

She felt Sadie nod. Any thoughts of death seemed to have passed.

Out beyond the mouth of their cove, across what looked like miles of open water, the horizon began to glow with a pale light. Kris watched as the silver moon inched its way into the black sky. Like the stars before it, the moon was captured in the surface of the lake. The cool breeze picked up, rippling the water, and the moon's reflection dissolved into waving lines like a bad television signal.

Something was there, the hint of movement on the water, a pale wisp gliding over the face of the lake.

"Look," Kris said, pointing.

Sadie leaned out and peered into the darkness. "I don't see—"

"There. Just above the water."

Now Sadie did see it, a ghostly form rising into the cooling air. "Is that smoke?" she asked, slightly alarmed.

Kris shook her head. "Mist. It happens here almost every night in the summer. The valley cools down fast once the sun goes down, and as the water gets colder, the mist floats up. Kind of looks like the lake is on fire, doesn't it?" Kris pulled Sadie closer. "When I was your age," Kris said softly, "I would pretend the mist was the breath of a dragon that lived under the lake. And when everyone was asleep, the dragon would shoot up out of the water and fly through the night sky, breathing fire to keep the stars burning."

They stared out at the thickening mist as it whipped up into curling white tongues that licked the darkness. Kris draped her arm over Sadie's chest and could feel the quick, rabbit-like *pat-pat-pat* of the girl's heart beating. She was reminded of the profound moment when she heard that sound for the first time, when Sadie didn't even have a name, when she was only known as "the baby" or "baby girl" or "our little peanut." When they were a family. When, for a brief moment, she could not feel the shards of fear and sadness buried deep within her. When there was only love.

Sadie shivered suddenly.

"I'm cold," she announced, rubbing the sides of her arms with her hands.

"It stays kinda cool here, by the lake. Even in June," Kris said.

Sadie did not respond, but her hands worked harder to warm her goose-pimpled flesh.

Kris slipped her arm out from around the girl.

"Do you wanna go in?"

Sadie nodded. Her eyes caught the moonlight and glistened in the shadows.

"Okay. You go get ready for bed. Don't worry about showering tonight. You can do it tomorrow."

She nodded again and carefully slid down from her chair. The deck's wooden planks creaked faintly under her weight as she crossed to the back door and slipped into the house. The door clicked shut behind her.

Kris was alone.

She took a sip of her wine and rolled it lazily over her tongue as she listened to the symphony of the lake at night. The deep honk of the frogs and the buzz of the crickets had been joined by the rustling of windblown leaves, like a brush being lightly swept over a cymbal, and the occasional hoot of an owl somewhere deep in the low black mass that was the forest.

She could smell the entire world on the air: the sweetness of blooming flowers; the dry earthiness of dirt and rocks; the vibrant, ripe greenness of budding vegetation; the smokiness of ancient, twisted wood; the crisp, clean scent of lake water. This was the perfume worn by the best moments of her childhood, those summer nights when she and her parents would sit out on this very deck, the charcoal in her father's grill smoldering to ash, the neck of a Bud Light bottle clutched between her mother's fingers. And there was little Krissy, standing at the railing, counting fireflies.

Kris slid off the barstool and drifted over to the edge of the deck. Just as she had suspected, the railing was loose. It rocked easily back and forth in her hand, giving a few inches in either direction until the resistance of old screws finally stopped it with an irritated groan.

I can fix it, she thought, adding it to the seemingly endless list of home-improvement projects.

But that was for tomorrow. Or the next day. Or the next week.

Right now she wanted to do nothing but drink her wine and watch the mist swirl on the lake as the last hint of dusk faded into night.

She shivered. Sadie was right. It was getting cold.

Without warning, an unusually warm gust of air whipped up from below and wrapped Kris's body. It was as if someone had stepped up behind her and draped a blanket over her shoulders.

Kris closed her eyes.

"Hello, Mom," she whispered to the wind.

CHAPTER NINE

THE BOWL OF a flush-mount fixture hung from the ceiling, a single lightbulb filling it with a soft amber light, the dried bodies of dead moths silhouetted against its frosted glass.

Sadie sat on her knees on the floor beneath the light fixture. She had just finished placing the last pair of socks in the bottom drawer of the pink dresser. The rest of her clothes were already put away: shirts in the wide top drawer, pants and shorts in the middle, underwear in the small drawer on the bottom left and now socks on the bottom right. The few dresses and rompers she had brought were hanging on wire hangers in the mirrored closet.

All that was left was to find the perfect spot for her beloved stuffed animals.

As she glanced around the room, she picked up the purple frog with the crooked eyes and goofy smile and clutched him tightly to her chest.

His name was Bounce, and Daddy had won it for her at the fair. He had given the man with the yellow teeth five dollars and thrown three softballs into a stack of plastic bottles. The third ball hit just right and the bottles went flying, going *plink-plonk-plunk* as they rattled across the wooden floor of the yellow-toothed man's game booth. *Anything from the middle row for the big winner*, Mr. Yellow Teeth had announced.

She had scanned the collection of animals packed tightly into the third row: tigers and monkeys and even a green space alien wearing the kind of round helmet the old-timey astronauts used to wear. But when she saw the big silly grin on the froggy's face—and he was purple, her favorite—she knew this was the one. This was her prize. From her daddy.

She had snuggled into the frog's shaggy fur, knowing full well that frogs didn't have fur, except this one did, this one was different—this one was *lucky*. She had watched two other people play that game before Daddy and neither of them had won anything. And there she was, bouncing gently in Daddy's arms as he carried her away from the row of carnival games—from the ring toss and the duck pond and the one where you squirted the clown in the mouth and a balloon grew bigger and bigger and bigger over his creepy clown face—out to the center of the fairgrounds where lights flashed and metal cars full of screaming kids swung by on all sides and in every direction.

She had heard Mommy lean in to Daddy and whisper, "That thing looks like it has some kind of frog disease. Its eyes aren't even sewn on straight." And she had hated Mommy a little in that moment. Just for a second. But it was long enough for hot anger to reach deep into her chest and down to the pit of her stomach. Until then, she hadn't noticed that Bounce's eyes weren't quite straight or that the threads at the corner of his smile were beginning to pull loose and a little bit of white stuffing was poking out. Until then, he had been perfect.

She remembered shrugging and telling herself that she didn't care what Mommy thought. She loved Bounce. She would love him more *because* of his crooked eyes and stringy smile. She would love him most of all.

That had been almost two years ago.

The following autumn, the fair came through Black Ridge as it did every year, but this time Daddy didn't win any prizes. He didn't play a single game. She walked between her parents for most of the evening, until she got sleepy and Mommy carried her. Once she looked up and saw Daddy staring into the swirling silver cars of the Scrambler. The rest of the night he was either on his phone or strolling silently beside them with his hands in his pockets. He was there, but he wasn't there. That's how she had felt. He was with them, but he was also somewhere else, in his mind. Like he was daydreaming of a place he would rather be, like how Sadie's mind sometimes wandered at school. She knew she should be listening to her teacher, but the sunlight outside was dancing too pretty to look away.

The fair would come through again this fall. Maybe she and Mommy would go. But not Daddy. Not ever again.

Sadie wrapped her arms even tighter around Bounce. His soft purple body squished flat in her hug. She buried her face in his matted fur, just as she had that evening when Daddy had won him for her. She closed her eyes, and the tears that caught beneath her lids stung as they searched for a way out. She did not want them to escape. She was afraid that if one slipped free, she would not be able to stop the rest. She would cry until her bedroom was filled with tears, and she would be stuck there, at the bottom of that ocean, hugging her purple frog with the crooked eyes and wishing that nothing had ever changed.

A wet, hot line streaked down her cheek.

Sadie whimpered and pressed her face deeper into Bounce's limp body. His stuffing crunched softly inside. Another white clump had found a small hole on the frog's back and poked up like a pimple ready to burst. Sadie felt that single tear reach the line of her jaw where it hung, just for a second, before splashing to the floor below.

She glanced down.

The wetness from the tear was already fading, like the floor was drinking it up.

And then she heard it.

A whisper.

No, that wasn't quite right. It was almost like the memory of a whisper, a sound echoing to her from the past.

Sadie cocked her head, listening, even as she became certain that it wasn't her ears that had detected the sound.

As quickly as it appeared, the strange whisper was gone, whooshing away like air sucked back through an opened door.

She sat perfectly still, Bounce all but forgotten in her hands. She listened for that sound.

She wasn't sure what it was, but she longed to hear it again.

CHAPTER TEN

GRABBING HER PHONE from the kitchen counter, Kris turned and found herself staring through the archway to the great room, at the four paneled windows standing like strange glass sentinels. Their bodies were black against the night.

She needed to call home. She needed to touch base with Allison, let her know they made it okay, make sure everything was under control at work.

She tapped the face of her phone with her thumb and it illuminated to reveal several alerts on the lock screen. Since leaving home, she had set the phone to Do Not Disturb. She knew that word of their abrupt departure would travel like lightning through their hometown, and from the alerts greeting her, she had been right. Texts and missed calls from friends and nosy neighbors hungry for gossip. A voicemail message from Jonah's favorite aunt who lived in the foothills outside of town, the one who always referred to Kris as "that girl" and now pretended to be a sympathetic ear just so she could feed off of Kris's pain like a leech. More reasons not to be in Black Ridge. More reasons to leave the phone on Do Not Disturb.

Ignoring the alerts, she typed in her password, opened the Phone app, and navigated to Favorites. She pressed the entry for "Allison" and raised the phone to her ear.

The number began to dial over hundreds of miles to a modest two-examination-room veterinary clinic in the small mountain town of Black Ridge, Colorado.

A click, and the distant ringing was replaced by the barking of dogs. A woman's voice spoke sharply, "Dr. Barlow?"

"Hey, Allison, we're here," Kris said.

"Just one second."

On the other end, a door swung shut, and the barking became muffled, as if through a wall. Allison spoke again, this time less distracted, the usual chipper tone in her voice.

"Sorry. Everyone in town decided to go on vacation at the same time. No more room at the inn. Place is a little nuts." Then, realizing how that must have sounded, she added, "But it's all under control. No reason to worry. Dr. Nichols is cool, as usual."

Kris sighed. "Dr. Nichols is not cool."

"Okay," Allison admitted, lowering her volume just in case Kris's fellow veterinarian was nearby. "Wrong choice of words. Dr. Nichols is as crotchety yet competent as ever."

"I shouldn't be gone for so long," Kris said. Forgetting her responsibilities back home had been easy when she'd kept herself isolated, but talking to Allison made her truly feel the distance. She had built that practice herself, and now . . .

"It's all good," Allison insisted.

"People hate Nichols. I know that. I should have kicked him to the curb a long time ago. If he's an emotionless dick to everyone this summer, I'll lose half my patients to the Aspen clinic."

"Dr. Barlow, for real, relax. I'll give everybody some extra lovin' to make up for that prick. He's a good vet. The animals are taken care of. That's what matters." Then, eager to change the subject, she asked brightly, "So how was the trip?"

The glass of wine still clutched in her hand, Kris traced a single finger over the knife marks on the butcher-block surface of the island. There were decades of gouges, but they felt as though someone had taken a single blade and slashed the wood over and over and over.

"We drove all night but we made it," Kris told her assistant. She could picture Allison standing in an empty exam room, the brown roots showing in her purple hair, the sleeves of her scrubs pulled up to the elbows to reveal what appeared to be a random collection of frivolous tattoos. Kris could hear the faint click of fingernails being bitten, a nervous habit that left Allison with rough edges at the end of each finger. For some unexplained reason, only her ring fingers avoided this habitual assault.

Allison made a soft spitting sound and then asked, "How's the house?"

"It's . . . not exactly how I remember it. But it's good. Just needs a little TLC."

"Good."

There was the sound of a door opening, and then the humorless monotone of Dr. Nichols said, "Allison, we need you at reception."

Allison's voice was muffled as she spoke away from the phone. "No problem, Dr. Nichols, just talking to—" The thud of the door swinging shut, and then into the phone again, her voice clear and bright. "Dr. Barlow. That's what I was going to tell him. That I was talking to you." A rush of breath as she sighed. "He's gonna fire me."

"He's not going to fire you, because I won't let him," Kris assured her. "He works for me." From farther in the office, in what she assumed was the direction of the waiting room, she heard the incessant yap of a Chihuahua. "Lucky you. Sounds like Toby is back. What is that, five times this month?"

"Six, if you count the time Mrs. Stevenson brought him in twice in the same day. I keep telling her there's nothing wrong with him, if you ignore the fact that he's a serious asshole. I'm starting to think we've got a case of Munchausen by Proxy."

Kris chuckled. She liked Allison. Allison was what Kris's mother had called "good people." "Well, I better let you go—"

"How's Sadie?" Allison asked abruptly, following it with a quick, self-conscious, "I'm sorry, I don't mean to—"

"She's the same."

"Is she talking more?"

"Not really," Kris admitted. "I don't know. Maybe this was a mistake."

"It wasn't a mistake. But . . ." Allison took a breath, once again unsure if she was overstepping. "If Sadie won't talk to you, maybe you should, you know, think about letting her talk to someone else."

Kris cupped a hand over her mouth and the bottom half of the phone, just in case Sadie was standing in the darkness of the hallway, attempting to listen in. "She doesn't need therapy. She lost her father. What she needs is her mother. And I—"

"I know. I know." Allison's words were overly enthusiastic in the hopes of conveying undeniable support.

At the center of the butcher block was an unusually deep cut, either from the direct impact of a knife's tip or from the heat of multiple humid summers warping its surface. Kris slid the nail of her index finger into the slit, working it in deeper and deeper until one false move would snap her fingernail in half.

"I better go, Allison."

"Okay."

"I'll call in a few days to check in. If you need to call me for any reason . . ."

"We won't. I mean, of course we would call you, but . . . we won't. Don't worry about us. You take care of Sadie. And yourself."

Kris closed her eyes. "Right. I will. Bye, Allison."

"Bye, Dr. Barlow."

A soft click, and Allison was gone.

Sadie was all ready for bed, her teeth brushed and face washed. She was dressed in her favorite pj's, the matching pink-and-gray camouflage outfit that her grandmother had given her—Jonah's mother—for her last birthday.

She motioned to the mattress, still in need of fresh bedding.

In the bedroom doorway, Kris snapped her fingers, remembering. "Right," she said. "One second."

She hurried out into the great room and over to the small pile of things she had brought in from the Jeep. Her own duffel bag was there, packed full of clothes and a couple pairs of shoes, as was a backpack filled with toiletries, a cardboard box marked "Bedroom Stuff" in black Sharpie, and a few pillows. She had planned on bringing in the rest of their stuff this evening, but like everything else, it would have to wait until tomorrow. This was enough to get them through the night.

She pulled open the box top and dug into the soft, cottony contents until she found what she was looking for: Sadie's sheets, the ones from her bed at home, the blue ones covered in white and gold Wonder Woman symbols. Kris grabbed the sheets, a thick crocheted blanket, two pillowcases, and two pillows, then crossed back to the hallway.

Sadie had not moved. She stood motionless beside the bed as though frozen in time. Kris tossed a pillowcase straight at Sadie's face, and she whipped up her hands, catching it before it hit her. She smirked as her mother dropped the rest of the bedding onto the floor.

Kris picked up the fitted sheet and shook it open.

"You do the top corners. I'll do the bottom."

They had the sheets and the crocheted blanket on the bed in less than a minute. Kris jiggled the pillows into their cases and laid them at the head of the bed, one on top of the other. She folded down the blanket and top sheet and patted the mattress with an open hand.

"Come on. Bedtime."

For a moment, Sadie did not move. She looked from her mother to the turned-down bed as if she were being asking to walk the plank. Then she crouched down, scooped up the purple frog with the crooked eyes, and crawled hesitantly onto the bed. She slipped under the covers as Kris pulled them up to her chin.

"I'll be right down the hall. Okay?"

Sadie gave a sharp nod. Her hands gripped the top of the blankets and her eyes darted around the room as if she expected something terrible to come lurching from one of the corners.

For the second time, Kris snapped her fingers as she remembered something. She left the room once again, and when she returned, she held a night-light in the shape of a ceramic angel with golden wings and a flowing white gown. Mounted behind the angel was a four-watt bulb. Kris plugged it into an outlet between the bed and the dresser and flicked the switch. The bulb popped on. The angel glowed faintly.

Kris looked over at Sadie, who was staring over the edge of the bed.

"Better?"

"I want you to sleep in here," Sadie said. Her weak voice trembled.

"Honey, I—"

"Just for tonight."

Kris sighed. She pulled her phone from her pocket, and the screen instantly illuminated. Displayed against her wallpaper—a photo of her and a smiling Sadie beside the Continental Divide sign at Independence Pass—was the time: 8:56 p.m.

You still have to clean the master bedroom, that annoying, chiding voice reminded her.

Despite the warmth of the house, Kris shivered. She thought of the half-open door to the master bedroom and what lay beyond it.

It's just a bed.

It's her *bed*, her shadow voice said.

"Please, Mommy?" Sadie was beginning to whine. It was the immature tone she adopted when even she knew she was trying to play her mother.

Kris pushed away the image of the door at the end of the hall. She forced the edges of her lips to curl into a smile.

"Okay," she told Sadie. "Just for tonight."

Halfway through brushing her teeth, it hit Kris how truly exhausted she was. She had only had one glass of wine, but her head was suddenly so heavy, it bobbed on her slender neck, and she had to concentrate to keep her eyelids from sliding shut.

She did a quick pass over her bottom teeth and spat a bubbly mixture of toothpaste and saliva into the sink. Cupping a hand under the faucet, she slurped cool water into her mouth. She spat the water out and rinsed the sink before turning the faucet off.

On the floor beside her was her toiletries backpack. Its top was unzipped. It drooped wide open, revealing a cloth makeup bag decorated with blazing suns and packed full of foundation, blush, concealer, mascara, eye shadow, lip gloss, and various other bottles and tubes. Half of these things she would probably never even bother opening. Her beauty regimen would consist of a layer of sunscreen in the morning, a reapplication in the afternoon, and face wash and moisturizer at night.

She stared into the open bag and decided to skip the last step. She was too tired. Like Sadie, she would let their late afternoon dip be her bath, even if it meant going to bed smelling like lake water.

Dipping a hand into the backpack, she rifled through the contents, her fingers passing over nail clippers and lotion bottles and a brush with bristles entwined with long strands of her reddish-brown hair until she felt the slick plastic cylinder of a pill bottle. She took out the bottle, pressed the childproof cap against her palm, and twisted it free. She dug a finger inside and fished out a single yellow pill.

Xanax. 0.5 milligrams. Prescribed to her after the funeral by a concerned uncle of Jonah's, a family doctor. Kris was reluctant to take the medication. She told herself she wasn't struggling with anxiety. She was angry. She didn't need pills; she needed to punch a wall until her knuckles bled and scream until her throat was nothing but a raw curtain of ragged flesh. Still, she had the prescription filled just in case, only taking two or three of the pills in the days after they lowered her husband into the ground.

She held the pill out before her, pinched between her thumb and index finger.

Bottom's up.

She opened her mouth and tossed it to the back of her tongue, cupping her hand under the sink faucet, and washing it down with a palmful of water. Her body shivered.

She set a mental regimen. She would take one pill every night before bed. And one with breakfast. Two per day. She did not need more than that. They were just to take the edge off. And when they were gone, they were gone. The lake house would be her medication. Bringing it back from the brink of death would be her therapy.

She stripped out of her now-dry jeans and tank top, unhooked her bra and let it fall to the floor. She kicked the heap into the pile with her other clothes, then pulled on a soft cotton V-neck shirt and thin plaid cotton pajama bottoms, which she'd grabbed from her duffel bag in the great room.

She flicked off the bathroom light behind her, and she was immediately swallowed by darkness. She had never found the switch for the hall light, she realized. What little illumination had lit the hall had come from sunlight drifting in from the great room and the two bedrooms. Now the sun was down, and the hallway was pitch-black.

Holding a hand out in front of her for protection, Kris carefully crossed toward the faint glow of Sadie's bedroom night-light.

Sadie was still awake, but her eyes looked as heavy as Kris's felt. The sleepy little girl scooted closer to the wall to make room for her mother on the narrow mattress.

The bedsprings squeaked faintly as Kris slid under the covers. Instantly, Sadie's arms were around her, the girl's small body conforming to hers. Kris could feel the ends of Sadie's curls tickling her cheeks. She gently brushed the hair aside, running her fingers through her daughter's twisted locks.

Sadie sighed, content, and nuzzled even closer.

Except for the weak sphere of amber light cast by the angel night-light, the entire house was dark. Kris could barely see the back of the bedroom door, still open a few inches, but beyond it there was nothing.

The lake house ceased to exist. It had been swallowed by an abyss. Kris wished she had left one of the lamps on in the great room, just enough light to give dimension to the space outside the bedroom door.

From high up in that darkness, something creaked.

Beside her, Sadie sucked in a sharp breath.

"It's just the house settling," Kris said.

Sadie pressed her lips close to Kris's ear. Her breath was hot and wet.

"Why does it do that?" she whispered.

"The wood. During the day, the heat makes it expand, you know, get bigger. When it cools down at night, it shrinks a little, which makes the whole house sort of . . . shift."

Sadie did not respond. The explanation, while certainly confusing for an eight-year-old, must have at least seemed reasonable coming from her mother.

For a few minutes, they lay in silence, listening as the random sounds, the pops and creaks and groans, echoed through the house. Outside, the wind picked up and whistled over the roof.

Suddenly Kris was aware of a new sound—the steady rhythm of air drawn in and out, in and out, like the lazy lapping of rippled water against a lakeshore.

Sadie was asleep.

Closing her eyes, Kris imagined her daughter's breaths to be the gracefully sweeping hands of an orchestra conductor. And then she was sailing into an empty, dreamless slumber. Her breaths fell into perfect sync with Sadie's as mother and daughter drifted away together, bodies side by side.

CHAPTER ELEVEN

SHE WOKE TO find the pink room bathed in pale light.

Rolling onto her back, Kris stretched her arms and legs to each corner of the bed and felt the comforting tingle as her muscles pulled taut and then relaxed. She had slept hard but well. She had no idea what time it was, but she knew it was morning. She was ready to take on the new day. She was—

Confusion rippled through her as she realized she was taking up the entire bed.

She sat up, blinking away the last remnants of sleep as she glanced around.

The bedroom door was wide open.

She was alone.

"Sadie?" she called out.

Her voice was swallowed by the empty house.

Kris tossed back the covers and swung her feet off the bed. Her naked toes touched the cool wood floor and the board—like so many other boards in the old house—creaked under the weight.

She waited, listening for any sign of movement.

There was none.

She called again—

"Sadie . . ."

—even though she knew there would be no answer.

The invisible arms of sleep tried to pull her back toward the bed as she shuffled to the doorway. She wandered out of the bedroom and through the entryway at the mouth of the hall.

A cool breeze curled around Kris's ankles, gently rubbing against the bottoms of her cotton pj's like an invisible cat. The French doors were wide open again. Sadie was on the back deck, staring out.

The lake was gone.

Even as her mind tried to make sense of what she was seeing, something drew her forward, a command that did not seem to come from her brain. Yet her legs obeyed, the involuntary action moving her across the room, to the open doorway.

She stepped over the threshold and onto the deck. Tiny splinters of wood bit at the bottoms of her bare feet.

You're dreaming, her timid voice insisted.

But she knew this was not true. She was awake. What she was seeing was real.

The lake had disappeared in the night, replaced by a layer of drifting cloud. Or else the lake was still where it should be and the house itself had moved, had somehow lifted into the sky and was now resting precariously on a foundation of mist thirty thousand feet above the earth.

She stepped up behind Sadie. Her daughter did not seem to sense her presence. Sadie was lost in thought, staring out at the thick fog that swirled over the spot where the lake should be. She was still dressed in her pajamas. Her hair was matted on one side, giving her head a misshapen look as if some blunt impact had caved it in.

Like she's been in a car crash. Like the mushy side of Jonah's skull—

Kris stopped the thought cold, refusing to let it go further.

"Sweetie?" she asked. "What are you doing out here?"

Sadie's body flinched, the sound of her mother's voice startling her. She glanced back over her shoulder, the hair cutting down across her face so that only one green eye glimmered amid the red tangles.

"We're floating," she said. She raised a single finger and pointed out toward the lake.

Realization washed over Kris, the strangeness of waking alone and wandering through the dreamlike rooms fading away as her mind began to make sense of what they were seeing.

"It's the mist, remember? It was just starting last night, but now . . . now it's covering the whole lake."

Sadie gave a small nod, although Kris doubted she fully understood what had happened.

For a few minutes, Kris stood at her daughter's side, staring out at the thick white fog drifting over the lake's surface and listening to the breeze slip through the treetops. From within that earthbound cloud, a single bullfrog called out in its deep, throaty voice, mourning the end of the night. Then it fell silent.

They said nothing as they watched the sun rise higher behind a thin veil of morning clouds. Already the temperature had risen a good five degrees since Kris first stepped out onto the deck. The fog was beginning to burn off, bare patches revealing the rippling waters of the lake. The dark head of a turtle peered up from the shallows, then ducked down, out of sight, sending a ring expanding in all directions.

Kris placed a hand lightly against Sadie's back.

"You hungry?"

Sadie shrugged unenthusiastically.

Well, we're up, Kris thought. *Our first official morning here. So what now?*

Her gaze drifted away from the lake, up the bluff to the stone path that led to the deck. Just before the back steps, there was the faintest hint of a part in the weeds. Her eyes followed this across the yard, past the overgrown garden and the rickety swing set, toward the edge of the forest.

And just like that, she remembered.

"Go get dressed," she said. "I want to show you something."

They stepped down from the back of the deck and onto the trail of flat stones that would have taken them over the edge of the slope and down to the dock. But halfway along the path, Kris abandoned the stones altogether, directing Sadie into that barely recognizable break in the billowing tallgrass. The budding tops of knee-high bluestem brushed against their legs as they cut a trail between the old garden and the swing set.

Kris glanced over at the rectangle of railroad ties to her left and the mountain of weeds that called it home.

Hey, Mom, she thought as she gave a little nod to the girl following closely behind her. *This is your granddaughter. This is Sadie.*

They left the garden and swing set behind them. The weeds and tallgrass gave way to an uneven length of brown earth that crumbled beneath their feet. The beginning of the forest was only a few yards away. The breeze rustled the leaves around them. To Kris, it sounded like overlapping voices whispering. It was too low to make out the words, yet she understood it, in her heart, in her soul. It was a spell, an incantation, and if they allowed it to be cast on them, everything—the lake house, the town, Black Ridge, Jonah—all of it would be gone. They would belong to the forest.

Kris stopped and pressed the knuckle of a bent finger against her lips as she scanned the trees.

"I think . . . it's somewhere around . . ."

"What?" Sadie asked. The sun was a quarter of the way into the cloud-littered blue sky. Tiny beads of sweat dotted her forehead.

There.

Kris reached into a tangle of kudzu and low-hanging branches at the edge of the forest and swept it back as though she were parting a green velvet curtain. Before them, like magic, was a tunnel of Osage trees, their long, skinny branches bending to the ground like the lowered heads of petrified swans.

Sadie gasped, and the sound made Kris smile.

"Let's go," she said as she led her daughter into the woods.

It was all coming back to her.

Passing through the tunnel of trees was like stepping back in time. Kris emerged on the other side with the scent of honeysuckle in her nose and the sound of rustling branches in her ears. She was ten years old again, walking the same path she had wandered down that bittersweet summer when love and darkness became one.

Twigs snapped under their shoes as Sadie followed her deeper into the forest. There was no discernable trail, but Kris remembered the landmarks from her youth: the massive, moss-covered boulder that used to paint her palms green as she scrambled to its top; the ring of saplings that had once been a circle of children listening to Miss Krissy, their teacher, during story time, now a crowded cluster of towering sycamore trees; the sloping hillside dotted with wild berry bushes where she once fed a friendly box turtle; the deep ravine where a patch of earth had slid free, her secret tunnel through the forest. Just as one natural marker fell behind them, another would appear. Many had changed in size over the thirty years since Krissy walked the woods—some larger from decades of growth, others chiseled away by wind and rain—but she recognized them all.

Finally. She was home.

The descent of the ravine carried them down into a twisting chasm of sandstone. It was much cooler there. What sun was able to penetrate the canopy of leaves was blocked by twenty-foot rock walls. They passed through shadow, the chasm narrowing until the overlapping armor plates of sandstone were within arm's reach.

"I remember . . ." Kris began before she even knew what she was going to say. "I remember pretending this little canyon was alive and . . ." The words trailed off as she glanced at the ground, looking for something. She bent down and picked up a fallen branch from one of the trees above. She tested it, gripping it at either end and bending it slightly. The wood creaked but the stick did not snap.

"What's that for?" Sadie asked. Her soft, sweet voice bounced about the chasm.

"I'll show you," Kris said, holding the stick in one hand and taking Sadie's hand with the other. "Careful."

The dirt floor of the chasm became rockier until stones the size of watermelons began jutting up from the earth. Their edges were jagged and rose to points like sharks teeth. At the same time, the space between the sandstone walls grew tighter. It nearly brushed their shoulders as they passed.

Kris helped Sadie maneuver between the sharp stones. When she reached the canyon's narrowest point, Kris told Sadie, "Stay there," and she lifted the stick horizontally above her head. The sides of the stick screeched as Kris wedged it between the rock walls. Flakes of sandstone dusted the air.

She gave the stick a little tug. It held.

Kris turned back to Sadie, and the confusion on her daughter's face amused her. "That's so the rocks can't eat us."

Sadie frowned and glanced away, not allowing herself to fully believe what her mother had just said. But there was something tugging at her expression, a desire to give in, to go with it, to be an eight-year-old kid. Without raising her head, she looked up, her eyes finding the stick Kris had left between the canyon walls.

"Can I do one?"

Kris nodded. Together, they searched among the stones until they found another stick of appropriate length. Sadie stepped into the narrowing chasm and, just as her mother had done before her, raised her stick into the air.

Kris waited patiently as she watched her daughter work the branch into place.

Stepping back, Sadie admired her work. The stick was crooked and much lower than the one Kris had placed. There was a good chance it wouldn't stay put for more than a few minutes. But seeing the two branches together—one tall and secure, the other short and delicate—filled Kris with a sensation that she could only describe as a "glow," a light she knew was growing stronger within her every hour they were there.

"It's perfect," she said.

About fifty yards past the narrowest section of the canyon, the sandstone walls began to descend until they slid beneath the surface of the forest floor. With little warning, the woods expanded infinitely around them in all directions, and Kris and Sadie found themselves at the center of a grove of towering oak trees. High above them, sunlight filtered in through the thick canopy of rippling leaves. Morning glory bloomed along stretches of ivy that twisted through the wild grass and around rough, sturdy tree trunks. A swallowtail butterfly fluttered from flower to flower, its yellow and black markings brilliant against the blue of the morning glories like a drop of sunshine dancing through the air.

The ground cover was thick. Green, leafy fronds created a soft padding that occasionally snagged the toes of their shoes or tugged at the loops of Kris's shoelaces. Kris let her hands lift at her sides so that the tips of her fingers grazed the serrated edges of leaves sprouting up from low plants. She breathed in the morning air through her nose. Her nostrils filled with the scent of earth still wet with dew. She imagined she could hear the narrow shafts of sunlight vibrating like harp strings as she moved through them.

Her right hand knocked the top of a dogwood shrub, and hundreds of unseen leafhoppers hiding within erupted into a green mist around her. The miniscule insects clung to her clothes, leaping about in a frenzy. Kris laughed, both out of surprise and giddiness, as the leafhoppers went bounding wildly away into the open air, disappearing into the moss-colored shadows below.

"So?" Kris asked. "What do you think?"

Sadie did not reply. She moved silently through the army of oaks that stood at motionless attention.

Kris followed. Around her, the huge tree trunks groaned softly, like grumbling old men, as the wind tossed their bushy, outstretched arms.

The flap of wings shot overhead. Kris glanced up just as a large black shape glided beneath the swaying branches. It swooped up into what must have been the largest, oldest oak tree in the entire forest. Unlike the others, with their perfectly bulbous crowns, this oak's branches spun wildly off in all directions. It was as if a thousand years ago, a tentacled beast had exploded from the depths of the earth and become petrified at the first contact with open air.

From the fat, malformed ledge where a branch connected to the trunk like a deformed shoulder, the black shape danced excitedly from foot to foot. It clacked its obsidian beak and shrieked in a voice that cut to the bone.

A blackbird.

It hopped a few inches farther down the branch and into a shaft of sunlight. The tightly packed feathers around its neck glistened with a deep purple hue that stretched like an executioner's hood over the top of its head. It stared down at her with a single glowing golden eye pricked at the center with a black pupil. Even from that distance, she could see that its other eye was pinched shut.

It cried again, tilting its purple head to get a better look at something below.

Kris followed its gaze, down to the base of the treelike beast, down to where something pink and fleshy was being devoured by its trunk. A smiling, freckled face peered out from within the shadows of its open maw.

Sadie was standing in a large hollow that cut deeply into the pulpy flesh of the gargantuan oak. The cavity was as deep and wide as the trunk itself, large enough for Sadie to easily stand inside it.

The doorway, Kris thought, and the words plucked a string far in the dim recesses of her mind.

"Mommy, look," Sadie called. Her voice reverberated inside the tree.

Kris trudged through the foliage toward the unruly oak.

"Come in with me," Sadie said.

Kris touched the rough hide at the edge of the hole. "I don't know if I'll fit."

Sadie said nothing, but she scooted over to one side of the hollow to show that there was plenty of room.

"Okay."

Taking a breath of warm, summer air, Kris slipped into the oak's gaping mouth.

The hollow was much larger than Kris had assumed. She barely brushed shoulders with her daughter as they stood side by side.

"What was this place, Mommy?" Sadie asked.

A doorway, Kris thought again. *A doorway to . . .*

And then that single note vibrating from that distant memory became a chord that rose, louder and louder, until it enveloped her, like the sustained blast of a pipe organ in the sanctuary of a church.

Her eyes scanned the dark chamber within the tree.

"This tree . . ." she said. "I remember playing in here. I . . ."

She heard the words escape her lips, but she was not entirely convinced she had spoken them.

"I thought . . . I thought I had to guard this place."

Sadie cocked her head, confused. "Why?"

"Because it's a doorway. That's what I used to believe. It's a doorway." She turned to face the back wall of the hollow. The memory was controlling her now. She was ten years old and standing inside a tree that reached all the way up to heaven. It was the first tree to ever sprout from the earth. Before humans, before dinosaurs, before that first slimy beast pulled itself by its flippers onto solid ground, this tree had twisted like a green finger from the dirt. Its roots reached too deeply, their tips had slipped into other places—other *worlds*—and that's when its trunk had yawned open for someone, a ten-year-old girl named Krissy perhaps, to step inside and become the temporary owner of its power.

"If you close your eyes and think of a place," Kris explained to her daughter, "the back of the tree will open and when you step through, you'll be in that place."

"Any place?"

Kris reached out and touched the craggy back wall of the tree. She gave a small, embarrassed laugh.

"Well, I mean, that's what I used to pretend."

She watched as Sadie mimicked her action, hesitantly reaching out to trace the folds in the tree's husk.

"Do you want to try it?" Kris asked.

Sadie thought for a moment, and then her eyes narrowed as if she felt a sudden sharp pain. She shook her head, letting her hand drop down to her side.

"All right," Kris said. "Another time, maybe."

The Wishing Tree, as Sadie began to call it, marked the far edge of the oak grove. Another hundred feet and the forest opened up to a sea of wildflowers. Their tops blew in the wind, undulating waves of yellow and red.

Just as it had done to the mist on the lake, the blinding sun had burned off most of the clouds in the sky, although the coolness of early morning had not entirely been chased away.

Around them, the tops of flowers buzzed with honeybees, legs fat with powdery yellow pollen. They hovered around, their stingers quivering excitedly as they investigated each bloom.

Sadie tightened her grip on Kris's hand.

"Don't worry," Kris assured her. "They won't bother you if you don't bother them."

Sadie nodded. She made sure to keep hold of her mother's fingers, but her grip loosened ever so slightly as they cut a path through the wildflowers.

Just like the area behind the lake house, the land began to slope down as they neared the clear, lapping water of the shore. The overgrown vegetation thinned, and the dry ground transitioned to wet clay and water-smoothed stones. Kris held Sadie's hand as they stepped from rock to rock to keep the black mud from smudging their shoes. They stopped at the edge of the water and stood in silence. Lost Lake was before them, its crystalline surface sparking in the midmorning sun.

Without a word, Sadie raised a hand and pointed a single slender finger out toward the center of the lake.

Kris looked. At first she saw only the skeletal branches of sub-merged trees reaching up in jagged black lines from below the surface. But . . . there was something beyond this.

The tiled peak of a rooftop.

"A house," Kris said aloud, the words unlocking yet another door in her memory.

Sadie's brow furrowed. "In the lake?"

Kris swept a hand from one side of the lake to the other. "My daddy, he told me. He said a long time ago, this used to be a river. A few people lived out here, along the banks. But when the lake was made, the houses got flooded."

"Their *houses*?" Such a possibility was unimaginable to the little girl. "Why didn't they move?"

"Well, it happened fast. The lake sort of made itself. The water came out of the ground and the river turned into this, into a lake, the way it is now. That right there . . ." She pointed to the rooftop sprout-ing from the water like a wooden iceberg. "That's one of the houses. There are a lot more down there. A general store, too, I think. It's what they called Lower Basin Road. It's all under the water."

Kris watched as Sadie poked her head forward, her eyes narrow-ing to see those other phantom homes beneath the lake's surface. Kris knelt down so that she was cheek to cheek with her daughter, their gaze at the same level, staring out at the roof that stood like a monument to the lost community.

"We used to pretend that was a mermaid's house," Kris said softly.

"Who?"

"Me, when I was little."

"No. Mommy. You said, 'we.'"

Kris cocked and lowered her head, as if she were attempting to reel back her words. "I guess . . . I guess I meant . . ."

What had she meant? She was always alone when her parents brought her to the lake house. There were other kids in town—swimming at the beach, having a cone at the ice cream shop, playing at the park, or eating pulled-pork sandwiches at the Pig Stand—but Kris had never been in Pacington long enough to become friends with them. The lake house was family time.

And yet she could not shake the feeling that there had been some-one playing alongside her. Two voices, intertwined.

For a split second, a memory streaked through her mind like a shooting star: she was a little girl, peering down into the surface of the lake as small waves tore at her reflection.

"Mommy?" Sadie was looking up at her, concerned.

Kris pinched her eyes shut, trying to force open a door that refused to budge. Finally, she sighed. "I don't know, honey. I think I just misspoke. That's all."

There was no response. Only the soft lapping of water on the shore and the tossing of nearby branches.

Kris opened her eyes.

Sadie was leaning over the edge of the lake, staring down at her reflection. The wind picked up and sent a shiver across the water's surface. Sadie's reflection rippled until everything that made her "her" was obscured—the bright green eyes that sparkled with creativity and wonder, the curly red hair that framed her delicate, freckled skin.

Kris looked into the water, and a faceless girl stared back.

Across the street from the north end of Jefferson Park was the Pig Stand. There was no indoor seating at this establishment, so it was only open from the first of April to the first of November. But during those times, the Pig Stand became the nucleus of activity for those not out on the lake or swimming just off the man-made beach on Jefferson Park's southern tip. By the time it opened at noon, the savory aroma of smoked meat beckoned those in the park and the edge of downtown like an invisible finger to the small square shack where the owner, Ricky Redfern, waited at the open window with a smile, his sandy-blond hair pulled back into a ponytail, ready to take orders.

Kris remembered the line to the Pig Stand could stretch past the six wooden picnic tables on the front porch, all the way out to the curb. So it was a bit of a surprise when she pulled the Jeep into a parallel spot directly in front of the Stand and saw only a small cluster of people on the porch. Within five minutes, Kris and Sadie were stepping up to the window marked "Place Yer Order Here" and telling an eternally cheerful Ricky Redfern, his ponytail now gray and threadbare, what they would like for lunch: a hamburger with ketchup for Sadie, the house special pulled-pork sandwich for Kris, and a basket of curly fries to share. Another ten minutes, and they were seated at a picnic table at the edge of the deck and looking across Center Street at Jefferson Park while they ate their food.

One taste of the sweet, smoky sandwich dripping in barbecue sauce with a sharp vinegary bite, and Kris was struck by a ravenous hunger. She hadn't eaten since dinner the night before. Even then, after their long drive from Colorado and a day spent cleaning, she hadn't been particularly hungry. Her taste buds exploded like the tops of poppies in bright summer sunshine.

She was down to her last bite when she noticed Sadie picking halfheartedly at the basket of fries. There were two nibbles taken out of the edge of her hamburger; otherwise it had gone untouched.

Kris wiped her sauce-smeared lips with a much-too-thin paper napkin and asked, "Not hungry?"

Sadie shrugged, her eyes on the mound of curlicue fries piled high atop a square of greasy waxed paper in a metal basket.

Back to this, Kris thought. *The shrug. Always the shrug ever since . . .*

The incident, Timid Kris proposed in her squeaky, annoyingly helpful voice.

Shadow Kris chuckled, the sound echoing from the depths. *Incident? Is that really what you're calling it now? Do I need to remind you about his teeth? They were above his lips. His teeth were above his lips.*

Kris clenched her jaw and tried to force the door closed on that voice. Yet it would not be silenced.

He shouldn't have even been in that car. He should have been home. In bed. With you.

From nearby came a playful mixture of laughter and feigned terror.

Kris glanced to the park across the street.

A little boy, no older than five or six, was racing wildly in a lopsided figure eight while his father, a stout, balding man in his mid-thirties, gave chase. Just as the father would reach the boy, he would fall back so that his swipes barely brushed the child's back. Each time, the boy gave a giddy scream and cut sharply to the side, around the top loop of the figure eight, and the pattern began again. Seated nearby on a red-and-black checkered blanket, under the shade of a drooping cottonwood tree, was a woman with short brown hair and contentment in her eyes. Kris assumed this was the boy's mother. Above her, the branches swayed in the breeze, white tufts of cotton pulled free to drift lazily away into the sunny summer afternoon.

Just as the little boy shrieked, Kris looked back to Sadie and noticed a nearly imperceptible flinch. It was subtle, but it was there. There was no confusing it for anything else. It was a painful reaction to the sound of the little boy's joy as he pretended to fear the advance of his loving father.

Kris set down the last bite of her sandwich, then picked up a Wet-Nap package from atop a stack of paper napkins and tore it open. She wiped the sticky barbecue sauce from her fingers and under her nails, then balled it up and tossed the moistened towelette onto the table. "If you're done, we can go."

Sadie nodded and set her hamburger down on the brown paper in which it had been wrapped. Kris watched as her daughter mimicked her previous routine, tearing open her own Wet-Nap and thoroughly scrubbing every little finger from nail to knuckle, even though she had barely touched her food. When she was finished, she squeezed the towelette into a ball, just as her mother had done.

As they carried their trash toward the large trash can at the edge of the porch, Ricky Redfern thrust a hand out of the open window and shook it wildly in an exaggerated wave. "Y'all come back!" he called out. His smile was so big, Kris swore she could see his back molars.

She waved back politely and quickly dumped their trays into a metal trash barrel. She hoped Ricky hadn't seen Sadie's uneaten burger. If he did, he showed no sign of it. Ricky rested both hands on the inside counter and leaned forward to grin out the window at the Pig Stand's nonexistent patrons.

She waited for the click of Sadie's seat belt, and then Kris put her hand on the gearshift, about to slide it into Drive, when she happened to glance over at the right-side mirror.

A man was walking up beside the Jeep. His large frame was tightly bound in a tan County Sheriff's uniform. Above his right breast pocket was a brass name tag engraved with black letters: "Deputy B. Montgomery." Behind him, parked parallel to the curb just like Kris, was his cruiser, a white Dodge Charger with a gold stripe down the side and the word "Sheriff" floating in black block letters over this.

Kris's grip tightened on the oversized plastic knob on top of the gearshift.

It's nothing, she told herself. *He's just going to grab some lunch. He'll walk right by in a second.*

But then Shadow Kris purred awake in the darkness. *You know what cops bring. Bad news. Terrible news that shatters your world.*

She sat frozen behind the wheel as Deputy Montgomery reached the side window. He glanced down at something on the lower front half of the Jeep, then stopped and turned to peer in through her window. His eyes were shielded by the stereotypical aviator sunglasses that begged him to be cliché, but his chin, jaw, and lips were covered in a thick black beard. His cheeks were pocked with acne scars.

He motioned for Kris to roll down her window.

Kris thought, *Shit*, although she had no real reason to be concerned. She fumbled for the automatic window button on the armrest, found it, and pushed it. Across from her, the passenger-side window slid smoothly down.

"Ma'am," Deputy Montgomery said, his voice as rough as a burlap sack full of rocks.

Kris could sense Sadie's unease from the back seat: *Mommy is in trouble, Mommy did something wrong; even Mommy makes mistakes.*

That's right, Kris thought. *Even mommies and daddies make mistakes.*

And then the thought was gone as the face of Deputy Montgomery filled her view.

"Morning," Kris said, then shook her head, realizing. "I mean, afternoon."

"Afternoon," he replied. Behind that thick overgrown bramble patch of beard, his lips remained perfectly straight in a tight, emotionless line.

Kris tried to muster up a friendly smile. "Something wrong?"

Deputy Montgomery craned his neck, looking into the back seat. "Hello there," he offered in a much softer tone.

Sadie sank back as if she were trying to slip down into the crack between the back of her booster and the seat.

Deputy Montgomery glanced from Sadie to Kris, and for one brief moment, he seemed completely confused, as if the sight of them together had thrown him off. Then he recovered and tapped the window frame with large calloused fingers.

"Don't worry, you're not in trouble," he assured her in his gravelly Kris Kristofferson voice. "I just noticed the donut there on your vehicle. You been traveling long on that?"

The memory came flooding back to her: the tire blowing somewhere in Central Kansas; digging the spare out from under stacks of boxes and bags; gritting her teeth as she forced the lug nuts loose.

She let out a sharp sigh.

"Right. The donut. No, not too long. We had a blowout on the way to town."

Deputy Montgomery gave a low, "Uh-huh," then took another quick look down at the spare tire.

Kris shifted uncomfortably, as if fearing what she had just told him wasn't the truth, even though she knew it was.

"You staying here in town?" he asked finally.

Kris nodded a bit too enthusiastically.

"Yes. For the summer. We live in Colorado. But actually I'm from this area. Blantonville, originally."

Deputy Montgomery gave an ambiguous, "Hmm."

Once again, Kris found herself rambling to fill the air. "We're staying on River Road. The last house before you hit the park."

Deputy Montgomery raised a finger into the air, pointing to something only he could see. "River's End?"

"Yeah. That's it. Forgot people around here call it that. It belonged to my father. The lake house. River's End. I used to come here in the summer when I was a kid."

"Not as many summer folk as there used to be," he said. He cleared his throat as if saying this out loud had been a mistake. He rapped his fingers on the window frame once more. "You shouldn't put too many miles on that donut. You'll want to get a new tire on as soon as possible." He took a step back, up onto the sidewalk, and motioned back toward downtown. "There's a place just down the road, on Sycamore. The Auto Barn. Guarantee they can hook you up."

"Thank you," Kris replied. "I'll take care of it. Promise."

Deputy Montgomery scratched a dirty fingernail into his overgrown beard. Kris could not see his eyes through the mirrored lenses, but she felt as though he were taking an extra moment to glance at

Sadie in the back seat. Then he nodded, offered an obligatory, "You have a good day," and marched across the Pig Stand patio to where Ricky waited in the order window.

They decided to get ice cream, even though it was breaking the rules. Back in their old life, Kris rarely suggested getting dessert after lunch. Dessert was a dinner thing, and not an after-every-dinner thing. But this wasn't their old life. This was something else. And this something else called for ice cream after lunch—after every single lunch, if that's what it took to find flickers of joy.

She had already parked in an angled spot, both of them standing on the sidewalk as she pressed the key fob to lock the doors, when she realized that the ice cream shop was still half a block up.

"It's okay. We'll walk," she told Sadie.

From where she stood, Kris could see the shop's painted sign—in the shape of a bowl heaped high with a melting mound of vanilla—swinging slowly back and forth beneath a blue awning. Its all-too-clever name adorned the side of the bowl in crude calligraphy meant to look elegant: Dairy Godmother.

She remembered this place.

The ice cream shop.

A treat on a summer day.

A treat for after.

After what?

After a visit to the talking doctor.

Kris came to a sudden stop.

Slowly, she turned to her right, to where a doorway trimmed in stained redwood, so deep that it was almost a shade of purple, led up a steep flight of stairs to a business on the second floor. A bronze placard was mounted on the brick wall next to the doorway: "Clear Water Counseling—Alice Baker, Psy.D."

You've been here.

She saw herself, or a wisp of herself, like a figure made from dissipating smoke. She was holding her father's hand. He was telling her that this was a good thing. This would help.

Little Krissy stopped on the first step just inside the doorway. Daddy sensed her apprehension. He did not want to force her. He wanted her to feel comfortable.

Kris watched as Daddy knelt beside her younger self so that they were eye to eye, just as she did with Sadie when she wanted the child to feel like there was no hierarchy at play. His sandy-brown hair was thinning at the crown. The sunlight caught the pale patches of scalp beneath. Kris knew what Daddy was saying.

This was a place where they told her she could talk about anything. She could share her secrets.

She could tell them about—

"Mommy?"

Sadie was standing at the edge of the curb. She pointed impatiently to the other side of the street, to the next block where that Dairy Godmother sign called to them like an oasis in the desert.

"I'm coming," Kris said, yet she did not move. Not yet.

You can tell her anything.

"Mom-my . . ."

"Okay, okay."

Kris hurried over to her daughter and took her hand. Even as they crossed the street, she could still see that doorway in her mind, its edges rimmed in deep red.

Kris got a single scoop of butter pecan, Sadie a double scoop of chocolate fudge and cookie dough. They sat at the counter, paper-wrapped cones clasped in their hands, while the bell over the door dinged each time a new customer entered. Kris watched as Sadie crouched over her scoop and took a few small licks as if giving herself permission to enjoy the taste.

Even inside the store it was warm, the heat radiating off the large sunlit windows that lined the front wall. Every now and then, a puff of cool air would blow over from the refrigerated cases of ice cream.

Kris felt her uneasiness fade away with each lick of ice cream. Gone was the happy couple spending a carefree day at the park with their son. Gone was Deputy B. Montgomery knocking on her car window. Gone was the red-rimmed doorway leading up to the talking doctor's office. This place—the ice cream shop—was, by its very nature, a place to escape troubles.

We came here, Kris realized. *Mommy and Daddy and me. We sat at this very counter and we ate ice cream and Mommy made a joke about Daddy's tummy and Daddy said it wasn't ice cream he was worried about,*

*it was beer, and we all laughed because we were happy. Because I didn't
know. I didn't know what was really happening. But they did. They . . .*

She pinched her eyes shut and pushed away the thought.

Not here. Not in the ice cream shop.

She looked over at Sadie. Unlike her disinterested nibbles of
burger at the Pig Stand, Sadie was eagerly lapping at the top mound of
chocolate fudge. If this was her lunch, then so be it.

"Good?" Kris asked.

Sadie nodded between licks. A line of cookie dough cream
coursed over her knuckles. A second later, the same thing was happening to Kris, white streams of butter pecan slipping from the glistening
ball atop the cone like floodwaters over a dam.

"Hurry!" Kris cried. "Lick! Lick! We can't let the ice cream win!"

They tried to eat quickly, but the ice cream melted quicker, running down the sides of the cones and between their fingers. By the time
they were done, both Kris and Sadie were a mess, their hands smudged
with sticky cream, Sadie's mouth covered in brown chocolate from her
lips all the way to the middle of both cheeks.

Kris wet a napkin on her tongue and threatened to wipe Sadie's
face with it, an act that had always elicited a frightened giggle from
the girl. Now it barely got a smile, but the hint was there, tugging as
always at the edge of her lips. The hint would do, Kris decided. The
hint meant the possibility of smiles down the road.

She took the wet, mushy paper that had been wrapped around
Sadie's cone and nodded toward a hallway at the back of the store.
"Why don't you go wash up?"

With the brown smudges beginning to dry on her fair skin, Sadie
slipped off her stool and trotted away down the hall. A moment later
came the click of a bathroom door opening and closing.

Kris stayed at the counter, nibbling at the last of her sugar cone.

"She's a beautiful girl."

Behind the counter was a young woman of nineteen or twenty.
She wore chunky black glasses with lenses so thick, her eyes looked
like blue pails lowered to the bottoms of deep, dark wells. Her plump
cheeks were marred by clusters of pimples, not nearly as bad as the kid
at the supermarket, but her greasy flesh still begged for a good, soapy
scrubbing. Pulled down to the top of her eyeglass frames was a tan cap

embroidered with the business's name in the same amateurish script as the sign out front.

The name of every store in this town is a ridiculous pun, Kris thought, and then she scolded herself. It was supposed to be cute. It was supposed to hearken back to a simpler, less cynical time. A happier time.

When everything was swept under the rug.

"Are you visiting or . . ." The young woman let her words drift into the warm air as if there were no second option.

This was not the same person who had waited on them when they arrived, Kris realized. That had been a rail-thin girl of high-school age with her hair pulled into a sloppy side ponytail and bangs cut an inch too high on her forehead.

"Visiting," Kris said, trying to hide her confusion. "For the summer."

The young woman did not reply. For a few moments, Kris sat in silence while the young woman rinsed the ice cream from used metal scoopers, the hot water from the faucet billowing steam around her face.

"You know, you ought to keep an eye on a little girl like that in this town." The young woman was facing Kris. She held a scooper in her hand, seemingly forgotten. Milky white water dripped from its tip.

"What?"

The woman cocked her head, those tiny, faraway eyes staring off in the direction of the restrooms.

"She's been in there a long time," the woman said.

Invisible fingers traced the back of Kris's neck. She began to get up from her stool, the toes of her shoes just touching the ground, when down the hall one of the restroom doors opened and Sadie reappeared. She obediently crossed the empty store, the skin around her mouth red from being wiped clean with a rough paper towel.

"Better?" she asked, lifting her face to show off her clean skin.

Kris nodded. "Much." She stood and tightly gripped Sadie's hand. "Ready to go?"

Sadie pushed the front door open, the bell giving a pleasant *ding*, thanking them for their visit.

Over her shoulder, Kris called back, "Have a nice day."

Behind the counter, the young woman smiled, but to Kris, it looked more like a grimace, as if she were trying to ignore a pain eating away at her gut.

The words continued to ring in Kris's head as they stepped into the sunlight:

In this town.

She was just trying to be helpful, the timid voice scolded.

Kris couldn't recall exactly when she realized she thought in different voices. One day her thoughts had simply taken on distinct tones. They sounded like different versions of her. There was the timid voice that pestered her, lecturing her in its passive-aggressive tone. This voice always tried to see the bright side. It was the one she had listened to for much of her life, the one that had told her everything was fine with Jonah, that his late nights and foul attitude meant he was working hard, nothing more. This voice made her feel like a child. She hated it most.

And then there was the dark voice, the shadow voice that echoed from a great distance. It was the voice behind the door. This one made her skin prickle and the muscles in her neck and shoulders tingle. This voice spoke the truth, even when she didn't want to hear it. *Especially* when she didn't want to hear it. It said things like *He doesn't love you anymore,* and *Your daughter hates you,* and *Your mommy is turning into a monster.*

Kris did not hate this voice. She feared it. She feared it most when she didn't understand it, when it seemed to know more than she did. This voice was more like her than the other voice. Sarcastic. Sometimes profane. Full of attitude.

She's not trying to be helpful, this voice said now. *That asshole is trying to scare you.*

"Can we go back to the house now?" Sadie asked. She had already started down the sidewalk, toward where the Jeep was parked across the next street.

This town, Kris heard the young woman in the thick glasses say again.

She hurried to catch up to her daughter.

CHAPTER TWELVE

THEY NEEDED TO have some fun. No more cleaning. No more worrying about the dirt and the weeds and the spiderwebs. The minute they got home, Kris led Sadie straight to the back doors and out onto the deck.

"Where are we going?" Sadie asked, her voice barely a murmur through tight lips.

"On an adventure," Kris told her.

They reached the top of the slope behind the lake house, and Kris peered down, her eyes falling upon a black mound rising from the rocky ground a few yards from the water's edge. It was a plastic tarp, and she knew that beneath it was—

Jonah's body

—the rowboat her father had bought shortly after purchasing the lake house.

In Kris's memory, in that scrapbook of yellowing images from her childhood, the rowboat was a single, curved piece of sleek, shiny metal with freshly painted red-and-white oars resting in steel rowlocks. What she saw as she stripped away the black tarp vaguely resembled that recollection, but time had taken its toll on the boat, just as it had with the lake house and the dock. The vessel's once-pristine hull was rough with rust and riddled with dents where the wind had knocked it against the side of the dock. The floor was covered in rotting leaves from so many autumns past. Black ants scurried across the slick surfaces, and a fat black beetle attempted to crawl up the curving side of the hull, only to fall onto its back as it must have done countless times before. Wet, torn leaves clung like leeches to a set of oars, their red-and-white paint flaking away to reveal the splintered gray wood beneath.

Kris felt Sadie hug closer to her.

"It's just some leaves," Kris assured her.

Grasping the lip of its bow, she dragged the small boat across the short stretch of shoreline to the water's edge. Rocks screeched as they scraped across its metal belly.

"Help me push."

Sadie obeyed, falling in beside her mother as they shoved the boat the rest of the way into the water.

From the corner of the boat, Kris dug out one of the oars and used its flat head like a shovel to scoop and toss clumps of wet leaves into the water. She watched as they drifted away like the dead bodies of strange, misshapen fish. It wasn't long before the mud-streaked metal floor began to reveal itself.

When she was done, she tossed the oar aside and climbed up onto the dock. She crouched down, tipping the side of the boat toward the surface until water slipped over its edge. It filled the hull like a flooded river breaching a dam. With a grunt, she lifted her side high enough for the water to pour over the opposite edge, carrying with it a wash of mud and the last remaining leaves, as well as ants and millipedes and a few wolf spiders. They stretched their spindly legs out as far as they could and remained perfectly still as they floated helplessly out into the lake.

Kris repeated this action several times until the inside of the boat was wet but clean.

She held out a hand to her daughter, who pinched her bottom lip between her teeth and eyed the boat with trepidation.

"Come on, give me your hand. I'll help you in."

Sadie sat on the forward thwart, her hands gripping its front edge tightly. Flecks of white paint clung to her skin, the contrast bringing out a pinkish warmth in her flesh.

Kris took the bench at the center. She slipped the mooring rope from the last piling and pushed them away from the dock. Carefully, she lowered the oars into the rowlocks. She lifted the handles out level with her shoulders and let the ends dip down into the cool water. Then she pulled them close to her chest, her biceps tightening beneath the sleeves of her T-shirt. Soon the dock behind them became smaller and smaller until it disappeared from sight.

Kris fell into a steady rhythm as she guided the boat out of their cove, toward the center of Lost Lake, concentrating on the soft lap of the oar cutting through the surface. The sound was hypnotic. The muffled whoosh as its flat head caught the water beneath and pulled against it. The gush of oar emerging once more into the air, droplets falling like rain from the cracked wood and splashing back into the lake.

They sat in silence as the familiar shore behind their lake house fell into the distance, revealing what they had thought to be the entirety of the lake as only one of several coves that jutted off in irregular shapes from a much larger body of water. At the edge of the cove, the hang-dog arms of willow trees swayed lazily in the warm summer wind, and then they were away from the forest and out into the lake—into the honest-to-God lake that seemed to stretch an impossible distance to the blue horizon.

With each pull of the oars, Kris felt the fear and dread that had been building up inside her slip away. Each breath was a little bit slower, a little bit deeper, until her respiration mimicked that of pleas-ant slumber.

Every now and then, the shadowy form of a fish would cut silently through the water beside the boat. Each time, Kris noticed that Sadie leaned a little closer to the edge in hopes of catching a glimpse of the darting creatures. Sadie's grip on the edge of the thwart loosened until only her fingertips grazed its side.

"I used to take this boat out all the time when I was just a little older than you," Kris said suddenly, breaking the silence.

"By yourself?" Sadie asked.

Kris nodded.

"Did you ever fall in?"

Kris grinned. "No."

"Could we fall in?"

"No."

"How do you know?"

"Because I won't let that happen."

To their left were the usually red hills, now a burnt orange in the bright light of the sun overhead. To their right, on the other shore, was a low wall of bulrush and cattails that quivered like a single, shud-dering beast as the breeze swept through. About a half mile down, the emergent plants came to an abrupt end, and the rocky shore smoothed to a stretch of blond sand. A white-and-blue braided rope cut a perpendicular line into the lake, dotted every twenty feet or so by an oval buoy. This was the designated swimming area just off the man-made beach at the far end of Jefferson Park. The roofline of downtown could barely be seen peeking over the top of the park's sloping lawn.

When they reached what felt like the center of the lake, Kris lifted the oars from the water and swiveled the rowlocks until the oars rested along the top edge of the boat. They drifted a bit farther before slowing to an imperceptible crawl. On the very tip of the bow, a powder-blue dragonfly landed and watched them with eyes like gilded armor.

A comfortable fuzziness enveloped Kris. It was the same sensation she usually needed two or three glasses of wine to experience. But not here. Not out on this peaceful lake with her perfect little girl. Out here, the things on land could not bother them. Out here there was no "Back home," there was no "I'm so sorry to hear about Jonah," there was no "In this town." There was only Kris and Sadie and the summer breeze tousling their hair and the water softly lapping against the side of the boat like the gentle licks of a friendly hound.

Out here, they were safe from everything.

Kris leaned back and closed her eyes, turning her face toward the sun. It warmed her freckled cheeks. She knew they shouldn't be out long. They both burned easily in direct sunlight. *Like a couple vampires on vacation*, Kris thought with a soft chuckle. But they were okay for a little bit longer.

"We can go fishing one of these days," Kris said, her eyes still closed, her face to the sky. "And we could get a few board games or puzzles from the toy store in town. Do one of those thousand piece monsters on the floor of the great room. Take as long as we want to finish it. And there are plenty of trails to hike. You still haven't been into the hills. There are caves on the other side."

In the distance, seemingly beyond that place where the water and the horizon met, she heard the cry of a bird.

A small hand gripped Kris's wrist.

"Mommy. Look."

Kris opened her eyes.

Somehow, in that short amount of time, they had drifted to the mouth of another cove, a horseshoe tucked away on the east end of the lake. The other side of the lake, *their* side, looked as though it were a hundred miles away.

Sadie was pointing at a white buoy bobbing gently in their path. A few yards past this, another buoy rose above the surface like the head of a turtle. From what Kris could see, there were five buoys in total, not in a straight line but seemingly placed at random around this section of the lake.

It took a moment for Kris to realize why.

"The houses," she said quietly. "They mark where the houses are, the ones flooded by the lake. So boats will know they're there. So they won't run into the roofs if the water is too low."

Gripping the metal edge, Sadie carefully leaned over the side. Her eyes widened. Her jaw dropped open.

"Wow," she whispered.

Kris slid over beside her. Just like her daughter, she held on to the side of the boat as she peered into the water.

At first, all she saw was her own reflection, her auburn hair falling down around her searching eyes, and for a brief moment, she was sure it was not her face she saw in the water but that of another girl, staring back at her.

Then, beneath her reflection, a shape began to take form.

Like the tip of an enormous arrow pointing up at them.

"I told you," she said.

She squinted, peering deeper into the depths.

A thick layer of dark green algae covered the roof of the house. At its base, patches of pondweed waved slowly as if tossed by an underwater breeze. Silver torpedoes shot past the collapsed brick chimney as a school of perch swam by. Beyond this, farther down a gentle curve that had once been Lower Basin Road, the dark shapes of two more roofs pointed toward the surface.

"Were there people in them? When it happened?" Sadie asked. Her voice was surprisingly even. There was no fear or horror. She was asking out of pure curiosity, the way an adult might ask about the weather.

Kris slowly shook her head. "No. No, the people weren't home, honey."

There was a jolt and the entire boat shuddered, the side of the metal hull screeching angrily as it slid along the plank lining the dock.

They were back.

Kris dropped the oar handles into the belly of the boat and quickly looped the mooring rope around the first piling. She gripped the side of the dock with one hand, holding the boat steady, and grasped Sadie's arm with the other.

"Careful."

She waited until Sadie was safely on the dock before standing. As she did, she felt the bottom of the boat give slightly under her weight. A shallow pool of water appeared around her foot. She gave a gentle bounce, and a crack in the rusty hull revealed itself just a few inches away from the toe of her shoe. More water rushed in, swirling the remnants of mud and dead leaves into a light brown soup.

Jesus, she thought. *What if we had been out on the lake when this happened? What if the entire bottom gave out?*

You didn't even bother with life jackets. It was the chiding voice, the scolding voice.

"Can I go inside?" Sadie asked. She was already backing off of the dock and onto the path leading up the slope to the lake house.

Kris nodded and exhaled a barely audible, "Yeah."

The calm she had felt at the center of the lake, the peace she had experienced for one exhilarating moment, was evaporating. The day felt oppressively hot. Her skin was sticky with sweat and dirt.

She watched as Sadie reached the top of the slope and hurried up the back steps to the deck. She heard the sound of the French doors opening and closing.

To her side, something bobbing in the clear water below the dock caught Kris's eye.

It was the black beetle she had spotted when they first got to the boat, the one that had been trying desperately to crawl up the slick metal side.

It was dead. Drowned. It floated on its back, its crooked legs jutting into the air at odd angles.

Kris watched as the rippling water slowly carried the dead beetle under the dock and out of sight. And then the water settled, the surface of the lake becoming smooth and still.

True to its name, the E-Z Lite charcoal went up like a Christmas tree in February. Within twenty minutes, the flames were dying down into a mound of orange coals dusted with pale gray ash.

From the great room, a bouncy guitar, one of the most famous riffs of all time, drifted out through the open French doors. The ragged voice of Warren Zevon began to sing.

"I saw a werewolf with a Chinese menu in his hand . . ."

For the past forty-five minutes, Kris had been on the back deck, cleaning the charcoal grill, stripping its legs of spiderwebs, dumping ancient ashes from its basin into the towering weeds below the deck, scrubbing clumps of incinerated grime from its grates.

It was finally ready for them. For their summer.

Four dogs went rolling onto the grill with an angry hiss. It wasn't long before their skin was beginning to blister. Hot, clear juice spurted from jagged splits in the charred casings.

One by one, Kris jabbed the hot dogs with a fork and nestled them down into buns lined up in a row on a paper plate.

Sadie had managed to move from the armchair inside to a seat at the bistro table on the deck. She stared out at the still waters of Lost Lake, its surface reflecting a purple sky.

"Here we go."

Kris set the plate down in the center of the table, flicked open the top of a squeeze bottle of Heinz ketchup, and ran two red strips down either side of a hot dog, just the way Sadie liked it.

Without a word, Sadie picked up the hot dog and took a small bite from one end.

Kris held her breath. Watching. Wondering if they would have a repeat of lunch, with Sadie immediately losing interest in her food.

The little girl chewed the bite slowly, swallowed, then took a larger bite.

Good enough, Kris thought.

From inside came the softly strummed chords of an acoustic guitar and the longing voice of David Gilmour.

"So. . . so you think you can tell . . . heaven from hell . . . blue skies from pain . . ."

Kris reached over and swept a spiraling strand of hair out of Sadie's face. She watched as Sadie took another bite, even larger this time, shortening the hot dog to half, and listened to the gentle smack of her lips as she chewed.

"Did you like coming here when you were a kid?" Sadie asked suddenly after a moment of silence.

"Yes," Kris replied. She paused, thinking, then said, "That room upstairs, that was my secret playroom. I used to pretend it was a place where only I could go. No grown-ups allowed. You had to believe in magic to pass through the door."

"And grown-ups don't?"

"Believe in magic?"

Sadie nodded. She was staring into the empty space before her, her brow furrowed as if she couldn't imagine ever outgrowing something so sacred.

Kris let out a sigh. "It's hard, Sadie. You know, life . . ." She let her words drift away before taking a different route. "When you're little, you tell yourself you'll always remember what it's like to be a kid. But the truth is, most grown-ups forget. They get busy with work and family and bills and all of those grown-up things that seem to take up every minute of every day, and they forget to look for the magic."

"But it's still there?"

Kris thought, *I don't know. I honestly don't know. It might dry up and disappear forever like a puddle of water on a hot day. Or maybe it was never there in the first place.*

What she said was, "Yes. It's still there. If you believe."

They fell silent once more.

Inside, a jangly guitar churned out power chords over driving drums and cymbals that crashed like waves.

Kris knew the song immediately. She winced in a mixture of pleasure and pain, her mouth opening in a silent "Oh!"

"Moving forward, using all my breath . . ."

Pushing her chair away from the table, Kris slipped down to her feet.

"Come on," she said, holding a hand out to Sadie.

The little girl stayed put.

"Oh, so that's how it is." Kris stretched her arms out over her head, her body swaying. "Okay. You think you can actually listen to this song and *not* dance. Cool. Let me know how that works out for ya."

The chorus kicked in, and Kris sang it to her daughter, loudly and more than a little off key.

"I'll stop the world and melt with you! You've seen the difference and it's getting better all the time."

A smirk tried to force its way onto Sadie's lips. She covered her mouth with a hand, but there was little she could do to fight it.

Kris tilted her head back to sing to the sky. "There's nothing you and I won't do . . ."

Even with the music blaring, she heard the faint sound of chair legs scraping across wood. Sadie stepped up to her, and Kris took the girl's hands, twirling her around and around until that smirk turned into a beaming smile.

"I'll stop the world and melt with you!"

They danced, their fingers clasped, Kris moving her daughter's body to the beat, just as Kris's mother had danced with her on those summer nights when the music settled on their skin.

God, she loved this song. Because it was more than a song. It was an anthem. A triumphant celebration.

It was perfect.

"Dream of better lives, the kind which never hate, trapped in the state of imaginary grace."

Sadie's body suddenly grew still.

"Who's that?" she asked.

Kris stopped dancing.

"Who are you talking about, sweetie?"

Sadie pointed to the opposite side of the lake. "There. That woman."

Kris searched the black forest on the other shore but saw nothing.

"She's watching us," Sadie whispered, more to herself than to her mother.

A chill ran through Kris. "Sadie, I don't see—"

There it was. Through a narrow break in the wall of featureless black trees that spread across the shore like smeared ink was a light, burning brightly. A single fixture was mounted above the back door of another lake house, and silhouetted against its glow was a dark form, watching. The distance was too far and the night too dark for Kris to see her clearly, but there was no doubting it was a woman, tall and thin with hair hanging like black sheets of rain around her shoulders. Her arms were down straight at her sides, and the featureless void where her face was seemed to be staring straight at them.

"It's just someone else who lives on the lake," Kris said, a little too quickly for her own liking.

"Why is she watching us?" Sadie asked.

Kris was suddenly acutely aware of her situation—alone with her eight-year-old daughter in a small house in the woods—a house with a single dead bolt on the front door, and weak latches on every other door and window—on the outskirts of an equally small town that was not their own.

Stop, she warned. *You're trying to scare yourself.*

She shook her head to dislodge the thoughts burrowing into her mind. "She's not watching us, Sadie," she said. "She's just on her deck, like we are, looking at the lake. She can't see us. It's too far away."

"We can see her."

"Not really. She's just a shadow."

"It feels like she's looking at us."

The hairs on the back of Kris's neck prickled. Sadie was right. It felt like they were being watched, like two eyes were boring into them with an intensity as inexplicable as it was undeniable.

Before Kris even realized she was moving, she had stood up from her chair and was collecting the things from the table.

"Come on," she said, nodding toward the back door. "It's getting late, and I still need to bring in the rest of our things."

Sadie obeyed without fuss, stuffing the last bite of hot dog bun into her mouth and trudging back into the house.

As soon as they were inside, Kris closed the French doors behind her and twisted the lock. She leaned back against the cool panes. It was better in here. Safe.

Kris glanced over her shoulder and found herself staring through her own reflection. It was like peering through a ghost.

Across the lake, the porch light shimmered in the darkness. But the woman was gone, if she had really been there at all.

The back hatch of the Jeep was beginning to sag. The old hydraulic hinges always did this in cold weather, and even though the June night was far from what Kris would call "cold," it was considerably chillier on the lake once the sun went down.

Propping the door up with one hand, she stretched out with the other until her fingers grazed the cardboard side of the last box. She slipped her fingers over its top edge and pulled the box closer. There was a clank as the items inside shifted. She tipped the box toward the dome light at the center of the Jeep and was immediately reminded of what she had packed in this particular box: a stack of ceramic plates, and beneath these, a random collection of silverware.

Good. No more eating off paper plates. Just because their stay was temporary didn't mean it had to feel like it.

She let the hatch door slam shut on its own as she turned toward the house, the box pressed securely to her chest.

Around her, a night breeze rustled the branches of the endless forest. The weed-infested yard emitted a rhythmic drone as if the very ground were vibrating. It was different from the song of the bullfrogs out back. This was a soft buzz like an electrical appliance idling. It was the lullaby of content crickets nestled into the still-warm earth.

Before her, Kris could barely make out the brick path leading up to the front porch. She gripped the box tighter as she carefully navigated the uneven terrain.

From high overhead, there came a loud bang, like a fist against glass.

She glanced up at the house.

The windows on the second floor were dark.

She kept her eyes on them as she picked up her pace, staring at their black panes as if at any moment she expected to see someone peering down at her.

Above the oval window on the far right, on the gable's peak, something shifted, a black shape that danced in place along the ridge. Its movements were jittery, like a filmstrip with multiple frames excised at random. It cocked a small, pointed head, eyeing her. Just as she reached the overhang of the front porch, the thing gave an abrasive shriek.

Another blackbird.

Kris snorted, irritated.

The bird cried again.

"Kiss my ass!" she yelled up at it.

The bird kept its eyes trained on her. Its head was now cocked at such an angle that the ebony spheres set into its dark skull caught slivers of moonlight.

Kris stepped onto the porch, thankful to be hidden beneath its roof. Balancing the box with one hand, she twisted the doorknob with the other and flung open the front door. From above, the unseen bird gave a final *awk*, just for spite, as she entered.

She set the box on the kitchen island. The other boxes and suitcases were stacked in a heap behind the leather couch in the great room.

The music was still playing, now halfway through a song by the Cure. How many tracks had her mother crammed on to this tape? Kris recalled many cassettes being inserted into and ejected from the boombox during their long summer days, but her mother always returned to this mixtape.

When Kris was little, these were simply the songs her mother enjoyed. Bands like the Cure and the Smiths and Fleetwood Mac may as well have been items from the adult menu at a restaurant, and so Kris had disregarded them as such. They were not for her. But listening to them now, as a forty-one-year-old woman, Kris was reminded of how goddamn cool her mom had been. She was young when she was first diagnosed with cancer, just shy of her thirty-sixth birthday, and Kris was now a full year older than her when she died. She had officially outlived her own mother. As Robert Smith moaned his way through "Inbetween Days," Kris was struck by how frightened her mother must have been. She was just a kid, only three decades into a life that should have lasted at least another half century more. She loved her family and the outdoors and bittersweet songs that bravely faced life's coldest, darkest hours.

"Sa-die," Kris sang loudly.

Crossing quickly to the fireplace, she punched a fingertip down onto the Stop button. There was a sharp click, and the music ceased.

The house was still.

From the corner of her eye, Kris caught a glimpse of her reflection in the towering windows. Her transparent form—this other, hollow self—matched her movement for movement as she slipped past the arm of the couch and stepped into the entryway to the hall. She yelled loud enough for her voice to carry upstairs, "Sadie! Time to get ready for bed!"

"I am."

The voice was right beside her.

Startled, Kris whipped around.

A face was peeking out of the hall bathroom, half hidden by the doorframe. A toothbrush, still wet and sudsy with toothpaste, was clutched in Sadie's hand. A thin line of slick white foam ran from the corner of her mouth to the edge of her chin.

Kris reached out and wiped it away with her thumb.

"Let's get you in bed."

She waited for Sadie to finish rinsing at the sink, and then she guided her across the hall and into the pink bedroom. Kris pulled back the covers and waited for the little girl to climb up onto the bed, but she never arrived. Kris could feel Sadie standing behind her, motionless.

She turned back.

Sadie was cradling Bounce in one arm, her other hand gently stroking his patchy fur. She stared down into the frog's crooked eyes. Her own eyes were beginning to swim with the first threat of tears.

"Honey?"

Sadie's bottom lip trembled.

She's fighting it, Kris realized. *Oh, my sweet baby, she's fighting it. But she's losing. She's losing.*

Carefully, as if she were afraid the girl would startle, Kris dropped down onto her knees and reached out to touch Sadie lightly on the arm. The second her fingers made contact, the girl's entire body began to shake as her grief—held so long and so tightly within her—uncoiled like a frayed knot. Tears slipped free, flooding down her cheeks.

Words attempted to push through lips thick with mucus.

"I miss Daddy," Sadie whimpered.

"I know," Kris said.

"I miss Daddy."

"I know, baby. I know. I know."

A horrible, shuddering bellow erupted from Sadie's open mouth.

Stop, Kris thought desperately.

Sadie fell against Kris, her face pressed hard into mother's shoulder, her hands gripping for any hold. She was adrift in grief, untethered. Her teeth pressed against Kris's neck as an animallike moan escaped her lips.

Please stop. Please stop please stop please stop!

The sound of Sadie's wailing seemed to fill the entire house. It echoed off the walls of the bedroom, ricocheting violently until it found the open doorway and careened wildly down the hall, a spirit summoned without consent, desperate to escape.

Kris could feel Sadie's cries, actually *feel* them pressing like invisible fingers that wormed deep into her ear canals.

A ridiculous thought popped into Kris's mind: *She was happy yesterday. This was working. This was going to work.*

But had she ever truly believed that it would be that easy? That she could drive Sadie five hundred miles away from her pain and it wouldn't follow her?

Glistening ropes of saliva stretched across Sadie's gaping maw, her face bright red and locked in a silent scream.

All Kris could say was, "I know." Over and over. "I know. I know. I know."

The space within the house felt as though it were pushing against them, constricting them, squeezing the air from their lungs. It was going to crush them, this collapsing force. And then, with a snap like a buckling twig, it was gone.

Sound found its way to Sadie's lips, and she shrieked with a force that left Kris's ears ringing. It was a terrible sound that no child should ever make.

It was pain and suffering and the death of magic.

PART TWO

IN BETWEEN DAYS

CHAPTER THIRTEEN

SOMETHING HAD CHANGED. She couldn't put her finger on it, but when Kris woke on the third day, once again in Sadie's bed—this time with Sadie breathing softly beside her—the house just felt . . . lighter. The weight that she had felt the previous night, the intense pressure that had attempted to push every square inch of breath from her lungs while Sadie sobbed in her arms, was gone.

No, not just gone. Replaced. Replaced by a lightness that made Kris feel as though the weight of her body had no effect on the tired springs of Sadie's mattress.

Sadie's mattress. After only two nights, it's her mattress now. Of course it is. This room is hers and everything in it.

She breathed in this new lighter air. It tasted purer across her tongue. It felt cleaner in her lungs. She had never smoked, except for the few random cigarettes she'd snuck as a teenager beneath the bridge where Overlook Boulevard crossed Sycamore Creek, but she assumed this was the sensation she would feel after two weeks of kicking the habit, the tar flaking away from her blackened lungs to reveal healthy, hopeful pink tissue beneath.

A line of sunlight streamed through the narrow slit between the yellowed drapes, and as Kris stared at the beam cutting across the dim room, she realized it was completely void of dust motes. It was a strip of flawless gold.

This is it, Kris thought. *This is how we'll feel every morning for the rest of the summer. Like we're on vacation.*

Because last night, Sadie had finally allowed herself to expunge the pain she had held deep within her tiny body. She had flushed it out of her soul with a shower of tears. And her release was exactly what Kris had needed too, to take that much needed next step forward. They could both move on now. Not completely. Not all the way to the finish line. She wasn't naive enough to think that either of them was done dealing with the loss of Jonah, but she was certain that this . . . *lightness*—there was no other way to describe it—that this lightness was a sign of healing.

And they would heal together.

This summer.

Kris took another long, joyous breath, savoring its freshness.

This house is clean, she thought, and she had to clamp a hand over her mouth to keep her laughter from waking her sleeping daughter.

When Sadie woke almost thirty minutes later, she let out a long, contented sigh, as if she awoke to the same easiness that had greeted Kris. There was a casualness to her, to the way she stretched her arms wide and yawned a big gaping-mouthed yawn, to the way she blinked in the sunlight as her vision cleared.

"Good morning," Kris said softly.

Sadie turned her head toward the voice. For a moment, she stared at Kris as if she couldn't quite place her own mother's face. And then she gave another lazy stretch, like a cat waking from a nap.

"What time is it?" she asked.

"Time to get up," Kris told her.

Sadie's appetite was back as well. In the kitchen, Kris broke out one of the pans she had brought from home, heated it up on the electric range, tossed in a spoonful of butter, and cooked up two scrambled eggs. Within five minutes of sliding the fluffy eggs onto Sadie's plate, Kris realized she had underestimated the girl's hunger. There was a frantic scraping of metal across porcelain, and then Sadie's plate was as clean as if it had just come out of the dishwasher.

Kris quickly beat two more eggs into the pan. While she was waiting for the eggs to cook, she dropped two pieces of whole-wheat bread into the toaster.

Sadie ate it all. Four eggs and two slices of buttered toast.

Things were back to normal. They were *better* than normal. It was as if a fever had broken, and they were both filled once again with energy. With appetite. With *life*.

Kris poured Sadie a glass of orange juice and then whipped up a batch of eggs for herself. She cracked four, just to be safe.

That afternoon, Kris and Sadie did another pass on the first floor. They started just inside the front door, catching all of the things they had missed the first time: a pile of dead leaves that had blown into the corner of the narrow foyer; cobwebs floating loosely between the coat hooks mounted on the wall; a layer of dust, imperceptible to the naked eye, that covered the walls. They moved into the kitchen, Kris once more ignoring the sagging, crooked cabinet doors, instead doing a quick wipe-down of the countertops before focusing more time on the overlooked breakfast nook. On the booth seats, beneath flattened tan cushions, they found three dead crickets, one dead roach, a live earwig, twenty-six cents, and enough crumbs to build an entire slice of bread. But when they were done, the nook was as clean as the rest of the kitchen, and Kris was content knowing that they no longer had to stand at the island while they ate their breakfast.

While they cleaned, the mixtape unspooled slowly through more of Side B: the dreamy one-two punch of Sweet's "Love Is Like Oxygen" and April Wine's "Say Hello"; the distorted power of Jimi Hendrix's "Spanish Castle Magic"; the eerie brilliance of U2's "Mothers of the Disappeared"; the throw-your-fist-in-the-air stadium anthem of Journey's "Only the Young"; the bittersweet nostalgia of Big Star's "Thirteen"; the fall-on-the-floor-and-die genius of Prince's "Purple Rain." When Side B reached the end, Kris would eject the cassette, flip it over, and press the door shut. The Smiths would drift from the speakers, and the musical journey left by her mother would begin all over again.

By midafternoon, Sadie was ready for a break. She retreated to her bedroom just as it dawned on Kris that there was nothing left to clean. Not downstairs, anyway.

You're forgetting something, the shadow voice purred from the abyss.

She froze.

The master bedroom. She still had not even entered it.

You don't have to. It was her timid voice, stretched thin by fear. *You can keep staying in Sadie's room.*

"Not all summer," Kris answered aloud.

From the depths of her mind, Shadow Kris called her bluff. *Sure you can. Just don't use that room. Close the door and never go inside. Sleep in Sadie's bed or on the couch. That makes sense, right? That's not crazy at all.*

She knew she had to clean the master bedroom, but not just so she could finally move out of Sadie's room. The house needed to be perfect—the entire house—just like how she remembered it. Kris would help the house, and in return, the house would help Sadie. Just like it had done for her, back when her mother was little more than a moaning corpse at the end of the hall.

Piled in a metal bucket under the kitchen sink were plastic bottles and the remaining clean rags and sponges. She lifted the bucket up, set it on the counter beside the sink, and began to unload the contents one by one until everything was arranged in a neat, evenly spaced group. Flicking the faucet handle up, she waited until the water was nice and hot, and then she gripped the handle hanging down on one side of the bucket.

"It's just a room," she said to herself.

She placed the bucket under the running water and squirted in a stream of liquid soap until it was filled with steaming suds.

Carefully, Kris gripped the heavy bucket by its handle and carried it across the great room. Clutched in her other hand was a plastic bag containing the rest of the supplies.

She paused at the mouth of the hall.

At the other end, the door to the master bedroom stood half open, its hinges backlit by bright sunlight.

She glanced quickly over at Sadie's bedroom door. It was closed, but she could still hear the soft rustle of pages as Sadie flipped through a book.

Good. Sadie didn't need to help her. Not with this room.

You need to do this alone, she told herself.

Taking a deep breath, Kris crept quietly down the hall.

CHAPTER FOURTEEN

SADIE HEARD HER mother passing by, the creak of the wood floor under her shoes, the soft slosh of water in a bucket. And then the sounds were lost as a breeze suddenly swept over the lake and up the slope to hum across the steep roof of the house.

Arranged before her in rows, like students in a classroom, were her stuffed animals. Bounce sat in the front row, eager to listen to the story Miss Sadie had chosen. In her hand, Sadie held a battered paperback copy of *The Berenstain Bears and the Old Spooky Tree*, one of her all-time favorite books. She had had it since kindergarten, and its cover was bent, the corners of its pages tattered.

A few moments ago, she thought it would be fun to play "Teacher" with her toys. She had even started to read the first few pages in a hushed voice:

"Three little bears. One with a light. One with a stick. One with a rope. A spooky old tree. Do they dare go into that spooky old tree?"

On the next page were the words: *Yes. They dare.*

But Sadie suddenly found that she could not say them. She didn't want them to go. She wanted them to stay in the light. Because once you went into the darkness, you never came out. That's how these things worked. They swallowed you and kept you forever.

Like the hole in the ground.

The one that Daddy lived in now.

Sadie closed the book and let it slip from her hands.

Outside, the breeze died down.

In its place, another sound lingered.

Sadie cocked her head.

It was a familiar sound. She had heard it before.

That impossibly faint whisper that seemed to be far away and close all at once.

Sadie rose, making sure to give Bounce a pat on the head to let him know he was, as always, a good boy.

She pushed her door open and paused, listening.

The whisper flowed away from her, like a leaf carried away on a gentle stream.

Quietly, she slipped out of her bedroom and tiptoed down the hall. On her right was the partially open door to the master bedroom. To her left, the hall turned sharply. She could see the edge of a step peeking out from around the corner, the polish on its surface worn.

A board groaned under the heel of her shoe.

Sadie froze. She did not know why she didn't want Mommy to see her out of her bedroom, but something—that beckoning voice perhaps—warned her not to get caught.

She stood perfectly still, only allowing her head to turn slowly toward the master bedroom door.

There was Mommy, on her hands and knees, scrubbing at a stubborn patch of dirt with a filthy rag. Like the other rooms, this one only had a few pieces of furniture and almost no decorations of any kind. It would not take Mommy long to clean it. If Sadie hoped to follow the sound to its source, she needed to move quickly.

Lifting up onto her tippy-toes, she crossed in staccato steps to the foot of a staircase. The stairs stretched up high above her. At the top was a landing painted in the same gold light that had cut a swath through the curtains in her bedroom.

Her small hand gripped the handrail. She let her palm slide across it as she ascended the stairs, and the scratchy wood scraped harmlessly at her flesh like the hairs on—

On Daddy's head. When he shaved it that one time. Because you told him that he was going bald. And Daddy got mad. Daddy didn't like being told that. Daddy didn't want to be old. It made him sad. You made him sad.

The whispering voice grew louder, as if the connection had suddenly become more secure. But she still could not make out what it was saying. The voice was nothing more than waves lapping against rock.

Her hand bumped into the edge of the top post. She had climbed the entire staircase without realizing it.

Below, in the doorway to the master bedroom, there was no sign of Mommy. Not a shadow. Not even her voice calling out to make sure Sadie was okay.

Sadie was above now. On the second floor.

You shouldn't be here, she thought.

But that didn't make sense. This house was where they were going to live for the whole summer. This was their "get away" place. She had heard Mommy say that on the phone before they left, when she was talking to Miss Allison at Mommy's office: "We just need to get away for a while." So why should Sadie have to stay on the first floor? Mommy had never said she couldn't come up here. The entire house was theirs.

But you're being sneaky, she told herself. *You're sneaking and you don't want Mommy to find out.*

Knowing this made Sadie feel sad. But it wasn't the regular kind of sad, like when she watched a movie where an animal died or read a book with a mean sister in it. This was a special kind of sad, as if a little part of her kind of enjoyed feeling this way. There was a word for this feeling. She had heard Mommy say it once when she was talking about how Daddy felt sometimes. Melon-something. Melon . . .

Collie. Like the dog. Like Mr. Brubaker's dog when he brought it to Mommy's work, that time it tangled with a porcupine. It had those thorny things in its nose. Miss Allison had to hold it down while Mommy plucked them out, one by one, with tweezers.

Mommy didn't know that Sadie was listening to her talk to Miss Allison, but she was, and she heard Mommy say that word that sounded like "melon collie." Mommy said that Daddy liked feeling that way because it made him seem romantic.

Sadie stood hesitantly on the landing and tapped the toe of her shoe against the floor's uneven planks. Directly ahead of her was an archway constructed of knobby white wood, its pale bark dotted with dark, twisted knots. To Sadie, it looked as if two trees had bowed their heads to form a frame.

A picture frame.

But the picture inside was moving, like those paintings on the walls in Hogwarts, just the slightest hint of movement from the curtains flanking the windows along the north wall. One of the windows must have been open, because the curtains knocked softly in a breeze, shifting shadows around the room.

Through this magic tree-lined picture frame, Sadie started into a large rectangular room that appeared to be used mostly for storage. The larger items had been shoved to either side, creating a straight, narrow pathway to the far side of the room. The items were odds and ends, a random collection of things no longer wanted downstairs. Folding chairs. A mirror in a strange, twisty steel frame. The heads of animals—a wild cat, a deer with pointy horns—mounted on shiny wooden shields, their artificial black eyes glistening like marbles.

Sadie sucked in a frightened breath.

Suddenly the touch of an invisible finger was under her chin, lifting her head so that her line of sight was straight and level, so that she was peering directly to the far side of the room.

There was a small square door, no more than three feet by three feet. It was set into the wall on brass hinges. A sliding steel latch was mounted on the wall to one side. The bolt rested against the loops, not through them.

It was open, just an inch or two.

Inside that doorway was darkness.

Sadie stepped forward, through the archway, through the magic picture frame, her tiny form slicing narrow streaks of sunlight to send dust motes swirling away like ghostly fingers clawing at the air.

CHAPTER FIFTEEN

THIS IS YOUR mother's room.

Kris clenched her jaw and pushed the thought away, as she had done a hundred times since entering the master bedroom. She focused on the work, on scrubbing at the grime-covered mirrors lining the closet doors. She put her weight into the damp rag and yet she could not seem to remove a stubborn patch of film from eye level.

Others had stayed here. She knew that. In the thirty years since she and her father had walked out the door, Mr. Hargrove had initially rented the house to who-knew-how-many summer people until her father abruptly ordered him to stop. The master bedroom would have been the first and most obvious choice for them to sleep, and so it belonged to everyone.

And yet the voice in her mind persisted.

The shadow voice. It reminded her, over and over, with more than a hint of pleasure: *This is your mother's room.*

Kris knew it was right. Because her mother had been the only one to truly claim the room as her own, to claim it with her laughter, with her pain, with her tears, with her screams.

With her life. But most importantly, with her death.

There, the voice purred. *In the bed. It's right there. Beside you. Look at it.*

Kris scrubbed harder, concentrating on that goddamn smudge that turned the reflection of her own face into a blurry blob. The rag in her hand was beginning to fray.

Look at it!

The voice's shout was so loud, so sudden, that for a moment Kris was convinced she had actually heard it, not reverberating off the walls of her mind but off the hard wood planks lining the bedroom, its percussion echoing down the hallway like a shotgun blast.

Look at it.

This time it was her own voice. Soft. Patient. Comforting.

Look.

Kris took a long, slow breath—in through her nose, out through her mouth—and then she turned toward the bed.

There were no horrors waiting for her. Only a simple metal frame supporting a fabric-covered box spring that was worn through in multiple areas to reveal the wood beneath. Above this, a lumpy blue comforter was tucked over the queen-sized mattress. At the head of the bed, two mismatched pillows rested against the rustic headboard—the one in a yellow case was as thin as the comforter upon which it sat; the other, sporting a decorative slip covered in various types of fishing lures, as fat as the first was thin. Kris did not recognize the pillowcases or the comforter, but all would be stripped and replaced, just as she'd done to Sadie's bed.

For a long moment, she sat on her knees, the dirt-smeared rag in her hand forgotten, and stared at the bed as if waiting for the covers to rise up and the thing beneath them to turn its head on a neck like a crooked twig as the sheets slipped away from a face more skull than flesh, cheeks sunken into shadowy graves, skin as gray as smoke and marred by red sores, the wet, raw meat glistening. And those eyes, the hazel eyes that had once stared lovingly down at her when she was a baby, now bulging and wide as if lidless, seeming to float in the sockets of that flesh-draped skull.

This did not happen, even as Kris waited another full minute, listening to the pull and release of her soft, steady breaths.

It was a bed. Nothing more.

For better or worse, it was her bed now.

Twenty minutes later, Kris had finally managed to clean the smudge from the mirrored closet doors. She could see her own face, although the sight made her uneasy. It was like staring into the face of someone who looked exactly like her, but someone who had a completely separate life. As if the smudge had been trying to protect her from her own insignificance.

She turned back to take in the enormity of her task.

Hanging on the wall directly across from the foot of the bed was a painting in a distressed frame. In the picture, a young girl stood at the end of a dock. Lily pads dotted the still blue water behind her. She was facing straight ahead, but the wind had blown her brown hair across her face. Only one of her blue eyes was visible through the stray locks. She was staring up at something in front of her, just out of frame.

This had been her mother's favorite painting. It had been here when her father bought the lake house. Kris didn't know if the real estate agent had hung it to stage the house or if the previous occupants had left it behind, but she did know that her mother wanted it to remain in that exact spot. She did not want it taken down at the end of each summer to travel home with them to Blantonville. Her mother wanted it in the lake house, so that it could greet them when they returned every June.

Kris recalled, as a little girl, peering up at the painting and only seeing the girl in her pretty dress and the lily pads. She loved the painting because her mother loved it. But the last time she had seen this particular print was thirty years ago, and now she looked at it not through her mother's adoring eyes but through her own, through three decades of her own pain and joy, her own hopes and fears. There was something about the girl's posture—one foot behind the other as if she were backing up, a hand raised slightly as if preparing to defend herself—that made Kris uneasy. The girl seemed to have been backed to the end of the dock, her one visible eye peering not at the viewer of the painting but at something beyond, the thing that had made her run in the first place, the thing that was now creeping cruelly toward her.

Kris gripped the painting on either side of the frame and lifted it from its hook. The picture wire gave a soft twang as it came loose, like an out-of-tune guitar string. She carefully slid the painting under the bed until only the edge of its frame could be seen in the thick shadows beneath.

Guilt rippled like faint thunder through her chest, and she felt her heartbeat quicken, ever so slightly, knocking against the backside of her rib cage.

You are trying to forget her, Kris's mind accused.

"No," Kris whispered to the empty room, and she knew it was the truth. She did not want to forget her mother. She wanted to forget the pain.

Kris turned back to the wall. There was a clear rectangle of darker paint where the picture had hung, and of course the naked hook remained, but at least the painting was gone. It was a start.

Taking a step toward the master bathroom, she saw that the details were the same as when she was a child: a long, narrow room lined with darker wood panels than the rest of the house; a small shower tucked into one corner where a large round showerhead protruded from walls of smooth river rock; a steel sink set into a rustic wooden cabinet in the same grayish-brown shade as the walls; and a pocket door that opened to a tiny water closet containing a simple porcelain toilet. The toilet paper holder was shaped like a largemouth bass, its head and tail turned forward so that the wooden spool fit between them, its body hand-painted and covered in a shiny resin finish.

Yet what had been, in her memory, a quaint space now had a strange, unsettling quality to it. The single frosted window set between the sink and the shower provided little light. Its pale glow actually contributed to the bathroom's gloomy appearance. And then there was that fish, that bug-eyed, gape-mouthed fish, staring out from the shadows of the water closet.

She decided to focus on the positives. For being left unattended for God knows how long, the master bathroom was in surprisingly good shape. There were no signs of mold in the shower, no creeping mildew like they had found in the hall bathroom, no rotting wood to suggest the steady drip of a leaky pipe. It should take no more than fifteen or twenty minutes to clean. Another fifteen to mop and dust the bedroom, five to put fresh sheets on the bed, and then cleaning this room would be thankfully behind her.

As she stepped into the bathroom, the toe of her sneaker squeaked as it scuffed the limestone tile floor, and Kris was suddenly aware of how intensely silent the house had become. The gust of wind that had whipped over the house a few minutes before had vanished. Even the occasional knock of Sadie's movements in her bedroom had ceased.

Kris moved quickly out of the bathroom and over to the bedroom doorway. She leaned out.

"Sa-die . . ."

From above came the faint sound of muffled laughter.

Crossing to the staircase opposite the master bedroom, Kris quietly crept up the steps to the second-floor landing, where she found herself staring through an archway constructed from ghostly white birch trunks. The room before her was cluttered with random, unwanted items from the house.

Again, the soft sound of a child giggling came from nearby, like the tinkling of glass.

At the end of the room, a small passageway had opened low on the wall. Sunshine spilling in from a row of double-hung windows on the north side of the house hit the far wall at such an angle that the pale plaster around the tiny doorway seemed to glow. Yet the space inside the passage remained infinitely dark.

Kris stepped through the archway and began to cross the room. Her eyes never left that black square cut into the wall.

Alice, she thought suddenly, and the name confused her. The memory of a taste, of something sweet, slipped across her tongue.

Cake. Chocolate cupcakes with rubbery chocolate frosting and two thin white lines that zigzagged across the top, intertwining again and again like the bodies of mating snakes.

Hostess Cupcakes. The kind Dad always packed as a snack for the road. The perfect items for a tea party, for Alice to bring as she passed into Wonderland. But to get to Wonderland, she first had to crawl through that strange little door. She had to shrink down, smaller than small, and enter the darkness.

She was a child again—eight years old when she first came to the lake house, when she discovered the entrance to the extra storage area beyond the main room. The same age Sadie was now.

That's where she is, Kris realized. She had found it on her own. She had found her mother's secret place.

Kris knelt down next to the opening in the wall, trying to be as quiet as possible. The tips of her fingers licked the darkness, but she did not move any farther.

She listened.

Sadie's soft voice floated, disembodied, in the blackness. At her age, almost everything she said had a singsong quality to it. Yet since Jonah's death, Kris had heard that dancing lilt begin to fade, like the song of a bird that had finally accepted it would never escape its cage.

But there was no denying it: the melody of hope and innocence once again played through Sadie's voice, even if her words were too faint to make out.

Kris felt the edges of a smile push at her cheeks. There was a spreading warmth as the muscles attempted to resist, but she welcomed it.

She leaned in closer and closed her eyes, listening to the sweet sound as Sadie's voice lifted into a question punctuated by giggles.

Kris raised a hand from where it rested at the edge of the doorway and reached forward, watching as the darkness consumed first her fingers, then her hand, and finally her forearm up to the crook of her elbow. The disappearance of the appendage was absolute; one minute her flesh was illuminated by the warm glow of sunlight and the next it was gone. She knew it was still there; she could feel it reaching into air that felt strangely thick and held a chill even as the rest of the house remained warmed by the summer heat. Her brain could not reconcile what her eyes were seeing, the blackness that seemed to slice her arm cleanly so that only a stub remained. She clenched her invisible hand into a fist.

Pull it back! her mind cried out in irrational terror.

Kris ignored the voice.

She crawled into the darkness.

She knew what she was seeing was impossible. A fat, pale moon hung above her in a starless night sky. Two lines intersected it, slicing it into four equal pieces, as if she were looking at the moon through the sight of a rifle. The walls, if there were walls, could have been as close as an inch away, or they could have been hidden on the other side of an unseen horizon line. The impression was that of being plunged into an infinite void, of an astronaut taking that first step out of the safety of the shuttle to float freely over endless darkness with only a single safety cable to keep her from drifting off into space.

Except Kris had no safety cable. She had not even bothered to retain a grip on the doorframe before plunging into the abyss.

Panic ran its frozen fingers down her spine, and she glanced quickly to the doorway.

It was still there, less than a foot away, yet like the full moon that shone down on her now, its light did not seem to actually penetrate the dark. It was held at bay as completely as if the door had been shut.

Kris swallowed hard and forced her vocal cords to produce a single word: "Hello?"

If this were indeed Wonderland, then she had tumbled through at the darkest hour of night. She tried to recall if Alice had ever stayed in that other world after the sun went down, and what creatures crawled out with glowing yellow eyes and clicking claws to greet her.

It's not a fantasyland from a children's story, she reminded herself. *It's a storage room. A small one. You know this. You were here when you were little. And you know that there is a light right above you, if you can just find . . .*

The string.

That's right. Dangling somewhere above her was a string with a small metal clasp at the end. One tug, and a bare bulb mounted to the ceiling would pop on, driving the darkness away to crouch as little more than shadows in the corners.

Carefully, Kris extended a hand into the space directly above her. She could not recall how low the ceiling was and whether or not her fingertips might collide with its rough, splintered surface. When she had her arm completely stretched out and still hadn't felt wood, she began to wave her hand back and forth, first in front of and behind her, then side to side, hoping at any moment her fingers would grasp that dangling string and the room would fill with light.

From somewhere in the blackness before her, she heard the slow movement of steady, patient breaths.

At the same time, her hand bumped into what felt like an unusually thick length of spider silk. She grasped at it with trembling fingers and yanked, hard.

A fine line of flame exploded within the dingy bulb, and a harsh cone of light blasted down around her.

She was not in some nightmare version of Wonderland, nor was she drifting helplessly through an endless vacuum. She was in the extra storage room, accessible only through that small door, a narrow rectangle that ran from the front of the house to the edge of the great room, directly above the kitchen. The walls were unfinished, the studs exposed, the old wood split in places by poorly driven nails. Hovering above was not a full moon but the round casement window she had seen when she arrived. It quivered gently in its frame as the breeze outside knocked softly against it.

Sadie was sitting in a small red chair at a round play table positioned below the casement window. Across from her was an empty chair, this one painted a light purple. A sheer cream-colored sheet was suspended from a hook driven into a crossbeam above. It draped around the table like a canopy. Like everything else in the house, clumps of gray dust clung to its fabric.

Kris let out a breath of relief.

"Hey, sweetie. What are you doing up here?"

Sadie remained silent, but her eyes darted quickly to the empty chair across from her.

Crawling over to the chair, Kris held out her arms. "Come here," she said, letting the little girl slip down into her arms. She felt Sadie's small hands stretch around her and grasp the back of her shirt, holding on tight.

Overhead, the lightbulb buzzed like a hovering insect.

Kris rested her cheek against the soft mound of Sadie's curls.

"How did you find this place?" Kris asked.

She felt Sadie shrug. "Just found it, I guess." Then, as an afterthought, "Did you know it was here?"

"Yes," Kris said.

The truth was she hadn't remembered until a few minutes ago. But like many things since returning to the lake house, the details were quickly coming back to her.

She remembered her father bringing the play table from their house in Blantonville. She remembered him setting it and the chairs below the windows in the larger room, before it was cluttered with unwanted things from the rest of the lake house. She remembered sitting in that blue chair the first time she glanced over and spied the silly little square door in the wall.

She remembered dragging the table over to the tiny door and turning it sideways so that it would fit through.

She remembered bringing in the red chair and then the purple one, and placing them across from each other so Alice could have a tea party in Wonderland.

But Alice was alone. Even though she filled her secret play space with dolls and stuffed animals, she could still hear Alice's howls of pain, the desperate cries to be let go, to be allowed to leave that awful, miserable place.

She remembered crying when she realized there was no Wonderland. And she was not Alice. And no matter how dark that slender room seemed when the sun drifted over to the other side of the house, it did not compare to the true darkness that awaited her in the real world.

Stretching out a hand, Kris pointed toward the square of light illuminating the doorway to the other room.

"Come on, honey. I'll get dinner ready."

One by one, they crawled out of the tiny room, first Kris, then Sadie. As Kris was rising to her feet, she noticed Sadie glance back into the darkness inside the door.

There was a glimmer behind her eyes.

A spark.

And then she was marching off, ahead of her mother, toward the landing at the top of the stairs.

CHAPTER SIXTEEN

TUESDAY, JUNE 11, marked a full week at River's End. It was also the first inarguably hot day since their arrival. Even the air blowing up from the lake held little of the water's coolness.

A trip into town was in order. Since their visit to the Dairy Godmother for ice cream cones, the Jeep had remained parked in the jagged weeds sprouting up through the broken concrete driveway. But today they would pull the poor Grand Cherokee from its grave. It was time to tackle some of the bigger projects in the house, and to do that, Kris would need the proper tools from the hardware store.

From above came the sound of laughter.

Sadie was back upstairs. Kris had seen her carrying an armful of chapter books up the staircase—*The Magic Treehouse*, *Ivy and Bean*, *Junie B. Jones*, and some of her other favorites from home. Kris had crept up the stairs to peek around the edge of the landing. Sadie was lying on her stomach in a swath of sunlight in the main room, her books spread around her as she read out loud in a hushed voice. Nearby was one of her notebooks, the one with a unicorn farting a rainbow on the cover. The image never failed to elicit a giggle from Sadie. Scattered around the notebook was a random collection of crayons and magic markers.

Kris slipped silently back down the stairs. They would go into town, but not just yet. She wanted to give Sadie this time to herself, to play.

True Value Hardware was one of the few chains in Pacington. As if to make up for this, and justify its existence to the town's proud citizens, it shared half of its square footage with a locally owned furniture store called Verdigris Valley Home Furnishings. Both were housed in a large rectangular warehouse made entirely of corrugated steel on Overlook Drive, just half a mile up Highway 44 from Hope Church.

Kris weaved the Jeep through the obstacle course of cars, picking a relatively sensible spot at the curb in front of the store. She killed the engine. The cool air blowing from the vents cut out, the heat outside instantly penetrating the glass of the windows. It hit Kris like a boiling wave.

It was even warmer outside than it had been in the Jeep. Kris stood on the sidewalk near the front entrance and waited for Sadie to slam the back door shut and hurry up to her side. Without a word, Sadie took her mother's hand. The girl's fingers were surprisingly cool against Kris's sweaty palm.

Opening one of the double doors at the center of the building, Kris led Sadie into the warehouse. Compared to the tiny shops of downtown, this place looked like an airplane hanger. Rectangular fluorescent lights hung from the rounded steel ceiling that reached in a high arc overhead.

If the air conditioning was on, it was barely making a dent in the hot, stuffy air. Silver whirlybirds mounted to the roof spun overheard, casting circles of strobing shadow and light across the concrete floor as they attempted to suck out the heat.

To their right was the official domain of Verdigris Valley Home Furnishings. Each department was marked by a wooden sign affixed atop a metal pole, giving the space the appearance of a grid of crisscrossing streets lined with furniture instead of houses.

To their left was True Value Hardware, with its traditional rows of shelves dividing the area into aisles marked, among many others, hardware and tools and lumber.

Straight ahead was a bank of four checkout counters, only two of which were manned by employees: a twentysomething girl in a brown Verdigris Valley polo and an elderly woman with a gray perm wearing the red vest of the opposing team. Neither bothered to look away from the individual spaces of nothingness they were staring into as Kris and Sadie passed by. Even the clatter as Kris pulled a stubborn plastic basket from a stack near the first register failed to get their attention. The two women seemed to be lost in their own separate but equally uninteresting daydreams.

Hitting the hardware aisle first, Kris tossed various boxes of nails, screws, bolts, and nuts into the basket. She curved in and out of the next few aisles as Sadie followed silently behind her, checking off the major items she knew she needed from her mental list. The basket in her hand grew heavier and heavier, but the weight of it felt good. It felt like progress, like the next step in returning the lake house to its past glory.

If the mixtape and the overgrown garden conjured up memories of her mother, then this hardware store with its unique cologne of wood and leather and steel reminded her of her father. She could still hear the shrill cry of a table saw blade coming from the workroom behind their garage as it sliced through lengths of pine. She could still see the swirling clouds of sawdust twisting in shafts of sunlight from the small window on the garage's side door. Her father was a self-taught handyman, learning from trial and error until the successes outweighed the failures. Her mother lovingly joked that Daddy always made things worse before he made them better—but make them better he did. Repairing dry-rotted boards in the attic. Replacing warped molding in the hallway. Planing and rehanging the back door after a particularly humid summer left it off-kilter, refusing to budge.

Eventually her father began to spend more and more time in the workroom, even when there were no home repairs on his to-do list. He was transforming from handyman to craftsman, using his skills not just to maintain but to create. His first project was typically ambitious: a rocking chair for little Krissy's room so Mommy could rock her to sleep. When it was finished, both Krissy and Mommy immediately noticed that the chair rocked a bit to one side, but neither of them said a word. They snuggled in the chair every night before bedtime, knowing that Daddy was standing just outside the doorway, watching them with a contented smile.

When Krissy was old enough to swing a hammer, Daddy began to pass on what he had learned. He started with simple things—the difference between a flathead and a Phillips screwdriver, locating a wall stud, wielding a caulking gun. But as she got older, the lessons became more advanced. By the time she was nine years old, Kris was manning the table saw by herself, wood chips bouncing off the plastic shield of her safety goggles and sticking in her wild, curly hair, while her dad focused on another step of whatever project they had taken on together.

"Don't be afraid to mess up." He told her this over and over. It was his truth. His mantra. "You can always drive a new screw or patch a hole. You just have to have the confidence to fix it."

Back then, she believed her father could fix anything.

But there was one thing, her shadow voice whispered. *There was one thing even Daddy couldn't fix. He couldn't fix Mommy, could he? No one could fix Mommy.*

"Something I can help ya find there, miss?"

The man seemed to have materialized out of thin air. One moment, Kris was walking toward a gap between two shelving units that led to the section marked Tools, and the next a short man with deep-set eyes and wearing a sweat-stained Kansas City Chiefs baseball cap was standing directly in her path. Like the old lady at the front counter, the man wore a red True Value vest.

Kris stopped cold, the basket swinging suddenly at her side, its weight nearly tearing it from her fingers. Her other hand instinctively shot back behind her to shield her young daughter from any danger this man may pose.

"Uh," Kris stammered as her mind tried to piece together the words the man had said.

The man grinned to show that he meant no harm, but it only served to reveal more of his crooked, strangely pointed teeth.

"You looking for your husband?" he asked. "I'm happy to page him if you like. You know how men get in hardware stores."

A sharp, humorless laugh cut between Kris's lips. Instantly, her confusion cleared, replaced by cold irritation.

"No, I'm good. Thanks."

Taking Sadie by the hand, Kris attempted to move past the man, but he did not take her cue. He remained in her way, blocking the entrance to the next section. He nodded that ratty ball cap toward a metal sign hanging from a rope that spanned the entryway.

"This here's the power tools. Is there another section you're lookin' for?"

Okay. It's gonna be like that, Kris thought.

She glanced down at the name tag pinned to the left breast of the man's vest. It read simply: Tommy.

In her mind, Kris gave a snort.

This guy hasn't been a Tommy in forty years.

She forced herself to fake a warm smile.

"Actually, Tommy, you can help me."

Tommy threw his shoulders back straight as if to assure her that he was a good little soldier, at her service.

"I'm gonna go grab some new hardware for my kitchen cabinets, after all, it is my favorite room in the house, and a pair of work gloves. You do have pink for the ladies, right?" Tommy opened his jagged, rodent-like teeth to offer a reply, but Kris cut him off. "Now if you could do me a solid and find a cordless drill—nothing under twenty volts, I don't need it crappin' out with an inch of screw left to drive—a sheet sander, two extra packs of medium grit, two packs of fine grit, a hundred-foot extension cord, and a double-bladed Weedwacker, that'd be super. I'll meet you at the counter and we'll see if we can get one of those assholes to stop staring off into space and ring me up. Cool?"

Kris did not wait for a reply. She took Sadie's hand, spun in the opposite direction, and marched away to find her last remaining items. She could feel Sadie's wide eyes staring up at her in shock.

"I know," Kris said, "Mommy shouldn't have said 'assholes.' But if everyone in this store wasn't acting like an asshole, I wouldn't have to call them that."

She waited until Sadie had looked away, then stole a glance at the little girl.

An excited smile played at the corners of Sadie's mouth.

From the entryway to the Tool section, Tommy called out, "What brand do you prefer?"

"Surprise me, Tommy," Kris replied without looking back.

CHAPTER SEVENTEEN

THE FIRST TIME down Center Street, Kris completely missed the turn for the Auto Barn. It wasn't until after she stopped into You Old Sew and Sew to ask for directions that she saw the narrow drive partially hidden by a row of wax myrtle hedges.

Sadie shifted restlessly in the back seat as they turned off Center Street and rolled slowly up the drive, its loose concrete temporarily held in place by a thin layer of shale. Sadie had taken the news of the extra errand surprisingly well. It didn't hurt that she was still in shock at her mother's performance back at the hardware store. But Kris knew the girl's patience would not last long.

Up ahead, a tall, slender woman was sweeping out the barn's first stall. She glanced up at the approaching Jeep, and the breeze lifted her straight black hair away from her face. She was in her mid-thirties, her skin a rich brown, her eyes a good two shades darker. She was dressed in a black Western shirt with the sleeves rolled up to the elbow, tattered blue jeans, and square-toed cowboy boots. She leaned against the handle of her broom and raised a hand to shield her eyes from the sun's intense glare.

Kris swung the Jeep to a stop directly in front of the first stall and rolled her window down.

The woman smiled warmly, still squinting in the sun. "Hey there." She had an accent thicker than most in the area, a friendly twang, Southern Oklahoma or Texas perhaps, which turned a simple "hey" into an elongated "ha-ey."

Kris glanced over her shoulder to Sadie in the back seat. "Stay put," she said quietly but sternly.

Sadie sighed impatiently, but she obeyed her mother's orders.

Kris opened the driver's-side door and stepped out into the Kansas heat.

The woman introduced herself as Camilla and gave Kris's hand a hearty shake. She nodded toward the donut. "Looks like you're needin' a new tire."

"Had a blowout on our way to town," Kris explained. "No idea what I hit."

Camilla tucked her black hair behind her ear. "Let's have a look."

Kris raised the back hatch, reached in, and dragged the damaged tire toward them.

Camilla ran a finger over the jagged edge of a hole the size of a fist. She whistled in resignation. "Whelp, that one's toast."

"Yeah?"

"Oh yeah. Dead as a motherfucker."

The comment caught Kris off guard, and she gave a startled laugh.

Over the top of the rear seat, Sadie's face peeked up, eyes watching, suddenly interested.

Camilla clapped a hand over her mouth. "Oh shit, I'm sorry." And then, upon realizing her repeated mistake, she followed it with a self-scolding, "Son of a bitch, I did it again."

Kris's body shook with laughter. It felt good. It felt goddamn good to laugh so purely, so unexpectedly. She put a hand on Camilla's arm and managed to choke out "It's okay."

"Hi," Camilla said sweetly, giving a little wave.

Sadie hesitantly raised a hand and waved back.

"That's Sadie," Kris told her after she had recovered.

"Well," Camilla said to them both, "I apologize for anything you may or may not have heard."

There was no reply from the back seat. Sadie was little more than a pair of green eyes staring over the headrest.

Camilla gave the expired tire a hard slap. "We got a salvage yard on the other side of the barn. We can hook you up."

Kris smiled a true, warm smile that made her cheek muscles ache from lack of use. "Thank you."

"Not a problem," Camilla assured her before walking back toward where she had left her broom propped against the building's chipped red brick.

Kris heard her call out in a gentle but commanding voice, "Jesse."

From the second stall came the clank of tools tossed onto the surface of a workbench. A moment later, a man emerged from the shadows, wiping his grease-covered hands on an old red rag. He was older than Camilla, as much as ten years judging by the gray that was creeping through his black hair and down into his thick sideburns. Jesse was tall and lean, but time was clearly catching up with him. The bulge of a gut showed beneath the buttons of his denim shirt. His shoulders slumped forward slightly as if carrying an invisible weight. His dark eyes were set deep beneath a brow that appeared to be frozen in a furrow.

Tucking the rag into his back pocket with one hand, he gave a small wave with the other, mouthing the word "Hi" without actually saying it.

Kris started to wave back, then paused, suddenly unsure if Jesse was waving at her.

Of course he's waving at you, her mind scolded. *Who else is here?*

There was Sadie.

Kris glanced over her shoulder.

The girl had ducked down even lower, hiding. A single eye peered through the space between the seats.

When Kris looked back, Jesse was deep in conversation with Camilla. Their voices were a low, indecipherable murmur carried on the soft breeze. Jesse ran a calloused hand over his mouth and then motioned outside, in the direction of the field that bordered the property to the east. Rusting barbed wire stretched between crooked wooden posts separating the field from a small gravel lot that served as both a parking lot and temporary holding for vehicles in need of pick up or further repairs.

At the center of the field, something moved, a brown shape staying low behind swaying stalks of prairie sandreed. As Kris watched, the object rose up above the grass's splintered tops, and shining black eyes stared out at her. Dark nostrils flared as the creature gave a curious snort.

A horse. A jagged white line ran from just above its gray nose and narrowed as it cut across the animal's tan forehead, coming to a point at the center of its forehead like a lightning bolt. A pale white mane billowed up behind its eyes and fluttered gracefully down its muscular neck.

The horse snorted again, but it did not look away.

"Mrs . . ."

The voice, unexpectedly close, made Kris flinch.

Camilla had returned. Behind her, the second stall was empty. Jesse was gone.

"Barlow," Kris managed to say, hoping she didn't look as startled as she felt. "Kris Barlow."

"Kris, you're in luck. My husband thinks there's a tire out back that's a perfect match. Shouldn't be more than an hour and we'll have you all fixed up. He just . . ." Her voice trailed off. She glanced down, either out of frustration or embarrassment or some combination of the two. "He needs to feed the horse first."

"That's fine," Kris said.

Camilla was still staring at the ground, her sharp words spoken into her chest. "I told him I could do it, but he insists . . . He likes to be the one."

"Really, it's okay," Kris assured her.

Camilla looked up, and her thin lips flattened into a small, appreciative smile. "Thank you."

Movement caught Kris's attention. The horse was trotting away through a sea of yellow grass, toward the wood-shingled roof of a nearby stall.

"Quarter horse?" Kris asked.

Camilla tilted her head curiously. "Yeah. You have one of your own?"

"No. No, I'm a vet. Back . . ."

Don't say "home," she warned herself. *This is home until the end of the summer.* She quickly changed the subject. "Boy or girl?"

"Boy. His name's Cap. Short for 'Cappuccino.' My daughter, she thought his face looked like the foam on the top of a cappuccino, you know, with the white streak against the tan."

"Cap," Kris said, testing it out. "It's perfect. Your daughter must love him very much."

Camilla gave a stiff, affirmative nod, but she said nothing. Her brown eyes were staring down once more.

CHAPTER EIGHTEEN

LOOSE GRAVEL SHIFTED under Kris's shoes as she and Sadie made their way down the Auto Barn's long drive toward Center Street. Flanking them on each side were rows of eighty-foot maple trees stretching into the cloudless blue sky like billowing green smoke.

Even though it was only ten in the morning, the day was hot and getting hotter, the perfect excuse to indulge in some pre-lunch ice cream. But the thought of returning to the Dairy Godmother and that odd young woman with the sunken eyes made Kris shiver despite the heat.

"You ought to keep an eye on a little girl like that in this town."

No, there had to be a better place to pass the time.

Suddenly a cluster of concrete and gravel went bouncing ahead of Kris.

She looked over at Sadie, who was trudging along beside her. With every other step, the little girl let the toe of her Converse dig into the uneven ground, unearthing a clump of stones and sending them skittering across the cracked, buckling drive. Her arms were folded across her chest, her eyebrows pinched into a sharp V, her ruby lips pursed in a childish pout.

"We had to do this at some point," Kris said. "We couldn't keep driving on the spare. It wasn't safe."

Sadie said nothing. She kicked at the ground, and a ball of dirt and gravel exploded into shrapnel around the toe of her shoe.

Like most eight-years-olds, Sadie had a fairly basic range of interests. She liked plush toys, cartoons, coloring, YouTube videos of funny animals, books—

An image flickered to life across the dark screen of Kris's mind, a memory of walls lined with the spines of books, of a strange little house on a street corner where the books lived.

"I know what we can do," Kris said with a smile.

Despite the deep shadows cast by the monstrous maple trees, Sadie's face brightened.

The Book Nook was another block down, on the corner of Center and Willow. Housed in what was once a residential home, the bookstore stood out from the rows of uniform 1950s-era buildings that gave the rest of downtown its quaint consistency. Whoever had claimed this land first, whoever had built this structure as a home, they were long gone, and the inside of the two-story Victorian had been invaded in the name of commerce. Each room had been cleared of furniture; walnut shelves lined each wall, filled end to end and top to bottom with a combination of new and used books.

The front room was devoted to Fiction. Tabs of white paper displayed the subcategories of each section in an elegant, handwritten script: *Mystery*; *Romance*; *Western*; *Science Fiction*; *Historical Fiction*. Past this, an archway opened to a living room with scuffed wooden floors partially covered by a decorative rug. This room was evenly split between *Classic Literature* and *Nonfiction*. A sign taped to the wall beside the entrance to a short hallway read: *Children's Section in Back Room*.

They wiped their feet on the front doormat, even though it had not rained a drop since they'd arrived in town and the sidewalks were pristine, free of even a single orphaned cigarette butt.

"Can I get a book, Mommy?" Sadie asked as Kris began to scan the shelves in the front room. There was the rare vibration of excitement in the girl's voice.

"Yeah, you can get something," Kris assured her.

She followed Sadie through the archway and into the living room. It was bright and warm thanks to a large half-moon window over the tops of three bookshelves. Dusty shafts of sunlight streamed in through the beveled glass.

She noticed the man behind the counter a split second before he welcomed them with a cheery "Hello!" He was in his sixties, dressed in what she could only think to call a "spiffy" plaid sweater vest and striped button-down shirt. A thick wave of silver hair curved down over the purple frames of his round eyeglasses. He was very tall and very thin. What muscle there was on his body clung tightly to his bones like the dry meat of an overcooked chicken wing.

"Hello, hello, hello," he sang as he slipped out from behind the ornately carved credenza that served as a front counter. "Welcome to the Book Nook, and, don't tell me, you two are sisters, am I right?"

Sadie glanced back at her mother, confused, and Kris shot her a knowing smile that said, *He's joking*.

The man crouched down so that he was level with Sadie's wide green eyes. "Are you her big sister?"

Sadie gave her head an unsure shake.

The man took a moment to study the little girl's face. Finally, he said, "How old are you? Twenty-five? Thirty?"

"She's eight," Kris answered for Sadie.

"Well," the man said, "in that case, there is a whole room down that hall with books just for you." He pointed to the short hallway leading to the back room. "Do you like to read?"

Sadie nodded.

"What do you like to read?"

Sadie once again looked to Kris. Stranger Danger alarms were obviously ringing loudly in her head.

"*Ivy and Bean*," Kris suggested. "And *Judy Moody*."

The man kept his gaze on Sadie, as if she had been the one to speak. "You have fantastic taste, my friend. Fantastic taste. I think you'll find that we have many, many books for a sophisticated young lady like yourself. Would you like to take a look?"

Sadie did not move.

"Go on," Kris told her. "I'll be back there in a minute."

It was all the encouragement she needed. Off Sadie went, hurrying down the hall.

The man clapped his long bony hands and rubbed them together as if to warm them. "So. What can I help *you* find?"

"I'm just kind of looking, if that's okay."

"That," the man assured her, "is more than okay. If you need anything, I'm here. My name is Phillip Hitchens. My friends call me Hitch. And you are?"

"Kris."

"Krissss." He elongated the name, dragging out the end like a cartoon snake. "Well, Kris, now we are friends. And as a friend, I will leave you the heck alone."

Kris gave an appreciative chuckle. "Thanks."

"De nada."

Hitch walked briskly across the room and slipped back behind the credenza. He took a worn paperback book from a large stack and scribbled a price on the inside cover, then set it aside and reached for the next book.

For a moment, Kris pretended to scan the shelves of books as she studied Hitch out of the corner of her eye. Surely, if she had met this peculiar man when she was little, she would remember him. Something told her this was their first introduction. Someone else must have worked the register when she was a child. The previous owner perhaps, or an older relative of Hitch's. His mother or father.

Hitch looked up suddenly, catching Kris's intense gaze.

"Something on your mind?" he asked, unfazed.

"How long have you lived in Pacington?"

"All my life," he said.

Kris nodded, digesting this fact. "I came into this bookstore when I was little," she told him.

"And when was that?"

"Late 1980s. My last summer here was '88."

"Well, then there is a good chance we've met before."

"But I don't remember you."

Hitch drew a long, slow breath in through his nose like a somme-lier scrutinizing a glass of wine. "The mind does that. Buries things it deems unnecessary. Not to worry, I am not in the least offended. If we did meet back then, I'm sure I'm there, somewhere, in your mind, high on a shelf, collecting dust."

"Not you, Hitch," Kris said with a playful smile. "Never you."

Hitch gave a sharp laugh. He shook his head as he picked up another book, checked its spine for creases, flipped through its pages for tears or pen marks, and jotted down an amount in the inside cover.

Kris strolled down to the next row of books. On a strip of tan masking tape, written in black Sharpie, was: *Local Interest*. She pulled a random paperback from the closest shelf and was surprised to find that she had selected a book called *Pacington: The Land of Hidden Waters*. She flipped to the center where there were several pages of glossy reprinted photos. A hand-drawn map of the area along the Verdigris River before European settlement. A faded sepia tone circa 1900 featuring the first businesses on Center Street. A black-and-white photo dated 1951 of the Army Corp of Engineers days before they began the first phase of their planned reservoir. The only existing photograph of the aftermath, a crane on its side, its neck submerged in the unintentional lake. A 1960s shot of Lost Lake in all its glory, the accidental vacation destination, rowboats and canoes crisscrossing its clear water, fishermen lining its shores.

Kris closed the book and turned it over in her hand. She ran her thumb over its glossy cover, rubbing the surface of the lake in the photo as if for luck.

"Can I ask you something else?" she asked suddenly.

Hitch smiled warmly. "Anything, my dear."

"Last week. There was a woman. Down the street, at the ice cream shop."

The older gentleman's nostrils flared. He seemed to sense where this was headed.

"She said something . . ." Kris continued.

"Amy Witherspoon," Hitch nodded. "Congratulations. You met the biggest gossip in town. I'm surprised Amy has any time for shifts at the ice cream parlor. It seems sticking her nose into other people's business is her full-time job." He sighed wearily. "What did she say?"

"She said . . ." Kris paused, suddenly reluctant to say the woman's words out loud. "She was talking about my daughter. She said, 'You ought to keep an eye on a girl like that in this town.' Do you know what she meant by that?"

Hitch's head bobbed up and down several times on his thin neck before he spoke. "Yes," he said.

When he did not continue, Kris asked, "Can you tell me?"

"Yes," Hitch said reluctantly. "But I feel I should tell you, first and foremost, anything Amy Witherspoon says should be taken with a grain of salt the size of a bowling ball. She is, if you will pardon my

French . . ." He lowered his voice to a whisper. ". . . batshit crazy." He cleared his throat and tugged at the bottom of his sweater vest, straightening nonexistent wrinkles. "She gets it from her mother. I'm afraid there wasn't any hope for the poor thing."

"What did she mean?" Kris asked.

"It's nothing, really. Pure coincidence. Nothing to worry about at all. Just . . ." Hitch paused, choosing his words carefully. "Over the years—many years, mind you—there have been . . . well . . . incidences." He said that last word as if it were underlined.

"Of what?"

"Of . . . things . . . happening."

She waited silently for him to finish the thought.

Finally, in a pointed whisper, he said, "To girls."

Glancing down the hallway, Kris was relieved to discover that she could see directly into the back room where Sadie was sitting in a small chair and thumbing through a chapter book. The little girl's lips moved slightly as she read to herself.

Lowering her voice, Kris asked, "What do you mean? What 'things'?"

Hitch wrapped his hands around himself and rubbed his arms as if warding off the cold. "I really shouldn't have—"

"Please," Kris said. "Tell me."

"There is nothing to worry about, I want to be very clear about that. Pacington is a wonderful town and an absolutely fantastic place to live. I've known the area all my life. I was born just down the road, in Cherryvale. And if you know the story of the Bloody Benders, you'll know that bad things can happen anywhere, at any time. There is no rhyme or reason to bad things. The fact is they happen much less frequently than good things. Maybe we just get too used to the good things. We forget to notice them. Maybe it takes the bad to make us see the good again."

Kris took a step toward Hitch, the book in her hand all but forgotten. "What happened here?" she asked.

Now it was Hitch's turn to check Sadie's whereabouts, although this time it was to make sure she was safely out of earshot. He cleared his throat and then said in a whisper, "We have . . . lost . . . a few girls over the years. If this were a big city, it would be no less tragic but more, well, expected, I suppose. But here in our little town, it has"—he searched for the perfect words—"an effect."

Lost a few girls, Kris thought. As if they were items that had been misplaced. She braced herself for what was to come, suspecting that the tale was about to get much worse.

Hitch held up one finger. "Ruby Millan. Eight years old. Climbed out of her bedroom window in the middle of the night."

A second finger joined the first. "Sarah Bell. Nine. Walked away from her elementary school at recess."

A third finger. "Megan Adamson. Just shy of her tenth birthday. Her mother took her shopping for a present downtown. Mama looked away for one second, and little Megan was gone."

Another finger went up. Four. "Poppy Azuara. This was just . . ." He closed his eyes as he counted in his head. "Four years ago this August. Poppy was with her parents over in Jefferson Park when she wandered off. Pacington is not a big place, as you know. You can walk it end to end in half an hour. An hour after she went missing, the entire town was out looking for her, although those of us old enough to remember the others knew where to look."

Hitch paused. If it was for dramatic effect, he was being unnecessarily cruel.

Kris opened her mouth to ask *Where?*, but before the word could escape her lips, Hitch answered: "The lake. That's where we always ended up looking, the other times. So with Poppy, a group of us just decided to go there first."

"Did you find her?" Kris's throat was suddenly dry. She tried to swallow and felt her throat constrict tighter.

Hitch slowly shook his head.

"And the others?"

"Oh yes, they were found. Poor things."

"Were they—"

Suddenly Hitch's attention shifted to something behind Kris. His body stiffened, his lips clamping shut in a tight, forced smile.

Kris heard the sound of light footsteps hurrying behind her. Something tugged on the back of her shirt.

Sadie stared up at her. In the girl's hand was a thin paperback, its spine tattered, the title barely legible.

Just like Hitch had done, Kris willed herself to smile. "You find something?"

Sadie nodded. She held the book closer for Kris to see.

It was not a novel at all but a leather-bound journal filled with blank pages of rough parchment. Stamped into the corner of the cover was a single flower blooming at the end of a twisting vine.

Sadie clutched it tightly in her hands, waiting patiently.

"Yeah, of course," Kris said. Her words were barely a whisper. She cleared her throat and repeated, "Of course. You can get it."

When Kris looked up, she found that Hitch had already returned to the front counter. It was as if he had never left, as if he had not been standing with her only a moment before. He rapped his fingers on the credenza's dense surface and smiled warmly. "Will that be it? Just the two?"

It took Kris a few seconds to understand what Hitch was referring to. She had completely forgotten about the book clutched in her hand. "No, just the journal," she said, and quickly returned the book to where she had found it.

Hitch happily punched the keys of a massive antique register as he rang up the journal. "Eight dollars even," he announced, his smile widening to reveal large, smoke-stained teeth.

Nodding, she reached into her purse. Her hands were shaking, both from the awful tale Hitch had told and the unexpected surprise of seeing the item Sadie had chosen—a journal, its pages ready to be filled with drawings and stories and anything else her young mind could dream up. Kris's trembling fingers found her wallet but refused to grip it. She balled her hands into fists and let out a slow, quiet breath. She opened her hands again. They were steady.

She paid with cash, dropped the wallet back into her purse, and handed the journal to Sadie. The little girl clutched it to her chest as if it were her most prized possession. When Kris turned back, Hitch was leaning over on one elbow, his face surprisingly close.

"I'm sorry if I upset you," he whispered. "I wouldn't have said anything, but you did ask, so . . ."

"No, it's okay. I wanted to know." She began to ask something else, although even she was not sure what it was. She wanted to know more. She wanted to hear the rest of the story, to find out what exactly had happened to Ruby and Sarah and Megan, but a larger part needed to leave, to flee this strange little store that wasn't quite a store, this house that wasn't quite a house.

She turned to follow Sadie, who was already halfway to the front door.

Behind them, Hitch picked up a paperback from the stack at his side and opened its cover. "Stay away from Amy Witherspoon," he said without looking up. "She'll only upset you." He quickly scribbled a price in the top right corner of the title page, set the book on the opposite stack, and reached for another.

CHAPTER NINETEEN

OUTSIDE, THE WIND had picked up. It whipped past the buildings along Center Street, twisting around light poles and howling over the tops of parked cars. It spun like a cyclone around a man in a green-and-yellow John Deere cap, forcing him to quickly clap both hands on top of his head to keep the wind from snatching his hat.

The air was warm and humid with an unmistakable wetness that dampened the skin. Kris wiped at beads of sweat that had suddenly sprung on her brow and beneath her eyes. She lowered her head against the onslaught, her hair lifting off her shoulders and flapping behind her like a short reddish-brown cape.

She no longer wanted to be there. She wished they were back at the lake house, the doors locked, the windows latched, sitting together on the couch as they listened to the walls creak like the hull of a ship as the furious wind beat against them.

Are you sure? It was the voice from the darkness, purring like a cat. *Are you sure the lake house is where you want to be?*

Where else is there? she asked the voice.

Home.

This is home.

The voice retreated into the shadows, but she had a feeling it was not fully satisfied with that answer.

She clutched Sadie's hand tightly as they made their way down the sidewalk, back in the direction of the Auto Barn. With every townsperson they passed, Kris found herself staring a bit too long, studying their faces as if they were disguised guests at a costume party. Their smiles seemed genuine enough, their eyes friendly and bright. The ones who returned her gaze did so with expressions meant to imply a compassionate sense of disbelief at the shared assault they were all experiencing. *Can you believe this wind?* they seemed to say. She forced herself to search for anything hidden behind their polite expressions—a crack in a smile, a twitch at the corner of an eye—something to suggest the masking of some untold pain.

Reaching the familiar row of hedges, Kris turned left, steering Sadie alongside her. The crumbling road seemed longer than before and a good deal darker. The trees to their right caught the sunlight and held it, refusing to let it pass any farther.

"Mommy." Sadie sounded apologetic, as if she were sorry for having to speak up. "You're squeezing my hand."

Kris said, "Oh," and loosened her grip ever so slightly. But not completely. She wouldn't until she had her daughter safely back in the Jeep.

At the far edge of the driveway, the shadows arced away and sunlight illuminated the bright red face of the barn. Kris realized that a window on the second floor looked into a modern office where Camilla sat behind a sleek steel desk, her face unusually pale in the glow of a computer monitor. She seemed to sense that she was being watched, for at that exact moment, she glanced up, and her slack expression rose into one of recognition and understanding. She held up a finger to signal that she would be down in one moment.

"It's fixed," Sadie said, pointing.

The Jeep was parked perpendicular to the first stall. All four tires gleamed in the sunlight thanks to a heavy coat of Armor All. If she hadn't taken the flat off herself, she would have been hard pressed to say which tire was the replacement.

"You're all set," Camilla called as she emerged from a darkened stairwell just inside the first stall. The wind caught her hair and brutally flattened it across her face. She swept it away with both hands, quickly tying it into a ponytail with the ease of someone who had performed the task countless times before.

"How much do I owe you?" Kris asked.

Camilla waved a hand in the air once her hair had been secured. "Don't worry about it."

"No. I can't let you do that."

"It's a tire from the salvage yard. It didn't cost us anything, it shouldn't cost you anything."

"But the work—"

"Took Jesse longer to find the god . . ."—she glanced down at Sadie, catching herself—"gosh darn thing than to put it on. Really. It was nothing."

"You sure?"

Camilla smiled, relenting. "Tell ya what. You take the tire, and the next time Cap tangles with a porcupine, you come down and help me pull out the quills. We don't have a vet in town, and hauling a half-ton horse to Fredonia ain't exactly my idea of a fun afternoon."

With a sharp laugh, Kris nodded and said, "Deal."

She felt her hand pull away, as if on its own accord.

She looked down.

Sadie had taken a few steps to the side and was staring off toward the field, where Cap stood with his head stretched over the barbed-wire fence. His lower jaw moved slowly in a semicircle as he lazily chewed a piece of grass.

"Would you like to see him?" Camilla asked.

Sadie thought for a moment, and then she nodded.

Cap did not seem too concerned by their approach. He raised his head a few inches and snorted, but otherwise he showed no signs of fear, even as Sadie reached the fence and held out a hand to touch his wet, dark nose.

"He's a good boy," Camilla told her, as much to reassure Sadie of her safety as to give Cap a well-deserved compliment.

Kris watched as Sadie's fingers grazed the wiry hair of the horse's cheek. He leaned his head into her touch so that his face rested in the palm of her hand. Sadie rubbed a thumb along his snout, and Cap's eyes closed. He gave a soft, contented snort.

"He likes you," Kris told her.

The wind swept under Cap's mane and lifted it into the air so that it fluttered like a thousand fingers waving to the horizon.

"Before I forget," Camilla said, holding out a business card in the same shade of white as the jagged lightning bolt that cut down the center of Cap's face. "Just in case you have any other car trouble while you're here."

Kris took the card, offering a quiet "Thank you" as she slipped it into her purse. She glanced down, catching a glimpse of the Auto Barn logo, which featured the same vintage convertible seen on the sign on the front of the building. Below was Camilla's name—Camilla Azuara—and two phone numbers, one labeled "Office" and the other "Cell."

Azuara.

Poppy Azuara.

The business card slipped from Kris's numb fingers and disappeared into the open mouth of her purse.

She looked up, at her own daughter still lovingly stroking the horse's cheek. A horse named Cap. Short for Cappuccino. Their daughter's horse. Poppy's horse. Poppy, who had never been found.

And there it was, what Kris had looked for on the faces of every townsperson they passed.

There, at the corner of Camilla's smile—a nearly imperceptible quiver, like a rubber band stretched to the breaking point.

She did not remember the next few minutes. She had no memory of loading Sadie into the back of the Jeep, or listening for the click of the little girl's seat belt, or pressing the ignition button to wake the engine. She simply heard the engine let loose its throaty growl, and threw the gearshift into drive.

The next thing she knew, she was driving down Center Street, the row of hedges marking the turn into the Auto Barn becoming smaller and smaller in her rearview mirror.

She was moving away. That was all that mattered.

The sand-colored buildings of downtown slipped away. There was the Pig Stand on her left. And across the street, the green expanse of Jefferson Park appeared, ending in a small section of public beach that lined this bit of the lake's shore.

Jefferson Park.

She heard Hitch's voice, barely a whisper.

Four years ago this August, he had said. *Poppy was with her parents over in Jefferson Park when she wandered off.*

She didn't want to look. And yet some force pulled her, like a magnet, turning her face until she was no longer looking at the road. She was staring out across the sloping grass.

How could anyone disappear there? With the exception of a few lone trees, it was wide open.

How could someone have taken her without her parents noticing? *Unless she wanted to go. Unless she knew the person taking her.*

You watch too many true crime shows, you know that?

This was not her voice. It was not Timid Kris or Shadow Kris.

It was Jonah. He'd say something like this anytime she expressed suspicion about the neighbors or concern about being home alone with Sadie late at night.

Maybe if you came home earlier, she had suggested.

Maybe if you turned the TV off and read a book, had been his reply.

I do read a book. In bed. While I wait for you to get home.

She looked at the well-maintained acre of grass outside the passenger-side window. She could almost see Camilla and Jesse Azuara there, four years younger, back when they smiled and actually felt it, when joy warmed their chests and fear was something only big-city folks felt.

They had turned their backs for one second, and Poppy was gone.

CHAPTER TWENTY

THE PALM SANDER shook wildly in Kris's grip as it passed over the surface of the wooden seat. Sawdust billowed in the air, which was thick with heat and sunlight.

Kris moved the sander in clockwise circles, instantly chipping away stray splinters as she wore the seat down to a layer of smooth, pale wood. In less than five minutes, it was reborn, a slick wedge of pine suspended between rusty chains. She could clean the chains in vinegar, but having the proper length cut at True Value would be even easier. She would take care of that the next time they were in town. For now, she had eliminated the threat of jagged slivers of wood slicing into Sadie's flesh. Having the girl's hands stained orange from rust was the least of Kris's problems.

Stepping back from the swing, Kris let the electric sander drop to her side as she examined her work.

The swing, or at least its seat, had been reclaimed. She could stain it. Yes, she could pick up a weatherproof sealant from the hardware store to add that finishing touch.

Sadie moved up behind her, swishing through the tallgrass.

"Not yet," Kris warned her. "Just give me a second . . ."

Bending down, Kris fished into a socket wrench set and selected two wrench heads that seemed like a good match.

The second head slipped easily over the hexagonal end of the bolt on the inside of the swing set's frame. With one hand holding a set of pliers in place, Kris twisted the socket wrench back and forth until she felt the bolt tightening in the nut.

"Hey, baby, could you push on that leg of the frame as hard as you can?"

Sadie did as asked, pressing her palms against the inside of the leg and pushing with all her might.

At the same time, Kris cranked the socket wrench back and forth, back and forth, until the wrench would twist no more. She did the same to the bolts on the opposite side, then gave the frame a good shake. It was still a bit crooked, but the connections would hold.

Kris plopped down on the wooden seat. Good. The chains were still strong.

She stood and took a step back from the swing set.

"Give it a try."

Carefully, Sadie lifted herself up onto the sanded seat. She gripped the rusty orange chains and pumped her legs, slowly at first, then leaning back to stretch her feet out toward the shining waters of the lake. Soon she was swinging in a wide arc as the chains clanked against the metal eyelets twisted into the beam overhead.

A long, satisfied sigh escaped Kris's lips.

This was progress.

This was something.

She glanced over her shoulder, toward the lake house, and her gaze fell on the weed-filled garden contained within rectangular stacks of railroad ties.

You're next, Kris thought.

Clumps of dried dirt clung to roots as she yanked the weeds from the outlying edges of the garden. Old plants began to emerge from the overgrowth: stubborn lavender bushes, clumps of mint, a cluster of black-eyed Susans, and a single blueberry bush, devoid of fruit but still alive. All had been planted by her mother over thirty years ago, withered but alive.

Behind her, Kris could hear the squeak of metal chains as Sadie swung herself higher toward the cloudless blue sky.

Sweat trickled down the sides of Kris's face as she took hold of another thick patch of weeds with gloved hands. Gritting her teeth, she pulled until she felt the roots let loose from the thirsty soil.

She held the plant up to examine her handiwork.

One of the roots moved with unexpected life, stretching out to point at her like an accusatory finger. It twisted in the open air as it attempted to grasp some desired object just out of reach. And then it gave up and pulled its glistening, dirt-specked body back toward the other dangling roots.

Not a root, Kris realized. *A worm.*

She watched as the earthworm retracted farther, curling back into the cluster of roots and earth dangling beneath the fistful of weeds. Carefully, she pinched the end of the worm's twisting, mucous-slicked body between two gloved fingers and unwound it from the roots until it dangled from her fingertips.

"Here ya go, bud. Have fun."

She set the worm down into the crater of earth left by the extracted weeds. It instantly curled into a fleshy pink ball in some sort of pathetic defense mechanism, then stretched its rippling head into the loose, parched ground, trying to dig back into the soil.

Kris brushed her fingers over the dirt at the edges of the crater, sending it cascading down into the shallow pit until the earthworm was completely covered, buried alive in the comfort of its grave.

With the worm successfully extracted, she tossed the handful of weeds into a growing pile just outside the railroad tie border and attacked a new section. She had managed to clear two square feet in less than ten minutes. Soon the garden would be completely free of weeds and ready for new plants. She thought back to the other things her mother planted during their summers together: peonies and snap-dragons, tomato vines and strawberry bushes.

Wrapping her gloved fingers around a thick section of thorny weeds, Kris leaned back and yanked, hard. The weeds tried to maintain their hold on the earth, but Kris's strength proved too much for their pitiful pale roots, and the weeds finally gave up their hold.

The sudden release of the roots sent Kris stumbling backward. She tossed the clump of pulled weeds into the growing pile and was reaching for the next section when she noticed a hint of purple peeking out from the dried brown stalks.

She parted the weeds. There at the center of the garden was a patch of purple flowers. Yellow heads peered out from their rich petals.

She recognized them immediately. She had helped plant them. Violets. Her mother's favorite.

Kris stared down at the weathered planks. She was afraid to take a closer look at the pilings for fear that they, too, would need to be replaced. But she thought that with a fresh sanding and some sealant, she could give the planks a few more years before they were ripped from their beds.

Because in this town . . .

She buried the dark thought just as she had the worm and slipped a square of sandpaper from its cardboard package. She secured it to the bottom of the power sander and gave the extension cord a yank, pulling a few more feet away from where it was plugged into an outlet at the back of the house.

She began at the first plank. Crouching down at the edge of the dock, she put her weight onto the sander and switched it on. The tool vibrated beneath her hands. Flakes of white paint and sawdust billowed into the air. It fell upon the surface of the lake like ash. Fresh beads of sweat instantly sprang from her brow and trickled down her forehead to slip into the line of her eyebrows. She paused long enough to wipe the sweat away with her bare forearm, and then she went back to work.

After a few minutes, Kris sat back. Her chest heaved as her lungs sucked in quick breaths of hot summer air. She ran a hand over her work. Not a single splinter snagged the soft leather of her work glove. The wood was nice and smooth.

She was about to move on to the other half of the plank when suddenly she was overcome with the feeling that she was being watched.

Confused, she turned off the sander and glanced down the long wooden dock. Its white boards shone in the sunlight like bleached bone. Beyond the dock, the impossibly clear water of Lost Lake glistened.

"No one's there," she said quietly.

Yet she could not shake that feeling.

In her hand, the electric sander was all but forgotten. She quickly scanned the opposite side of the lake, searching its rocky shore and the edge of the forest beyond.

Nothing.

No one.

Letting out an irritated sigh, Kris set the sander facedown onto the plank, her finger on the power switch as she prepared to go back to work.

Just then she saw someone.

Across the lake, past the swaying arms of a weeping willow tree, was another lake house. It was much more rustic than River's End, a simple rectangle, its walls constructed from stacks of round logs barely cleaned of their branches. The windows were framed in chunky unpainted timber. The roof peaked sharply into a tall, narrow A, its tip disappearing into trees whose leaves were thick with webworm nests. A crumbling redbrick chimney jutted from uneven wooden shingles at a strange angle. It was as if the chimney had plummeted from the sky and buried itself through the cabin's roof. She searched her mind's eye, but for whatever reason, the house did not exist in her memories.

A small square deck stretched out from the back of the cabin. Beneath it, deep shadows cloaked the wooden posts supporting it, creating the illusion of a cave under the deck that seemed to stretch into the dark bowels of the earth.

On the deck, just below a porch light that burned inexplicably in the daytime, was the woman Kris and Sadie had glimpsed on their first night. She was too far away to make out any significant details, but Kris could see her long, black hair drifting in the light breeze, she could see the oval of her pale face, she could see the blue denim shirt and blue jeans that hung loosely from the woman's skeletal body.

Kris could not see the woman's eyes, but she could *feel* them. Staring out across the lake. Staring straight at her.

Kris raised a gloved hand and gave a friendly wave.

The woman did not return the gesture. She remained motionless. Staring.

"Whatever," Kris grumbled. She turned her attention back to the plank, powering up the sander once more and smoothing another section of damaged wood.

She could still feel the woman watching. Those unseen eyes were boring into her from a quarter of a mile away. She tried to lose herself in the work, driving the sandpaper harder and harder over the plank, minute grains of dust drifting up into the air around her. But the woman was watching. She knew it.

An invisible hand began to creep up her back to the base of her neck. She focused on the steady rhythm of the sandpaper eating away at the jagged, uneven surface of the plank.

The flesh on the back of her neck prickled as that invisible hand gripped her in its cold fingers.

She's watching you, her shadow voice taunted. *She's still watching you . . .*

"Dammit," Kris exclaimed sharply. She switched the sander off and tossed it onto the dock. It bounced across the next few planks before coming to a stop, sandpaper-side up, like an overturned turtle.

Kris looked to the woman across the lake. Still there. Still staring. *In this town . . .*

"Time for a break," she said aloud as if to give herself permission. She stood up, her knees and back aching from holding her crouched position.

She called out, "Sadie," as she walked away from the dock and the lake and that damn staring woman.

Sadie was no longer swinging. She sat on the freshly sanded seat, the tips of her shoes barely touching the ground beneath her. Her head was turned. Kris could not fully see the little girl's face, but there was movement in her cheeks and at the corner of her mouth, as if Sadie were speaking aloud to the empty swing beside her.

CHAPTER TWENTY-ONE

THEY ATE DINNER at the breakfast nook instead of their usual spot at the bistro table on the back deck. Kris told herself that it was too hot to eat outside, despite the fact that the evening had brought with it a cool breeze that tossed the tops of trees and rippled the water.

Sadie could barely sit still during the meal. She bounced in her seat, holding her fork like a weapon, shoveling mounds of spaghetti into her mouth until it overflowed with stringy noodles dripping with thick red marinara.

"Slow down. You'll choke," Kris warned her.

Sadie chewed the mouthful of pasta and swallowed hard.

"Done," she said, pushing the plate away. She quickly wiped her mouth on a paper towel, balled it up, tossed it on top of the remaining spaghetti, and hopped up from the bench. She dashed away, through the great room and down the hall.

"Where are you going?" Kris called after her, even though she already knew the answer.

"To play," Sadie's voice called from the end of the hall.

Kris looked down at her own plate. She had barely touched her food. The mound of red sauce atop the noodles was beginning to congeal. She drained the last sip of pinot noir from her wineglass and reached for the bottle at the center of the table. Barely an inch swirled at the bottom as she lifted it toward her glass.

When they'd sat down for dinner, there was still three-quarters of a bottle left. Had she already drunk the whole thing?

A wave of shame washed through her, but it quickly retreated, dulled by the buzz of the alcohol. She forced herself to eat a few bites of pasta before finally crossing the kitchen and dumping what was left in the trash can under the sink.

From overhead came the drumming of footsteps. Kris looked up at the ceiling, tracking the sound as it raced from one end of the second floor to the other. Suddenly there was a shriek of laughter, so loud and unexpected that it sent an electric jolt surging through Kris's body

"Jesus," she muttered, a smile creeping to her lips as the shock was replaced by joy.

It sounded as though Sadie were playing a game, tag or hide-and-seek. Kris stood with her hands resting lightly on the edge of the kitchen sink, listening as Sadie's laughter drifted down through the floor above.

She was sure that it would take multiple requests for Sadie to come downstairs at bedtime, but surprisingly, at ten minutes to nine, she was already in her room, under the covers, teeth brushed, face washed, pajamas on.

"I'll be ready for bed soon," Kris told her.

"You don't have to sleep with me tonight," Sadie said in that matter-of-fact way.

Kris cocked her head. "Oh. You sure?"

For almost two weeks, this had been their nightly routine, both climbing into bed in the dim pink room, Sadie falling asleep as she stared up at the ceiling, Kris on her side looking out into the darkness beyond the reach of the night-light.

But now Sadie nodded enthusiastically, seemingly eager to have the room to herself.

"Okay," Kris said, still thrown by the sudden request. She kissed Sadie on the forehead, pulled the covers up over her shoulders, and walked out of the bedroom. She swung the door shut until the latch bumped gently against the jam, so it would stay open just a crack.

In the bathroom, Kris was reaching for her toothbrush when, for no discernable reason, she paused. She rested her hands on the edge of the sink, her back hunched slightly.

For a solid minute, she stared at herself in the mirror.

A strange sensation began to worm its way under her flesh. She felt herself separating from that reflection, the face opposite her becoming its own entity. She could feel it staring out at her from that two-dimensional world behind the mirror, its gaze unbroken, its eyes scrutinizing her as she scrutinized it.

The face seemed slightly older than hers. The hint of shadowed circles hung under its eyes. Shallow lines cut away from the edges of its eyes. Its hair, a dull reddish brown, the color of an old penny, brushed its shoulders like the brittle branches of a wilting plant.

This was not her face.

The longer she stared at it, the more she hated the thing in the mirror. What right did it have to pretend to be her? What reason could it possibly have for this cruel masquerade?

She felt a disorienting sense of vertigo, and her scalp prickled.

Gripping the edge of the sink, Kris closed her eyes and tried to regain her balance. For a moment, she was sure she would faint. She dug her fingers into the sink's porcelain lip until the dizziness subsided. Only then did she open her eyes again.

She was staring down at the hands of the mirror woman, blue veins rising across their backs, thin fingers swollen slightly at the knuckles.

They're your hands, Kris, her shadow voice purred.

Yes. There was no denying this. She owned them, just as she owned her face and her body and every second of the forty-one years that had brought her to this moment.

"Life is a vampire," she whispered.

Snatching the pill bottle from her toiletries bag on the floor, she quickly popped the top and tossed a Xanax onto her tongue. She swallowed it dry, wincing at the bitter taste. She started to replace the lid, then paused.

She could take one more. Just for tonight. She might need it if she was really going to sleep in that bedroom.

No, she told herself. Stick to the routine. *One in the morning. One at night.*

Twisting the lid back into place, she dropped the plastic bottle back into her bag before she could change her mind.

Her own sheets were in the same cardboard box where she had found Sadie's on their first night in the house. Since then, she had unpacked most of their things, putting everything in its proper place. Filling shelves and cabinets made the house feel lived in. It felt like it was *their* house. But this box she had simply shoved around the side of the leather couch, out of sight, and forgotten about it. It was still there when she trudged into the great room. She knelt down beside it, unfolded the cardboard flaps, and scooped up the bedding. A waft of air found her nostrils. The sheets still smelled like the house in Black Ridge, like lavender laundry detergent and mountain air and a hint of the cedar chest where she stored her bedding back home.

She stripped the old bedding as quickly as her sluggish body would allow. The mattress beneath was showing its many years, threads sprouting from the seams, the impression of coiled springs pushing up beneath its yellowed surface. Over this, she struggled to slip on her own fitted sheet. She felt as though she were trying to make a bed under water, her arms unusually heavy as she flung the sheets over the mattress and tucked them into place. When she was finally done, she sat down on the edge of the bed and held her head in her hands.

That's when she realized she had completely forgotten to brush her teeth. She ran her tongue over teeth she knew were stained gray by wine.

Her eyelids were hundred-pound weights, her vision reduced to thin slits as she freed her feet from her shoes and slipped out of her jeans. The T-shirt she had been wearing all day smelled of soil and sweat, so she awkwardly stripped it off, her elbows getting caught in the arms of the shirt before she was finally able to pull it over her head and drop it to the floor. She searched blindly through a dresser drawer until she found a fresh shirt and pulled it on.

She paused, standing at the foot of the bed.

Climb in, her mind commanded.

But she did not want to. Despite the numbing sensation of the booze and the meds, she felt her heart begin to pound harder.

Don't think about it. Just do it.

She crawled across the bedspread and slipped under the covers. She stretched her bare legs down deep into the cotton sheets, and the mere fact that she was no longer on her feet sent a rush of endorphins flooding her brain. Her eyes were already closing, blocking out the light from the nightstand lamp that she had forgotten to turn off. Her hands slipped under her pillow and lifted its soft body up to conform around her face. She was sinking, drifting down, down, into a place where only dreams could keep her afloat. The mattress seemed to hug the sides of her slender body as if it were a mold cast in her image. The springs sank weakly beneath her, here on the right side of the bed, where she had laid for days at a time, never moving, never getting up, the pain keeping her trapped in the bedroom that even in the bright summer sun became a tomb, in the indentation in the mattress that fit her perfectly from head to toe, like a corpse in a coffin.

Kris swam desperately up from the depths of sleep and forced herself to roll out of the dip in the bed and over the side. She tumbled to the hard, wooden floor with a loud, painful *thunk*.

She was awake again, her heart racing, a fresh layer of sweat slicking her flesh.

The horror dawned over her like a bloodred sun rising over jagged black mountaintops.

That dip in the bed, that was the exact spot where her mother had been bound by her illness for weeks, unable in her final days to even get up to go to the bathroom.

That was the place where her mother had died, where Kris, moments before, had been drifting off to sleep.

She scooted away from the bed, the back of her head thumping hard as she collided with the wall. Her body trembled. She wrapped her arms around her bare body, but she could not stop shaking.

"Fuck," she snapped through quivering breaths. She clenched her fists tight, cords of muscle twisting up along her arms. "Fuck," she said again, but the word did not hold enough power to express the revulsion she felt.

She could flip the mattress. She could flip the mattress and the indention would be gone. It would be like new. It would be like—

Like your mother never died in this room.

Kris pressed the palms of her hands against her eyes, fighting back the threat of tears, willing the medication dissolving in her stomach to flood her bloodstream faster and kill these thoughts.

She focused on the rhythm of her steady breaths, the sound that meant she was not her mother, that she was alive. After a moment, her heart began to calm. The sweat on her skin evaporated into the warm night air.

Crawling on her hands and knees, she reached up onto the bed and yanked the sheets away, stripping the mattress once more in a single stroke. She snatched down the two pillows and tossed them ruthlessly into the corner of the room. There was no way she was sleeping on that mattress. Not tonight. Not ever.

Her fingers fumbled across the smooth ceramic body of the night-stand lamp until they found the switch, and the lamp clicked off.

Darkness enveloped the room. For a moment, she saw nothing. And then her eyes began to adjust. Faint, ghostly streaks of moonlight materialized.

She crawled over to the corner of the room where the bedding was now piled in a heap on the floor. She pulled the sheets around her, tucking them between her body and the cool wood. She burrowed the side of her face into the pillows and let out a long, exhausted sigh.

Every vein and artery in her body seemed to buzz like neon tubes. Her skin tingled as the hard floor began to fall away beneath her.

Out in the hallway, a board creaked.

Kris stared with drooping eyes toward the black rectangular void that she assured herself was the bedroom door.

She lay perfectly still, listening. At first there was nothing but the normal snaps and pops of the house settling. And then a board groaned a low, gruff voice. It was just outside the door.

Her heavy eyelids wanted desperately to close, but she forced them open as she stared at that black doorway.

Waiting.

Waiting.

For what felt like hours, she stared into the abyss. When sleep overtook her, it did so immediately and absolutely.

She sat up into a warm beam of sunshine. Sheets dampened with sweat tangled around her shivering body. Her chest rose and fell rapidly as she sucked in desperate breaths.

From her pallet of sheets on the floor, her eyes flashed to the bed. The bare mattress rested on the bedframe like a skinned animal.

She had been dreaming. In the dream, she had been in this exact spot, wrapped in sheets, yet she had been frozen, unable to move even her eyes. They had been trained on the bed, just as they were now. Except in the dream—

Nightmare, she corrected herself.

In the nightmare, the old sheets were still on the mattress, and there was something beneath them. A lump, the size and shape of a person curled into a ball.

There was nothing she could do but watch as that shape rose up, higher and higher, the sheet sliding slowly away, revealing first a head of ratty hair and then glaring black eyes. They stared at her from over the top of the sheet.

The sheet billowed as hot breath pushed words up from dry, leathery lungs.

"You left me," the thing hissed. "You left me here alone . . ."

That was when her eyes had opened, and she had realized it was not the dead of night but morning, and the bed was empty, even of sheets.

She clenched her teeth as an unexpected rush of anger flooded through her.

This was insane. Sleeping on the floor. Plagued by nightmares of things that even death could not touch.

The fury burned hotter in her flesh.

There was still one thing she had to do to truly clean the bedroom.

Launching herself up from the pallet of blankets, she gripped the mattress by the edge of its lumpy belly and, with all of her strength, flipped it over the other side of the bedframe. The mattress tipped up onto its side and toppled over onto the floor. It came to rest at an awkward angle against a closet door on the far wall.

Kris stormed around the foot of the bedframe, which now held only a fraying box spring, then dug her fingers into the corner of the mattress and yanked it toward the open door. She had to angle it just right to make the turn from the doorway into the hallway, maneuvering it around the foot of the staircase and around the corner. Once the mattress was lined up perfectly with the entryway to the great room, she moved behind it and shoved hard. Whether the indention she felt the night before had been real or imagined, the mattress began to sag in that exact spot, drooping until one side kissed the hallway wall.

With a furious grunt, she planted her bare feet into the wood floor and rammed her shoulder into the end of the mattress, driving it all the way down the hall like a linebacker with a practice sled. Only once the mattress was through the entryway and into the great room did she stop. She stood, panting in her T-shirt and underwear, her hands clenched into fists at her side, and watched as the thirty-something-year-old mattress crumpled pathetically to the ground.

Now she just had to get it out the front door and onto the porch. From there, she didn't care what happened to it. There was no way she could navigate such a cumbersome object over the crooked path leading to the front drive. She decided she would simply drag the god-damn thing to the edge of the porch and toss it into the weeds. All that mattered was that it was out of the house.

Kris backed into the hall and paused at the door to Sadie's room. It was open just an inch, exactly as Kris had left it the night before.

"Sweetie?" she called through the door.

She was answered by silence.

"Are you okay?"

She reached out and gave the door a gentle nudge. Its hinges squeaked faintly as the door swung open.

Sadie's bed was empty.

From upstairs came the sound of footsteps racing by. Sadie's laughter echoed down the staircase at the end of the hall. The sound should have filled Kris with warmth, but it made her hands tremble like vibrating piano wire.

You're losing it, the shadow voice taunted her.

It was the nightmare, that's all. She had woken in a fit of panic and she couldn't shake it. She just needed to calm down, to get herself under control. She needed—

It's morning, she realized with sudden relief. *You can take another and you won't be breaking the routine.*

Spinning quickly, Kris marched into the bathroom, flicking the switch as she entered. The fluorescent light flickered to life over the sink.

She thrust a hand into the backpack on the floor and found the pill bottle. She swallowed a Xanax before she knew she had even popped the bottle top. Its powdery coating left a taste like dandelion stems on the back of her tongue.

Any second.

Any second now.

Without warning, a pleasant tickle rippled up from Kris's stomach and into her chest and arms. She sighed in relief as the pill did its job. Her fingers relaxed against her thighs, the trembling gone. For the moment, her body was numbed like a bad tooth.

CHAPTER TWENTY-TWO

TOMMY SAW THEM the instant they entered the store, but he quickly pulled his sweat-stained Chiefs hat down to shield his eyes and turned toward the nearest shelf, pretending to busy himself with a display of landscaping lights.

Kris couldn't have cared less. She wasn't there for tools or hardware. She headed straight to the Verdigris Valley Home Furnishings side of the warehouse with Sadie trailing slowly behind her.

A row of mattresses on steel frames lined the far wall. Signs taped to the ends of the mattresses touted each brand's *unbeatable pillow tops* and *space-age memory foam* and *patented* Therm-a-Rest Technology.

Kris couldn't be bothered with the details. She climbed onto the very first queen mattress and stretched out on her stomach. She looked to Sadie, who was standing impatiently at the foot of the bed, and patted the empty space beside her. Sadie crawled up next to her mother and tested the mattress with a small bounce.

"What do you think?" Kris asked.

Sadie lay down on her side and rested her cheek against the raised diamond pattern stitched into the fabric.

"It's comfy."

"Yeah. It is."

"How much money is it?"

Kris reached out and gently swept a stray curl from Sadie's face.

"Who cares?" Kris whispered with a mischievous grin. "I like it. I'm getting it. And you're getting one, too. It's time to stop sleeping on crappy old mattresses, don't ya think?"

Sadie smiled back.

They were passing through downtown on their way home when Kris saw her. Her name was Alice. Kris could not recall her last name, even though she had read it just two weeks before on the bronze placard mounted outside the redwood door leading up to her office.

Dr. Alice. That's what Kris called her when she was little. It made her giggle, thinking of Alice in Wonderland all grown-up and through med school.

"She's not that kind of doctor," her father had told her. "She's like, a doctor for the mind. You can talk to her."

"A talking doctor?" little Krissy had asked.

"Yeah," her dad had said with a smile that held no joy. "A talking doctor."

Daddy took you to see her. To talk about Mommy.

And now there she was, Dr. Alice, thirty years older and just as elegant as Kris remembered. She had to be nearing seventy, but her shoulders were as straight as a board, her hair only showing a few stitches of gray among the black.

Kris watched her stroll confidently down the sidewalk, waiting to see if she would glance over, if by some chance she would recognize Kris. But she did not turn her gaze from the path before her. Only when Alice reached the end of the block did she glance quickly to the side to check for the nonexistent downtown traffic. She crossed the street to the next block and, halfway up, she slipped through the red doorway, disappearing up the stairs.

It did not even occur to Kris to go straight down Center Street toward Jefferson Park, or to pull a U-turn and head back toward the fork that would take them to the beginning of River Road. Her mind was still on Dr. Alice. Kris was engrossed in her own thoughts as she took the next left onto Beech Street and eased the Jeep to a soft stop at the intersection. She barely took notice of an old bearded man in grass-stained coveralls and clear plastic safety glasses, trimming the overgrown weeds along the curb with a gas-powered Craftsman edger that belched puffs of black smoke into the breeze. The man paused long enough to give a friendly wave, but Kris did not return the gesture. In her nostrils was the scent of mahogany and leather, and in her mind's eye was Dr. Alice perched on the edge of a couch cushion, silhouetted against a tall, narrow window.

Kris was not fully conscious of her whereabouts until she had already turned left onto Birmingham Drive and felt the car angling away from downtown as it followed the curve of the road.

She attempted to conjure up an overhead view of the town, but since arriving, she had never left Center Street. Birmingham appeared to cut a diagonal through the perpendicular layout of Pacington, bucking the system of east-west numbered avenues and north-south streets named after trees.

As Birmingham carried them farther from downtown, the frayed edges of Pacington began to appear. Overgrown lawns. Crumbling driveways. Shingles hanging crookedly from roofs like scales shedding off a lizard's back. They had barely traveled half a mile and yet Kris felt light-years from the meticulously trimmed grass and pristine sidewalks of Center Street.

By the time Birmingham cut an odd angle across the 800 block of North Willow Street, there was more wood or cardboard filling window frames than glass. Some of the houses had been completely abandoned.

It's a mirage, she realized. Downtown was for visitors, for the summer crowd, for those few vacationers who still journeyed to Lost Lake to escape the Kansas heat with a few months of boating and swimming. But the rest of the town of Pacington, well, it was an old, moth-eaten sweater, unraveling into a pile of threads. Its glory days were long gone. No amount of weed whacking could change its downward trajectory.

On the dilapidated porch of one of the last holdouts on the block, a man in a grease-stained tank top pointed at Kris with two fingers clamped around a cigarette.

"What the fuck are you waiting for?" he yelled. "Go. Go!"

Kris hit the gas, cranking the wheel to the left, onto Willow. She had to get off of this street. She didn't care if a dead end rammed the Jeep into the hillside. She could not spend another second on Birmingham Drive.

The next intersection was coming up quickly. Kris slowed just enough to check for pedestrians and oncoming traffic, and then she rolled through the stop. In a yard on the corner, a mangy dog ran to the length of its chain and barked wildly at the Jeep as it passed. Kris thought she caught a glimpse of its owner watching, confused, from the front porch, but she did not look. Her eyes were on the line of downtown rooftops in the distance.

Only a few more blocks.

"Mommy?" There was fear in Sadie's voice.

"It's okay, baby."

Third Street flashed by, then Second, and Kris was suddenly at the corner of Willow and Center Street.

Tires chirped on the hot pavement as she brought the Jeep to a sharp stop. She let out a rattled breath.

On the opposite corner stood the out-of-place Victorian house that was now the Book Nook. That structure had seen the growth of the town from a quaint village along the muddy Verdigris River to the roaring vacation destination brought about by the accidental creation of Lost Lake. And now it sat perched like a vulture, watching as its beloved community died from the outside in.

Kris flicked on her turn signal. She tapped the steering wheel impatiently as she waited for a late-nineties Ford Expedition to rumble by, and then she turned quickly onto Center and pointed the Jeep toward home.

"Home," she whispered, testing it.

The word tasted like a bitter pill on her tongue.

She pushed the car faster as the town of Pacington fell away behind her. She wanted to leave it in the rearview mirror.

That place is rotting, too. Just like Daddy's lake house. Just like Mommy in her grave.

Her foot pressed down harder on the accelerator, sending the speedometer creeping past sixty. She wished she could abandon the voices in her head as easily as she had just abandoned the town.

She reached the spot where the highway forked, and slowed the Jeep just enough to safely swing a hard left onto River Road. Sunlight strobed through the trees as the car sped toward the lake house. There was the gap in the embankment where the gate should have stood.

But it fell down, didn't it? That rotten gate. That rotten gate at a rotten house outside a rotten town that not even the lake would want to swallow.

She cranked the steering wheel, the back tires slipping on the dirt road as the Jeep fishtailed through the gap. Only when she could see the house before her did Kris hit the brakes. The Jeep skidded to a stop in the gravel drive, kicking up a fresh cloud of powdery dust.

The second the car came to a halt, Sadie was unbuckling her seat belt, throwing open the door, leaping out. She raced up to the lake house before Kris could even put the Jeep in park.

"Sadie!"

Kris felt the all-too-familiar thud of her heart against the wall of her chest as she slammed the driver's-side door shut and hurried across the overgrown yard. Brown grasshoppers fluttered out of her way as she pushed through the weeds. She was forced to slow as she navigated the obstacle course of tangled weeds and loose bricks along the path to the front porch. She glanced up at the front door, expecting to see Sadie waiting with an impatient scowl for her mother to unlock it.

The door was wide open.

Icy needles of panic pricked her flesh.

Had she left the door unlocked? She tried to recall the twist of the key, the thunk of the dead bolt sliding into place, but everything before that moment was a blur.

She stepped into the dim threshold between the sunlit porch and the shadows of the claustrophobic foyer. Her hand gripped the door jamb as if her body were trying to keep her from entering.

"Sadie!" Her voice was swallowed by the empty house.

From somewhere farther inside, she heard the mischievous giggle of a child.

Kris felt the warm rush of anger course swiftly through her body. She drew in a breath as her parental gears shifted from protector to disciplinarian.

See? It was not her own voice. It was Jonah. *It's a pain in the ass, isn't it? Having a kid. If we didn't have her—*

"There is no 'we,' you cocksucker," Kris whispered, and the words cut the air like a freshly sharpened blade.

She stepped into the house and instantly came to a stop again.

What was that smell?

It wasn't the foul stench of a rotting bird that had greeted her when they first arrived, but it was just as surprising, just as unexpected.

She sniffed deeply, and the sweet odor of perfume tickled her nostrils.

Someone was inside! This was no longer Jonah's voice. This was panicky Kris, fearful Kris. God, she hated that voice.

Yet she couldn't deny the thought made sense. The unlocked door. The lingering scent of perfume.

What if someone had been in the house?

What if they never left?

Or perhaps she had simply left the front door unlocked, the latch not fully catching, and the wind had pushed it open while they were gone.

The gears shifted once more, and the engine inside her growled, low and menacing, as the disciplinarian became a warrior. She wasn't taking any chances.

She marched into the kitchen, swerving left at the island as if on a preset track. She yanked open a drawer. Metal utensils clanked inside. She quickly scanned the random items and snatched up the one good knife she had brought from home, a boning knife with a slender seven-inch blade. For some reason she couldn't explain, it was her preferred knife in the kitchen, her go-to. She used this knife for everything.

Never this. This is a first, she realized.

She slammed the drawer shut, not caring if the intruder heard the sound, in fact hoping that any noise might send them fleeing out into the woods.

With the knife gripped tightly in her hand, Kris moved like a predatory animal into the great room. The perfume smell was stronger there. The air was heavy with its sickening sweetness.

Across the room, sunlight hit the back windows at just the right angle to turn them into four fiery pillars. They looked like something out of a pagan ritual. Yet even against their dazzling brilliance, Kris could see that the French doors were shut tight. She moved quickly between the furniture and the fireplace and gave the door handle a sharp yank.

Still locked.

She was letting go of the handle, her body turning back toward the center of the room, when she heard it again.

The playful laugh of a little girl.

Kris spun around, her fingers curling tighter around the knife's black plastic handle.

She was still alone.

She could feel the heat from the windows against her back, the intense warmth cutting through her thin T-shirt. Her entire body suddenly seemed in danger of going up in flames like a smoldering log. Another moment, and the heat would ignite her.

The blade stabbed the air at her side as she stormed across the great room and into the hallway. The overwhelming odor of perfume wedged in her throat. She winced, pressing a fist to her nose to fend off the assault.

She managed to force out a single "Sadie!" as she leaned into the bathroom and flicked on the light.

Empty.

"Sadie!" she called again.

"Mommy! In here!"

Relief rushed through her. Her body immediately began to tremble as every muscle, up to now clenched tight, relaxed. In an awkward mix of leap and stumble, she crossed the hall to Sadie's room.

Her daughter smiled up at her, completely oblivious to the fear that had gripped her mother.

"Look," she said. Her sweet, innocent voice sounded awful, like an insult, against the horror of the moment. "Aren't they pretty?"

Not perfume, Kris realized. *Flowers.*

Her fingers went limp and the boning knife fell from her hand. It landed blade down, the tip perfectly burying itself into the wood.

Spread across the floor of Sadie's bedroom were dozens of purple wildflowers. Clumps of fresh dirt clung to roots like pale, malformed limbs.

Violets.

Her room was filled with violets.

PART THREE

BLACKBIRD

CHAPTER TWENTY-THREE

SERIOUSLY, DOES THIS town have only one cop? she thought.

Kris was relieved to see him, nonetheless. Deputy Montgomery was a hulking presence as he clomped down the wooden path, his shoulders broad, his belly a bit thick over the black leather belt that cinched his gray trousers. There was something about his scraggly beard that made her think he was a no-bullshit kind of guy. At some point in his career, some higher rank must have ordered him to be clean-shaven like every other officer. A mustache was fine, but not that patch of overgrown brown weeds hanging from his chin. And yet Deputy Montgomery had obviously said no. The beard stayed.

Kris and Sadie stood on the front porch, mother and daughter, clutching each other in such a stereotypical "save us" fashion that Kris found herself wanting to push the girl away, to show Deputy Montgomery that while they desired his assistance, they were not scared. They could take care of themselves.

But you can't, her shadow voice whispered.

Fuck off.

You're in over your head.

Fuck. Off.

Deputy Montgomery put one black boot up on the first step, but he came no farther.

"Break-in?" he asked. His voice was deeper than she remembered, and rough, like someone who hadn't slept well in years.

Kris nodded, saying, "Yes," then, thinking better of it, "Well, actually, I don't know."

She told him about the front door, how it was unlocked, how she was sure she had locked it before they drove into town.

But you're not. You're not sure.

She told him about the flowers they had found strewn about on Sadie's bedroom floor.

Deputy Montgomery asked them to stay on the front porch while he "checked things out." Kris noticed that his hand was placed on his holstered sidearm as he moved past them into the house.

For at least ten minutes, Kris stood with Sadie on the porch. Every now and then, Sadie would shuffle her feet in exaggerated impatience. The rubber soles of her shoes made a squeak-scrape sound against the rough wood of the front porch until finally Kris shushed her, demanding she stand still. Kris was listening for . . .

What, exactly?

Sounds of a struggle? Of a police officer being ambushed? Of Montgomery yelling at an intruder to "stay where you are" and "put your hands up?"

You overreacted and he knows it, the shadow voice hissed from behind its little door.

Someone put those flowers there, Kris shot back. *I sure as hell didn't do it. And Sadie . . .*

She glanced down at Sadie, who had taken a few steps away from her mother and was picking at the seam on the side of her rainbow leggings, her face hidden by her hair.

This was taking too long. Even if he were checking every closet, every nook and cranny, that would only be, what? Ten minutes? Fifteen? She looked at her watch. When had she called him? It felt like ages ago. Half an hour, at least. Had he really been in there that long?

Somewhere in the woods surrounding the house, a bird shrieked, its harsh call cracking the silent day like a stone against a windowpane.

Just as Kris was about to call through the open doorway, to ask if everything was okay, Deputy Montgomery returned. His hand was no longer on his firearm. His mirrored sunglasses were folded and placed in his breast pocket. His eyes were the same shade of brown as his beard, she noticed.

"There's no one in the house," he said.

Kris frowned, both needing to believe and disbelieve him at the same time. "Are you sure?"

"I checked out every single room, including the extra storage space upstairs. Had a hell of a time fitting through that little door. Every window is locked. The back doors are latched." He seemed to sense her frustration and held out a hand. "I'm not saying someone wasn't here. I'm just saying they're not here now."

"But—"

"I'm positive, a hundred percent," he said, and she knew he meant it.

"Okay," Kris said. "Okay. But . . . someone *was* in there."

"Does anyone know you're here?"

"Only people back home. In Colorado."

"Have you met anyone in town who may have taken an interest in you or your daughter?"

Kris considered the question, a gallery of faces flashing through her mind: the waitress at Patty's Plate, the odd way Darryl Hargrove had reacted to Sadie at Safeway, the sunken-eyed girl in the ice cream shop, Hitch in the bookstore.

The woman across the cove.

"Mrs. Barlow?"

"No," Kris said a bit too quickly.

Deputy Montgomery ran a hand over his beard, digging his fingertips in to give his chin a contemplative scratch. When he spoke, his voice was lower, his words intended only for Kris.

"I hate to ask you this, but I'm just trying to eliminate all possibilities here. Are you absolutely sure it couldn't have been . . ."

His eyes pointed to Sadie.

Kris was surprised to find that her first instinct was not to defend her daughter of the accusation but to consider it. Could she have done this? When would she have had time? And why? The pieces just didn't fit, and yet she could not help trying to force them together. Finally she shook her head, telling him, "No. No, she was with me the whole time."

They stood in silence, listening as grasshoppers chirped in the yard. Then Montgomery nodded and gave a quiet grunt as if confirming an opinion. He pulled the sunglasses from his breast pocket and put them on as he stepped off the porch and into the afternoon sunshine. He glanced back, twin images of the lake house captured in his mirrored lenses.

"I'll do a sweep of the exterior of the house and the edge of the woods," he assured her. "And I'll do a pass down River Road every hour on my regular route. But I wouldn't worry too much, Mrs. Barlow. Probably just a prank, local kids trying to scare you. They test the front door, find that it's open, use the place to hang out and drink beers. Wouldn't be the first time. A lot of these lake houses are empty, even in the summer. They're easy targets for turds with too much time on their hands."

The front door wasn't unlocked, Kris wanted to say.

From his other breast pocket, Deputy Montgomery produced a business card featuring a large gold shield, below which was his full name and information.

BEN MONTGOMERY
DEPUTY
GREENWOOD COUNTY SHERIFF'S OFFICE

In the lower right corner was a phone number for the main office. He assured her that if she called, dispatch would connect her straight to him or another officer on duty.

"Thanks, Deputy Montgomery," Kris said softly, turning the card over in her hand.

"Please. There's barely a thousand people in this town, and that's counting the summer folks. You can call me Ben. Everybody else does."

She gave an appreciative smile. "Okay. Thank you, Ben."

"I almost forgot," he said, unfastening the top of a small leather pouch on his utility belt. He took out a thin square of paper with a shiny silver object on the front and held it out to Sadie.

"We're a little shorthanded, even for a speck of dust like Pacington. I could use the help, if you're up for it."

Hesitantly, Sadie reached out and took the square of paper. At its center was a detachable sticker shaped like a police badge. The words "Pacington Police Department" arced across the top edge of the badge. At the bottom, in the same official-looking font, was "Junior Deputy."

"What do you say?" Kris prodded.

"Thank you." Sadie's voice was barely louder than the breeze whispering across the porch.

Ben Montgomery gave them both a nod and was turning back to the brick path that cut between the bushes and wildflowers when something stopped him. His brow furrowed, his head cocked slightly. Kris followed his gaze across the front yard to where a ridge of white rose up above the tops of billowing tallgrass.

The mattress.

Kris had dragged it to the edge of the porch, lifted it up onto the railing, and flipped it into the untamed foliage below. That's where it remained. Even in the bright sunlight, its white fabric was dull and aged, like the graying bones of a long-dead animal.

Don't, Kris pleaded in her mind. *Just keep walking.*

For another unbearable moment, Ben remained motionless, focused intently on the unusual presence of the mattress. And then he seemed to hear Kris's plea, for suddenly he turned as if he had never paused, and walked away toward his cruiser, first with the thud of his boots on brick and then the crunch of gravel.

Kris slowly let out a breath.

He was almost to his patrol car when another thought buzzed through Kris's mind like an annoying insect.

Ask him about the girls. It was her timid voice. Her chiding voice. The voice of her fears and insecurities.

No.

But he'll know. He'll know the truth. Not just gossip. He can tell you if there's anything to worry about. Maybe the flowers—

Have nothing to do with that, she finished the thought.

But how do you—

I don't want to know about any missing girls.

She knew this was a lie. She had been telling herself a lot of lies lately.

Far in the recesses of her mind, she heard a chuckle at this.

Lately.

Try your whole life.

Kris did want to know about the girls. She hadn't truly stopped thinking about them since leaving Hitch's bookstore. Four girls. All around Sadie's age. One never even found. And the others . . . She was curious. She couldn't deny it. And all she had to do was ask Ben.

Kris opened her mouth, but no words escaped.

If she knew the truth, that might be the end of—

Of what? The end of what?
Everything.
Don't be melodramatic. Once again, it was Jonah in his most condescending, dismissive tone.

Her body clenched like a fist. She wasn't being melodramatic. She came here for a reason—to this town, to this house—and if there was any hope of healing this summer, she needed to believe that this place was good, that it was safe.

She watched as the cruiser backed out onto River Road and drove away, out of sight, leaving only a puff of dust hanging in the warm air to prove Officer Montgomery had not been a figment of her imagination.

In a shallow closet nestled between the kitchen and the small foyer, Kris had hung the broom and dustpan on two thin nails driven into the flaking plaster. She took both down and closed the closet door, turning to Sadie, who was standing just inside the closed front door.

"Wait in the kitchen. I just want to clean those . . ."
Violets.

For some unknown reason, she couldn't bring herself to say the word aloud.

"That mess, and then you can go play. Okay?"
She was answered only by an annoyed glare.

Kris held her daughter's gaze until finally the little girl glanced away, defeated.

That's right, Kris thought. *Don't give me that look. I'm still the one in charge.*

Grabbing a white, plastic trash bag from under the kitchen sink, Kris hurried to the hallway and into Sadie's room.

The dead, drying flowers were beginning to lose their potent aroma, but the sweetness hanging in the warm air still bit into the back of Kris's throat. She tried to take short, shallow breaths as she cut through the scattered mess with the broom. Purple petals fell away from blooms, mixing with bushy green leaves and clumps of soil, filling the dust pan with a heaping mound of eviscerated vegetation. It only took a few minutes before Kris was dumping the last of the flowers into the half-filled trash bag.

She surveyed the bedroom floor with a sense of desperate relief. It needed a quick mopping before she could truly call it clean, but at least it was back to how it looked before . . .

Before someone was in your house.

Kids, she assured herself. It was common in this area. That's what Ben had said. She would just have to make sure the house was locked up tight the next time they went into town.

Kris grasped the bag with one hand, the broom and dustpan clutched in the other, and backed through the bedroom doorway.

From the corner of her eye, she caught sight of a small, slender figure in the hallway.

"I wanna go play," Sadie said.

That nagging feeling returned. Kris's mind tugged at it like a loose string.

"Sadie, you . . . you didn't do this. Right?"

Sadie stepped back. "No."

"Promise?"

Something farther down the hall caught Sadie's attention. Her eyes darted up toward the second floor.

"Sadie?"

"I promise," she said. Her head tilted as if she were trying to make out a distant sound. Then she was off, scampering down the hallway, the soles of her Converse squeaking like excited rodents as she went.

Kris listened as her daughter's footsteps thundered up the staircase, then padded quickly to the opposite side of the house. There was the sharp slam as she pulled the door shut to the tiny room behind the wall.

And then the house was silent save for the whistle of the wind.

"It's not the same."

Kris shut the master bedroom door so that Sadie couldn't hear her side of the conversation.

On the other end of the line, seven hundred miles away, Allison shushed a barking dog and then pressed her lips closer to her cell phone. She spoke in a hushed tone, as if afraid of being caught on a personal call, even if it was with the boss.

"Of course it's not the same," she said. "It's been years. And that part of the country's been hit hard. Businesses move away. People move away. You can't expect it to stay, like, frozen in time."

Kris sighed, frustrated. "It's not just the house. Or the town. It's—"

Allison cut her off. "I do this all the time, Dr. Barlow. I build something up so big that when it happens, it's a letdown. Like my birthday last year. It never could have lived up to my expectations. I mean, twenty-nine's huge, you know? It's like a milestone."

"Twenty-nine. Seriously, why do I call you thinking it'll make me feel better?"

Kris felt the tickle of Allison's laughter against her ear, and she was surprised to find herself smiling. She felt a little better. For the moment.

"My point is," Allison continued, "everything changes. For better or worse. It has to."

Kris sighed and sat down on the edge of the box spring. The new mattresses still had not arrived, despite the store's assurance that they would be there that day.

"I don't know, Allison, it's just . . . I feel like everything here is just . . . strange. It all looks right; it just feels . . ."

There was a pause, then a sharp click, and Kris knew Allison was biting the nail of her index finger. "Have you ever done sensory deprivation? You know, like the tank and water? The whole bit?"

Kris shook her head. "No."

"I tried it in college. For fun."

Now it was Kris's turn to laugh. "You are so weird."

"I was dating a psych student, okay? They had one of those tanks in the lab in Denver. I go in, and the water's so saturated with salt, it's like I'm floating on air, and there's no sound and only darkness. But after a while, I started to hear things. And then I started to *see* things. Like, beyond the walls of the tank. And I knew they weren't real, so there could only be one other explanation: I was losing my mind. I was going crazy. When he finally opened the tank, I was in a full-on panic."

"And you immediately dumped Mr. Psych for talking you into that."

"No. I let him buy me a nice dinner that night as an apology. And then I dumped him." She paused for dramatic effect. "Okay, I slept with him and then I dumped him." Then her voice lowered to a whisper, as if she were sharing secrets she had held for too long. "But I was only in that tank for an hour. Imagine being in something like that for thirty years."

"So, what? Everyone here has been in a sensory deprivation chamber since I was a kid?

Something clicked again on the other end. Allison was still chewing her fingernail. "No, not the town. That town, it's real. But what you've got in your head, the way you remember it when you were ten, the town that you haven't let change . . ."

Her words trailed away, but Kris knew where she was going. "That's the crazy part."

Kris could picture Allison recoiling in embarrassment. "I didn't mean—"

"No. You may be right."

There was a moment of silence, and then Allison spoke in a warm, reassuring tone: "I'm not saying you're losing it. I just mean that if you don't allow your mind to let go sometimes, it can really start to mess you up. I remember reading somewhere . . . someone said even insects dream or else they would go crazy."

Dreaming's not the problem, Kris thought. *It's what's in the dreams.*

She closed her eyes, just for a moment, and even though the old mattress was now the property of insects on the side of the house, Kris again saw a shape rising up behind her, the thing under the covers, peering out over the top of the sheet with cold black eyes.

The thought sent an involuntary jolt through her body, and she stood up quickly from the box spring.

Allison was speaking again: "Just . . . don't hold on to what doesn't exist for too long. At some point, you have to let it go and accept the reality of what it's become."

There it is, Kris thought. *That's why I call this kid. Because sometimes she's twenty-nine and sometimes she's eternal.*

"How's . . . everything else?" Allison asked hesitantly.

Kris knew what she was getting at. She took a moment to choose her words.

"Sadie seems to be doing better."

"Seems?"

Kris sighed. She had wanted Allison to pick up on her skepticism, but now she had to explain it.

"She spends most of her time alone, up on the second floor. It's like her playroom. I've checked on her, just to make sure she's okay. Her art stuff is up there and some of her stuffed animals. But . . ."

Allison waited, giving Kris the time she needed.

"It's already the middle of June. She'll have to be back in Colorado for school in a couple months. I just hope it's enough time."

On the other end came the sound of a door opening, the barking of dogs suddenly louder. Allison remained silent as someone passed by. When she spoke, her voice was quieter and closer to the phone.

"How exactly did you expect this to go, Dr. Barlow?"

"I guess . . ." Kris tried to conjure up an honest answer. "I mean, I understand her feeling like she needs to hole up, away from the world. I just . . . I thought we would face it all together."

"Grief takes a lot of different forms," Allison assured her. "It might not be the way you want it to be, but maybe it's the way it has to be."

They talked for another ten minutes. Finally Allison signed off with a "Take care, Dr. Barlow," even though Kris had told her assistant countless times to call her by her first name.

Kris tapped end on her phone, and the cellular lifeline that connected her to the world she had left behind was instantly cut. Around her, the house creaked quietly in the gentle June breeze.

From outside, there came the sound of a child's muffled voice.

Kris turned her ear up toward the second floor, listening for the telltale signs of Sadie at play.

There was nothing. No footsteps. No laughter.

Had she come downstairs at some point? Had she passed by the closed door to the master bedroom, tiptoeing to make sure any squeaky boards wouldn't alert her mother to her presence?

Kris kicked aside the jumbled pile of sheets on the floor and stepped up to the window. Fifty yards away was the beginning of the forest. Buried somewhere in there was the break in the trees that led to the trail of bowing Osages. She listened, and there was the sound again, even and calm.

She moved to the far-left side of the window, pressed her cheek against the wall, and peered out at as sharp an angle as possible. From there, she could just see the edge of the swing set. Sadie sat motionless on the first swing, just as she had the day before, her hands gripping the links of chain on either side. Kris could barely make out the second swing, but it was clearly empty. Yet Sadie spoke to it as if a friend sat beside her. As Kris watched, she realized that what she had glimpsed the day before was not a misunderstanding. She could see it clearly now. The little girl was chatting away in an endless stream to the empty swing, pausing only to pretend to listen to a comment from her invisible companion.

An intense feeling of déjà vu swept over Kris. It was as if she were spying on herself as a child, as if the window looked out not on to the present but thirty years in the past, when she was the curly redhead, and her friend . . . her friend . . .

She could picture her younger self playing with another child, although the memory was so old and faded that it refused to focus into more than a blur. She must have played with other children during her summers at the lake. Had that helped her cope with her mother's illness? She couldn't recall for sure.

A high-pitched squeak blew in on the breeze, then it was gone, then back, then gone, a steady rhythm like clockwork gears in need of oil.

With her cheek resting against the sun-warmed glass, she watched as Sadie swung back and forth, back and forth, her legs pumping as she pulled herself higher and higher into the air. Beyond her was Lost Lake glistening in the bright midday sunshine. She could hear her daughter's excited yips as the swing carried the girl closer to the sky.

The wind must have picked up, because the empty swing beside Sadie began its own small arc over the weed-infested ground. Back and forth. Back and forth.

Like a friend is swinging with her.

But something was wrong.

The weeds.

They were motionless.

Kris glanced quickly over to the forest and the cover of trees thick with leaves. Not a single branch swayed. Not a single leaf fluttered. There was no wind.

She raised a fist to knock on the window, knowing damn well the noise would be too faint to get Sadie's attention, but just as her knuckles kissed the pane, she froze.

A face stared out of the woods.

It looked as though it had sprouted from a cluster of buds, the green perfectly framing flesh as gray and bloodless as a slaughtered pig. Half-moons of shadow hung under each eye. The eyes themselves were icy blue, like the water that had sprung up from the depths of the pre-historic lake hidden beneath the Verdigris River.

It was the face of a woman, and she was watching Sadie.

"Oh God!" Kris cried out, her voice echoing through the empty house.

She spun, her knees knocking awkwardly against each other, her entwined legs nearly sending her crashing to the floor, as she bolted from the bedroom. Her bare feet thudded across the hard wood as she rounded the corner at the mouth of the hall. She was across the great room in three leaps, twisting the latch, throwing the French doors open.

On the swing, Sadie had already begun to slow. She looked over as her frantic mother bounded across the deck, hopping down the back steps and onto the path leading to the lake.

"Get inside!" Kris commanded.

"What—"

"Get in the house!"

Sadie did as she was told, not waiting for the swing to come to a full stop before hopping to the ground.

Cutting sharply to her left, Kris abandoned the path and raced through the knee-high weeds, toward the edge of the woods. The teeth of spiny thistles bit into the soles of her feet.

She searched the forest for what she had glimpsed from the house.

The face was gone.

Confused, she slowed to a jog, her heart racing.

There. Behind the wall of trees. A shape. Moving quickly to the north.

"Hey!" she yelled. She picked up speed again, not caring as the dagger like edges of rocks gnashed at her soles.

She raced along the outer edge of the woods, tracking the shadowy shape. It, too, quickened its pace.

She shouted once more, "Hey!"

To her left, the lake house fell away. She was now in the front yard. Her feet were bleeding, she was sure of it. She could feel stones and spiky plants digging into her flesh.

Up ahead, the forest came to a sudden stop where River Road cut through the countryside. The embankment of dried clay and twisted roots created a natural wall along the far end of the property, with only the slim opening where the rotted gate had fallen away allowing entry to the road beyond. Kris sprinted away from the trees and toward that open passage. She pounced—there was no other word for it, for she felt like an animal tracking prey—into the middle of the road and glared down at the neglected street twisting into tree-shrouded darkness.

No one was there.

She stood, panting, her mind racing, trying to piece together the logic that had allowed the woman to escape her.

Behind her, there was the crunch of gravel under her shoes.

Kris spun around.

Two figures were moving up the road, away from her. One was the person she had seen peering out of the trees, a young woman in her twenties dressed in blue jeans and a ragged white shirt. The other woman was older and slightly taller with straight black hair that draped down to her waist and swung like a pendulum of shadow. The older woman had one hand on the younger girl's arm, the other around her shoulders, quickly leading her away.

"Hey, you!" Kris cried out, still sucking in air as she tried to catch her breath.

The girl started to glance back, but the older woman tightened her grip, stopping her.

They were nearing another break in the trees farther up the road.

"Hey! Answer me!"

The older woman picked up her pace as she guided the girl off River Road and onto a dirt path. Just as they began to pass out of sight, the woman glanced over her shoulder. Her dark eyes found Kris, and her leathery, weathered face wrinkled up in disgust. And then the forest folded them in, and they were gone.

Kris stood in the middle of the road, staring in confusion, the breeze tossing her hair across her face. In her mind, she followed the two women down the path and around the curve of the lake shore.

Unless that path suddenly cut sharply to the west, the only place it could possibly take them was—

The other side of the lake.

There was a nearly audible snap as another piece of the puzzle fell into place.

The woman's long, dark hair. Her tall, slender form.

It's her, Kris thought.

She was certain of it. It was the woman from the cabin on the other side of the cove, the woman they'd seen staring at their lake house as if waiting for it to sprout wings and fly away.

But who was with her? Who was that girl?

Call the police, her timid voice pleaded. *Call Ben.*

She knew she could. He had given her his card for this very reason. But what would she say? A woman has been standing on her own deck a lot lately? Another woman, her daughter maybe, was walking in the woods, on public land?

"What am I doing?" she asked out loud. Chasing a girl who, as far as Kris knew, was out on a hike. Screaming at neighbors who were just curious about the new family across the cove, who probably came over to introduce themselves.

The surge of adrenaline that had carried Kris to this point suddenly subsided, and in its wake was left a dull throb that worked its way from Kris's battered feet up her calves to her knees. She stumbled backward just as her legs gave out, and she plopped down hard against the ridge of the embankment.

Around her were the sounds of the woods—the buzzing of insects, the chattering of birds, the rustling of leaves.

Not since the night of Jonah's death had she felt so alone.

CHAPTER TWENTY-FOUR

BY THE THIRD week of June, Kris had managed to tackle most of the home improvement projects remaining on her to-do list. Every loose board had been secured with a few carefully driven nails and a healthy dollop of wood glue. The wiggly stones on the fireplace hearth were cemented in place thanks to a caulking gun and two tubes of anchoring adhesive. The drooping edges of peeling wallpaper in the master bedroom were glued back to the wall, straight and mostly wrinkle-free. By duct-taping several broom handles together, she was able to reach the highest corners of the great room's cathedral ceiling to swipe at the last of the spiderwebs. The new mattresses had arrived, and the delivery men graciously hauled Sadie's old one away. Kris did not bother telling them about her old mattress. She hoped they didn't spot it in its grave of weeds on the side of the house as they drove off.

The deck railing had been her final project, at least for the time being. She had slathered on the SPF-50, pulled the brim of her fraying Denver Broncos cap down low to shield her face and, with the boombox moved to just inside the back doorway and tuned to a rock station out of Wichita, she spent several hours driving six-inch wood screws through each slat and securing the corners of the railing with galvanized steel braces. When she was finally done, every inch of her skin was covered in sweat and sawdust, and a long, damp peninsula ran down the back of her tank. She tested her work by leaning all of her weight against the rail, even stretching her arms out as far as they would reach to put as much pressure on the railing as possible. The wood creaked in protest, but the screws and braces held.

As she was packing up the drill and the rechargeable battery, she noticed the beetle. It was crawling down one of the balusters, away from the top rail, stopping every now and then to swipe the air with furry antennae as if trying to pick up a signal. It was modest in size, barely the width of a dime, with a glossy black end and a pale yellow thorax. At the center of its thorax, just above its head, was an odd dark splotch like an ink drop. It looked like a mini Rorschach test. The shape made her immediately think of a plump bird just beginning to unfold its wings as it took flight.

Kris could name over forty breeds of cats and more than two hundred breeds of dogs off the top of her head, as well as more facts that she ever thought she would know about birds, horses, sheep, and goats. Being a vet in Colorado, she was no longer surprised by what constituted a "pet." She didn't have enough fingers to count the number of times a sick boa or python or bearded dragon had been carried into her office. But insects she knew little about unless they were commonly burrowed into or nibbling on the flesh of her patients.

This one looked harmless enough, though. She watched it curiously as it carefully traversed a split in the wood to make its way to the edge of the bottom rail. There it paused, its front legs reaching into the open air in a hopeless attempt to span the distance to the deck floor.

Kris lowered her hand down under the beetle. It reared back slightly, alarmed by the close movement. But after a moment, it dangled its front legs once again into open air until the prickly points of its front claws found her smooth flesh. She waited until it had pulled itself the rest of the way onto the base of her index finger before moving her hand down to rest atop the deck floor.

The beetle did not move. It remained perched on her palm as if afraid to venture farther.

With the back of her thumb, she gently nudged its butt until finally it got the hint and crept carefully off her hand and onto a wooden plank. It paused, raising its head high into the air, its antennae twitching, and then it slipped into a hole about the size of a quarter and disappeared into the darkness beneath the deck.

She sat back next to the open drill case and found herself hoping she had sent the beetle off in the right direction. She hoped it was scurrying along the underside of the deck, that it would find the lattice work that lined the lower half like a skirt, that it would make its way down to the dead grass below to whatever stone or hole in the earth that it called home. It was silly, wasting thoughtful wishes on a bug, but Kris had been that way since she was a child, always wanting to help every creature in need. It got to the point that her mother would always make sure there was an empty coffee can in the car, numerous holes poked into its plastic lid with an ice pick, just in case Kris spotted a box turtle on the side of the road during one of their summer drives, or a tarantula crossing the highway on its autumn journey to find a mate. Her father told her she couldn't save them all, and she knew he was right. But she could save one or two, the ones that desperately needed her help, right then and there. She knew the one thing she couldn't do was pass it by. She could save it. She could fix it.

Like you fixed Jonah, the taunting voice purred from far off in the darkness.

She tried to ignore the comment. There was no need to enter into a mental debate. Jonah was his own person. He had made his own choices.

And so the voice turned the screw tighter: *Like you're fixing Sadie.*

Kris clenched her eyes shut and imagined her thoughts to be daggers, cold and narrowing to a razor-sharp point, as she hurled them blindly into the recesses of her mind: *I'm not trying to* fix *Sadie, I'm just trying to . . . reset. That's all. To hold down the power button and let our regular life shut down. And after this summer, I'll fire it back up, and we'll go home. And maybe, just maybe, everything will run a little more smoothly. Maybe the pain will be a little less.*

And if that doesn't happen? the taunting voice asked. She had never associated a face with this voice, but something about its tone convinced her that if there was a face, it was smiling.

She's playing, Kris thought, more to herself than to the disembodied voice in the darkness. *I'm giving her space and it's helping. She's playing and laughing. She's pretending. Using her imagination just like she used to. That means something, right? That* has *to mean something.*

If her playing is a good thing, the shadow voice asked, *then why does it scare you?*

Kris knew that the voices in her head were are part of her, that they were fractured pieces of a single mind. Yet this comment felt completely detached. She had never thought of Sadie's activities as scaring her. Troublesome? Maybe. Annoying? At times. But scary? What reason did she have to be scared?

Ask Camilla that question, her shadow voice whispered.

No. Such thoughts would do no good. Kris pushed them all—Sadie, the lost girls, the sadness that hung over the town—out of her mind.

Focus on the work, she commanded.

Through the boombox speakers, an overly amped DJ suddenly began to holler in a high-pitched twang that if they were the tenth caller to name the next song, they would be rewarded with two free tickets to the "most bitchin,' hardest rockin' show to invade the Intrust Bank Arena all mutha-effin' year." He assured them this life-altering event could only be provided by K106.7, the Blade, and then his thin, nasally voice was replaced by aggressively assaulted guitar strings descending in a surprisingly thoughtful, melodic riff.

"Foo Fighters," Kris announced to no one. "'Monkey Wrench.'"

She had just allowed herself a momentary fantasy—picking up her cell phone, dialing the radio station, hearing her own voice through the boombox speakers as the DJ declared her the winner—when, from somewhere inside the house, there came a thump.

She paused, listening.

It had been a door closing, but the sound had been distant, not from just down the hall.

There was only one door on the second floor. The small square door to the room behind the wall.

Kris glanced back over her shoulder, through the open French doors, her eyes rising slowly up to find the section of wall above the entryway to the kitchen.

Behind that wall was the extra storage space.

The secret room.

Reaching for the boombox in the doorway, she twisted the volume knob all the way to the left, silencing the music. She tried to force all other sounds away—the whisper of the breeze, the rustle of leaves, the buzz of insects in the grass, the lap of water against the lakeshore. She tried to focus only on that wall and what lay beyond it, out of sight.

A song.

Someone was singing, their voice light and ethereal.

It was a child. A child was singing.

No, she realized. Not singing. Humming. As one might hum along to a favorite tune.

She leaned farther into the great room. The outside sounds fell away. The humming was louder but still muffled. She looked slowly around the room, tracking the sound like a fly. Once again, she found herself staring up at the section of wall above the kitchen entryway.

There was no doubt. It was coming from there.

The song was familiar, although she could not hear enough of it to place it.

She could not even be sure that it was an actual song. It could have been a random tune, made up by Sadie as she played or read a book. But her delivery of it was growing in confidence as if she were learning each note, practicing it over and over.

Careful to not make much noise, Kris tiptoed past the leather couch and over to the kitchen entryway. She was directly under that section of wall now, staring up at the mere inches of wood paneling that separated her from Sadie as she hummed her sweet little tune, pausing only to start it all over again.

What was that song? She knew she had heard it before. Many times, in fact. There was a repetition to it, the same simple cycle hummed over and over. If only she were upstairs, standing just outside the tiny door instead of downstairs.

Without realizing what she was doing, Kris took a step backward, and she felt the floorboard give just the slightest bit beneath the heel of her shoe. It squeaked, not loudly, but enough to make her wince.

Above her, the humming stopped.

The entire house had fallen still.

Outside, in the distance, a bird gave a sharp cry—once, twice—but it was answered only by silence.

CHAPTER TWENTY-FIVE

IT CAME TO her as a thought, like the other times when she was alone in her room or on the swing or up in her secret playroom.

At first Sadie was sure they were *her* thoughts, but those had always sounded just like her own voice. These sounded . . . different. Not completely. The voice of these thoughts was still a little girl, like her, but it was . . .

She paused, trying to find the right word.

Stronger. That was it. The voice was stronger. Like when the older girls spoke to her on the playground at school. Most of them were nice, like this voice, but they had a way of talking that made Sadie feel even smaller.

This thought had asked her a question. Now it was waiting. She could almost hear it breathing.

Can thoughts breathe?

It was a silly thing to wonder, and yet it sent a shiver through her small body.

"Because I heard something," Sadie replied out loud. She was careful to keep her voice just above a whisper. She was sure Mommy was downstairs listening. Mommy was always listening, waiting for a reason to ask if she was okay. She was okay. She was better than okay.

It wasn't only because of the new voice in her mind. Sadie was beginning to see something, too. She couldn't look straight at it. Looking straight at it made it go away. But if she stared straight at something else—the wall or her ceiling or a book she was pretending to read—she could see a fuzzy shape out of the corner of her eye.

Like right now, as she sat in the circle of sunlight shining through the oval window above her play table. In the middle of the table was a glass jar she had found in a lower cabinet in the kitchen. It was one of those old-timey jars that grandmas put homemade jam in and adults younger than her mommy used for drinking alcohol. These types of jars had a name. On the side of the jar, in swirly, bubbly letters, was the word "Ball," but she knew that was not its name. She had heard it before, although she couldn't remember where or when. But she was pretty sure it started with an "M."

Mason.

That was it!

Mason the Jar.

She had set Mason the Jar on her table like a vase, and in it she had placed one of the purple flowers from her bedroom, one that Mommy had missed when she was sweeping up the mess. Her broom must have knocked it under the bed, but Sadie had found it, and here it was. She had put a little bit of water in Mason the Jar so the pretty flower could drink when it got thirsty.

If she looked right at that flower and did not, for any reason, let her eyes move away from it, she could see the blurry shape standing beside her.

Her friend.

The girl who talked to her in her mind.

Sadie could feel the shape staring at her, as if, up until then, she, too, had been nothing but a sound or a feeling in the house. But now they could see each other!

The flowers on her bedroom floor had been a present. A friendship present. Like the Rainbow Loom bracelets her best friend, Charlotte, had made in the first grade.

She missed Charlotte. She missed her other friends from school. She missed going to the park and climbing on the yellow-and-green thing with steps and the bars and the pole she could slide down when Mommy wasn't looking, because Mommy was afraid she would lose her grip and fall.

She missed home.

But this was home now, wasn't it? For the summer, this was her home.

And then you're going to leave?

It was her friend's voice again, as strong as it was sweet. But now it was so clear, so real. Not the *feeling* of what her friend meant but actual words. They were no longer in Sadie's mind. The voice was in the room with her.

"We have to," Sadie whispered.

She could see the blurry shape moving closer. Her friend's face was almost pressed up against hers.

But we have so many games to play.

Sadie grinned, and her chest suddenly felt warm and tingly. She loved their games. She never got tired of playing hide-and-seek or tag or World Record. And she still wanted to play the game her friend had put into her mind like a note slipped in class, Ghost in the Graveyard, even though Sadie had sensed that this game was most fun when played at night.

But she knew Mommy was getting worried. She saw it on Mommy's face and heard it in her voice when she called out Sadie's name.

I don't want you to leave again, the shape of her friend whispered in her ear. *I want us to play forever, Krissy. Forever and ever and ever.*

Sadie frowned. She turned her head, her eyes leaving Mason the Jar, and her friend instantly vanished as if someone had flicked a switch.

"My name isn't Krissy. It's Sadie," she said to the empty air.

She waited for a response, for that wonderful voice to speak again, but there was only silence.

Sadie looked back at the jar. The blurry image of her friend returned to the corner of her eye, but it was farther away, as if it had taken a few steps back. The shape cocked its head, confused.

"Kris is my mommy's name," Sadie offered, answering a question that had not been asked.

The shape remained motionless, staring, its head cocked at that odd angle.

Sadie was suddenly filled with a terrible fear that made her tremble, like when she ran too far ahead in a department store and realized suddenly that she was lost and alone.

She's mad at me, she thought, even though she could not figure out why. The possibility that she had ruined this new friendship made her want to burst into tears.

As if hearing this thought, the shape straightened its head.

Where is Krissy? it asked.

Sadie sighed with relief. There was no anger in that voice.

"That's my mommy's name," she replied.

The woman downstairs?

"Uh-huh. That's my mommy. Her name's Kris. I'm Sadie."

The shape fell silent once again.

Outside, the wind picked up, gently rocking the house. The exposed roof beams overhead creaked softly as they held their place.

Sadie kept her eyes locked on the purple flower in the jar. It was beginning to droop over the lip of the jar. She blinked, and in that split second, her friend was once again beside her, so close that Sadie imagined she could feel hot breath on her cheek.

I want your mommy to play with us, her friend said.

Sadie felt a sourness in the pit of her stomach. It was the same feeling she had when she saw Charlotte playing with other girls at recess.

"Why?" she asked. She did not mean to sound angry, but she couldn't help it.

It'll be fun. You'll see.

"I don't think she wants to play. She's busy. And . . ." Sadie paused, afraid that the thing she was about to say would hurt her friend's feelings. "I don't think she'll believe you're real."

Once again, the room grew still. Sadie was afraid her friend had left, even though she could still see the fuzzy shape standing right beside her.

Then the voice in her mind said, *We'll make her believe.*

Sadie couldn't be sure, but she thought she saw the red smear of a smile rise up on her friend's face.

The thought of making her friend happy made that yucky sourness in Sadie's tummy go away. She stared harder than ever at the purple flower poking out of the top of Mason the Jar, and she was filled with a happiness that tickled her skin.

Sadie began to hum again, the song she had just learned, the song her friend had taught her.

CHAPTER TWENTY-SIX

IN THE DISTANCE, a flash of lightning split the sky.

Kris brewed a fresh pot of coffee, poured herself a steaming mug, and stood at the towering windows along the far end of the great room, watching as the sky turned from blue to a sickly green until it was finally overtaken by the thick cluster of charcoal-gray clouds that rumbled in like a smoke-streaked locomotive.

She sipped the black coffee, careful not to burn her tongue. Steam curled up around the sides of her nose. The coffee was bitter, but she relished its harshness. It jolted her senses, only to settle into the burn of a smoldering fire in her belly.

Thunder rumbled through the storm front, and the rain fell suddenly in one incredible, dense sheet. The lake was transformed into a million shattered mirrors. The trees in the forest lining the shore bowed obediently to the onslaught.

Across the cove, lights shimmered through the deluge, like a torch flickering behind a waterfall.

Windows. Illuminated from within.

The cabin. Her *cabin.*

Kris lowered her mug. The bitterness of the coffee no longer tasted pleasant. There was something off about it, a rottenness that crept up from her throat and over the back of her tongue.

Leaning closer to the window, she attempted to peer through the rain-streaked glass. The downpour was much too heavy to see the other side of the cove in any detail, but every now and then, she felt she caught a wavering glimpse of a figure standing in one of those windows, a woman with straight black hair draping over her back. Staring. Watching.

It's your imagination, her chiding voice scolded her. *It's like you want the woman to be there. You need her to be bad, because you chased her, you chased her away. . .*

Behind her, a floorboard creaked.

In the window pane, Kris glimpsed the reflection of a small form creeping through the great room.

She turned just in time to catch the shape of a child ducking behind the leather sofa.

"Sadie?"

"Mommy, quick! Come hide with me!"

"Why don't we play a board game?" Kris suggested. "We could play Clue. You love Clue."

Sadie popped up just enough to glare over the top of the couch. She whispered sharply, "Mommy! Come on! Hurry or she'll know where I am!"

Across the lake, a streak of lightning cut a jagged line behind the gypsum hills.

Kris flinched at the sudden flash of light, and fresh anger slipped under her skin like a hot poker.

"Who are you talking about—"

Sadie pressed a finger flat against her pink lips. "Shh!" Nodding her head as if picking up some inaudible rhythm, she began to mouth numbers as if she were counting along with someone else calling out from deeper in the house.

Eleven.

Twelve.

Sadie's eyes were fixed on something across the room.

Kris followed her gaze. In the hallway, the doors to the bathroom and both bedrooms were shut. The hall was an endless black tunnel.

Sadie continued to mouth the words:

Thirteen.

Fourteen.

Kris stared at the black void, as if she expected someone to emerge from it, to come racing out in a wild fit and charge at her.

That's crazy. We're the only ones in the house.

And still Kris did not look away.

Fifteen.

Sixteen.

Seventeen.

Hide, her timid self cried out desperately in her mind. *Quick, she's coming!*

Kris heard herself expel the word on a breath: "Who?"

But there was no answer for this question. She knew this was just another of Sadie's games, one of her fantasies. And yet Kris could not help but feel her skin tightening as Sadie drew closer and closer to the final count of twenty.

Eighteen.

At her side, Kris's hands clenched, clutching the edges of the sleeveless flannel that hung down over the top of her jeans. Without even realizing it, she began to twist the fabric between her fingers.

"Sadie, enough."

Nineteen.

"I want you to stop this."

"Shh!"

Twenty!

Sadie ducked behind the couch, out of sight.

Overhead, a fresh sheet of rain thundered against the roof. The sound echoed down from the vaulted ceiling and filled the house with the steady, powerful rhythm of its attack.

Kris could not look away from the impenetrable blackness within the hall.

She's coming, the frightened voice warned.

Who? Kris shot back.

From behind the couch, Sadie giggled nervously.

She's going to find you.

In her hand, Kris twisted the end of the shirt so tightly that the collar began to tug at her neck.

Something was building inside her. It began deep in her chest and then rose up her throat to the back of her tongue, burning like hot bile. It felt like a shriek that had been hiding within her for years. It needed out, and there was nothing she could do to stop it.

She opened her mouth, and the first blistering-hot word began to form on her tongue.

And then Sadie screamed.

The sound pierced so deeply into Kris's ears, it felt like needles driven savagely into her ear canals, the tips scraping at the folded lobes of her brain. Her entire body seemed to short-circuit.

Go, her mind commanded. *Help her!*

But just as the sensation of stunned paralysis faded, Kris heard her daughter's screams transform into laughter. Without warning, Sadie raced out from her hiding place behind the couch, shrieking "No! No!" as she bowed her body forward as if someone were right behind her, reaching out to tag her. She was a blur as she sprinted across the great room and disappeared into the blackness of the hallway.

"Mommy, come on! We're it!" Sadie's voice echoed from far away.

And then all was silent.

Kris took a step forward, her legs quaking as if they might give out at any moment.

"Sadie!" Kris yelled.

The wind shifted outside, sending thick drops of rain thudding against the great room's windows.

An image flickered through Kris's mind: the handprints she had found on the glass when they first arrived, the remnants of a thousand childlike hands pounding desperately to be freed.

Quietly, cautiously, she moved toward the hallway. A floorboard creaked under her weight, and Kris flinched. She was immediately ashamed. She knew there was nothing waiting for her in the darkness.

Then why are you afraid?

Like a steam engine propelled across tracks, Kris crossed the rest of the way to the hall. She reached into the inky black and searched the wall with her hand until she found the switch. She gave it a hard, irritated flick.

Light exploded into the hallway, driving the dark away until it was nothing more than quivering shadows.

No one was there.

"Sadie? Sa-die . . ."

At the top of the staircase, a board gave a telltale squeak. Kris listened patiently as footsteps crept down the stairs until a pale form, barely visible in the thick gloom, appeared at the end of the hall.

"Mommy?" Sadie called.

"Yes?"

"Do we have tea? Like hot tea? Like we have back home."

It took a moment for Kris's confused mind to understand what Sadie was asking. Then she thought back to the things she had bought at the supermarket.

"Yeah," she said. "We have tea. You want me to make some? We can sit in the kitchen or at the coffee table."

Sadie shook her head. "I want you to bring it upstairs," she said. "I want to have a tea party with you."

There were no teacups and saucers in the lake house, and Sadie's plastic play set was on a shelf in her bedroom back in Colorado, so Kris had to improvise with two mismatched coffee mugs. But the tea smelled wonderful, a mixture of citrus and wildflowers that curled up into the air on ribbons of steam.

Sadie was waiting in the main room upstairs. Her plush animals were arranged in a semicircle with Sadie at the center. In her lap was Bounce, his head hanging low on his thin neck. His crooked eyes stared in two different directions.

Rain tapped against the windows along the north wall. It sounded like the fingertips of some unknown visitor asking to be let in.

Kris placed a folded paper towel on the floor in front of Sadie and sat one of the mugs—a low, wide cup with sloping sides that looked most like a teacup—on top of it. She raised her own mug to her lips and blew softly across the surface of the tea before taking a sip.

"It's still a little hot," she told Sadie.

Nodding, Sadie looked down at her mug but did not attempt to touch it.

They sat and listened to the rain tapping on the window above the dresser like a friend asking to be let inside.

"This is nice," Kris said, breaking their silence.

Sadie nodded, but she did not look up from her mug. She seemed entranced by the finger of steam twisting into the air.

"It sounds like you've been having a lot of fun lately."

Again, Sadie nodded.

"What have you been doing up here?"

"Playing," Sadie said.

"Playing what?" There were no board games up here. No toys beyond the stuffed animals. In all their weeks here, Sadie had never asked once for the iPad still stashed away in the Jeep's glove compartment.

"Tag. Hide-and-seek."

Kris glanced around the room at every possible place to hide: the furniture still draped in sheets, the small square door to the secret room.

"Is it fun playing those things by yourself? I mean, would you want to go to the park sometime and see if there are other kids to play with?"

Sadie started to respond, then her eyes darted away from the mug as if something had caught her attention. When she looked back at her tea, she appeared slightly withdrawn.

Chastened, Kris thought, even though it made no sense.

"No," Sadie said softly. "I like it here."

Kris took another sip of tea, letting the moment linger. Then she said, "Don't you get lonely?"

Sadie slowly shook her head. Her lips bunched tightly as she fought a little smile.

"What?" Kris asked brightly, as if she were in on the joke. "What's funny?"

"Nothing," Sadie said, but the hint of the smile lingered.

Kris glanced down at Sadie's mug. The steam was a mere wisp.

"It's probably cool enough now."

Carefully, Sadie wrapped both hands around the mug and lifted it up from the paper towel. She took a hesitant sip. As she did, she glanced ever so slightly to her left, her brow furrowing as if she had heard something that concerned her.

"What's the matter, sweetie?" Kris asked.

Sadie seemed to be processing a thought she was afraid to say out loud.

"If there's something on your mind, you can talk to me. You know that. You can talk to me about anything."

"What happened to your mommy?" she asked suddenly.

The question took Kris completely by surprise. She had expected Sadie to ask about Jonah, about how he died or *why* he died. In that moment, Kris's mother had been the furthest thing from her mind.

She cleared her throat and resisted the urge to pull away.

"Well, I told you, she was very sick."

"What did she have?"

"Cancer."

"What's cancer?"

Kris bit the corner of her bottom lip between her teeth.

"Cancer is a disease that some people get from smoking or being in the sun too much or sometimes for no reason at all, like what happened to my mom. It's like a little part of your body goes bad, like when a piece of fruit gets a dark spot on it, you know?"

"Like rotten?"

The word struck a flat chord inside Kris. She swallowed and forced herself to nod.

"Yeah. And sometimes no matter what the doctors do, it just keeps getting worse and worse until your body can't take it anymore and . . ."

Kris stopped herself, not because she was afraid of scaring Sadie but because she did not want to continue down that road.

"Were you sad when your mommy died?" Sadie asked.

"Yes, I was very sad. I loved her very much."

The back of Kris's throat clenched. She took a gulp of tea to loosen it. For a moment, she thought she was going to choke. There was a bitterness to the tea that she had not noticed before. It reminded her of the time when, as a very young child, she had picked a dandelion and pinched the end of its stem between her lips. She remembered spitting it out as its shocking bitterness invaded her mouth. Finally Kris's throat relaxed, and the tea slipped down, the aftertaste making her wince.

"Did she die here?"

Kris looked up. Sadie was staring at her with intense interest.

"What?"

"Your mommy. Did she die in this house?"

"Sadie, I—"

"You said anything. You said I could ask you anything."

Setting her mug down, Kris took a deep breath.

"Yeah. I said that. But . . . why do you want to know about *that*?"

The little girl's eyes flicked briefly to her left again, as if she were looking to someone for guidance.

Kris did the same, noticing that the square door in the wall was open just a crack. Through that sliver, she could see only the darkness of the secret room.

Kris turned back just in time to catch Sadie nodding toward the storage door. Her cheeks quivered with a suppressed smile.

"Are you sleeping in the room where your mommy died?" she asked.

We're done, Kris thought, and before she could question herself, she was snatching up their mugs and rising to her feet.

Sadie stared up at her, confused.

"Where are you going?"

"I just . . ." Kris clenched her teeth. She could *feel* the tiny square door to her side and that sliver of darkness slicing into the white wall. She had been cautiously optimistic when Sadie invited her upstairs, but now Kris wanted to get back downstairs as quickly as possible. "Why don't we take our tea down to the breakfast nook? We can talk down there."

Sadie's grin was gone. Her bottom lip began to tremble.

"No. She wants you up here."

"Who?" Kris asked, confused.

Once more, Sadie glanced over to that little door for approval.

"What are you looking at, Sadie?" Kris knew there was anger in her voice, but at the moment, she did not care. "Why do you keep doing that? Why do you keep looking at that door?"

Whatever Sadie heard, it made her expression harden, the sadness that had moments ago threatened to overpower her gone in an instant. She glared up at her mother.

"You said I could ask you anything."

Bounce tumbled to the floor as Sadie hopped up. She was out of the room before Kris could even call her name. She listened as Sadie bounded down the stairs. A few seconds later, the slam of her bedroom door echoed through the house.

Kris looked down at the limp body of Bounce the purple frog sprawled at her feet.

Sadie was not getting better.

It was time to admit that.

The Xanax rattled about the bottom of the plastic bottle, skittering away from her fingertip as she attempted to snatch one out. She was surprised to find so few left. It seemed just yesterday the bottle was still a third full, but now . . .

She peered in and quickly counted the yellow pills.

Seven.

A week, if she took only one a day. Two weeks if she could confine her usage to every other day.

She scanned the label on the side of the bottle. *Quantity: 80.*

Eighty pills when the prescription was filled. Could that be right? Had she gone through that many in two weeks?

She attempted to do the math in her head.

When had she first dipped into the meds? The first day? Or had she waited? And how many had she taken before leaving for Kansas?

Did it really matter? Even if she gave herself the benefit of the doubt and said she had arrived with sixty pills, over the course of fourteen days that was about four pills a day. And she knew for a fact that in the beginning, she was only taking two per day. That had been the deal she made with herself. Those were the rules.

There was only one explanation. In the past week, there had been days when she popped five or six in a twenty-four-hour period. There were times when she was running on a solid three milligrams of Xanax, not to mention the amount of wine she was downing every evening.

"People heal in different ways," someone had told her after Jonah's funeral. "Let it take whatever course it takes."

But had they meant this? Isolating herself and her daughter in a cabin in the woods and numbing herself with pills and alcohol?

For a moment, she stood motionless, her finger still plunged into the pill bottle.

Then without another thought, she tossed the benzodiazepine into the back of her throat. Her mouth instantly filled with spit, and she swallowed it down.

Six pills left.

People heal in different ways.

She could accept that. But this way would require a refill of medication soon. She wasn't too keen on contacting Jonah's physician uncle out of the blue and asking if he could call in a prescription. That would require two things she wanted to avoid at all costs: informing more people—and family members at that—of her location, and answering the most irritating question anyone dealing with grief is expected to answer: "How are you doing?"

Well, my daughter is ignoring me, I've been spending all my time repairing a house I don't intend to live in past August, and I'm calling you for more drugs, so how the hell do you think I'm doing?

Allison. She could ask Allison to call something in. They prescribed Prozac for people's dogs all the time. Just last month, she wrote a prescription for a Pitt mix when it looked like training alone wouldn't keep the high-strung pooch from nipping at neighbors who came too close to the fence. She could—

Kris slipped a hand around her forehead and pinched her temples, hard, as if trying to keep the rest of the thought from fully forming in her brain.

Prozac for dogs? How goddamn desperate are you?

Kicking off her shoes one by one, Kris climbed onto her bed fully clothed, then buried her hands under the pillows and pulled them against her cheek. The new mattress was still a bit too firm for her liking, but compared to the deathbed she had tried to sleep on that first night, it was heaven.

She lay on her side and listened to the rain pelt the windowpanes.

The pills weren't the problem, she realized, as the one she had just consumed began to work its way into her bloodstream. No, the real issue was *why* she was taking the pills. And it had very little to do with Jonah, if she were being completely honest.

As much as she did not want to admit it, she knew that the more her daughter laughed and played, the more Kris popped and drank.

That's shitty, her mind scolded. *That is an absolutely shitty thing to think.*

But it was true, wasn't it? The constant sound of Sadie's laughter, the flash of red hair as she raced by, her muffled voice floating down from upstairs as she carried on an animated one-sided conversation with no one. The more dependent Sadie became on this routine, the more Kris craved the bitterness of a Xanax on her tongue.

It shouldn't be this way. She knew it was wrong. But right or wrong, this was the way she felt. Her daughter's happiness had become the reason for her own unhappiness.

Deep in the black abyss of her mind, a door creaked open.

You're a bad mother, that taunting voice purred.

No.

You're selfish.

No. I'm trying to deal.

So is she. And you hate her for it.

I do not hate her! I love her!

You resent her.

Kris shut her eyes and pressed her face into the pillow.

She resented Sadie. She resented her resilience. She resented her innocence. She resented that she could not be that young again with all of her choices yet to be made.

And what would you choose? the voice behind the door asked. *What would you do differently?*

Kris's scalp was beginning to tingle. The medication had found its way to her synapses.

I would have never married Jonah.

She rolled onto her back, her head sinking into the pillow.

Across the room, the window lit up as lightning flashed through the darkened storm clouds. Thunder rumbled angrily from one side of the world to the other, rattling the windowpane. Rain continued to pummel the roof, although Kris barely noticed it.

The task of keeping her eyes open was becoming too much to bear. Her vision blurred, the bedroom becoming a blur of shadows. She closed her eyes.

She waited for the stuffing inside the pillow to finally bring her head to rest, but she continued to sink and sink and sink, farther and farther until she was beyond the pillow, and the bed beneath her. She was drifting down into a place below it all.

Below the floor.

Below the house.

Below the ground.

Into a place of ancient rock and primordial darkness, where pristine water flowed up through slits in the earth's crust that looked like the petrified gills of some long-extinct sea creature.

The voice behind the door was down there with her. It had never sounded so close.

She was in its realm. Behind the door.

But if you never married Jonah, you never would have had Sadie.

She felt her body settle against a ridge of stone.

Maybe that would have been okay.

Maybe . . .

Kris never remembered finishing the thought.

In the days that followed, she liked to think that it was not sleep that had stopped her. She had purposely cut that thought short. She knew that what she was thinking was wrong. Because in the light of day, without a pill numbing her mind, she would never even entertain such thoughts.

Not her.

A mother could never think of abandoning her child.

CHAPTER TWENTY-SEVEN

KRIS SAT STRAIGHT up in bed, her lips attempting to drag air down into her lungs. She sucked in breath after breath, her mind trying to twist itself around the irrational fear that the room was running out of oxygen.

She had been dreaming that she was at the bottom of the lake.

Wait, that wasn't quite right. She had been deeper than that. She had been *below* the bottom of the lake, staring up through a jagged hole in its bed to the faint shimmer of the surface far above. But she had been able to breathe down there, or perhaps it just hadn't been necessary. And then, suddenly, her chest was heaving, her lungs were collapsing. She needed air.

But it was just a dream, and not the first in this house to send her lashing wildly into consciousness, panting and drenched in sweat.

After a minute, the panic dissipated like fog. Kris pulled her damp hair away from her face and leaned back against the headboard. The bedroom was dark save for a shaft of pale moonlight falling in through the window. Outside, the rain appeared to have stopped.

Snatching up her phone from the nightstand, she tapped the screen, waking it. A photo of Kris and Sadie was set as the wallpaper, Sadie on her lap, smiling, Kris hugging her daughter tightly as they rode a gondola to the top of a mountain in Breckenridge. It was from two summers before, and somehow those two years made them both look impossibly young. Hovering over this picture was the time: 11:35 p.m.

"Shit." Kris hopped off the bed and rushed out of the bedroom.

The walls of the great room were stained with swaths of shadow cast by the lamp on the end table. She must have left it on when she went into the bedroom. Up ahead, to her left, Sadie's door was open just a crack. The light was off.

Kris tiptoed to the door and gently nudged it open a few more inches. In the faint glow of the night-light, she could see Sadie in her bed, the comforter pulled up to her neck. One hand was outside of the covers and hung limply over the side of the mattress. Her chest rose and fell with steady, peaceful breaths.

Guilt stabbed Kris in the chest like a knife. Rather than wake her mother, Sadie had put herself to bed. She had come downstairs to find Kris passed out in the master bedroom and had brushed her teeth and washed her face and changed into her pajamas before finally crawling into her bed without so much as a kiss on the forehead.

And you fell asleep thinking about what your life would be like if you'd never even had her . . .

Kris pulled Sadie's door almost all the way shut. She quietly crept down the hall and into the great room. Through the rain-specked windows, she watched as the last of the storm clouds floated silently by. Their bellies were still an angry gray, but at the edges, the clouds thinned to wisps of moonlit white.

She clicked on the standing lamp beside the fireplace. The two illuminated lamps created intertwining globes of warm light that floated like colliding stars in the shadowy room. She sat down on the hearth and felt the cold stones through the butt of the jeans she had worn to bed.

The house was quiet. Not even the usual creaks and pops of the contracting wood broke the stillness.

This was all she had wanted—peace from the incessant racket of Sadie's games—but the hush that had fallen over her now felt more like a punishment than a reward. It was not the sound of life at rest. There was a tension to it, a deliberateness, as if something were biding its time, waiting patiently for the perfect moment to shatter the silence.

She wished the rain were still falling or the thunder were rumbling or even that Sadie were up so that this stillness could be broken by the thumping of her footsteps upstairs.

You wished she were gone, the chiding voice continued. *Your own daughter. In this town, of all places.*

This town. Where girls as equally loved as Sadie vanished.

Kris slipped her phone from her pocket, unlocked the screen, and opened the browser. She paused, unsure of what to type into the search window. Finally she typed: *missing girl pacington kansas*

Her thumb tapped Go.

The first two search results were a lost and found post about a missing German Shepherd puppy named Gracie, and a tweet from a local high school boy missing his out-of-town girlfriend. But the third result was exactly what Kris both hoped and feared she would find.

Missing Girls–Does Anyone Care?!

It was a post on a local message board, wedged between the much more innocuous announcements of Hope Church Quilting Group Fundraiser and Pothole on 4th Street Needs Repair Now! The missing girls post was dated August 21, 2004. It was a single line:

"Why has no one found out what is happening to our girls?"

It was signed simply *V.*

There were no responses to V's post.

Kris scrolled through a few more pages of results, but none of them had anything to do with missing girls in Pacington. She closed her eyes tight, trying to recall the names Hitch had mentioned to her.

Sarah. Sarah was one. What was the last name? It started with "B."

Bell. Sarah Bell.

Kris typed the name into the search window, along with the name of the town.

She read the first result and her heart sank.

Pacington Girl Found Dead Near Lost Lake

She forced her thumb to tap the link. A page from *The Eureka Herald* began to load. It was a brief article from September 16, 1998, but as Kris read, she realized it was not about Sarah Bell.

Pacington, KS — The body of a nine-year-old Pacington girl was found Tuesday morning in the woods near Lost Lake. She has been identified as Megan Adamson, daughter of Tera Adamson, of Pacington, and Don Adamson, of Chanute. Local authorities had been searching for the girl since she disappeared from a downtown store around 1:00 on Sunday afternoon. According to Greenwood County Sheriff Jim Conners, it appears the girl wandered into a section of the

forest known locally as Blanton's Pass. "She must have gotten up on the cliffs there and fell onto the rocks below," said
Conners. "She was deceased when we found her." Conners
says there is no reason to suspect foul play. There is also no
apparent connection to the disappearance of Sarah Bell in
1992 or that of Ruby Millan in 1989. Both girls lived in
Pacington, and both were found dead near Lost Lake.

A search for "Megan Adamson" only resulted in information
about her memorial service at Hope Church, and a search for "Ruby
Millan" resulted in nothing except the article Kris had already read.

Ruby and Sarah died before small-town newspapers like *The
Eureka Herald* had a presence on the web. Their stories might still exist
on microfiche at the public library or yellowing in a cardboard box in
some dark, dank basement, but there was nothing more to learn online.

Three girls dead.

But there was a fourth.

Camilla and Jesse's girl.

Poppy.

She typed the name: "Poppy Azuara." Her thumb hovered over
the Go button. This felt different. It seemed like a betrayal. She had
met Poppy's parents. She had sensed the pain hidden just below the
surface.

And yet she wanted to know.

She tapped the button.

Her stomach dropped as she saw what she had both desired and
feared. There were multiple results for Poppy. One by one, she clicked
the links. The sources were all different—*The Eureka Herald*; *The
Montgomery County Chronicle*; *The Wichita Eagle*—but the information
was the same she had learned from Hitch: Poppy Azuara, eight years
old, missing from Jefferson Park and never found. A photo accompanied the articles. Seeing it was worse than learning something new
about Poppy's disappearance. It was a school photograph of the young
girl, her hair and eyes as brown as her mother's, her smile wide and
bright. She looked nothing like Sadie, and yet there was one undeniable similarity. She had that spark that lit up her entire face, the same
spark that Sadie had lost when Jonah died, the glimmer of which had

returned only in the past few days when Sadie began spending so much time upstairs.

Kris could not stand to look at Poppy's sweet face any longer. She lowered her phone. With it went the glow of its screen. Her face was left in darkness.

Mom, where are you? her mind called. *If you're here, if you've ever been here, please, I need you.*

Kris's body shivered, the movement threatening to send her sliding off the edge of the hearth. She flung her hands backward to stop herself. The side of her right hand collided with something that went skittering noisily across the cold stone. She glanced over at the object.

It was the case for her mother's mixtape.

As she reached for it, her gaze fell upon the boombox a couple feet away. A plastic case rested on top of it, directly above the left speaker.

Her brain seemed to misfire as it tried to reconcile the sight of the two cases.

Sadie had only found one in the cabinet. Kris was sure of it. It was the only tape they had played the entire time they had been at the lake house. They had listened to it from end to end, over and over, taking breaks to dial in nearby radio stations before eventually returning to her mother's mix and the opening chords of The Smiths' "There Is a Light That Never Goes Out."

Yet now she held a second tape in her hand.

She turned the case over. Through the smoky plastic backing, she could see a ladder of black lines where the track and artist names could be written. But unlike the other cassette, these lines were blank. The spine of the tape was also untouched.

It made no sense. If Sadie had found another cassette, why hadn't she said something?

Or maybe she discovered it while Kris was asleep and set it on the hearth for her mother to find.

The numbness brought on by the medication she had taken before bed had completely subsided, allowing this sudden confusion to completely grip her mind in a quivering fist.

Slowly, she opened the case and slipped the cassette out.

Its body was white plastic, yellowed slightly with age, just like the other tape. One side was labeled with a large A, the other a B, but otherwise there was no indication of what—if anything—had been captured on the magnetic tape strung between its spools.

She felt as though she were still in a dream, her movements requiring unusual effort and concentration as she reached over to the boombox and hit eject. The cassette door popped open. Inside was her mother's mixtape.

At first her fingers refused to grasp it, but finally they took hold, sliding the cassette out from between the plastic guides. She set the mixtape on the stone hearth and removed the new mystery tape from its case. She dropped it down into the boombox's gaping mouth and pressed the door shut until it clicked softly into place.

Her finger found the play button, but she couldn't bring herself to push it.

It could be blank, she told herself. *Or it could be more music. Mom just never got around to labeling it.*

Her shadow whispered giddily from behind its little door: *Or it could be a recording of her voice, begging to die . . .*

Without warning, Kris jammed her finger down on the button. Through the clear door on the front of the boombox, she watched as the cassette's spools began to turn. There was the familiar hiss of empty tape. And then the finger-picked strings of an acoustic guitar floated from the stereo's small speakers, accompanied by the clean, precise click of a metronome.

She instantly recognized the tune.

It's their song.

The gentle voice of Paul McCartney began to sing:

"Blackbird singing in the dead of night . . ."

Kris raised a trembling hand to her mouth.

". . . take these broken wings and learn to fly . . ."

Her vision began to blur. At first, she was not sure why, and then she felt the first tear escape and roll down her cheek to the line of her jaw. It dropped like rainwater onto the hearth's cool stone.

". . . all your life . . ."

Suddenly she was painfully aware of the last time she heard this song, not the last time she *listened* to it on the radio or playing randomly on some Spotify playlist, but the last time she truly *heard* it, as she had come to know it: as their song, their shared favorite, the song they had danced to at their wedding, the link between her mother's love of rock and her father's stubborn allegiance to all things country and western. He had played this song endlessly that final summer at the lake house, turning the boombox up so loud that the music seemed to emanate from the very walls.

He turned it up so Mommy could hear it.

Because Mommy was in the bedroom.

Because Mommy couldn't leave her bed.

Because Mommy was dying.

But that didn't make sense. The boombox was small and portable. He could have carried it into the bedroom. He didn't have to play it so loud.

". . . you were always waiting for this moment to arise."

Kris was frozen in place. She could not move. She could only sit on the hearth and listen as the song played through to its final gentle chords.

Against the blackness of her mind, she saw herself as a young girl, racing through the woods. The lake house was completely hidden by the forest, but she sensed that it was behind her. She was running away from it. And someone was running ahead of her, leading her deeper into the trees.

The buzz of blank tape broke the spell.

Kris raised a hand to her cheek, and her fingers slipped across damp flesh. She had cried throughout the entire song, completely unaware as more tears slipped free.

She was reaching for the stop button when the song began once more.

The same plucked strings. The same tick of a metronome.

"Blackbird singing in the dead of night . . ."

Her father had dubbed the song twice in a row. It could have been a mistake. Or perhaps he had filled the entire tape with this song—their song—so that it would play over and over for her mother to hear.

Another piece of a long-unfinished puzzle snapped into place in her mind.

It was for her in the beginning. But by the end, it was for us. To drown out her screams.

From the darkened hallway came the sound of soft, shuffling footsteps.

Kris looked up just as a pale shape emerged from the shadows.

It's Mommy. You called to her and she came, Kris thought as the pale thing lurched into the light.

It was not her mother. It was Sadie. And even though the girl's eyes were open wide, her irises as perfectly round as green buttons, she did not seem to see anything before her. She came toward her mother in strange, lurching movements.

"Take these broken wings and learn to fly . . . all your life . . ."

"I know this!" Sadie screeched.

Startled, Kris leapt to her feet. The cassette case slipped from her fingers and fell to the floor with a hollow clank.

"I know this!" Sadie cried out, over and over. "I know this!" Her eyes were still staring straight ahead, into nothingness, but she cocked her head toward the sound.

". . . take these sunken eyes and learn to see, all your life . . ."

Kris took a step forward, her hand stretched out in a pitiful attempt to stop what was happening.

"Sadie! Wake up!"

Even though the girl's eyes were clearly open, Kris was convinced she was sleepwalking. It was the only explanation. Sadie was lost in some all-consuming dream, unaware of her actions even as she shuffled farther into the dim light of the great room.

"Sadie!"

"I know this!" Sadie raised a hand and pointed a single quivering finger toward the boombox. Her wild eyes found her mother, and for the first time since entering the room, she seemed to focus on the object in front of her.

"This is *her* song!"

The words brought Kris to a sudden halt. *Her* song. Mommy's song. But how could Sadie know? Kris had never really told Sadie about her last summer. How could she? Even to Kris, those final days were murky.

Her voice warbled as she asked, "Sadie, what are you talking about?"

". . . you were only waiting for this moment to be free."

A strange little smile suddenly played at Sadie's lips, made all the more disturbing by the madness in those green eyes, as if her brain squirmed with fever.

"I know this!" she shrieked. "This is her song!"

"Blackbird fly . . ."
"Sadie, stop!"
"Blackbird fly . . ."
"It's her song!"
"Sadie, wake up!"
"Into the light of a dark black night."

Lunging forward, Kris grabbed her daughter by the shoulders, stopping her terrible, lurching march.

A bird was chirping, right there in the room with them. Not the harsh shriek of a grackle but the tweeting of a songbird.

Sadie looked up into her mother's eyes. Her lips peeled away from her clenched teeth into an awful imitation of a smile. And the little girl began to laugh.

On the boombox, the guitar returned, joining the chirping bird in a duet. It curled around the sound of Sadie's manic laughter like smoke twisting in darkness.

"Stop it!" Kris commanded.

Grasping her daughter's shoulders tighter, Kris gave her a sharp shake, then another.

"Wake up! Sadie! Wake up!"

Sadie's eyes opened so wide, it was as if someone had cut the lids away. The wet orbs looked as though they were about to fall out of their sockets.

Her upper body began to shake with laughter, the sound forced mercilessly through teeth clamped like a triggered animal trap.

"Stop it!" Kris screamed. "Wake up! Wake up!"

Before she was even aware of what she was doing, Kris spun around and leapt toward the boombox. She jammed a finger down on the stop button.

"Blackbird singing in the dead—"
Click!

The music abruptly ceased. Silence rushed in to fill the void.

It was as if a spell had been broken. Sadie's eyelids drooped. Her lips relaxed. Her laughter faded away like an echo into open air. Her brow furrowed in confusion as she turned to Kris.

"M-Mommy? What's happening?"

On the couch's cracked leather cushion, Kris's cell phone began to ring.

Kris glanced down just as the screen lit up, displaying the caller ID. The area code was 620. A local number.

She and Sadie stood in confused silence, listening to the steady rhythm of the phone vibrating against the leather cushion. Finally, it fell silent. A second later, the phone gave a pleasant *ding* as a notification appeared on its screen: "1 Missed Call."

"Sadie—" Kris began.

The phone started to ring again.

With an irritated snort, Kris snatched up the phone.

Sadie slowly shook her head. "Mommy, don't . . ."

But Kris had already tapped accept.

"What? Who is this?" she barked angrily into the phone.

On the other end, there was only the distorted sound of wind blowing. Then a man's gruff voice spoke up: "Mrs. Barlow." He quickly corrected himself: "*Dr.* Barlow?"

Kris stared down at the floor, confused. "Yes?"

"This is Officer Montgomery."

"What . . .? Is . . . is something wrong?"

There was another pause. Only the wind filled the void.

And then Officer Montgomery said grimly, "Dr. Barlow, I'm afraid we could use your help."

CHAPTER TWENTY-EIGHT

"STAY IN THE car," Kris said to Sadie in the back seat. She did not wait for a reply. She stepped out of the Jeep and slammed the driver's-side door shut, locking the doors with the key fob as she hurried across the drive.

The last of the storm clouds were drifting slowly away to the northeast like the dark forms of whales swimming off into an even darker sea. Over downtown Pacington, stars had begun to reclaim the sky, blinking out of the blackness.

The thunderstorm may have passed, but its presence was still felt in the way Kris's boots sank into the soggy earth and the fallen branches that snapped under her weight as she made her way toward the field. The lights of the Auto Barn burned in the gloom, the mirrored image of the sign reflected in two deep, rainwater-filled tire ruts. The warmth of the previous day had been swept away by the downpour. A cold breeze blew through, carrying with it hints of honeysuckle and wild lavender. Kris shivered, her bare arms prickling into thousands of goosebumps. She should have grabbed a sweatshirt before she left, but she had been too distracted by the call from Officer Montgomery and Sadie's bizarre behavior.

Raindrops dripped from the rusted points of barbed wire as Kris neared the fence. Three figures were standing in the field beyond. The tallgrass surrounding them drooped low, weighted down by rainwater. Each of their faces was a study in contrast, one side glowing with the yellow light cast by security lamps, the other completely lost in darkness. They all wore the same expression—mouths pulled down at the edges as if by gravity, brows furrowed into peaks of pure helplessness, watery eyes staring at something large on the muddy ground before them.

Kris heard it before she saw it—the sharp snort of nostrils, the desperate breaths of a body in shock—and she knew what held their attention.

Ben was the first to look up. He offered Kris a faint smile of appreciation. It was all the joy he could muster.

"Thanks for coming," he said. "There's no vet here in town, so you were the closest—"

"It's no problem," she assured him.

The sound of her voice got Camilla's attention. She glanced up at Kris with puffy, bloodshot eyes. It took a moment for her to place Kris's face, and then recognition washed over her. She let out a long, trembling sigh, her eyes shining with fresh tears.

"Oh God, I'm so glad you're here," she said. "Please, you have to help us. You have to do something."

Beside her, Jesse knelt down and cradled the head of the thing in his arms. It did not seem to know he was there. Its brown eyes bulged behind long tan lashes. Thick lines of saliva ran from its open mouth, its cheeks puffing rapidly in and out with shallow gasps, its brain running its most basic program: stay alive, stay alive, stay alive.

Kris felt her stomach become suddenly awash with acid as dread took hold of her.

Lying on its side in the rain-soaked grass was the quarter horse. Their daughter's horse. Cap, short for "Cappuccino." His eyelashes flickered above brown eyes wide with terror. Something had ripped angry red gashes across the adorable pale lightning bolt that cut down the length of his snout. His white mane was stained with blood.

Kris attempted to speak and found that she had no breath to back her words. She swallowed and tried again. "What happened?"

"Must'a been the storm," Camilla said. Her Texas twang, once so comforting, now clashed mercilessly with the pain in her quavering voice. "Something spooked him and he . . . he . . ."

"It wasn't the storm," Jesse shot back. He was angry, not with Camilla but with fate, with God, with whatever cruel power had allowed this to happen. Cap nuzzled his wet nose into the crook of Jesse's elbow, his panicked eyes narrowing slightly as he was allowed the tiniest bit of comfort. Jesse stroked the horse's forehead, softly shushing the beast, whispering, "It's okay, it's okay," even as his chest hitched with fresh sobs.

Ben planted a boot down onto the second row of barbed wire and pulled up on the line above it, widening the fence just enough for Kris to slip through. "You should see this," he told her.

Careful to avoid the fence's barbed tips, Kris stepped through the opening. The wires sang a soft falsetto note as Ben released them and they snapped back into place. Kris was now in the thick of the field, the drooping tallgrass wiping tear streaks across the legs of her jeans. Before her was the horse, its massive body outlined by stalks of arrow-feather and bottlebrush. There was nothing outright troubling about this image. The horse could have simply been resting on its side, its legs stretched lazily out beneath it, had it not been for the tattered drapes of flesh hanging down around the hole in its belly. Wet ropes of intestine twisted out from its shredded hide and curled into the weeds like obscene snakes.

"How did this happen?" Kris asked no one in particular.

Ben turned to face her and spoke in a low tone so that Camilla and Jesse could not hear. "We don't really know. One minute the horse was in its stable, and the next thing they knew, it had broken out and was trying to . . . well . . . it was trying to get free." He motioned toward a patch of barbed-wire fence a few yards down. The top two wires were bent from the weight of Cap trying to break through. Strips of bloody flesh hung from the barbs. "It was like he was reacting to something Camilla and Jesse didn't hear."

"I don't get it," Kris said quietly. "A horse doesn't just gut itself on barbed wire for no reason. He could have hopped that fence if he really wanted to."

"I don't think it occurred to him," Ben said. "I think he was in a panic. He was only thinking about one thing: getting out."

Camilla must have realized the two of them were having a private conversation, for she suddenly stepped closer, the harsh security light falling across her tear-streaked face. She reached out and took Kris's hands. Her grasp was icy, as if all of the blood had drained from her fingers.

"Please tell me there's something you can do."

There's nothing, Kris thought.

But she gave Camilla's hand a reassuring squeeze and said, "Let me take a look."

Kris moved around to the other side of Jesse and placed a hand on his back in what she hoped felt like support. He swallowed hard, choking back tears, and leaned back to let Kris get a good look.

It wasn't pretty. In addition to Cap's eviscerated bowels, the horse's front legs were shredded from knee to hoof. Most of the flesh had been stripped away from the bone. On the right leg, the femur was clearly fractured, bent unnaturally at the middle so that a shard pointed like a dagger into the darkness. The other leg looked as though the horse were wearing a sock whose elastic had given out; the skin sagged down around its ankle, revealing a thick stretch of severed muscle that dangled freely like a snapped rubber band.

But the wounds were only one thing. As she did with every animal facing a life-threatening injury, she moved around to face Cap head-on, taking his muzzle in her hands. A high-pitched whine twisted through his wheezing breaths. She looked directly into the horse's eyes.

"What?" Jesse asked, his voice breaking.

Kris sighed.

It just wasn't there. The will to fight, to put every ounce of energy into surviving this ordeal—there was not even the slightest glimmer in Cap's terrified stare. Instead, she saw resignation. She saw the desperate plea to end this horror.

Once more, Jesse asked, "What?" And once more, Kris ignored him.

She gripped Ben by the elbow and moved him a few steps away from the scene.

"His injuries are just too severe. Even if we could transport him to a clinic, there's nothing anyone could do. He's in pain. All we can do is stop it."

She glanced to the gun holstered at Ben's side.

"Will that . . . Will that be enough?"

It took a few seconds for Ben to make sense of what she was asking. He nodded, but his dark brown eyes searched for any other answer.

"I don't know if I can do it," he said.

"You're a country boy. Surely you've put down animals before," Kris told him. She did not mean this as a slight. She said it simply as a fact.

"This is different," Ben replied, his eyes locked on hers.

Kris nodded, understanding.

They both felt Camilla take a step in their direction, and their bodies stiffened defensively.

"What's going on?" she asked.

Neither Kris nor Ben answered. Now it was Ben's turn to take Kris by the arm and lead her farther into the field.

He said, "You have to understand. This horse . . . this was their daughter's. This was Poppy's horse. It's *all they have*." He said the last three words as if each were the end of a declaration: All. They. Have.

Kris turned back to Camilla and Jesse. She hated this feeling. She was sure there were people out there who were good at delivering bad news, those who had figured out the perfect balance of compassion and professionalism to make the worst outcome a bit more palatable. But she had never been that person. She understood the bond between people and their pets. She knew that the love they felt was not some desperate need for connection by the sad and lonely. That love was real. There was always that moment when the owners' eyes met hers, and Kris held their world in her hands. It was the same for any doctor. In those moments, the hierarchy dissolved and there existed a kinship in this awful power. They were either the bearers of good news or bad news. There was no in-between.

Kris felt that now, their pleading eyes on her, and she knew there was nothing to do but shake her head.

Jesse was the first to break down. He began to sob, pulling Cap's muzzle closer into his folded arm and kissing the horse on its blood-streaked snout.

"No," Camilla was saying. "No, no, no, there must be something you can do. You're a vet. You help animals every day—"

"Not like this," Kris told her.

Camilla closed her eyes and pressed her balled-up fists against her forehead. "But he's the last thing we have! Don't you understand? He's the last we have of her!"

Kris did not respond. There was nothing to do except give them their moment of unbridled grief. That was the most anyone in this situation could be granted.

Kris and Ben stood in silence, listening to the awful sobs of shattered parents and the quick, wheezing breaths of a dying creature.

"He's a fighter," Camilla croaked.

"But he's not going to win," Kris told her. "He's in your hands now. I know you didn't ask for this. But there's no other way. You have to let him go."

Camilla slowly shook her head, but Kris knew it was not a rejection of what she had said. It was Camilla's reluctant acceptance of a situation over which none of them had any control. The destruction of flesh they saw before them was the work of something bigger, something so removed from its own creation that it had become alien. When it looked down, it saw nothing more than scurrying insects.

Whoever lets things like this happen never knew pain, Kris thought.

As if sensing the decision that had been made on his part, Cap gave a resigned snort and rubbed his nose against Jesse's arm. Fresh tears flowed down Jesse's cheeks, dripping down onto the horse's cheek.

"Mommy?"

The child's voice broke through the moment like a gunshot on a still night.

Sadie was on the other side of the fence. Her hands were clasped in front of her as if to show obedience even as she clearly ignored her mother's one order.

"Sadie, go back to the car," Kris told her.

"What's wrong with the horse? Is he sick?"

"Go back to the car!"

"I'll take her." It was Jesse. He carefully set Cap's head down onto the trampled grass, gave the animal one last, loving stroke on its muzzle, and then he stood, resting his hands on his knees to keep his unsteady legs from buckling.

"Stay," Kris said.

But Jesse simply shook his head and trudged through the rain-slicked weeds, toward the fence.

Ben pulled up the second row of barbed wire like a bowstring. He planted his boot on the bottom two rows and shoved them down, creating a gap just large enough to slip through.

Jesse ducked down low, careful not to snag the back of his sweat-shirt on the twisted barbs. And then he was once again on the other side. He took Sadie's hand.

"Let's go, sweetie."

Kris watched as Jesse led her daughter off into the darkness, toward the Jeep. Sadie glanced back over her shoulder, and Kris mustered up a small smile, just to let her know it was okay.

Then Kris turned to Ben. She did not need to ask him again. She knew what his answer would be. She pointed to the Glock holstered at his side.

"Give it to me," she whispered.

Ben slowly shook his head.

"I'm gone at the end of the summer. There's no reason you should have to live here with this," she told him.

Ben's hand went to his sidearm. He took a deep breath, his chest heaving, then it fell as he exhaled.

"I can do it," he said.

"You have to have a steady hand—"

"I can do it." There was desperation in his voice. *I need to do it* is what Kris heard.

She turned and called over, "Come on, Camilla."

Camilla did not move. She was staring down at the bloody offense of Cap's shredded belly.

"Camilla," Kris called, louder.

"I'm staying," Camilla said softly.

Ben let out a sigh of objection. "You don't want to see this."

Camilla's voice rose, even as her gaze remained down on the suffering beast. "Poppy loved this horse, Ben." The breeze picked up just then, blowing strands of Camilla's long black hair across her face. They stuck to her tear-streaked cheeks. "She can't be here with him. But I'm here. And I'm staying. This time, I get to say good-bye."

Silent understanding fell over Kris and Ben.

Ben slipped his fingers to the holster strap and popped it loose. He slipped the gun free, keeping the barrel pointed safely down at the ground.

With her finger, Kris pointed toward the horse, tracing an invisible line across Cap's forehead.

"Draw a line from one ear to the opposite eye, then do the same with the other, and put the bullet right in the middle of the X," she told Ben.

He nodded and adjusted his grip on the Glock's handle. "You two step back and cover your ears."

Kris and Camilla did what they were told, although Kris stayed one step in front, hoping to block some of Camilla's view.

I'm sorry, she wanted to say. *I'm so, so sorry. This shouldn't be happening. None of this should have happened. Cap should be okay. Poppy should be with you.*

Over her shoulder, Kris saw Camilla press her fingers against her ears. Kris did the same, and the noise around them took on the sound of soft crunching, like boots in snow.

Ben wrapped his other hand around the first to steady the gun. His finger slid across the trigger as the barrel came up.

For an unbearable moment, he did not move. Kris thought he was going to back out, that she was going to have to do the deed after all, when without warning, Ben took two quick steps forward and pointed the gun directly at the center of Cap's forehead.

The horse seemed to sense the inevitable. He turned his wide, panicked eyes up toward Ben and slowly blinked his beautiful lashes once, as if to tell Ben that he understood what was about to happen. Cap's nostrils flared as he expelled a tired breath.

Kris saw the flash of fire explode from the gun a split second before she heard the sound. She watched as Cap's front legs jerked involuntarily, his hooves clicking. She let her fingers slip from her ears, and she could hear the gunshot echoing away into the darkness that had settled over the rain-slicked town.

The horse's eyes stared up into nothingness. There was a streak of red blood, like splattered paint, cutting across the lightning bolt of white just above his nose.

Behind her, Camilla began to bellow.

Kris knew she should turn around and offer words of comfort. Something. Anything to try to ease the woman's pain. But she could not look away from that streak of blood above Cap's muzzle. The tall-grass swayed slowly in the breeze around the horse's motionless body.

Reholstering his gun, Ben marched past Kris to Camilla. He caught her in his arms just as her legs gave out. Camilla gripped tightly to the back of his uniform as if she were afraid Ben would let her go and she would fall, fall, fall forever into her grief.

"It's over," he whispered over and over in her ear. "It's over. It's over."

Nothing about this feels over, Kris thought. Without a word, she spun around, the wet ground mushing under her shoes as she moved quickly to the fence. She crouched down to pass between the lines of barbed wire. One of the barbs grazed the back of her head and tugged at her hair. She gave her head a quick shake, and the lock came loose. When she was sure she was clear of the rusty barbs, she straightened up and walked briskly over the soaked grass and onto the gravel drive, attempting to leave the tragedy behind her. But there was no escape.

When Kris reached the Jeep, Sadie was already in the back seat. Jesse stood beside the closed door, his arms folded tightly across his chest. He was shaking as if bitten by a gust of cruel winter wind. His tear-streaked cheeks glistened in the light of the Auto Barn's security lamps.

Kris came to an abrupt stop. She reached out and grasped Jesse's forearm, squeezing it desperately.

He slipped a hand over hers, gripping her hand so tightly that the knuckles of his fingers turned bone white.

Kris's vision began to swim. Tears flooded to the edges of her bottom eyelids, but she pushed them back. This was not her pain. This moment was not for her.

The tears receded. Her vision cleared.

A face was staring out at her from within the dark car.

It was Sadie, her image distorted by the rain-streaked glass.

She was smiling.

PART FOUR

MOTHERS OF THE DISAPPEARED

CHAPTER TWENTY-NINE

KRIS MADE THE appointment with Dr. Alice Baker for ten on Friday morning, two days after that horrible night at the Auto Barn. Kris had hoped to get Sadie in earlier, but the receptionist at the main office in Emporia informed her that Dr. Baker would not be back at her Pacington office until then. And so Kris had no choice but to wait.

She did her best to keep Sadie occupied until her appointment. They stayed out of the lake house as much as possible, taking walks in the woods or playing board games on the deck. Yet she often caught Sadie glancing back at the house, staring at the windows as if something were standing inside, just out of sight. She saw the longing in Sadie's eyes, that desire to leave her mother and return to her games. Kris had to constantly remind herself that no one was watching them. She could not let herself be pulled into the little girl's fantasy.

Part of her hoped, when she was looking across the cove, that she would see the dark-haired woman standing on her back deck, watching them, as motionless as a statue. But if the woman was there, she was tucked away in her cabin, peering out from the shadows.

The Xanax helped, although it wouldn't for long. She could count the number of pills left on one hand. She was careful not to overdo it, only allowing herself one pill per day. Yet every time she swallowed one, it felt like a clock had ticked one minute closer to midnight.

On Friday morning, they left the lake house at eight o'clock and drove into town for a leisurely breakfast at Patty's Plate. The presence of others comforted Kris. The smell of bacon and biscuits, the clank of silverware on mismatched plates, the murmur of morning chatter—it was all a constant reminder that real, live people shared their world.

Sadie held her mother's hand as they walked down the street to Dr. Baker's office. Soon the red-framed doorway to Clear Water Counseling materialized from the tan brick of the other buildings lining Center Street.

As had happened several times since arriving in town, Kris was overwhelmed with the odd sense that she was experiencing a memory but from someone else's point of view. She was her father, walking a little red-haired girl to the doctor's appointment.

She felt something tugging at her, trying to slow her down, and she realized it was Sadie's grip on her hand growing increasingly tighter.

"There's nothing to be nervous about," Kris told her.

"What if I don't feel like talking?" Sadie's words were like timid little mice anxious to flee back down her throat.

"Then you don't have to talk. But listen . . ." Kris knelt down so that she was eye to eye with her anxious daughter. "When I was your age, I talked to Dr. Baker."

She saw Sadie's scrunched-up expression loosen just a bit.

"I was going through something pretty scary, too. My mommy was really sick and . . . and she died, and I was really sad, so my daddy thought talking to Dr. Baker might help."

"Did it?"

Kris nodded. "Yeah. It did. Dr. Baker is really nice. I think you're going to like her."

For a moment, neither of them moved. A few people drifted down the sidewalk, stepping around them with curious glances.

And then Sadie nodded.

"Okay," Kris said.

She let Sadie step through the doorway first, following closely behind as they moved carefully up the steep staircase. At the top was a small landing. To their left was a door with a large pane of frosted glass at its center. A flaking decal was peeling away from the other side. It featured a yellow sun rising over a body of blue water. Beneath this, several letters were missing from the decal announcing the name of the practice as "C—ar –at-r Co-ns—ing."

Kris raised a hand to knock, then paused, her own nerves fluttering like butterflies in her chest. She rapped lightly on the frosted glass.

Inside, a blurry shape moved by. A friendly voice called, "Come on in!"

Kris paused, giving Sadie's hand a little squeeze. "There's nothing to be scared of, okay?"

Sadie nodded, but her pale cheeks blushed pink and her eyes tilted down to stare at her shoes.

Kris opened the door.

Alice Baker was sitting in a chair upholstered with green-and-cream fabric featuring a menagerie of small woodland creatures. There was no waiting room. No receptionist. The door opened directly to a second-floor loft. On the wall facing Center Street, narrow windows ran from floor to ceiling. They were flanked on either side by thick, wine-colored curtains. These had each been drawn back and tied with a length of three-strand cotton rope, allowing the sunlight to fall in diagonal lines across the wood floor. The other walls were lined with heavy oak bookshelves, each shelf filled from end to end with medical journals, leather-bound novels, and random knickknacks—a Golden Gate Bridge snow globe, a small plate with a hand-painted illustration of Peter Rabbit fleeing Farmer McGregor's garden.

Kris took in a breath through her nose in an attempt to steady her own jangling nerves, and in that air she smelled something at once familiar and foreign. That single inhalation was a time machine, flinging her back to the moment when her father opened this very door and ushered her inside. It was an odor of leather and old books, of sunshine and dust, laced with the slightest hint of a sweet floral perfume.

Dr. Baker smiled warmly and rose from her chair. She was tall, a good five inches over Kris's own height of five six. As she watched Dr. Baker cross the room, she was hit with an image from her childhood of staring up at the doctor and thinking this was the tallest, most powerful woman she had ever seen.

"Kris?" Dr. Baker asked.

"Yes. Kris Barlow."

Barlow was Jonah's name, the voice in her mind scolded.

"I mean, Parker. It was . . . it was Kris Parker. Before I was married. I don't know if you remember, but I came to see you when I was little . . ."

There was a moment of confusion as Dr. Baker tried to connect the name to a long-forgotten memory. And then her eyes widened, her face growing even brighter. "Oh my, yes, of course I remember!" There was a slight quaver in her voice. "Kris! Why didn't you say something when you set the appointment?"

Kris shrugged. "I . . ." she began, only to realize she had no explanation. Perhaps there was part of her that was afraid to tell Dr. Baker.

You can tell her anything, she heard her father say.

Dr. Baker reached out and took one of Kris's hands in both of hers, giving it a pleasant squeeze. "Look at you. All grown-up. It seems like yesterday . . ." Then her expression changed, just slightly, allowing for a hint of concern. "How are you?" The question did not seem like mere pleasantry. It was an invitation to speak honestly.

"We've been better," was all Kris would say.

Dr. Baker nodded, understanding. She looked down at the shy redheaded girl standing at Kris's side. "Oh my goodness. This must be Sadie."

Kris nudged Sadie softly with her hip. "Say *hi*."

Sadie waved hesitantly and said, "Hello," in a voice as sweet and perfect as a gently pressed piano key.

"Well, Sadie," Dr. Baker said, "I wonder if you could help me with something." She motioned to a nearby shelf, upon which sat a small wicker basket. "I have some art supplies over there, colored pencils and crayons and notebooks. Do you think you could get them out for me and set them on the coffee table? Later, we can do some coloring."

Sadie nodded obediently. She slipped away from her mother and crossed to the shelf, removing the items from the wicker basket one by one.

Dr. Baker looked from Sadie to Kris, her eyes widening in exaggerated shock.

Kris nodded. "I know. She looks just like me."

"Exactly," Dr. Baker said in awe. "It's as if you walked in here after, what? Thirty years? And you hadn't aged a day."

They watched as Sadie leaned over the basket and collected loose pencils, putting them in a small pile on the floor.

"What is she doing that has you worried, Kris?" Dr. Baker asked, her voice low so Sadie couldn't hear.

Kris sighed, unsure of how much to unload on the doctor in this moment. She briefly filled Dr. Baker in on Jonah's death and her decision to spend the summer at the lake house, away from the constant reminders of their loss. She talked about her hope that this would be a time of healing.

"Just looking at her, you'd think it was working," Kris explained. "She acts happy most of the time. She's smiling and laughing. And *talking*. Right after Jonah's death, she barely said a word to anyone. Now she acts like she's forgotten all about the accident. She seems to love the lake house. Loves playing there. But . . ."

Dr. Baker gave Kris the time she needed to continue.

"She's always been a creative kid. And I know how important that can be, especially at times like this. But she's spending more and more time alone. *Playing* alone. I'm starting to think maybe I should try to find other kids in town because it seems like . . . like she's pretending to play with someone."

There was a slight change in Dr. Baker's expression. Perhaps her eyes narrowed just the tiniest bit, or her head tilted a half inch to the right. Kris could not be sure. But she felt as though the doctor were staring at her with a new sense of scrutiny.

"What are you talking about?" a soft voice asked them.

Sadie was back. She stared up at them as if waiting for an answer. Behind her, the art supplies were stacked neatly on the coffee table.

"Just catching up," Dr. Baker said. Crouching down so that they were on the same level, she looked directly into Sadie's eyes. "I knew your mother when she was about your age. She was a very special little girl. But she was going through kind of a scary time. Did she tell you about that?"

"A little bit," Sadie said.

"Well," Dr. Baker explained, "sometimes when we feel a little scared or worried, it's good to talk to other people. And sometimes it's easier to talk to someone who isn't your mommy or a close friend. That's why you're here today. I'm a doctor, but not like the kind that looks down your throat or gives you shots. I'm like—"

"A talking doctor," Sadie said suddenly.

The words caught Kris off guard. She searched for any recollection of telling Sadie this nickname for Dr. Baker.

From Dr. Baker's knowing smile, it wasn't the first time someone had referred to her as the "talking doctor."

"That's right," she said. "And that's why you're here. Just so we can talk. Is that okay?"

Sadie seemed to take the question very seriously. For a moment, she did not respond as she thought it all over. Then she gave a little nod.

Dr. Baker's smile widened. "Good. Good."

"So . . . should we sit down?" Kris asked.

"Actually," Dr. Baker said, rising up so she could lean in close to Kris's ear. She lowered her voice to a hush. "I would like to speak to Sadie alone, if you don't mind." She must have sensed the wave of uneasiness that washed over Kris, because she quickly added, "I find that children speak more freely when they don't have to worry about pleasing their parents."

Kris considered this briefly, then nodded. "Yeah. Yeah, of course."

She swept a finger across Sadie's cheek, tucking a few stray curls behind her ear. "I'm going to step out for a little bit, and you stay with Dr. Baker, okay?"

"Mommy—" Sadie muttered nervously.

"It's fine, I promise. I won't go far. I'll be back before you know it."

Dr. Baker motioned to an overstuffed leather couch opposite her chair. "We can talk about anything you want, Sadie. You can sit or you can lie down or you can jump on the couch for all I care. Just don't jump up to the ceiling fan. I'm tall, but I don't think I could get you down from there."

Sadie pursed her lips as she fought a smile.

The reaction was exactly what Dr. Baker had hoped for. She turned to Kris and said in a reassuring voice, "We'll be okay."

"Okay," Kris said, as if repeating the word made it all the more real.

She watched as Dr. Baker took Sadie's hand and led her to the couch. Turning back, the doctor mouthed, "Ten forty-five," to Kris.

Without another word, Kris turned to the office door and opened it. She paused just long enough to glance over her shoulder.

Sadie was standing before a large framed black-and-white photograph of a handsome African American man in his forties.

"That was my daddy," Dr. Baker explained. "He died when I was just a little older than you. I missed him very much. I still do. Missing people and being sad is part of remembering. That's our job, once they're gone. Our job is to remember."

For one brief moment, Kris was back in the cold steel room of the coroner's office, Jonah's smashed face staring over the top of the black plastic sheet.

And then she was stepping out onto the landing, Dr. Baker's office door closing behind her with a soft click.

CHAPTER THIRTY

PATTY'S PLATE WAS deserted save for a smattering of lone diners scraping forks across yellow smears of wet yolk and crunching on butter-slathered toast, whiling away their morning in anticipation of an equally uneventful afternoon.

At a small square table in the corner, Kris sipped a cup of lukewarm coffee that tasted like it had been brewed the day before. She watched two new mothers seated near the front windows as they attempted to squeeze in some "girl time" while obsessing over every move, every sound made by their newborn babies. Their youth seemed strangely out of place.

They held their infants and their coffees with equal adoration. The babies squirmed, every object and movement drawing their attention. Kris remembered those days. Despite Sadie's fussiness, there were still moments when she would snuggle into Kris's shoulder, her smooth, little nose pressed into the crook of her mother's neck, and Kris would close her eyes, listening to the gently lapping tide of Sadie's slow, content breaths.

Remember this, Kris would tell herself in those moments. *Remember this feeling. This love is all that matters.*

Jonah loved the quiet times, too, lying on the couch with infant Sadie stretched across his chest. For Jonah, those twenty or thirty minutes of calm were like teasing glimpses of how he had imagined every moment of parenthood should be. In his mind, an inconsolable baby was like a new washing machine that somehow always knocked itself off balance. The baby should "work right" all the time, not intermittently.

When Jonah would finally give up and leave the swaddled, wailing child in the Pack-N-Play they had assembled in the living room, Kris would scoop Sadie up and hold her just as closely as she did during more peaceful times when the baby was quiet and sleepy.

No, she corrected herself. *Closer.*

When your child is upset, you hold them closer.

So why did she feel further away from Sadie than ever before?

Because she's happy, her shadow whispered with a grin. *And you hate her for that.*

Kris forced the thought away. She checked her watch. 10:12. Two minutes had gone by since she sat down. She pictured Sadie alone in a strange room with a woman she had just met. Sadie was not a particularly outgoing kid even before Jonah's death. Kris wondered if she had spoken a single word in the last twelve minutes.

Dr. Baker has a way . . .

Yes, she did. Kris knew this firsthand. She hadn't wanted to talk about her mother, but Dr. Baker made her feel comfortable. She made young Kris feel safe. And Kris had opened up. She had told the doctor everything.

Dr. Baker could help them. She could get them back on track.

This summer will be good, she told herself.

This summer was not a mistake.

We are supposed to be here.

As if surfacing from a dream, Kris became aware of squeaking rubber soles inching toward her. She looked up.

Doris, the same waitress who had waited on Kris and Sadie during their first breakfast in town, was heading toward her, grinning over a carafe of steaming coffee clutched in one hand. She smiled, those red clown-like lips pulled back to reveal a smudge of lipstick across her front teeth.

"Freshen that up for ya?" she asked, not waiting for a reply before filling Kris's mug to the rim. Without turning her head, she glanced at the empty chair opposite Kris.

"Where's the little one?" she asked.

"It's just me today," Kris told her, hoping this non-answer would suffice.

"Ah," Doris said, nodding as if she knew something Kris didn't.

For a few seconds too long, Doris stared curiously at that empty seat. Then she shuffled away, passing the young mothers and their babies without as much as a glance, leaving the odor of old coffee and floral perfume in her wake.

The sound of the bell over the front door drew Kris's attention. A woman had just entered the diner, her back to Kris as she surveyed the many available tables with an inexplicable hesitation. There was something instantly familiar about her. The richness of her skin. The long, straight hair flowing down her back. The worn-in blue jeans and dusty cowboy boots.

Camilla, Kris realized.

She felt her grip tighten on the handle of her coffee mug. She suddenly wanted to be anywhere else in the world. She wanted to escape without being seen, to fade into the wall like a forgotten spirit.

But her gaze was locked on Camilla. She could not look away.

The easy joy that Camilla had exuded when Kris first met her at the Auto Barn was gone. Deep shadows hung below her dark brown eyes. Her shoulders were slumped forward in an attempt to protect herself from everything around her.

Look away, Kris's mind commanded.

But she couldn't.

Camilla scanned the room, her eyes finally falling upon Kris in the corner, watching.

There was a moment, brief yet unbearably powerful, like the splitting of an atom, when the women stared straight into each other's eyes and recognized the icicle that had been driven into each of their hearts. They were joined by the hurt life had inflicted upon them. They were sisters in sadness.

Camilla tried to muster up a smile to pretend like this were any normal run-in on any normal day.

"How's the tire working out for you?" she called over.

"It's . . . it's good. Still full of air."

Camilla gave a sharp laugh, the ridiculousness of the comment cutting through the tension. "Well, that's good since, you know, that's pretty much its only job."

"Yeah." Kris fell silent, unsure of what to say next. She took a sip of her coffee and glanced nervously over at the table where, moments before, the two mothers had attempted to chat while fumbling with their infants. They were gone. The table had been cleared, the silverware reset. It was as if, without Kris's attention to bind them to this world, they had vanished into thin air.

"I wanted to thank you." Camilla's voice was suddenly, startlingly close.

Kris turned to find her standing a few feet away.

"You know, for the other night. I know there was nothing you could do, but . . . I appreciate you being there. It was . . ."

Camilla's voice faded away, trailing off into the dark ether of memory.

Kris reached out and rested her fingertips on Camilla's surprisingly cold hand. She felt Camilla jerk slightly at the touch; then her body relaxed, the tension in her neck and shoulders seeming to loosen just a bit. Her eyes were instantly brimming with tears begging to be released. But she held them back. She was not ready to let them go. Not yet.

Camilla shook her head sharply to chase away the overwhelming emotions. She spotted the empty chair opposite Kris and realized this was her escape from the subject.

"Where's Sadie?" she asked, forcing a brightness into her words.

Kris was beginning to resent the empty seat across from her. She fumbled for a response. "Oh, um, she's . . ."

With the shrink. Because she can't talk to her mother, because her mother has failed her.

"Down the street," she said finally.

Camilla nodded as if that vague detail answered everything. "Well, you want some company? I mean, we're both here. Seems kinda silly to sit alone pretending the other doesn't exist."

"Yeah," Kris replied without giving the question much thought. "Yeah, absolutely. That would be nice."

Camilla slipped into the empty seat. She had barely settled into the chair when Doris reappeared without even the squeak of her shoes to announce her.

"Get ya something, Camilla?"

"Just a hot tea. English breakfast," Camilla said. "Thank you."

As it had done with the empty chair, Doris's gaze hung a moment too long on Camilla, her lips frozen in a smile, that smudge of lipstick peeking out like blood on bone.

"Thank you, Doris," Camilla said forcefully.

Doris's smile widened, a much too toothy grin that revealed the bottoms of gray gums. Then she was off to fetch the tea.

"Is Jesse working?" Kris asked, trying to start a conversation.

"No. He's . . ." Now it was Camilla's turn to grasp for an explanation. ". . . on a walk. He likes to get away from the shop sometimes to, you know, clear his head."

Doris returned long enough to deliver Camilla's tea, and then the two women fell silent, sipping their drinks.

Kris checked her watch. 10:16.

This was not lost on Camilla. "I'm sorry," she said. "I invited myself over here and—"

"No. Really. It's okay."

Camilla gave a long, exhausted sigh. "Truth is, I don't really feel like talking, but I also didn't feel like being alone."

"I totally understand," Kris assured her. She took a breath, opening her mouth to speak, then paused.

You can trust her, she told herself optimistically. She was surprised by how much she wanted to believe this.

"Actually," Kris said, lowering her voice, "I'm waiting on Sadie. She's down the street. With Dr. Baker."

There was a subtle but unmistakable reaction from Camilla. Her expression actually seemed to lighten, as if hearing that someone else had problems made her own feel just a tiny bit less suffocating.

Kris did not judge her for this. She understood perfectly. There was something comforting in knowing that you were not the only one being unfairly punished by fate.

"Is everything okay?" Camilla asked.

Kris wanted to say "yes." She wanted to lie and say that everything was fine. She yearned to turn the conversation to innocuous chatter about books and movies and the weather in June in Southeast Kansas.

Camilla sensed her apprehension. "You don't have to tell me if you don't—"

"My husband died in a car accident." The words seemed to explode from her lips like a bubble bursting. The release was strangely exhilarating.

She seemed to fall back away from her own body as she continued, listening to herself tell Camilla about the night the highway patrolman called her and the unbearable moments she waited for Sadie to wake so she could tell her daughter that Daddy would never come home. She heard the entire story pouring from her mouth in a great, uncontrollable torrent. She watched as Camilla's tea cooled, forgotten. Kris left some details out, of course. There was no reason to tell this stranger that she no longer loved her husband, that his death did not seem so much a tragedy as it did karma. But she did tell Camilla about Sadie's breakdown, and the moment after Cap's death when Kris realized her daughter needed help. Real help.

When Kris was done, she stared into Camilla's ashen face and thought, *She's going to tell you that she's sorry. She's going to say that she feels so bad that your life went to shit and that Sadie is a mess, and then she's going to make an excuse to leave, and the next time you pass her on the sidewalk, she will pretend she doesn't see you.*

Instead, Camilla said, "You need to get your daughter out of this town."

CHAPTER THIRTY-ONE

KRIS HURRIED DOWN the sidewalk along Center Street, but she felt like she was moving in slow motion. She was late to pick up Sadie, but an invisible rope was tethered around her waist, pulling her back to that table at Patty's Plate and the words of Camilla Azuara spoken in a hushed yet straightforward voice.

"There is something wrong with this place."

She could still see the fear on Camilla's face as she began to tell her tale.

"When we moved here, we didn't have kids," Camilla had said. "We weren't sure we even wanted them. We thought we could get the garage up and running. Turn it into a successful business. Maybe open another one in another town. Eureka or Yates Center or Cherryvale. And then I got pregnant, and before we knew it, we had our little girl, and Jesse and I couldn't imagine being complete without her.

"You know when you're a kid and you tie a string between two cans, and when you talk into one end, your voice travels down the string to the other side? Well, that's how it felt with her. She was the string that connected our hearts, and we were suddenly hearing each other in ways we never had before. She made our world more real than it had ever been.

"At the time, Jesse had a dog, an old bird dog named Speck. Jesse doesn't really hunt much anymore, but back then, he would go out every other weekend to hunt pheasant or quail. Speck was a good dog but he was a worker, not really a member of the family. He was an outside dog. Until we had our baby girl. The second Speck saw her, he became her protector. He would howl at night until we let him inside, and then he would curl up below her crib and stay there until morning. When our baby girl was old enough to sleep in a toddler bed, Speck would stretch out on the floor beside her. They were best friends.

"But Speck was an old dog—Jesse had had him since high school—and right around our girl's eighth birthday, Speck started eating less and sleeping more. Eventually his kidneys failed, and we had no choice but to put him down. Our sweet girl was devastated. She would take his collar to bed at night and curl up with it and cry. We'd never seen her so upset. But I guess it makes sense. Her best friend was dead. We shouldn't have expected her to just accept it.

"But then the crying got worse, to the point where we had to pull her out of school. She couldn't seem to snap out of it. We even took her to see Dr. Baker. Jesse hates shrinks and was totally against it, but I mean, what choice did we have?

"It helped for about a week, and then one night I heard her crying. She was in bed, curled up with Speck's collar clutched in her hand. She had the metal tags pressed against her lips.

"That was the first night she heard the song."

The memory made Kris's legs tremble, and she was barely able to make it to a wooden park bench at the corner of Center and Ash Street before they gave out completely.

The song.

Camilla could not describe it beyond that. Her daughter had mentioned it in those generic terms. It seemed to be a melody only she could hear.

"She told us the song was coming from the lake," Camilla had said, her eyes glistening with fresh tears. "She had such an imagination, always drawing and painting and making up stories. We thought it was just another one of her stories, you know? And she seemed happier. She still had Cap, and she would spend all day riding him, giving him kisses, hugging him. She was smiling again, but . . . when I think back on it . . ."

At this, a tear had spilled over the lid of Camilla's left eye and streaked down her cheek. She quickly wiped it away. She glanced nervously around, as if sensing the eyes of the other patrons upon her. Yet no one was watching. They were as good as alone at the table in the corner.

"I think of the *way* she smiled, and it was like when she knew her birthday or Christmas was coming up, like . . . like she was excited about something.

"One day we walked down to Jefferson Park, right by the lake. I remember the closer we got, the more excited and chatty she became, and I thought, 'She's finally over Speck's death. She's our sweet, happy Poppy again.'"

Hearing her name had made Kris's stomach clench painfully into a tight ball. She closed her eyes and Hitch was there, standing in the Book Nook, holding up four fingers. *Poppy Azuara. Four years ago this August. Poppy was with her parents over in Jefferson Park when she wandered off . . .*

The chatter of the other patrons, the clink of coffee cups, the ring of the cash register, all of the sounds of Patty's Plate had faded to silence. There had only been the voice of a grieving mother as she attempted to make sense of the unfathomable.

"We looked everywhere," Camilla had insisted. She was no longer talking to Kris. "The entire town looked for her. In the woods. On the lake. We went door-to-door, checking every single house, praying that she'd wandered into someone's yard and was found. I even started to hope she had been taken. How fucking awful is that? I remember there was a man named Charles . . . Charles something who took a girl from her front yard in Yates Center a few months before, but the police bungled the case and he went free. And I started thinking maybe Charles What's His Name was passing through town and stopped at the Pig Stand for a bite and he snatched up Poppy. I *wanted* that to be true. Because at least it meant she could still be alive. She could still be somewhere close, where we could find her. But she wasn't anywhere. She was just gone. How do you look away for one second and a little girl just disappears? How the hell does that *happen?*"

There on the bench at the corner of Center and Ash, occasional morning traffic cruising slowly by, Kris buried her face in her hands and wept. She wept for Camilla and Jesse Azuara. She wept for Poppy, still missing after four painful years. She wept for the other girls, for Ruby and Sarah and Megan. And she wept for the question she had forced herself to ask Camilla, the one she could not take back:

"Do you know . . . what happened . . . to the others?"

Camilla had nodded. Yes.

"We didn't know anything about them when we first moved here. No one said a word, and why would they? But when Poppy . . . Well, that's when we started to hear about the other girls. Everybody said there was no connection. But the way people looked at us, it was like we reminded them of something they had tried hard to forget."

Camilla's voice had dropped to a whisper so faint, Kris had to lean halfway over the table to hear it.

"Ruby Millan was the first. She was missing for over a week. She was there when her parents went to bed but in the morning, she was just . . . gone. Everyone assumed she had been kidnapped. It was the '80s, you know, faces on milk cartons and that movie, *Adam,* on the TV. Everyone was terrified their child would be the next to be snatched. Maybe that's why they didn't really bother searching the woods. It wasn't until a hiker took a wrong turn off the trail leading through Blanton's Pass that Ruby was finally found. She was—"

Camilla had swallowed hard, her throat trying to prevent the words from escaping.

"She was curled up in a hollow tree and she was looking out like . . . like she *expected* to be found. People said she still had a smile on her face."

A shudder had rocked Kris's body. She had tried not to picture the scene, but her mind was determined to form the image. A little girl's corpse, cheeks pressing against taut, sunken skin, eyes wide and staring from lidless sockets, lips pulled tight over baby teeth in a frozen grin.

"The police," Camilla had continued, "they assumed she had been dumped, but there was no sign of trauma. No wounds. No bruising."

At that point, Kris had begun to regret her question. Shame flooded through her. She started to say, "You don't have to—"

But the story poured from Camilla, just as sweat pours from flesh when a fever breaks. "It was like Ruby crawled into the hole in that tree and just stayed there until she died."

The tree, Kris had realized in that moment. *A hollow tree. Like the oak tree where you played. The Wishing Tree.*

Kris had wanted to vomit. Her mouth had suddenly filled with saliva. Her skin had gone slick and flushed. She took deep breaths in and out through her nose, in and out, in and out, trying to keep control of her body.

"Sarah Bell was Albert Bell's granddaughter," Camilla had explained. "Do you know Albert Bell? He cuts grass here in town. You've probably seen him in his coveralls, with his edger, cleaning up the weeds along Center. He's been out there every day since he retired. He does it all on his own. Nobody asks him to do it. Nobody pays him." She said it as if Albert's dedication to the town should have been a factor in his granddaughter's fate. "When Sarah went missing, the woods was the first place they checked. A few people in the search party went straight to that oak tree—"

Your tree, her shadow voice purred.

"—but she wasn't there. It wasn't until someone spotted a glittery purple bow dangling from the top of a milkweed plant that they realized they were looking in the wrong spot. They hadn't gone far enough. They should have kept going until they hit the wildflower field just before you get to the lake. You know that spot? Near where you can see the roof of that house poking out of the lake?"

Oh yeah, you know, the shadow at the back of her mind taunted. *Don't you, Kris? Don't you know?*

We used to pretend that was a mermaid's house, she remembered telling Sadie on an afternoon that felt like an eternity ago.

"There was a shallow hole dug in the middle of the field," Camilla explained. "You would have missed it unless you walked straight through the flowers. It was a hole about five feet long, about the size of a child."

Camilla had leaned in closer, her eyes wild, as the story poured out of her.

"It was a grave," she whispered sharply. "And they said it looked like Sarah dug it herself. There was a sharp stick nearby that she had used to start it, and a flat rock she used to dig it deeper. They said she had dirt under her nails and her fingertips were bloody and raw like she'd used her hands to do the rest. They found her there, just lying in that hole with her eyes closed like she had crawled in and gone to sleep. But she wasn't asleep. They said the bees had gotten to her. They were starting to make a hive in her . . . in her mouth . . ."

Camilla's throat had gone dry. She took a long sip of her tea before continuing.

"And a few years before Poppy, there was Megan Adamson."

At this point, Kris had cut her off. She could not bear to hear any more.

"I know about Megan," she had said.

Megan Adamson, her body found at the bottom of the sandstone chasm known as Blanton's Pass, where jagged rocks rose up from the earth like shark's teeth.

The place where Kris had shown Sadie how to wedge a stick between the narrow canyon walls to keep it from devouring you.

Now, at 10:56 in the morning, on a wooden bench in a small town in nowhere Kansas, Kris covered her face with her hands and wished she could forget everything Camilla had told her.

She had played in every one of those places. She could still see herself climbing over the jagged stones. Ducking into the hollow of the oak tree. Counting the bees as they hovered over the blooms in the wildflower field.

She could have been any one of those girls.

Kris felt fingers lightly touch her shoulder, and she flinched.

"Are you okay, sweetie?" It was an elderly woman's voice. Kris could feel her palsied hand twitching slightly.

Kris did not uncover her eyes. She spoke into her hands, "I'm fine."

"Are you sure?" the old woman asked.

"I'm fine. Please. I just need a minute."

"Okay. Okay, honey. You take all the time you need."

For several minutes, Kris focused on the sound of her own breaths, slow and steady and cool in her lungs.

When she uncovered her eyes, the old woman had moved on.

No one was there.

She checked her watch: 11:05.

Leaping up from the bench, she hurried down the rest of the block and across the next street until she found herself in front of the red-rimmed doorway leading up to Clear Water Counseling. She raced up the stairs, taking the steps two at a time.

When she rushed into Dr. Baker's office on the second floor, Kris found the doctor sitting with Sadie on the floor beside the windows looking out onto Center Street. Beside them was a stack of picture books. Sadie was slowly flipping through a book in her hands, her lips moving slightly as she whispered the words to herself.

They both looked up, startled, as Kris barged in.

"Mommy!" Sadie cried, the book instantly forgotten. She hopped up and ran to Kris, wrapping her arms around her mother's waist.

Kris buried her fingers deeply into her daughter's curls. "Oh, baby, I'm so sorry I'm late. I just lost track of time. How was it? Was it okay?"

She felt Sadie's head against her stomach as the girl nodded.

When Kris looked up, Dr. Baker was crossing quickly toward her. Dr. Baker's cheeks were high and shining in a large, warm smile, but her brow was furrowed.

"Kris? Are you all right?" she asked quietly, careful to not alert Sadie.

Kris suddenly imagined what she must look like—eyes wild, face flushed, chest heaving as she tried to catch her breath.

"Yeah, I'm fine. Just . . . realized I was late. I'm okay."

Okay. You're always "okay." Everything's "okay."

"How was she?" Kris asked, motioning to Sadie.

At first, Dr. Baker refused to accept the change of subject. She stared at Kris, her eyes narrowed with concern. Then she blinked, and her expression softened.

"Oh, we had a very nice chat. She's a smart, creative girl. Just like you were when you were little."

Crouching down, Dr. Baker spoke directly to Sadie. "Would you mind giving me a minute with your mommy? Why don't you go back and look at the books? You can borrow one if you want."

Without a word, Sadie slipped away from Kris and quickly crossed the room, back to the stack of books near the windows.

Once more, Dr. Baker's demeanor changed, her lovely face becoming sharper as her jaw clenched.

"I would like to see Sadie again tomorrow, if you'll allow it."

"Tomorrow?" Kris asked. Her pulse quickened.

"I'm in town for a couple more days, and then I'll be at my office in Emporia until next Friday. I really don't want to wait a week to see her again."

Kris could feel her heart thudding. If it pounded any harder, she was sure Dr. Baker would hear it. "Is there something wrong?"

Dr. Baker took a breath, thinking. Her hesitation only served to deepen Kris's anxiety.

"Have you talked to her about when you were here? When you were little?"

"Here?" Kris asked, confused. "You mean when I came to see you—"

"No. No, I mean, when you visited this town with your parents. Have you told her about the summer your mother was sick?"

The memory of the tea party in Sadie's room flashed through Kris's mind, but she did her best to ignore it. "I said she died of cancer, but that's about it. I didn't want Sadie to be scared of the lake house. I wanted her to see it as a happy place."

"But it wasn't a happy place, Kris."

"It was for me. I got to spend time with my mother. To say good-bye."

Dr. Baker cocked her head, eyeing Kris as if she were an exotic animal she had read about but never seen in the flesh. Then she blinked, and her curious expression was gone.

"You know, I see patients of all ages."

"No, that's okay," Kris said before she had a chance to give the invitation any real thought.

"Kris, your husband is gone. For someone who went through what you went through as a child, that has to . . ."

"This is about Sadie."

Dr. Baker pursed her lips. "Well then, as I said, I'd like to see you again tomorrow. Then we can set an appointment for every Saturday while you're here."

"That often?"

Dr. Baker shrugged. "These things take time."

Kris glanced across the room at Sadie, who was slowly turning the pages of a much-too-simple picture book.

She's broken, Kris told herself. *All because of you.*

Dr. Baker must have sensed Kris's unease, for she smiled sympathetically and made a point to add, "I'm not deeply concerned about this, Kris. It's just better to get to the root of her issues now, rather than letting them fester. It's like a bad tooth. In the beginning there might only be mild discomfort. You think you can live with it. But if it's not treated, the infection can spread. It gets in your blood. It gets in your brain. And the damage is done."

CHAPTER THIRTY-TWO

THE SECOND THEY got home from Dr. Baker's office, Sadie prac-tically begged Kris to play hide-and-seek. In any other situation, Kris would have been thrilled by this. But Sadie's behavior was unnerving. It was as if she were on the edge of a manic episode. Her emotions seemed like a great, rushing wave that was about to crash.

"I think you need a nap," Kris told her. "You're exhausted. You're acting—"

Sadie cut her off, screaming, "Why won't you just play with us?" before storming off down the hall and up the stairs to her makeshift playroom.

This type of behavior demanded consequences. But Kris stood motionless in the kitchen, the shadows of leaves playing across the countertops, Sadie's words ringing in her ears:

Play with us.

Beneath her chin, Kris's skin tingled as though an invisible finger were caressing her flesh, lifting her head, drawing her forward. Then, as quickly as it came, the sensation was gone.

Kris hurried through the great room and into the bathroom. She found the pill bottle, twisted off its cap, and watched as the last pill tumbled into her trembling hand. She stared at it with an irritating mixture of disbelief and inevitability. She had known this moment was coming. She had been way too liberal with the meds. What started out as a targeted way to take the edge off had become habit and then . . .

Abuse.

She instantly shook her head at the thought.

No. Carelessness. That's all it was. A need to keep her own anxiety at bay. But that anxiety was worse than ever. Everything around her seemed to be pressing in, suffocating her like an invisible weight on her chest.

You can leave, the timid voice in her mind suggested. *Pack up and go back home. This isn't working. This place can't be saved. It's rotten and it's rotting Sadie and it's going to rot you if you stay any longer.*

She knew this was not a rational thought. This was fear speaking. It was the horror of learning about those poor lost girls and the unnerving feeling that she had somehow been involved even though she knew this was impossible. She had been a teenager in Blantonville when the first girl disappeared. And when the others went missing, she had been off living her life, oblivious to the pain in this town, focusing only on her own path. She knew the places where the girls had been found, but many people did. They were familiar landmarks in these parts. She was sure that most kids who spent more than a few weeks in Pacington eventually found their way to the forest and down to Blanton's Pass or into the hollow of an old oak tree.

The lake house had called to her for a reason. She still believed that. There had to be brighter days ahead. But she could not let herself get lost in town gossip or in Sadie's fantasies.

Easier said than done, she thought as she pushed the last Xanax around in her palm. Her lifeline was fraying. Soon it would snap, and she would drift into the darkness.

It would not be pretty. She would be going off Xanax cold turkey. Her brain's receptors would cry out for the relief they craved, but there would be nothing to feed them. Her mind would become a bundle of raw nerves, a twisted nest of hot wires. The anxiety that the pills had kept at bay for weeks would collapse upon her like a freak thunderstorm on a cloudless day. It would pummel her until she could not breathe. Her stomach would reject anything that was not the medication, forcing back any food or liquid in a rush of hot acid that would singe her throat as it erupted from her mouth.

She had only one true option, no matter how crass and unprofessional it seemed.

Closing her eyes, she cupped her palm over her open mouth and felt the pill drop onto her tongue. She savored its bitterness.

It's an acquired taste.

The thought elicited a sharp, humorless chuckle. Then she swallowed it down.

She left Sadie playing upstairs. With her cell phone clutched in her hand, Kris marched down the back steps and across the stone path to the edge of the bluff overlooking Lost Lake. Everything seemed smaller. The dock was little more than a flaking wood board propped up on rotting posts over the still water. The cove was a narrow sliver off the main body of the lake, the opposite shore closer than she recalled. Even the red hills that met the horizon appeared lower and less impressive, like sloppy piles of unearthed rock on a construction site.

She lifted her phone into the air and checked its signal. Two bars flickered briefly to one, then back again. She hoped the connection would hold long enough for this one brief call.

Allison picked up on the third ring. Her voice was as wonderfully droll as ever, her sense of humor alive and well, but she seemed rushed, as if Kris had caught her at a bad time.

"Is everything okay there?" Kris asked her.

"Yeah. Yeah, of course. Just busy. Nothing to worry about."

Whenever Allison told her not to worry, Kris worried.

She forced herself to push these thoughts away. Whatever was happening at the office, she would deal with in August. She needed to be here, now, tackling one problem at a time.

Kris turned away from the lake house and lowered her voice, even though she knew there was no way anyone—especially Sadie—could eavesdrop on her conversation.

"Hey, I won't keep you. I just needed a favor."

"What's up?"

The story seemed to come from nowhere, but she knew it had been there for hours, maybe days, growing in the darkness.

"There's a couple here that we've gotten to know. Super-sweet. Own the garage in town. And they have this bird dog, a pointer named Speck, that's become more of a family pet. You know how that goes. But he's pretty high-strung. Doesn't take much to spook the poor guy. You should see him during a thunderstorm. Anyway, we were talking and I told them I could probably help them with that . . ."

Allison gave a sharp laugh, and Kris was sure she was about to call bullshit. Then she said, "Jesus, Dr. Barlow, you seriously can't go anywhere without finding some pitiful animal to help."

Kris chuckled, trying to sound at ease, all the while hating herself for the story she had concocted. "Yeah, well, it's a really small town. The closest vet is in Fredonia, I think."

"I'll take your word on that," Allison said. "So what do ya need?"

Kris felt her heart pounding in her chest. She knew there was no reason to worry. This was nothing. There was no way she could get caught. Yet in the fifteen years since starting her practice, she had never crossed a line like this. Not once.

You think this anxiety is bad, wait until the Xanax leaves your bloodstream. Then let's talk.

She pressed the phone closer to her mouth and said in a low but casual voice, "I was wondering if you could overnight me some Prozac. Fifty milligrams twice a day. Let's say a hundred count just to be safe."

"That's a big pointer. Definitely a house dog now. What are they feeding him, cupcakes?"

"Yeah, he's put on some pounds," Kris heard herself say. She suddenly felt far away from her own voice, as if she were back in the darkness, near the small door where her shadow lived. "You can send it to the lake house. 106 River Road. Pacington, Kansas. 67956. Can you get that out today?"

"Yeah, sure."

"Overnight."

"Yeah. No problem." There was a pause, then Allison asked, "Is everything okay, Dr. Barlow? You sound kind of—"

"Everything's as good as it can be, Allison," Kris said sharply, hoping her tone would dissuade Allison from inquiring further. "Thanks for doing this for me. I appreciate it."

She hung up before Allison could respond. She slipped her phone into her back pocket.

On the other shore, a breeze twisted through the weeping willow trees, their drooping branches parting like stage curtains to reveal the back deck of the rustic cabin. The dark-haired woman was not there. Kris could not even sense the woman's prying eyes.

She was completely alone.

Her scalp began to tingle, an unpleasant sensation that started at the top of her head and spread down her neck to her spine. It was as if thousands of fingers were tickling the underside of her skull.

It's already happening. It's the withdrawal, she told herself.

But she knew this could not be true. It was the town and the things she had learned and the creeping feeling that somehow she was a piece of the puzzle.

She saw herself, ten years old, staring over the side of the rowboat as the waves transformed her reflection into the face of a stranger.

The fingertips inside her head pressed harder, and Kris cringed, fighting it, desperate to keep the feeling from overwhelming her.

She was sick of it. The anxiety. The fear. She had come here to escape those things, but it was finally time to admit that this was not the same place she knew as a child. This was not the perfect haven that her mind had trapped in time. It was an abandoned place full of haunted people.

She could not let herself become one of them.

CHAPTER THIRTY-THREE

THE NEXT MORNING, Kris returned to the Book Nook. Hitch was exactly where she had last seen him, standing behind the counter by a stack of books and jotting prices in the corners of pages with a dull pencil. He looked up as Kris entered, and his eyes widened behind the square frames of neon-yellow glasses. His silver hair swooped down like a comma along one side of his oblong face.

"Welcome back, my dear!" he called out as if a lifelong friend had just walked in his door. "Where's the young miss?"

With her shrink.

"With a friend," she said.

Hitch winked as though this had answered everything. "Out on your own, eh? A little Mommy Time."

"Something like that."

Across the room, an elderly man shuffled past a doorway as he scanned the bookshelves. He glanced at Kris but did nothing to acknowledge her. Then he disappeared to the other side of the adjoining room.

Kris crossed quietly to the counter, just as Hitch closed the cover of a romance paperback and added it to his stack.

"What can I do ya for today?" he asked.

Kris glanced quickly at the doorway. The elderly customer was now at the far side of the next room, tracing a shaky finger over the spines of books lined up along a fireplace mantel. Any logs that had once filled the firebox below had been removed to make room for even more books.

Keeping her voice low, Kris said, "I wanted to ask you about something. But I know it's a delicate subject. I don't want to upset you."

Hitch's eyes grew wider, one side of his mouth pulling his thin lips into a mischievous smile.

"And what section should we move to for this conversation? Mystery? Romance? If it's Religion or Politics, I warn you, I may be the one upsetting you. I have some rather *unpopular* views."

"When I was here last time, you were telling me about. . ." Kris checked once more to make sure they were alone. "The girls."

Those two words were enough to wipe the smirk off Hitch's face. His eyes grew grave behind his cheerful yellow glasses.

"Piqued your interest, did I?" he asked.

From the far room, the elderly customer shuffled slowly in, carrying a stack of books resting against his chest.

Kris stepped back to allow the old man access to the counter. She waited as Hitch engaged in friendly chitchat while he rang up the man's purchases. The antique register chimed with each amount entered. The drawer shot out with a jangle of loose coins. The books were placed into a paper bag with the Book Nook logo (wooden legs sprouting from the bottom of an open book, giving it the impression of an easy chair) printed on the side. Hitch held it out for the customer to take. He trailed behind as the old man inched his way to the front door, wished him a good day, and pulled the door closed. Hitch twisted the latch, and the dead bolt slid into place. In the door window, he twisted a dangling sign around so that the word "Closed" faced out.

"What are you doing?" Kris asked. She hoped that the flicker of fear she felt could not be heard in her voice.

Hitch turned around, his expression once again grave. He swept that comma of gray hair away from his eyes with fingers that seemed too long for his hand.

"You want to know about the girls, don't you?"

Without another word, he passed through an archway to his right. Kris heard steps creaking as Hitch climbed to the second floor. She looked to the locked door. She could leave. She did not need her questions answered. This was not her town. These were not her problems.

But she did not leave. She stepped through the archway and stared up at the glow of a pale light at the top of the staircase. Then she gripped the bannister and climbed up to where she knew Hitch was waiting.

Kris imagined the second story of the Book Nook would be just like the first, more rooms filled with shelves of aging books. What she found was a narrow hallway with a warped, full-length mirror at one end and two doorways off the left side.

She could see that the far doorway opened to a small bathroom. A window composed of four squares of textured glass let in just enough light to reveal the mess inside: used towels crumpled on the tile floor; a nearly empty tube of toothpaste on the edge of a filthy sink, cap off, a glob of mint-green gel crusting on its mouth, its body squeezed thin and uncurled like a scorpion's tail; a raised toilet lid, its belly speckled with black mildew.

Inside the other doorway, the one closest to her, was a room that appeared to be empty. She could see Hitch standing with his back to her, waiting for her to enter.

She stepped up to the threshold and peered around the corner. It was a bedroom, furnished only with a dresser, a secretary desk and chair, a single nightstand, and a twin mattress on a simple metal frame. The bed was undone, the sheets crumpled at its foot and spilling over onto the floor. On the nightstand, a pile of tabloid magazines threatened to crowd off a tarnished brass lamp. There were several stacks of books placed randomly around the room. Unlike the books downstairs, these appeared to be Hitch's personal collection.

The state of the house's second floor provided a sharp contrast to the impeccably put-together man who lived there. Kris wondered if it meant Hitch put all of his effort into his appearance, or if the man he presented himself as downstairs was merely a facade, if perhaps this was who Hitch truly was on the inside.

The clap of hands made Kris jump. Hitch turned, rubbing his palms together as if preparing to do a magic trick. Her reaction to the upstairs rooms must have been evident on her face, for he offered an awkward smile and said, "Please forgive the state of things. I don't allow many visitors up to my private quarters."

"Of course," Kris said, still caught off guard. "It's. . ."

"A bachelor pad, I know." Hitch clasped his fingers and continued massaging his hands together as if putting on lotion. "I've just never gotten around to properly decorating the place. I guess I keep telling myself it's only temporary, that I am destined for greater things. Someday I will accept that this is my fate, and then. . ."

He twirled his hands out at the room like a sorcerer casting a spell.

Kris took a step into the room. It was bright, at least. Two large windows let in a great amount of sunlight that reflected off the unpainted plaster walls.

"So," Hitch said, getting down to business, "you want to know more about our angels."

Kris's brow furrowed. "Angels?"

"Well, what else could they be, my dear?" He inched back toward the secretary desk, the soles of his leather loafers sliding across the old hardwood floor. "You do believe in angels, don't you?"

Now was not the time Kris wanted to explain her complicated relationship with religion. She had gone to church as a child, although her parents were more the "Christmas Eve and Easter" types. Back then, she liked the idea of a higher power, of mystical forces that bound all living things together. She had believed in heaven and hell and dis-embodied spirits, some who made it to the Great Beyond, others who got lost along the way and wandered through the halls of crumbling mansions and abandoned farmhouses. When her mother died, she told herself that she could feel a presence, as if someone were watching her from far away. But now she was not so sure. Pacington was not a place that felt like it was being observed by benevolent forces. At some point, they moved on, if they had ever existed in the first place. This town was on its own.

Hitch did not wait for Kris to reply.

"You can't have demons without angels," he said. He rested his long fingers on the edge of the secretary desk. "And there is a demon in Pacington. Make no mistake about that."

Hitch turned and grasped two knobs set into the side of the desk. He pulled them, and the desk popped free. He lowered it until the surface of the desk was flat, supported by two metal hinges. Inside were several mail slots and, beneath these, a long, deep drawer. Hitch worked the stubborn drawer from side to side until he could reach inside. From within it, he lifted out a thick scrapbook. The edges of loose papers poked out of its sides. On its cover were classical illustra-tions of angels with feathered wings and flowing white robes.

He set the scrapbook down on the desk, but he did not open it.

"Before I show you what I have here, I want to get one thing straight: this is my *research*. If you want *gossip*, you can go back across the street and talk to Amy Witherspoon." He said the woman's name as if he had just taken a spoonful of strong medicine. "I was born and raised in Pacington. I love this town. And so I have taken on this duty of telling their story."

With that, Hitch opened the scrapbook.

Kris stepped up beside him and peered down at the first page.

Beneath a shiny layer of contact paper, four faces stared back. She recognized one of them instantly. It was the same school photo she had seen online: the innocent, smiling face of Poppy Azuara. Beneath her picture, handwritten on a strip of paper in an elegant script, was her name. A name accompanied each of the other photos. Ruby Millan. Sarah Bell. Megan Adamson. Except for their ages and their shared hometown, there was no obvious connection to make by simply looking at the girls.

Taking a step back, Hitch motioned toward the scrapbook.

"Please," he said.

Kris ran a finger over the edge of the page, digging a fingernail beneath it to lift it up from the others. She hesitated, unwilling to turn it just yet. She took one more look at the faces of those little girls, burning them into her mind. They would be this age forever. They would never grow old, never experience a first kiss, never graduate high school, never have families of their own. Kris thought of the crooked road of her own life and felt guilty for having lived even her worst days.

She turned the page.

Trapped under the contact paper were yellowing newspaper articles. These were not printouts from the internet or copies Hitch had found on microfiche at the Pacington library. He had cut these out by hand from the actual newspapers and meticulously arranged them in his scrapbook.

"Where did you get these?" Kris asked.

Behind her, Hitch was only a voice. "I tried something a little out of the box: I called the newspapers. You'd be surprised how eager they are these days to connect with actual readers. They dug up old copies of the dates I requested and mailed them straight to my door."

Kris leaned in closer to the page. Here and there, a word or sentence was circled in pencil. She thought of Hitch at the counter downstairs, methodically writing prices onto the title pages of used books. She glanced between the articles and found that several circled words appeared in all of them. "Woods." "Forest." "Near Lost Lake." "No evidence of foul play." "Young girl." "Child." "Only child." "Parents." "Father." "Mother." "Gone."

She ran a finger lightly over the clear cover protecting the articles.

"Do these mean something?" she asked.

"Everything means something," the voice of Hitch insisted.

Kris turned the next page and saw the first two words—Woods and Forest—written in large block letters at the center of a sheet of paper.

The next few pages overflowed with articles and photos, some photocopied, some cut from books and newspapers, as well as random thoughts jotted down at odd angles in a feverish scribble.

"The woods. That's where this all begins, wouldn't you say?" Hitch's voice boomed in the small bedroom, echoing between the walls until it seemed his words were her own thoughts as she flipped through the scrapbook. "The forest was here before our little town existed, and it will be here when we're nothing but a memory in the Almighty's mind. And every now and then, the woods like to remind us that we are mere guests. Hikers lose their footing and tumble into ravines. Hunters get a bit too excited about bagging a pheasant and shoot themselves in the leg. Drunks wander away from midnight revelries only to come face-to-face with a mountain lion. Usually these mishaps result in minor injuries. But sometimes the forest demands that a greater price is paid."

Kris turned the next page to find a map of the woods around Pacington, courtesy of the Kansas Forest Service. Down one side of the page was a handwritten list of every type of tree known to grow in the area. Three red Xs marked spots in the section of forest south of town. Kris did not need a key to know what these Xs represented. In her mind, she connected them like a navigator charting a course—from the canyon to the oak tree to the meadow at the edge of the lake. At the bottom of the page, a large question mark had been written in the same red ink and then traced over and over until the paper beneath had begun to tear.

Images flashes across the screen of her mind, so bright and unexpected that she winced as if they had hurt her eyes. Krissy running through the tree. Krissy hiding in the hollow of a gargantuan tree. Holding her breath as someone crept closer. Pale fingers curling around the bark as a voice sang, "Found you!"

As quickly as they appeared, the images were gone, her mind thrashing wildly to get away, to leave them in the darkness.

"Anyone who does even the slightest bit of digging would know that this land never should have been settled." There was pride in Hitch's voice, a need to brag about his accomplishment. "Now I know *you* are familiar with Napoleon Blanton. After all, he gave your hometown its name, after a coin toss of all things. Left up to chance. The same chance, perhaps, that led him through our little neck of the woods, if you'll pardon the pun, in 1871." There was a pause, and then the voice behind Kris said, "That's your cue to turn the page, my dear."

It reminded Kris of the read-along books she enjoyed as a child, the ones with the cassette tape that played while she followed along in the book, the narrator saying, "At the sound of the chime, it will be time to turn the page." But this was not a children's book. What she held in her hands was an obsession. Still, she did as she was told and found, secured under a wrinkled piece of contact paper, a chapter from an unknown book describing surveyor Napoleon Blanton's journey through Southeast Kansas.

"He loaned his name to us as well," Hitch explained, "for the limestone canyon we call "Blanton's Pass." But what most people don't know, what most people don't *bother* to learn, is that Blanton also gave us a warning. He knew there were things in this countryside that could not be explained."

Without warning, a long finger slithered out onto the page. Kris's body stiffened as she realized Hitch was standing directly behind her, reading over her shoulder. He traced a finger over cutout illustrations of what Kris assumed to be supernatural or mythical beings. Under each one was a name written in Hitch's precise penmanship. Dryad. Faun. Wendigo. Acheri. He tapped a spectral ball of light.

"Will-'o-the-wisp. Blanton claimed he followed one through the forest until finally he and his men watched as it sank into the muddy waters of the Verdigris River. He thought it was an omen."

She could feel his chest pressing lightly against her back as he ran his too-long fingers over the contact paper, as if caressing the pages of his beloved scrapbook.

"But we didn't listen, did we? No, not only did we insist on living here, we tried to *thrive.*"

His fingertip slipped under the edge of the page and turned it. A new chapter, the following pages filled with what Kris assumed was similarly disparate research. Near Lost Lake was another collection of history, water-related accidents and creatures said to dwell in lakes and swamps.

Hitch was so close that she could smell his breath over her shoulder, a foul waft of smoke and decay, like wet ashes. She wanted to push away from the desk, to send him toppling backward. But what if there were answers buried here? She told herself that she could tolerate Hitch for a bit longer, just enough time to reach the last page.

Fortunately, at that exact moment, Hitch stepped away, his voice retreating farther back into the room. Kris breathed in the fresh air left in his absence. When she looked down, she found herself staring at the same photos she had seen in the Pacington book she had flipped through that first day in the Book Nook. Only these had been ripped from their spine and preserved under clear plastic like cherished photos in a family album. Here were the men from the Army Corps of Engineers with their cranes and steam shovels, grinning proudly as they prepared to reshape the river to their liking.

Hitch's voice seemed impossibly distant, farther away than she knew the back wall could allow. "There are some things that are meant to be left buried. Sometimes nature itself turns the earth, opens chasms, all to swallow something that should not be. But Man knows better, doesn't he? There is something in us that *needs* to bring these things back into the light. And for what? A little less flooding, as if we know better than the river? A place for our speedboats and Jet Skis, as if everything below the water's surface is supposed to accept the havoc we wreak?"

"What do you think they found?" Kris asked. She was relieved to hear that her voice was steady, showing no trace of her growing unease. "What could this possibly have to do with—"

"It is all connected, *don't you see that?*" Hitch's voice was suddenly shrill, the cultivated ease of his usual tone gone in an instant. Footsteps clomped as he rushed up behind her, once again reaching over her shoulder. His long, slender fingers flipped the pages, faster and faster, Kris's eyes hurrying to catch all of the information as it flashed by.

A new chapter: No Evidence of Foul Play, containing a list of ways to kill someone without leaving any trace. Another chapter: Young Girl and Child, followed by a list of childhood mental disorders, as well as an article from *Psychology Today* entitled "Pedophilia and the Traits of the Psychopath." The chapter entitled Only Child was a strange combination of causes of infertility, the psychology of the only child and reports of infertility in Midwestern communities, caused by tainted groundwater and air pollution.

With each new page, Kris felt herself falling further and further into the mind of a madman. This was not "research." This was obsession.

By the time Hitch reached the final chapter—Gone—Kris's heart was thudding in her chest and a layer of warm, sticky sweat clung to her forehead.

"We take and take and never think about what we must give in return. But a debt requires payment. And we oblige so that we may live in the illusion of prosperity."

The spine of the scrapbook groaned as he forced the last page over. His fingertip slammed down on photos and headlines from the state's bloody past, his voice bellowing their names like a preacher at a revival.

"1863. Innocent boys massacred alongside their fathers as Quantrill burned Lawrence to the ground. 1872. Mary Ann Longcor, buried alive with the corpse of her father by the Bender Family in Cherryvale. 1974. Two sweet children slaughtered along with their parents near Wichita by the man who called himself BTK. Six years ago. Charles Carpenter snatched a child just a few miles from here . . ."

The voice of Camilla Azuara joined in, her words echoing to Kris from that day at Patty's Plate: *Charles What's His Name . . . Charles something . . . who took a girl from her front yard in Yates Center . . .*

"They say he did it when he knew the parents were home. To maximize their pain. Just as he did to three other girls near Kansas City, girls who were never seen again. And he walked free because the law failed us."

Kris shook her head. "This doesn't make sense. These things have nothing to do with each other."

"If you choose to be ignorant to the connection, then you will not see it," Hitch said. "But there is a line to draw between these things. The line is that of our burden. If we accept that our happiness has been on loan, then we will know when it comes time to pay the debt. Or we can let our ignorance—our *arrogance*—blind us. Just as it did that day when the men dug into the earth, and the water rushed up to reclaim what it once owned."

The air around them was completely still, the sunlight warming it until the room was an oven. A bead of sweat sprang from Kris's hairline and streamed down the side of her cheek.

"That's enough. I've seen enough," she said. She attempted to push away from the desk, but Hitch planted the toe of his shoe against the chair leg, holding her in place.

"But you asked about the girls, didn't you? You wanted to know what happened to our angels."

Hitch turned the final page, and Kris's breath caught in her throat.

Tucked lovingly under contact paper was a series of Polaroid photos of houses, first from the street, then from inside, including shots of four different bedrooms. The bedrooms of young girls. Kris knew if she studied them long enough, she would see details that would link each photo to Ruby, Sarah, Megan, and Poppy.

"They paid our debt with their lives." Hitch's voice was so close, she could feel hot breath on the back of her neck.

Once again, Kris tried to shove away from the desk. This time, she found that the chair slid freely backward. She nearly tripped over her feet as she stood and spun around.

Hitch was standing less than a yard away, his eyes dancing in those yellow frames.

"Where did you get those?" Kris asked.

Hitch appeared genuinely confused. "Get . . . I assure you, all of that research is the product of hard work and my own valuable time—"

Kris thrust a finger toward the Polaroids.

"Where did you get *those*? Those are not pictures from news articles. Someone took those."

Hitch seemed to be frozen, as if time had stopped and only Kris was free to move inside this space between seconds. Then he tipped his head back and said, "Ah, yes. Well. When one is attempting to solve a mystery, one must have access to every piece of the puzzle. Surely you understand, or else you wouldn't be here."

"Did you take them?" Kris could feel her flesh recoiling, as if it were trying to slither away from the man before her.

"Yes," Hitch said matter-of-factly.

"How?"

"I went into their homes and I took them. And then I left. They never even knew I was there, thank God. Those families have been through enough."

Sunlight caught in the lens of Hitch's glasses and transformed his eyes into twin suns.

Kris inched away from the secretary desk, but Hitch was directly between her and the open doorway.

"You broke into their houses," she said.

Offended, Hitch put a hand to his chest, those too-long fingers spreading out against his sternum like the tentacles of a sea creature.

"I did no such thing."

Leaning closer, he whispered, "You wouldn't believe how many people leave their doors unlocked these days. Though in their case, what did it matter? Their most precious possession had already been taken."

Kris glanced to the open door. She was sure Hitch planned to block her way. At her sides, she opened her hands, preparing to shove him as hard as she could in the chest, just enough to move him away from the doorway so she could slip through.

Before she could act, he stepped aside voluntarily and motioned toward the hall.

"After you," he said, the perfect gentleman.

Kris kept her pace slow and steady as she made her way downstairs. She half-expected a hand to clamp down on her shoulder and yank her backward, but the assault never came. She was at the front door before she accepted that she was getting away unscathed.

Her fingers found the latch and twisted it. The dead bolt retracted. She opened the front door and felt the salvation of sunlight and wind on her face. She stepped out onto the porch, forcing herself to maintain a sense of calm.

Hitch was in the doorway, his hands pressed against the frame, his oblong face jutting out mere inches as if he were magically bound to the building.

"They all want to forget, you know," he called out. "This town. They want to pretend that nothing bad happened here. But I won't let them forget. Because I remember. Don't be afraid to remember, Mrs. Barlow."

He stepped back, farther into the house.

"Thank you for stopping by," he said in a cheery voice, as if she were any other customer exiting the store. "Please, come again."

Hitch swung the door shut. He turned the sign in the window around from "Closed" to "Open" and offered the world an inviting smile.

Kris wanted to run. Her mind screamed at her to race down the front stairs and leave this awful place behind. Instead she took a breath, exhaled, and slowly walked down the steps one by one, refusing to give Hitch the satisfaction of knowing her fear.

CHAPTER THIRTY-FOUR

KRIS'S PULSE FINALLY steadied as she reached the second-floor door of Clear Water Counseling. She wiped her sweaty hands on the back of her shirt and knocked gently.

The moment the door opened, she could see that something was wrong. Despite Alice's attempt to conjure up her usual friendly smile, the expression seemed, for the first time, completely forced.

"What happened?" Kris asked.

Dr. Baker looked over at Sadie, who was stretched out on the office floor, her hair falling down around her face as she sketched in a notebook with a colored pencil. She was lost in thought, oblivious to the fact that her mother was standing in the doorway.

"Sadie?" Dr. Baker called out, completely ignoring Kris's question.

Sadie added the finishing touches to her picture and shut the notebook. She pushed herself up onto her knees, set the notebook on the nearby coffee table, and then rose to her feet.

Kris leaned in closer to Dr. Baker, anxious to get to the bottom of things before Sadie joined them.

"How did it go?"

"I think we made some progress," Dr. Baker said. Her lips were tight over her perfectly straight teeth.

Stepping up beside her mother, Sadie glanced down at her hand and realized she was still clutching several colored pencils. She made a soft, apologetic sound and held the pencils out.

"Keep them," Dr. Baker told her.

Kris shook her head in protest.

"We have plenty of markers and crayons already—"

Again, Dr. Baker pretended as though Kris had never spoken. She turned to Sadie. "You can color at home. Maybe bring me a picture next time."

She gave Sadie's shoulder a light squeeze, then stepped back, crossing her arms.

"Same time next Saturday?"

Kris stared dumbly at Dr. Baker as her mind tried to push away all other thoughts to comprehend the simple question.

"Yeah," she said finally. "We'll see you then."

With a nod, Dr. Baker turned and walked away.

Careful not to poke herself or her mother with the fistful of sharpened pencils, Sadie slipped out onto the landing and started down the stairs.

"Sadie, wait," Kris said, reaching for the doorknob and pulling the door shut. Just as it was about to close, she happened to glance back into the office.

Dr. Baker was standing beside the coffee table. She was little more than a silhouette against the warm sunlight shining in through the far windows. A glowing halo hovered over the top of her brown hair. She studied Sadie's notebook, now open in her hands.

They rode in silence as the last few houses of Pacington's residential streets disappeared behind them. As they neared Hope Church, she spotted a small playground consisting of a metal jungle gym and a row of swings. She slowed, scanning the area. She could stop, she realized. She could let Sadie play with children her age, maybe make some friends. But the playground was empty. From the weeds growing up around the equipment, it looked like it hadn't been used in some time.

Inside Kris's head, the voices began to chatter away like partygoers eager to spread gossip.

They were talking about you back there.

That's right. That's why Dr. Baker was acting so strangely.

She asked Sadie about you.

Yes, she did. And Sadie told her all about Mommy. She said that Mommy forced her come to this town.

She said that Mommy was too busy fixing up their shithole lake house to play.

She said that Mommy drank too much wine and swallowed pills when she thought Sadie wasn't looking.

I bet Hitch is making a brand-new chapter right now all about you.

Kris hissed through clenched teeth. She wanted to scream at the voices, to tell them to go to hell.

But what if they were right? She had gone to Dr. Baker for help, but what if Sadie had convinced her that Kris was the problem?

What if you are the problem?

She was so lost in these feverish thoughts that she almost missed the turn onto River Road. At the last second, she braked and cranked the wheel to the left. The tires slipped a bit as they left the asphalt for the uneven terrain of the long-neglected road, but then they found their grip once again, and the Jeep rumbled past the trees speckled with sunlight.

In the rearview mirror, she could see Sadie sitting in her booster seat, the colored pencils still clutched in her hand. Her face was turned toward the window, her reflection flickering in and out as dappled sunshine played across the glass.

"What did you two talk about this morning?" Kris asked.

Sadie shrugged and mumbled, "Stuff."

"What kind of stuff?"

Another shrug. "Just . . . stuff."

Liar.

The word was so clear and present that at first Kris was sure Sadie had spoken it.

She glanced into the rearview mirror.

Sadie was staring back, her brow furrowed in fear and confusion as if—

She heard.

She heard the voice, just like you did.

She heard it call her a liar.

Suddenly Sadie's gaze shifted. Her eyes went wide as she thrust a finger out toward the windshield.

"Mommy!"

Kris looked.

A girl was standing in the middle of the road.

There was no time to think. Her foot jammed down the brakes, her hands whipping the steering wheel wildly to the right. She felt the tires sliding again, except this time she feared they would never regain their hold.

In the back seat, Sadie screamed.

The blurry image of the girl flashed by, and then it was gone, and the Jeep was drifting straight toward the thick trunks of the trees that bordered River Road. They were going to hit them head-on.

Kris let up off the brake pedal long enough to give the steering wheel a sharp jerk in the opposite direction. There was a chorus of off-key screeches as the tips of outstretched branches scraped against the side of the car.

Then they were slowing, the Jeep arcing gently away from the wall of trees, back toward the center of the road. Finally, it came to a stop in a billowing cloud of dust.

Her fingers were gripping the steering wheel so tightly that her knuckles were as white as bone. Over the pounding of her heartbeat, she could barely hear the sound of herself panting as she tried to catch her breath.

In the back seat, Sadie was sobbing.

"We're okay," Kris said, her own voice seeming to come from somewhere far away. "We're okay. We're okay."

The girl, she suddenly remembered.

There was a girl in the road.

Twisting around in her seat, Kris stared through the back window as the cloud of dust slowly settled.

The road behind them was empty.

"What the hell?"

Her hand found the gearshift, and she threw the car into reverse as she hit the gas. The tires spun for a moment before catching on the parched earth. The Jeep rocketed backward.

"Mommy?" There was renewed fear in Sadie's voice.

Kris ignored her. All of her attention was on keeping the car straight as they shot back down the road.

The path flashed by so quickly, Kris assumed she had imagined it. But she slowed nonetheless, bringing the car to a full stop so she could shift into Drive. Slowly, she pulled the Jeep up until she was staring out the passenger-side window at a break in the trees.

Deep tire ruts cut a trail into a field of swaying tallgrass. Bees buzzed between the yellow and orange blooms of wildflowers. To the left of the trail was the cove. The field hugged its shore, following its curve south until both were overtaken by forest.

Within the tallgrass, something moved.

Kris rolled down the passenger-side window, and a breath of warm air rushed in. She leaned over, her eyes narrowing as she tried to make out the dark shape crouched down in the jumble of weeds.

Suddenly, from deeper in the forest, a voice broke the stillness.

Kris flinched, startled, and glanced over to see a woman marching out of the woods at the far side of the field. She was dressed simply in old jeans and a red-and-black plaid shirt. The breeze lifted her long, stringy black hair from her shoulders. Strands cut across her face like tendrils of a rotting plant.

It's her, Kris realized. *The woman from across the lake.*

The woman seemed oblivious to the Jeep idling, just out of sight, in the middle of River Road. She scanned the field, her eyes locking on the form hiding among the weeds. In a tone as sharp as broken glass, she called out a name just as a gust of wind blew through.

The seat belt cut into Kris's neck as she strained to lean closer to the open window. It was no use. The wind was carrying the sound away from her, back toward the edge of the forest.

Slowly, the dark shape rose up from its hiding place in the tallgrass. It was the girl Kris had almost slammed into moments before, the same young woman she had seen watching their lake house from the woods. She was dressed just as simply as the older woman, in jeans and a dingy white shirt.

The dark-haired woman barked the name again, and the girl began to walk obediently toward her, head bowed. The second she was within reach, the dark-haired woman clamped a hand down on her arm and yanked her toward the trees.

Sadie shifted nervously in the back seat. "Mommy, who are they?"

Without warning, the wind died down. The tallgrass settled. The world was still.

The dark-haired woman had also come to an abrupt stop. She glanced back over her shoulder, eyes darting wildly around the field until finally they found the opening to the road beyond.

She sees me, Kris thought, her pulse quickening.

She watched, frozen, as the woman raised a hand and extended a single finger toward Kris. She yelled something in her sharp, angry voice, but once again, as if on cue, the wind swept up her words and whisked them away.

"What do they want?" Fear gripped Sadie's words.

Kris watched as the woman slowly lowered her hand to her side, and then she turned away, dragging the girl with her, into the forest. A few seconds later, they were swallowed by the trees.

CHAPTER THIRTY-FIVE

SADIE STOOD IN the center of the upstairs room. All around her were the pieces of abandoned furniture—the unwanted things—most of them still covered in sheets. For some reason, Mommy had never bothered to clean upstairs. As far as Sadie knew, Mommy hadn't been up to the second floor since the day they'd had their tea party.

She liked being left alone upstairs. It was her very own special place. Her own world. It could be anything she imagined it to be. One day, it was a museum filled with works of art from long, long ago. Another time it was an old castle on a hill that the frightened people living in the village below refused to enter. It had been mission control for a rocket launch and an artist's studio in Paris and a maze where a snarling monster lived. But usually it was just her playroom, filled with plenty of things to hide behind, with corners to explore, with little nooks and crannies where she could disappear from the rest of the world.

She had this room all to herself. But she was never alone. Her friend was always there, first as a whisper she had mistaken for her own thoughts, then as a girl-shaped blur floating at the corner of her eye.

Lately, though, her friend seemed to be inching her way forward. Sadie no longer had do the trick she had taught herself, staring straight ahead while concentrating on the space beside her. In the past few days, she had been able to turn her head slightly and actually see the fuzzy shape standing nearby. Her friend still vanished every time Sadie looked directly at her, but she was sure that in no time at all—two shakes of a lamb's tail, as Gammie Barlow liked to say—she would finally see her friend clearly.

The thought of this had made Sadie's shoulders and neck tingle, like when Mommy used to run the tips of her fingernails over Sadie's back as they snuggled at bedtime. She was excited to really, truly see her friend.

She has a name, silly, Sadie often reminded herself. *You can call her—*

And then she would stop herself from even thinking it. She had made a promise. Her friend had asked her not to say her name out loud. Not yet, anyway. Sadie wasn't sure why. It made her think of that fairy tale about the mean little man who could turn straw into gold, the one who tricked a girl into giving him her baby. The story had scared Sadie, even though in the end, the girl got her baby back by guessing the man's name. She wasn't sure why the story had scared her. It could have been the way the librarian at the public library had made her voice all high and creepy as she read the story from a large picture book whose pages were painted a glittering gold on their edges. Yet Sadie had to admit, the voice wasn't *that* creepy, and it had been the middle of the day in a bright room of the library's children's section. No, there was something else about the story that dug under Sadie's skin and kept her from falling straight to sleep for a week.

It was the thought that a baby could be taken from its mother and carried off into the woods by a stranger.

Sadie knew this type of thing happened in real life. She heard it on the morning news shows that Daddy had liked to watch while he drank his coffee. Kids went missing. Sometimes they were found. Sometimes they were never seen again. She wasn't exactly sure why an adult would want to take a child. But there were ways to stay safe. Don't talk to strangers. Don't take candy from them. Don't ever get in a car with them, even if they say they're a friend or they're supposed to take you home from school or they say they want to show you the cutest puppy in the whole wide world. The rules made Sadie feel better about knowing that terrible things sometimes happened to kids.

The fairy tale, though, that was worse for some reason. Scarier. Because the baby wasn't just stolen when no one was looking. The mommy in that story *had* to give the baby to the man. There was nothing she could do.

Wait, that wasn't exactly true. There was one thing. She could say the man's name and he would have to go away forever.

Rumpelstiltskin.

That was it. When the mother said that name, the man lost all of his power.

Maybe it was like that with her friend. Maybe that's why she didn't want Sadie saying her name out loud.

And she hadn't. Sadie had kept her promise.

Until today.

She hadn't meant to say it. It just slipped out. Dr. Baker was so nice and she listened and Sadie really did feel a little bit better when she talked to her.

You only whispered it, Sadie told herself. *I don't think Alice even heard it.*

So why was Sadie afraid now? Why was she standing in the sunlight of the large room on the second floor and staring at the tiny square door in the wall, afraid to go inside?

Because she knows.

She knows what you did.

You broke a promise.

From downstairs came the sound of music. Mommy was playing the tape again, the one that her mommy made.

Sadie suddenly didn't feel like playing. She didn't want to be upstairs. For the first time since she'd met her friend, Sadie wanted nothing more than to go downstairs and be only with Mommy.

She started to turn away, back toward the entryway framed by those pretty white tree trunks and, just past this, the landing at the top of the stairs.

Behind her, she heard a long, quiet squeak, then a soft thud.

She froze.

Slowly, she turned back around.

The tiny door was wide open. Inside was the perfect blackness of the secret room behind the wall.

A breath caught in Sadie's throat.

Something was moving in there, in the dark.

The shadows seemed to peel away like drifting smoke as the shape crept closer to the edge of the doorway.

Sadie wanted to look away. She wanted to spin around and race toward the stairs. But every muscle in her body had locked. She was rooted to the spot like an ancient tree. Her heart felt as though it had thumped its way up into her throat.

It's her, she realized with an overwhelming sense of fear and wonder.

Two legs stood just inside the doorway. White tube socks rimmed with three black stripes at the top stretched up from dingy white sneakers. The elastic on one of the socks had loosened, and the sock drooped down to reveal a couple inches of pale skin. At the knee, the legs disappeared into the bottom of a purple dress. Threads hung from the frayed hem.

Where are you going? a voice asked from behind the wall.

Sadie's mind had gone completely blank. She had no memory of intending to go anywhere. All she knew was this moment, standing in a swath of warm sunlight, staring at a little girl's legs as the darkness within the secret room tried to reclaim them.

Don't you want to play?

Yes. She did want to play. That must be why she was up there. To find her friend. To find . . .

It's okay, the voice behind the wall said. *I'm not mad.*

A smile spread across Sadie's face, her cheeks blushing as they rose higher and higher. Her heart was pounding so hard in her throat, she could barely breathe.

You can make it up to me.

"How?" she asked.

Talk to me.

"About what?"

A bone-white hand reached out from the shadows.

Tell me about your daddy, the voice said.

Sadie's smile faltered. Her friend had asked about this before, but Sadie hadn't wanted to talk about Daddy. She wanted to play and have fun. She wanted to forget.

But Mommy wanted her to talk, didn't she? And so did Dr. Baker. Everyone wanted Sadie to talk about the things that made her sad.

From inside the doorway, she heard a wet, sucking sound, like when Mommy let her drink soda through a straw and she couldn't wait to slurp it all up.

Tell me, her friend pleaded.

Sadie took a step toward the door. She opened her mouth, the words tumbling out, and her grief lifted off her lips like a song.

CHAPTER THIRTY-SIX

A MIST OF gray wood billowed up into the air and drifted over the water like ash. Kris adjusted her safety glasses against her shoulder, and then she put her weight onto the electric sander, working it methodically across the first plank of the weathered dock.

Every so often, she glanced up to check the cabin across the cove. Neither the woman nor her daughter were there. Kris was alone with only her thoughts to keep her company. Too many thoughts. The events of the day were flitting like a school of panicked fish through her brain. She could almost feel them slithering beneath her skull.

With no more Xanax to pop, she needed something else to take her mind off things, just for a moment. That's when she had looked out the back windows and saw the edge of the old dock stretching out over the water. The rusty rowboat bobbed at its side.

That was something she could accomplish, one plank at a time. Just the thought of it had calmed her.

Kris ground the sandpaper harder into the wood, searching for the original glow dulled by three decades of boiling hot summers and brutal winters. She wondered what it would be like in December, to see the ice attempting to devour Lost Lake as the town of Pacington was wrapped in the perfect stillness of a fresh snowfall.

You'll never be back, she told herself. *Not after this*. And yet there was something tugging at the back of her mind, telling her that she could not leave until . . .

There it was. The thorn in her side. The *until*. She had only come to the lake house a handful of summers as a child, and still she could not shake the feeling that she and this place were bound together.

She released her grip on the sander, and it came to a gradual stop in her hand. She sat back and stared out at what may as well have been a million weathered planks.

Without warning, one of the ghosts returned.

He was crouching at the end of the dock, his face buried in his hands. He was crying. His back arched with each uncontrollable sob. When he raised his head, she found herself staring into the puffy eyes of her father. He forced a smile and said, "It's okay, baby. It's okay."

It's okay. Everything is okay. Isn't that what you tell a child?

Kris blinked, and the ghost was gone.

She stood up from the one sanded plank and began to wrap the power cord around the body of the sander.

That was enough work for today.

Inside, the house was impossibly quiet. Kris told herself that quiet was what she wanted. No clomping footsteps upstairs. No startling shrieks as Sadie played her games. Not even the hushed voice of the wind pressing against the walls or the creak of boards as they braced themselves against its impact.

There was nothing but pure, perfect silence. And yet she wondered what Sadie was doing upstairs. Kris glanced at her watch. It was almost six. How could that be? She needed to make dinner. She should check on her daughter, make sure she wasn't . . .

What? Having fun? Playing? Laughing?

Kris knew that even if she called out, Sadie would most likely ignore her. She would have to beg Sadie to come down and pick at whatever meal she had prepared. Was it worth it?

If she's hungry, she'll come down, Kris told herself.

On the kitchen counter, a bottle of cabernet stood with its cork wedged halfway into its neck. Kris picked it up and gave it a light shake. Dark liquid sloshed at its center. She took out a water glass and filled it halfway with wine.

She crossed through the great room to the fireplace. Warm evening sunlight fell upon the stone hearth in long, diagonal swaths of gold. She pressed the eject button on the boombox and removed the cassette.

The Blackbird tape.

The one she had been playing when Sadie emerged from the darkness of the hallway.

I know this! I know this song!

Kris quickly set the cassette down beside the boombox, picked up her mother's mixtape, and dropped it in, pushing the plastic door shut. She pushed play.

The tape picked up where they had last left off, halfway through a slow jam by Sweet.

"Love is like oxygen . . . you get too much you get too high . . . not enough and you're gonna die . . ."

With her glass gripped securely in one hand, Kris stepped up to the French doors and touched the handle, preparing to step out onto the deck.

Her first thought was that Sadie was outside, staring in. But the face she saw was transparent. She could see the sun-streaked boards of the deck through it.

It wasn't outside, she realized. It was a reflection in the glass. The girl was in the house, standing directly behind her.

Kris gasped, her hand slipped from the door handle as she spun around. Her eyes flashed about the great room, but no one was there. Unless . . .

Careful not to make a sound, she crept over to the couch. From there, she could see behind it, but at the far end, there was just enough space out of sight for a little girl to hide.

Kris moved down the length of the couch. She held the glass of wine tighter as she prepared for Sadie to leap out and startle her.

What if it's not Sadie?

Who else would it be? she wondered, but the voices in her head remained silent.

As she neared the end of the couch, she rose up on the toes of her shoes to peer over the arm.

No one was there.

"Jesus Christ," she said to the empty room, and she took a gulp of wine.

She decided to try sitting on the front porch, just to break up the routine. She left the front door open so the music could follow her outside. The insects seemed to sense the competition and buzzed louder, even as the shadow of dusk fell over the yard.

Kris's foot hit the package as soon as she stepped outside. She bent down and picked it up. FedEx. Overnight from Barlow Animal Clinic.

God bless Allison, she thought as she squeezed the shape of a pill bottle inside the padded envelope. She thought about ripping it open and taking one right there. But Prozac wasn't Xanax. It would need time to build up in her bloodstream—a week, maybe two, before she felt the full effects.

You asked your assistant to send you dog meds, the voice of Timid Kris chided. *You can wait until bedtime to take one.*

She tossed the package just inside the door and leaned against the side of the house. She sipped her wine and breathed in the scent of wildflowers on the summer air. The day had her head spinning. She could still feel the warmth of Hitch's breath on the back of her neck. The pages of his scrapbook flipped in her mind. Illustrations of monsters. Notes scribbled in a frenzy. Photos that should not exist. It was an artifact of madness.

His words echoed in her mind: *I remember. Don't be afraid to remember, Mrs. Barlow.*

Inside the house, the Sweet song came to an end, and the hum of blank tape was interrupted by driving bass and the jangly chords of a twelve-string guitar. The mournful voice of Ian Curtis began to sing:

"When routine bites hard, and ambitions are low . . . and resentment rides high, but emotions won't grow . . ."

Kris took another sip of wine, her tongue puckering.

Remember . . .

She was being chased through the woods. Laughing. Ducking into the tree. She was ten and her mother was dying, but she was not alone. Not anymore.

In the boat. Staring over the edge. Into the water. Her own face stared back. Something beneath the water stirred.

"Hey there."

The unexpected voice made Kris jump. Wine slipped over the rim of the glass and onto her fingers.

A man in dark brown pants and a tan short-sleeved shirt was making his way through the overgrowth of the brick path. He raised a hand in a friendly wave to let Kris know he meant no harm.

She let out a sharp, irritated breath.

"Jesus, Ben, you scared the shit out of me."

Deputy Montgomery stopped at the foot of the front steps and stared up at her through his mirrored sunglasses. He put a hand on the rail leading up the stairs but made no attempt to come closer.

"Sorry," he said in a voice as dry and cracked as a sunbaked country road. "I wasn't trying to sneak up on ya. Just thought I'd stop by to see if everything was okay."

Kris looked farther out into the yard. Ben's cruiser was parked just inside the opening where the gate had once hung. She hadn't heard him pull up or the slam of his door as he got out of the car.

She gave an exhausted laugh and expected it to stop at that, but the laughter kept coming until she finally buried her face in her hands to muffle the sound. Her body shook, her shoulders hitching as the mixture of embarrassment and relief worked its way through her.

When she looked up, she saw that Ben had removed his sunglasses and was staring at her with narrowed eyes.

"I'm okay," she assured him, the last of the chuckles rippling away like settling water. "I just . . ."

She just what? How could she possibly explain everything that had led to this moment? One dead husband. One rotting house. One daughter drifting further and further into a make-believe world. One doctor trying to fix said daughter. One bookstore owner with a dossier that screamed *child murderer*.

At that moment, the wind picked up, so quickly and so sharply that it sounded almost like a voice, a soft whisper, and yet it seemed to be coming from a distance. Kris waited for the breeze to sweep her hair up from her shoulders, for it to stream in thin strands across her face, but it remained where it was, draped just past her shoulders.

And yet she could still hear the whisper, so deep in her ears that it seemed as though it were coming not from the outside world but from inside her head.

The hushed sound folded in on itself, then folded again, until its overlapping rhythms formed a single word:

Krisssy . . .

"Mrs. Barlow?"

For the second time in less than a minute, Ben's voice made her jump.

She turned back to him, still standing at the bottom of the steps.

"I'm fine. I . . ." She pinched her eyes shut, thinking. "You mind hanging for a bit? It's just a little too quiet tonight."

With a simple nod, he stepped up onto the front porch, the wood groaning under the weight of his heavy black boots. He tucked his sunglasses into his breast pocket and looked straight at Kris with the sharp eyes of someone whose job it was to size up everyone he encountered.

"You haven't had any more trouble with—"

"Surprise flower deliveries?" Kris suggested, cutting him off.

"Yeah."

Kris shook her head.

"No. Nothing like that."

Her fingers curled tighter around her glass of wine, and she was suddenly reminded to ask, "Can I get you a drink? Wine? Coffee? Those are pretty much your options."

Ben raised a hand to wave away the offer.

"I'm good."

He leaned against the railing and cocked an ear toward the music drifting out from the open front door.

"Guess you've finally settled in," he said.

Kris sighed. "Yeah, well, the place was left—"

To rot.

"—in pretty bad shape. Just trying to make it feel like home. You know, give it some love. Bring it back to life."

"Yeah," Ben said weakly, as if he doubted that could be done. "I've always wondered what was going on with this place. Noticed in the past couple years that the weeds are higher and the shingles are a little more crooked every time I drive by. Not that I should be surprised. This place is no different than any other 'round here."

"What do you mean?" Kris asked.

Ben took another moment to collect his thoughts. "It's just not the same town it used to be," he said finally.

Kris waited for him to continue, but he did not.

"I'm getting you a glass of wine," she said, pushing away from the house and turning toward the doorway.

Ben held up a hand in halfhearted protest. "Nah, really."

"You're off the clock, right?"

"Well, technically . . ."

"Then I'm getting you a glass. And then I'm getting you to talk."

"Good luck with that," Ben chuckled as he followed her inside.

The wine bottle was still on the counter where she had left it. She twisted the half-sunk cork from its neck, then fished into an upper cabinet, found a random yet clean glass, and poured in a couple inches of cabernet.

She held the glass across the island to Ben.

"Thanks," he said, and took a polite sip.

Kris leaned back against the counter, swirling the wine around her glass.

"You from here?" she asked.

Ben nodded. "Been here my whole life. Went to high school here, when we actually had a high school. Now they bus all the kids over to Fredonia. Thought when I joined the Greenwood County Sheriff's Office, I would finally get out. Not far, but . . . well . . . far enough, I guess. But the Pacington Police Department went belly up in 2005, and who do you think the Sheriff's Office sent over to help keep the peace?"

"I'm assuming you?" Kris offered.

"You would assume correct. Called back to these crystal waters. Me and two other deputies have been on Pacington duty for over ten years now."

"What kind of things you have to deal with around here?"

"Mostly we just supply a police presence," he explained, "which for me means driving around with my Don't Even Think About It shades on." He tapped the mirrored sunglasses in his breast pocket. "I suppose that's why the sheriff lets me get away with the beard. When ninety percent of your job is intimidating small-town folks, it helps to look like you're half bear."

Once again, laughter found Kris Barlow, and she welcomed it like a patch of sunshine on a cool day.

Ben smiled easily, but then it began to retreat, little by little, until it disappeared into the bramble of his beard.

"Then there's the other ten percent. That's the part where you're glad you have a gun to go with the sunglasses. Lately it seems like more than ten percent. The fighting and the drinking and the drugs. A lot of drugs. Bad stuff that rots your brain, your skin, your teeth. People in this town, they don't have much to do except get drunk or high or fight. Jobs aren't exactly pouring in. The foundry shut down in '96. Seems like downtown has more empty space than actual shops. They hide it well by decorating the windows, and Albert Bell does his best to keep the sidewalks free of weeds, but take a good look and you'll see. This town is dying."

A chill crept across Kris's skin. She glanced over at the windows on the far side of the great room. The blue sky had deepened to purple as the sun slipped down toward the hills. It would be night soon.

Ben continued, "Sure, every time a new politician gets elected, they say they're gonna bring back the middle class. They talk about Main Street and the 'real America.' And then they zip past the turn-off to Pacington on their way to Topeka, never even knowing there's a little town here."

He must have seen the unease on Kris's face, because he suddenly leaned back and rubbed his hands together like a dealer leaving a poker table.

"I swear, I didn't stop by to bum you out."

"No, it's okay," Kris assured him. "It's not that. It's just . . ."

She thought of that room on the second floor of the Book Nook, the sun blazing on its white walls, the crinkle of contact paper as she turned the pages of the scrapbook, the sweet-sour stench of Hitch's breath over her shoulder.

"You ever go to the Book Nook?"

Ben drew in a deep breath, the buttons pulling his tan shirt taut as his broad chest rose and fell.

"Everyone knows Hitch," he exhaled.

"Do you think Hitch could have killed those girls?"

If the question surprised him, Ben showed no sign. He sipped his wine as he mulled it over. When he spoke, his voice was flat.

"No. I don't."

"He showed me a scrapbook—"

"I've seen it."

Kris shot him a confused look.

Ben shrugged. "He's pretty proud of that fucked-up thing. Thinks he's really onto something."

"He has pictures of their bedrooms, Ben. He went into their *houses.*"

Ben's back stiffened. "I know that. And I could have arrested him for it. Maybe I should've. But that would'a meant dredging up a whole lot of pain and ugliness that those families—and this town—don't need. He won't do it again. You can trust me on that."

Kris reached for the wine bottle and refilled her glass. She could feel the threads that she had been weaving over the past few days begin to unravel.

"Are you sure he had nothing to do with it?"

"Are you?" Ben asked pointedly. "You saw that scrapbook. You could have come straight to me. You got my number. Why didn't you?"

Kris did not reply, so Ben answered for her. "Because you and I both know he's just a crazy old bastard who spends too much time reading mystery books he should be selling."

"What about this Charles guy, then? Charles . . ." *Charles something. Charles What's His Name.* "Carpenter. Charles Carpenter. Both Hitch and Camilla—"

Ben gave a sharp laugh. "Wow, you really have been doing some digging, haven't you? You plannin' on solving three decades' worth of cold cases in one summer?"

Kris shook her head, realizing how all of this sounded. "I'm sorry. I'm not trying to do your job."

He laughed again, an honest-to-God boisterous guffaw that Kris never would have expected from the stoic deputy.

"Hell, you can have the job. I really don't mind."

Kris smiled, her stress easing up just a bit. She watched as Ben drained the last of the wine she had poured for him. He stared down at the bottom of his glass as if trying to make a decision.

She made it for him. Grabbing the bottle, she leaned over the island and splashed a bit more wine into his glass. When she looked up, she saw that he was watching her. A light seemed to flicker in those deep brown eyes.

"What?" she asked, feeling at once flattered and self-conscious.

"You got me talkin'," he said as he took another drink.

The second glass of wine was all Ben would allow. Kris followed him out onto the front porch. The last of the sun's rays painted pink slivers across the dark sky.

Ben had just reached the brick path at the bottom of the front steps when he turned around. There was something on his mind.

"Look, I appreciate what you're trying to do," he told her. "But this town is full of people with time on their hands. They've all got their own theories about what happened, and most of them are what I generously call 'out there.' Hitch isn't even the worst of them. Like I said, people ain't got much here. Not much but their imaginations."

"But what do *you* think?" Kris asked. Her voice was strong and clear.

Ben glanced up. His eyes were pools of shadow beneath his thick brows, but she could still feel their intensity.

"Ruby Millan's daddy drank himself into a rage every single night. Sarah Bell was being bullied so bad at school that she told her classmates she wished she were dead. Poppy Azuara's parents were stressed about money and fighting like alley cats. And Megan Adamson, well, from what people said, Megan wasn't too fond of rules and had a habit of wandering off." He sighed, and there was an awful finality to that weary sound. "I think they were all just their own separate tragedies. Maybe they were all accidents. Or maybe sometimes even a nine-year-old girl would rather die in a hollow tree than go back to the pain at home."

Tears stung Kris's eyes, but she fought them back.

Ben must have seen this, for his voice softened and he took a step toward her.

"I admit, Pacington has a lot of problems. But I promise you, I got an eye on things here. The rest of the world might'a forgotten about this town, but I haven't."

Neither has Hitch, Kris thought.

She gave Ben a nod. There was nothing else to say except, "Thank you."

"You've got my number," he reminded her. Then he nodded and began to cross the brick path, the overgrown bushes tugging at his pant legs.

He was halfway to his cruiser when he turned back. "You know, we've met before," he said. The casual warmth was back in his voice. "I mean, when we were kids."

"We have?" Kris asked, completely thrown by the change in subject.

"I wouldn't have remembered if I hadn't seen your daughter in the car that day. Took me a full twenty-four hours to figure out why she looked so familiar. And then it hit me. It was you. You looked just like her back then. You were the red-haired girl who would show up in the summer with your parents." The memory brought a smile back to Ben's lips. "I remember you always made me think of Charlie Brown. How he wanted to talk to the red-haired girl but he was too chickenshit to do it. And then one summer, you didn't come back. Never thought I'd see you again."

In her mind, Kris reached back to those summers so long ago, searching through memories of playing in the park or wandering the sidewalks downtown as if she were flipping through the pages of an old photo album.

She shook her head. "I'm sorry. I don't remember."

"That's okay. I wouldn't expect you to." Ben stood for a beat, pondering this thought. Then he nodded and offered, all business, "You have a good night."

A thought tugged at the back of Kris's mind. She called out, "Hey, Ben?"

Ben was standing at the driver's-side door of his car, the keys in his hand.

"You don't happen to remember me playing with other kids when I was here, do you?" she asked.

Ben gave it a thought, then shook his head. "No. You were kind of a loner. Kept to yourself. The few times your parents brought you into town, I mean. I think you spent most of your time at this house."

"Huh," Kris said, although she felt she had more questions than before.

She watched as Ben climbed the wheel of his sheriff's cruiser. A moment later, headlights split the darkness. Ben backed out onto River Road, and then he was gone.

At some point, the mixtape had reached its end, and the play button had snapped back into place. Kris thought about turning the tape over and playing the other side, but one glance at her watch reminded her that she needed to get Sadie into bed.

Setting the two glasses down in the kitchen sink, she turned to the FedEx package, which now rested atop the island. She grasped it in both hands, digging her fingernails into its padded sides, and pulled hard, feeling the satisfaction of plastic stretching until it snapped.

There was no prescription label on the side. Allison had filled it with samples from the locked cabinet at the back of the office. Kris pushed the lid in and twisted it free.

Unlike the Xanax, this medication came in a red-and-blue capsule. The mere sight of it sent a wave of relief rushing through her body. She tossed a capsule into her mouth, loosened its sticky body from her tongue with a bit of spit and swallowed it down. She paused, then fished a second pill out and quickly swallowed it.

Just to get the ball rolling, she told herself. *To take the edge off the withdrawal from the Xanax.*

Her shadow voice purred from the abyss. *Right. Keep tellin' yourself that.*

Kris slipped the pill bottle into her pocket, crumpled up the FedEx package, and tossed it into the trash can under the sink. Then she paused, her hand resting on the edge of the counter.

She had just stepped into the great room when she became aware of a sound, like the rush of air. Her first thought was that the cassette in the boombox was between songs, and what she was hearing was the white noise of blank tape. But the mixtape had stopped.

The sound grew slightly louder, a whisper swirling around her.

She had heard it before. Out on the front porch, just as Ben was making his way toward the house. As it had then, the whisper turned in on itself until it took shape, becoming something new, like a strip of paper folded into origami.

It was a symptom of withdrawal. It had to be. There was no other explanation for these phantom sensations.

The skin tightened across her scalp. She felt as though something were in the room with her, a presence that glared at her with hollow eyes.

From outside, there came the flapping of wings.

A black shape was flailing wildly on the back deck. It fluttered into the air, hovering long enough to squawk angrily before dropping back down, out of sight.

It's a bird, she realized. *Another goddamn grackle.*

Crossing to the window, Kris tapped her fingers against the glass hard enough for the bird to hear. But it was not concerned with her. It was focused on something between the wooden planks. It dug its pointy black beak down into the narrow space, snapping at something it couldn't quite grasp.

"Hey!" Kris yelled. She balled up a fist and pounded the window. "Go on! Get outta here!"

The grackle leapt into the air, closer this time, and squawked in protest. A few feathers shook loose as it flapped its wings to keep itself aloft. It cocked its head, spotting something below, and shot down as quick as a bullet.

Its sharp beak snapped again, then clamped shut.

The bird raised its head.

Something was squirming there, pinched tightly in its beak. Thin black legs kicked helplessly at the open air.

It was a beetle, exactly like the one she had seen while repairing the deck.

The grackle titled its head sharply to the side and stared straight at her with one yellow eye.

Then the bird's wings caught the wind, and it, and the beetle, were gone.

CHAPTER THIRTY-SEVEN

SUNDAY WAS THE hottest day since their arrival. The cool breeze they had enjoyed for most of June was now nonexistent. The river basin in which Pacington rested had become a cauldron. The hills trapped the summer heat so that even the dependably cool waters of Lost Lake offered no relief.

Kris woke to find her left leg hanging out of sheets damp with sweat. Her body had sought the relief of open air during the night. Yet there seemed to be no escape from the heat. It slipped in through unseen cracks in the walls to cup her in its suffocating hands like butterflies held prisoner in the grip of a sweaty, dirt-streaked child.

With no central air, not even a wall unit mounted somewhere in the house, Kris knew that their only option was to open all of the windows and hope for the return of a breeze.

She closed her eyes. The air in the room felt heavy, like a weight upon her chest.

An image began to form in her mind: a silver circle spinning behind a metal grate, a fan, turning its head slowly back and forth from side to side. The memory continued to take shape, expanding outward like a universe being born, revealing the stone hearth of the fireplace and the wood-plank walls of the great room. Her mother leaned in, letting the air from the fan lift her hair away from her face and shoulders. And then Kris was there, too. Seven years old. Before she knew about the sickness devouring her mother from within. Young Krissy put her mouth close to the grate and released a long, monotone, "Hellooo," the whirring blades vibrating her voice into something robotic and artificial.

The fan must still be somewhere in the house. Probably upstairs—

The excitement of the realization was cut short by a thought so sudden, it was as though someone else had just barked it into her ear.

Upstairs belongs to Sadie.

It took several seconds for her to realize how nonsensical the thought truly was. How could any part of the house *belong* to an eight-year-old girl? Even the pink bedroom wasn't solely hers, despite the fact that Kris referred to it as "Sadie's bedroom." If she wanted to get technical about it, the house belonged to Kris. It had since the day her father's liver finally tired of the incessant abuse and decided to shut down once and for all.

But Dad didn't want it even when he was alive. He wanted it to rot.

She pinched her eyes tighter.

She still didn't understand why he had done that. It made sense that he would stop using the place as a summer retreat. Kris was an only child living her life a state away, and Mom was long gone. He had no reason to return, especially in the last years of his life as his health worsened. But he could have continued to let Mr. Hargrove rent the place out. He could have taken Hargrove up on his offer to foot the bill for basic maintenance. No, her father had purposely abandoned the house. He wanted it to crumble to the ground. No matter which way she looked at it, the concept made no sense.

Then, from the pitch-black depths of her mind, a voice echoed, *He wanted it to rot because it wasn't his house anymore. It had been taken from him.*

Kris cocked her head, her cheek pressing into the zipper lining at the edge of her sweat-dampened pillow. She imagined him lying alone in a bed in a Blantonville nursing home, the medicinal stench of the room in his nostrils, his skin the color of dried mustard, his eyes equally jaundiced. She let her mind become his mind, as he turned away from the television mounted high on the wall across from his bed, one daytime talk show marching endlessly into another. What did he think about as he lay there, heavy with the knowledge that he was dying?

He knew that he would die alone.

Perhaps he hoped he would see his wife again soon. Or that his daughter would make an unexpected visit to check on her old man before he shuffled off.

But why even spend one precious second pondering the fate of the lake house? Why go out of his way to punish this place?

Kris's eyes flashed open, and she found herself staring up at a long, jagged crack in the plaster ceiling.

Because this was where the love of his life died, she realized.

This was where his sadness lived.

The thought of others entering this place and attempting to fill it with laughter must have seemed like a betrayal to him. So he decided to die comforted by the knowledge that the house would eventually be pulled board by board, stone by stone, back to the earth.

Except you came, that singsong voice chided. *You tried to fix this place. You betrayed your father's dying wish.*

On some level, Hargrove had known this. That's why he had tried to get Kris to stay somewhere else.

That wasn't quite right, she realized. He was happy to give her the keys to the house when he thought it was just her. It wasn't until he saw Sadie at the supermarket that he backpedaled. She wanted to know why.

Mid-Nation Realty was located in a narrow first-floor space on Center Street, two blocks west of Jefferson Park. Taped to the inside of the front window were sheets of paper featuring properties for rent and for sale in the Pacington area. Most of them had been in the window for a very long time. Strips of scotch tape barely held them in place. They sagged at odd angles, creating jagged lines across the glass. The photos of houses and apartments printed on the sheets were faded to unrecognizable pale blobs.

Darryl Hargrove was at his desk, clicking away at a game of Solitaire on his computer, when Kris entered with Sadie at her side. He quickly minimized the window and began shuffling papers into a pile as if this somehow implied that he was busy.

"Mrs. Barlow," he said, his voice cracking with surprise. "To what do I owe the pleasure?"

Kris motioned to a chair just inside the front door and whispered to Sadie, "This'll only take a minute."

Sadie shot Hargrove an irritated look, clearly blaming him for her being dragged away from the lake house, and then she climbed into the chair. She folded her hands in her lap, her legs swinging so that the toes of her shoes squeaked across the tile floor.

Taking a seat directly in front of Hargrove's desk, Kris conjured up what she hoped was a friendly smile.

"Sorry to bother you, Mr. Hargrove."

"No bother." He was already sweating. Kris could see it beading across a patch of sunspots on his forehead.

"There's just something I wanted to ask you, something that's been bothering me." She glanced over at Sadie, both to reassure herself that her daughter was still there and to make sure the little girl was not eavesdropping.

When she spoke once more to Hargrove, she leaned forward and lowered her voice, just to be safe.

"Why didn't you want us to stay at the lake house?"

The bluntness of the question brought more pearls of sweat to Hargrove's shiny brow. He wiped at them with his stubby fingers, then dried his hand across the leg of his pants.

"I'm not sure I understand . . ."

"Our first day here, when you ran into us at the Safeway, you said you could put us in another house closer to downtown. Why?"

Hargrove looked away, hoping Kris would do the same. But when he glanced back, he found that her gaze had not faltered. She stared straight at him, waiting for an answer.

He wiggled nervously in his seat. "As I said in my email, I knew River's End was not in, how should I say, peak condition. I just thought you and your daughter might be more comfortable—"

Kris cut him off. "No, see, that's the thing that's been bothering me. You didn't know I had Sadie with me until that day in the store. And when you saw her, something changed. You weren't just being polite. You seemed . . ."

She let her words drift away into the warm air.

Hargrove sighed with resignation. "Okay, look. Truth is that place wasn't renting even before your daddy asked me to pull the plug on it. I mean, sure, I had a few bites back when summers here were still . . ." He waved a hand in the air as if Kris knew exactly what he was getting at. "But no one stayed in that house for long. They always ended up asking to switch locations. Got to the point where I always made sure another rental was available because I knew eventually the call was coming."

Kris shook her head, trying to make sense of it. "Why? What reason did they give?"

"Well, I mean . . ." Hargrove gave a small, embarrassed laugh. "Most of them had some random complaint. The place was too small. The boats on the lake were too loud. There was a bad smell that was driving them bonkers."

The stench of the dead blackbird curled up into Kris's nose. She was sure she would gag. But then it was gone, as quickly as it came.

Hargrove did not seem to notice. "Some of them stuck it out, but most of them, especially the ones with children, well, they couldn't get outta there fast enough."

Again, Kris was struck with the need to check on Sadie, sure that this time, she would be gone, taken like the others.

To pay a debt, she thought, even though Hitch's words still made no sense.

But Sadie had not moved. She was in the chair by the door, staring down at the scuff marks left by the rubber soles of her sneakers.

Kris turned back to Hargrove. He looked tired, his face no longer able to muster up the fake cheer that was the true uniform of his profession. He seemed to sense the question that was forming in Kris's mind, and he answered it before it could be spoken.

"They said that the house felt sad. That's the word they used more than any other. As if there had been a great loss in that place."

His eyes softened, and for the first time, Kris saw how blue they were, like the cool waters of Lost Lake.

"I guess in a way they were right," he said. "But you would know about that better than anyone."

CHAPTER THIRTY-EIGHT

BY MONDAY MORNING, the heat was even worse and the Prozac still hadn't kicked in. Kris forced herself to keep to a regimen. Two pills a day. One in the morning. One at night.

Sadie was spending most of her time upstairs, although her games had become strangely muted. The house was no longer filled with the thumping of her footsteps and the squeals of her laughter. Every now and then, Kris would hear the creak of the floorboards above or the snap of the tiny door's latch clicking into place as Sadie withdrew to her secret room behind the wall.

By Tuesday, Kris felt as though her mind were filled with crossed wires. She knew the Prozac took time to become effective, but at this point, they may as well have been breath mints. It was as if all of the pain and anxiety Kris had managed to keep at bay with the Xanax was now crashing down on her in a single pummeling wave.

She tried to distract herself by sanding more of the dock, but every time she finished one plank, it seemed another had been added to the end.

At night, she tried to lull herself to sleep by recalling happier times in the bedroom, the few moments of bittersweet joy at her mother's bedside. She tried to imagine her mother's weak voice as she shared childhood stories in hopes that they would never be forgotten, as she recounted dates with Kris's father, as she relived beloved memories of raising their one and only child.

But none of those moments existed in Kris's memory.

On Wednesday afternoon, she officially gave up on sanding the dock. The wildfire that had ignited in her brain was raging.

This is not normal, she thought. *It can't be.*

It felt as though an invisible hand were reaching beneath her skull and gripping the spongy gray surface of her brain. It didn't make sense. She had never taken anything for depression or anxiety before Jonah died. How could a few weeks of usage result in such extreme withdrawal?

Picking up her phone from the coffee table, she checked the time. 3:17 p.m.

No one would blame her for having a drink.

She had just made it into the kitchen when she was engulfed by a maelstrom of sound. It was like walking into an impossibly thick cloud of gnats. The buzzing surrounded her, whipping by so quickly she swore she could physically feel it skimming the surface of her face.

And yet as the sound grew, so did the pressure inside her head, as if the swirling madness were looking for a way out.

Out.

Because it's not around you.

It's in your head.

It's all in your head.

You know it. Sadie knows it. Dr. Baker knows it. Even Ben knows it.

They know that you're the problem.

She threw open the refrigerator door. Frosty air wafted out. She dropped to her knees, losing herself in its coolness.

On the second shelf, a bottle of pinot grigio lay on its side. Its clear glass was misted with condensation.

Kris pulled the bottle from the shelf, took one more moment to soak in the cool air, and then she shut the fridge. She held the bottle's round, cold body to the side of her face as she moved around the kitchen in search of the corkscrew and a glass. Only when it was time to pry the cork from its neck did she lift the bottle away from her hot flesh.

She poured the wine as if she were filling the glass with water, stopping only when she realized just how closely it was coming to the top. She took a desperate gulp, savoring the mouthful of cold liquid as it slipped around her tongue. She swallowed, and the storm inside her mind seemed to calm ever so slightly.

Taking another smaller sip, Kris moved across the great room toward the French doors. She had already grasped the knob when she thought to stop and call back in the direction of the second floor: "Sadie?"

There was no response. Only this new, odd quiet that had settled over her playtime.

Finally, a muffled little voice called back, "Yeah?"

"You okay?"

Another pause, almost as if Sadie were conversing with someone before responding.

Then: "Yeah. I'm okay."

"I'm just going out on the deck," Kris told her. "Wanna come out with me?"

This time, there was no answer.

With a frustrated sigh, Kris opened the door and stepped outside.

The heat hit her like a slap in the face.

Shielding her eyes from the intense blast of sunshine, she stepped up to the deck railing and stared out at the landscape of wood and rock and water before her. The entire world seemed to be suffering, every weed brown and withered, every tree branch drooping as if desperate to reach shadow, every patch of dirt baking like clay in a kiln. Captured in the perfectly still water of Lost Lake was the blazing sun. This twin star sent a shimmer of heat rippling above the lake's surface.

Near the back steps, Kris spotted the freckled nose of a collared lizard peeking out from under a rock. The rest of its body was backed desperately away into cool shadow.

"Got any room under there for me?" Kris asked dryly.

The lizard flicked its tongue once and then crawled farther backward into the darkness.

Kris took another drink of wine. It seemed to be helping. She could already feel that familiar, wonderful numbness as the alcohol entered her bloodstream. The sound in her mind was also letting up, loosening like unraveling threads as it began to swirl away.

This was bad. She knew she could not continue like this. Popping one medication to treat another. Day drinking to drown her pain.

At some point, you'll have to face it, Timid Kris sang.

For once, the voice did not irritate the living hell out of Kris. She knew it was right. She couldn't busy herself with home improvement projects all summer. One of these days, she would have to face it all.

"Not yet," Kris whispered under her breath. Her lips found the glass again, her mouth sucking in more wine.

She swallowed.

She closed her eyes.

Not yet.

The fingers were back, creeping up the back of her skull, under the bone, across the fragile, wet surface of her brain.

Without warning, she was yanked away from where she stood on the back deck. The maelstrom raged around her as she was dragged by an invisible thread, thin as a spider's silk but as strong as steel, back across miles and weeks she thought she had left behind.

She was back in the frigid, sterile morgue of Howard Fox, coroner and medical examiner for Black Ridge, Colorado. She was leaning over the dead body of her husband, his face smashed into a barely recognizable mask of bone and blood and teeth where teeth should not be. Pebbles of safety glass glimmered in his hair.

"I'll never forgive you for this. Never," she hissed into an ear that hung from the side of his head like a loose button.

And then she was turning away, swiping angrily at the tears. She gave a sharp nod to Howard Fox and managed to choke out, "It's him."

Howard gave a sad, rehearsed sigh and reached out to touch her arm. "I'm sorry you had to do this." His hand was warm and clammy even in the freezing cold of the morgue.

Kris backed up a step so that his hand fell away. She crossed her arms over her chest, hoping Howard wouldn't notice as she casually rubbed away the lingering sensation of his moist flesh.

In the corner of the room, a light flickered behind a rolling partition. She had not noticed it when she entered, the white of the cloth stretching between two metal poles blending perfectly with the white wall. The light flashed again, illuminating the cloth with a soft yellow glow, like a burst of lightning behind the cover of thick, pale clouds.

There was something else behind that partition. Something that seemed to float in the air, flat on the bottom and gently sloping up on top, reaching its highest point at the opposite end.

Another gurney, she realized.

Another body.

"Is that . . ." Kris started to say.

Another voice interrupted her, a stern male voice from the opposite side of the room.

A police officer was standing in the doorway.

"Howard," he called, announcing his presence. The man was dressed in the tan slacks, blue shirt, and black flat-brimmed hat of the Colorado Highway Patrol. His thumbs were hooked behind his black leather belt, the pinky of his right hand habitually lingering on the gun strapped to his side. He nodded to Kris, but he did not look at her. He kept his gaze on Howard, clearly uncomfortable with making eye contact with the grieving widow.

"Just one moment," Howard told Kris.

She watched as he crossed to the patrolman, who lowered his head as he spoke, his words terse yet his voice soft.

He doesn't want me to hear.

Kris turned an ear toward the men, pretending to stare off in thought as she strained to hear their conversation.

". . . might wanna get her out the door," the patrolman was saying.

". . . don't want to rush her," Howard replied.

". . . other family on their way from the Springs," the patrolman informed him. "Don't want a scene . . ."

A jolt of electricity shot through Kris's body, every muscle painfully constricting as her suspicion was confirmed.

She glanced back at the cloth partition.

The light was on now, burning steadily. And below it was the shadow of the second body.

Her body.

It's her.

Kris had to see her. More than she had needed to see the body of her own husband. She wanted to stare into the destroyed face that, until hours ago, had been the other woman. The reason for Jonah's unnecessarily late nights. For the instantly deleted texts. For the work calls that Jonah could only take outside. The secret they both knew but of which neither of them ever spoke.

Howard and the police officer had turned away from her, the backs of their heads close together as they discussed their awkward situation.

With slow, light steps, careful not to let the bottoms of her boots squeak across the slick floor tiles, Kris crept over to the partition. She rested her fingers on the cold metal pole as she peered around it.

The body was covered from head to toe in a black plastic sheet, identical to the one draped over Jonah. A metal cart stood beside the body, its wheels locked in place, a collection of instruments meticulously arranged on its top shelf. Next to these was a simple industrial lamp with a bulb shining brightly in a steel dome attached to a long adjustable neck. Every now and then, the bulb flickered, threatening to go out for good. Shadows were born and destroyed with each flicker, creating the illusion that the shape under the sheet was moving.

Three fingers peeked out from the side of the sheet and dangled limply over the edge of the metal gurney. The middle and ring fingers were flawless, the skin smooth and delicate, the nails retaining the perfection of a recent manicure. A tiny painted flower curled elegantly across the glistening surface of the ring fingernail. But the pinkie destroyed the illusion that the woman beneath the sheet had suffered no trauma. It curled away from the other fingers at an impossible angle, the bone snapped free from its joint. The nail was identically painted, yet it dangled from the wet, exposed flesh, torn away from the cuticles that had once held it in place.

Kris had to see her face.

She lurched quickly forward, and the toe of her shoe caught the surface of the floor, giving a sharp squeak.

Kris winced.

"Ma'am?" she heard Howard call from across the room. There was sudden concern in his voice.

"I don't think that's a good idea," the officer added.

Fuck what you think, Kris thought.

She took another step.

"Ma'am!"

Howard was stomping toward her. The clack of the officer's hard soles followed.

Kris thrust a hand out, ready to grasp the plastic sheet, to pull it free from the mangled body she knew lay hidden beneath.

Her hand froze in midair.

Beneath her outstretched palm, the plastic sheet sloped upward slightly in a small hill. Right where the woman's stomach would be.

Kris's mind tried to make sense of what she was seeing. Her first thought was that something had been left on top of the body, a rag or an overturned bowl, something that caused the slight but unmistakable bump under the sheet.

And then the truth forced its way through the cloud of confusion.

"Oh . . . God . . ." Kris choked out, her throat tightening in horror.

A hand clamped down on her shoulder.

"Ma'am!"

As if willing herself awake from a nightmare, Kris forced her mind away from the moment. Suddenly she was leaving the mountains behind again, skimming over the flat fields of the Great Plains, over the rippling green earth of the Flint Hills, back to the small, forgotten town of Pacington, Kansas, and the lake that had once been a river before the earth had opened, before subterranean waters had exploded up from the depths to swallow everything in their path.

Kris opened her eyes.

The woman was watching her.

She was a speck of black, framed by the still-green tentacles of weeping willow as she stood on the deck behind her cabin. She was too far away to see in any detail, but Kris knew the woman was staring straight at her. She could feel the woman's dark eyes penetrating her.

Staring.

Judging.

Kris felt a wetness on her hot, dry cheeks and realized she had been crying.

"Mommy?"

Kris turned, her vision blurred by tears she did not remember shedding.

Two little girls stood in the doorway. They were identical in shape and size, but the one on the right was strangely out of focus. Her legs seemed to disappear into nothingness as if she were not fully there, like an image emerging from the blackness of a Polaroid picture.

Kris swiped at her eyes, quickly rubbing the tears away.

When she looked back at the doorway to the great room, there was only Sadie.

"What . . ." The word fell from Kris's open mouth, the confusion that gripped her mind refusing to allow her to finish the thought.

Sadie did not notice her mother's tear-streaked face or her wide-eyed expression. The little girl was glanced nervously to the empty space beside her.

"She wants . . ." The rest was lost in a mumble, as if Sadie did not truly want to say it. Something beside her seemed to get her attention. She took a breath and straightened, speaking with forced conviction. "She really wants you to play with us."

Kris's mind felt like a pinball machine, her focus ricocheting helplessly from idea to idea as she tried to bring them all into one coherent thought.

"Who?" she managed to ask.

Again, Sadie hesitated. Her hands here clasped obediently in front of her, her fingers intertwined so tightly that her fingertips pressed away what little color there was in her pale flesh.

Growing impatient, Kris glanced over her shoulder at the cabin across the cove.

The back porch was empty.

The woman was gone.

Sadie continued, "There's a game she wants you to play."

The paralysis lessened, her muscles tingling as she regained control.

"Sadie, I—"

"She said you love it. She will make you remember. It's called Ghost in the Graveyard."

Despite the heat, a chill ran down Kris's spine.

"What did you say?"

Without warning, Kris was assaulted by an image behind her eyes. She was a little girl. A couple years older than Sadie. She was in the forest, beside the great oak tree, the Wishing Tree, its trunk gaping like a hungry mouth. There was another girl standing in the shadows within the tree, dark eyes shining like light attempting to escape the pull of a black hole, ruby lips lifted into a playful grin.

She wasn't alone that summer. She had a friend. And her friend wore a light purple dress, the color of the flowers growing in Mommy's garden, the ones Daddy clipped and put in Mommy's room to cover the smell of death.

There was a sharp sound, like the snapping of fingers. All other thoughts were instantly gone. The other voices in Kris's mind—her timid self, her shadow self—abandoned her. They were hiding, refusing to take part in what was transpiring.

Sadie took a step backward. Her wide green eyes were locked on her mother. Her voice quavered as she forced herself to say, "She wants you to—"

"How do you know about that game?" Kris asked again, cutting her off. "Do your friends back home play it? Did Charlotte teach it to you?"

Sadie's body began to tremble. She was no longer listening to her mother. She stared at the space beside her, eyes brimming with tears.

"Why does she have to play with us?" she yelled at the empty air.

Kris took a step forward. "Sadie—"

"Why can't you just play with me?!" Sadie shrieked.

"Sadie, stop!"

Footsteps thundered and then Sadie was gone, racing down the hallway to her bedroom.

Kris heard the bedroom door slam shut.

Something brushed lightly against Kris's hair, and she flinched.

It was just a breeze.

Kris knew she should go after her daughter. She should comfort her. Talk to her. Make sense of everything.

But there was that voice that refused to stay silent, not her timid self or her shadow self. This voice was her own, and it repeated the two words Kris now realized it had been saying since she was a child:

Not yet.

Kris looked to the space to her right, just inside the open French doors.

Nothing is there, she told herself.

Nothing is there.

Yet she took a step back anyway, mechanically raising the glass of wine to her mouth for another drink.

Sadie finally came out of her room at dinnertime. The lake house was filled with the scent of melted cheese and browning bread. Kris slid a grilled cheese sandwich onto a plate and set it down on the breakfast nook table. She remained at the island, picking at her own sandwich while Sadie took a few uninterested bites.

"If you're not hungry, you can get ready for bed," Kris said finally.

Sadie rose from the table and marched out of the kitchen, her head low, chin against her chest.

Kris picked up the plate from the butcher block and turned to set it down in the sink. She paused, realizing other dirty dishes were already piled there. Food was crusted on plates. Glasses were smudged with finger- and lip prints.

She should wash them. She needed to keep this place clean.

"Why?" she asked the empty room. "What's the point?"

Let it rot, the voice in her mind said.

Carefully, she balanced her plate on the stack of dirty dishes and turned away. As she passed the fridge, she paused just long enough to open it and take out the bottle of white wine.

Her glass was where she had left it when she came inside, on the hearth, just to the right of the boombox. She picked it up and poured in the last of the wine, setting the empty bottle down where the glass had been.

The voice was still there, singing the words:

Don't you remember? Playing in the room behind the wall . . . in the pink bedroom . . . in the woods . . . by the lake where the mermaid lived . . . in the hollow tree . . . down in the narrow canyon between the sandstone cliffs . . . on the rocks that rose like teeth . . .

But the voice no longer sounded like her own. It was higher-pitched. Somehow fragile and strong all at once. It spoke as if it were Kris's voice, but it felt like an outsider. An invader. Something that had forced its way into her mind like a virus.

The rocks, the voice sang. *Where sweet little Megan Adamson died . . .*

Kris took a sip of wine.

Evening had brought a respite from the heat. The breeze rippled the surface of Lost Lake. It slithered through the cattails sprouting up from the shallow water. Even the turtles had decided to leave their hiding places in the cool shadows to drift like floating stones out to the center of the cove.

The French doors were still open, and the wind blew gently into the room, curling around her as she stood by the fireplace before disappearing like a fleeing spirit down the darkening hallway.

Without warning, the ghost was back. Her father was carrying in a handful of freshly cut flowers on his way to the master bedroom. She could smell their pungent sweetness hanging in the air.

Kris tipped the glass back and felt the last sip of wine slip past her lips.

She held the glass up and stared at it, confused.

It was empty.

The room was darker, too. Outside, the last glimpse of the sun could be seen over the silhouette of the hills.

How long had she been standing here? Twenty? Thirty minutes?

In the entryway to the hall, a floorboard creaked.

Sadie stood there, just at the edge of the light cast by the end table lamp. She was dressed in peach pajamas covered in the repeated image of a small grinning monkey.

"Good night," she said, her voice a cold monotone.

Still thrown by the missing time, Kris began to ask, "Are you all ready for—"

Before she could finish, Sadie turned and walked into the shadows. A moment later, her bedroom door clicked shut.

Without warning, another memory broke the surface of dark, rippling waters.

She was ten years old. She was standing at the mouth of the hall-way, just as Sadie had moments before. But she was facing the opposite direction. She was staring down the hall, and at the end, the door to the master bedroom was open just a crack, enough to let some light play across the wood paneling of the far wall. In the great room, the boom-box was blasting "Blackbird" at a volume that its meager speakers could barely handle. Yet Kris could still hear the low murmur of her father's voice coming from the master bedroom. It was soothing like the babble of a shallow creek flowing over water-smoothed stones. Every now and then, this peaceful sound was broken by the raspy shriek of her mother. Frightened. Confused. Wondering where she was—*who* she was—why she was in this place. This was not her home.

Their home was in Blantonville, forty miles down the Verdigris River.

And then her father was saying, "Shhh. Shhh." And her mother's terrified voice softened and grew quieter until it faded away completely. The tape in the boombox continued to play, but all ten-year-old Krissy could hear was the hushing of her father, all she could see was the light dancing across the wall at the far end of the hall, all she could smell were wildflowers filling the house with their sickly sweet scent.

Violets. They were violets from Mommy's garden.

Remember, the voice that was not her own said in her mind. *Remember that day . . . when you met her.*

Kris tightened her grip on the glass of wine just as it was about to slip from her fingers.

She looked around, back in the present, the memory already fading like a gunshot ringing in the distance.

Setting the glass on the coffee table, Kris hurried across the great room and into the hallway. She shot a quick glance at Sadie's door, making sure it was closed, and then she ducked quietly into the bathroom.

She turned on the switch.

The light over the sink flickered to life.

Kris dug into her pocket and pulled out the bottle of Prozac. Before she had time to comprehend her actions, Kris twisted off the lid and pressed its mouth to her lips. She heard the capsules slide like candy down the inside of the cylinder. One of them bumped against the front of her bottom lip. She tipped the bottle higher, and the pill slid into her mouth.

Stop.

She shook the bottle, loosening the clump of pills wedged against her lip, until another one found its way into her mouth.

Stop.

She jostled the bottle harder.

There were three now. Three capsules sticking to the wet surface of her tongue.

Stop!

Kris lowered the plastic bottle, letting the other pills slide back down to the bottom. She swallowed all three pills in a single gulp of warm saliva.

Her head was already foggy from the wine. She imagined the capsules landing in her stomach, a mixture of wine and acid melting their gelatinous bodies, their red-and-blue ends combining to create a new color.

Purple.

Violet.

She stretched out her arms, pressing her hands against the walls as she stumbled toward the master bedroom.

That alien voice tried desperately to push through the fog.

He was going to have a baby with her, it sang.

She reached the master bedroom and shoved the door open. Somewhere, a million miles away, she heard the doorknob bang harshly into the wall.

He didn't want a family with you. But he wanted a family with her. He was happy with her.

She started to pull her shirt over her head, then gave up, letting it fall back into place. She turned, and her legs gave out, her body plummeting backward onto her bed.

Not your bed. Your mother's bed.

Her eyelids were so, so heavy.

Not true, she managed to think. *New . . . New mattress . . .*

It will always be your mother's bed, the alien voice said. *Her deathbed. Can't you smell the flowers?*

Then the fog swept over them both, and all voices were gone.

Her mind was silent, just like the house around her.

Time passed. A minute. An hour.

It was dark now. The sun was down. Evening had abandoned her. Night engulfed the world.

A voice called her from the depths of sleep.

"Hello."

The sound was not in her head. It was in the room with her.

It seemed to take all of her strength for Kris to force her eyes open.

At first, she saw only darkness. And then things began to emerge in the pale glow of moonlight.

Her body, still clothed, resting atop the undisturbed covers.

The dresser where her empty pill bottle still lay on its side like a fallen soldier.

A girl, standing just inside the darkened doorway.

Kris blinked several times to clear her vision.

The outline of the doorframe came into focus, but the image of the girl remained blurry.

"What?" Kris asked. Her voice echoed as if she were far away from her own body.

"Hello," the girl said again.

The weight of Kris's eyelids was too much. She closed them and sank into the mattress, allowing herself to be pulled down by the strange gravity of some distant world.

A thought drifted through her mind like a kite whose string had snapped. This is what dying felt like, not the sensation of a soul fleeing the body but of being pulled down . . . down . . . down into darkness.

Kris had the faint awareness that somewhere out there, across the void, someone had stepped up next to the bed.

Small fingers slipped into her hair. Fingertips grazed her scalp.

Soft lips pressed close to her ear.

"I found you."

The sound of the girl's voice pulled her back from the depths of slumber.

Groggy, her limbs feeling like fifty-pound weights, Kris sat up and swung her legs over the side of the bed.

"I'm sorry, sweetie," she mumbled. "Are you okay? Did you have a nightmare?"

The girl stood silently before her.

With her eyes still closed, Kris felt around the open air until she found the girl's hand. She took it, flinching at the shocking coldness of the girl's flesh.

"Baby, you're freezing."

Kris pushed herself up from the bed and stumbled blindly toward the door. Each step was a Herculean effort. Those invisible weights tried to pull her to the ground, but she pushed forward, pausing only once she reached the doorway. She let go of the girl's hand to steady herself against the jamb. Then she took a breath and began the long journey down the hall.

She could hear the soft padding of the girl's footsteps beside her. She thought she could sense the girl looking up at her and smiling, but Kris could not open her eyes long enough to see more than a few necessary glimpses of the path ahead.

After an eternity, she reached the door to Sadie's bedroom.

"There you go." Her tongue was a thick, fat worm in her mouth. "Go back to sleep."

She bent over to kiss the top of the girl's head. Her scalp was cold beneath surprisingly straight hair.

"I'm sorry, I'm just so tired. Go back to bed, okay? I love you . . ." The words trailed away.

Kris fumbled blindly for the doorknob and pushed the door open. The little girl slipped into the dark room.

Kris pulled the door shut until she heard the latch click softly into place. Then she let herself tip against the wall, her shoulder dragging along the wood paneling as she struggled to make her way back to the master bedroom.

There was the bed. That wonderful bed—

Where she died

—where Kris could sleep forever.

She crawled onto the mattress, still not bothering to pull down the covers. Her head hit the pillow, and the world clicked off like a light.

Only Kris's steady breathing—along with the faint song of the crickets and the occasional bellow of a bullfrog in the lake—broke the silence.

All was quiet. All was well.

Sadie was screaming.

Kris pushed desperately up from the void, breaking out of the darkness like a free diver reaching the ocean's surface. She leapt out of bed, but her numb legs could not hold the weight and immediately buckled. Her knees slammed down into the hardwood. Pain shot like a lightning bolt through her upper body. The jolt momentarily swept the fog from her mind.

Her sweet girl was shrieking in terror.

"Sadie!"

Kris scrambled across the bedroom floor on her hands and knees, using the doorframe to pull herself to her feet. She leaned into the shadows of the hallway. Sadie's cries were unbearably loud, ricocheting off the walls like jagged shards of shattered glass. She was pleading with someone in the room with her: "Stop! Stop, please! You're hurting me!" And in the next breath, she was shouting, begging: "Mommy! Mommy! Help me!"

Lunging down the hall on unsteady legs, Kris reached the door to Sadie's bedroom and flung it open.

On the other side, someone slammed the door shut.

Kris twisted the knob, but the person on the other side was putting their full weight against the door.

"Sadie, let me in!"

Sadie was screaming, over and over, "Mommy! Mommy!" Her voice sounded strangely distant, as if she were on the opposite side of the room. Yet every time Kris tried to open the door, someone shoved back.

"Open the door, Sadie!"

"Mommy!"

"Open The Door!"

"Mommy! Help Me!"

Adrenaline surged through Kris's veins, countering the effects of the meds and the alcohol to bring the moment into terrible clarity. With a furious roar, she lowered her shoulder and rammed the bedroom door.

It flew open with a force that nearly ripped it from its hinges.

Kris flicked on the light.

Sadie was on her bed, her face drenched in tears. Her hair was a rat's nest, her elegant curls tangled into a wild, frizzy mess. She clutched a hand to one side of her head. Her body heaved as she sobbed.

Rushing to the bed, Kris took her daughter in her arms.

Sadie pressed her face into her mother's chest and wept harder.

A few seconds passed. And then Kris asked, "Why wouldn't you let me in?"

"It wasn't me!" Sadie shouted.

"Honey, I'm just trying to understand—"

"It Wasn't Me!"

"Then who was it?" She heard the anger that laced her words, and she took a breath, trying again, more calmly this time, "Who was it, Sadie?"

A bubble of mucus formed between Sadie's lips and popped as she pushed the name out with a wail: "Violet!"

A trembling breath worked its way up Kris's throat and out of her gaping mouth. She could not move. She was frozen in time, like this house, like this town. Her mind convulsed like a toad boiling in a pot.

"What . . ."

"She was here! She pulled my hair! She's mad at me! Because you wouldn't play!"

"Stop it."

"She's real!" Sadie cried. "Look! Look what she did!" She removed her hand from the side of her head and thrust it, palm up, toward Kris's wide eyes.

Her skin was smeared with blood.

"Oh my God!" Kris gasped. "Baby . . ." She took Sadie's head in her hands and began to part her tangled hair. The red curls made it difficult to find any traces of blood.

Kris's fingers brushed something wet. Carefully, she sank her fingers into Sadie's hair and parted it.

A bare patch stared back from among the curls, a glistening red wound where a small piece of the girl's scalp had ripped free.

Kris's stomach dropped.

"How did this happen?" she asked.

"She did it! She pulled my hair!"

She's lying to you. It was her shadow voice, back to twist the knife. *She wants to punish you for bringing her here.*

"Come on." Kris took Sadie's hand, pulling her from the bed. "We need to get you cleaned up."

As she neared the doorway, Kris's foot came down on something stringy and damp. She immediately hopped back, frowning as she peered down at the object on the floor.

It looked like the detached tail of a small animal. A rodent, perhaps.

Kneeling down, Kris pinched the soft end of the object between her fingers and lifted it into the light.

It was a clump of curly red hair. At its end dangled a tiny square of scalp, still wet with blood.

CHAPTER THIRTY-NINE

AT EIGHT THE next morning, Kris's cell phone rang. The sound woke her from a dreamless sleep. She reached out a hand, her fingers fumbling around the nightstand until they found the phone.

The screen illuminated as she lifted it up. The caller ID displayed a number Kris had just recently added to her contacts:

Dr. Alice Baker.

Kris raised the phone to her ear. "Hello?" Her voice was rough with sleep.

"Kris?" Dr. Baker asked on the other end. She did not wait for a reply. There was an odd urgency in her voice. "This is Alice. Dr. Baker. I . . . I'm going to be back in town this morning, and I wondered if I could speak with you. In person."

Kris pushed herself up against the headboard. Only then did she remember that Sadie was next to her, fast asleep on the other side of the bed. The girl's cheeks were still flushed from crying, but her expression was relaxed. She snored softly into the pillow.

Cupping a hand over the mouth of the phone, Kris asked quietly, "What is this about? Is something wrong?"

There was a pause, and then Dr. Baker said, "I would really rather talk to you in person."

"But . . ." Kris frowned, confused. "It's Wednesday. I thought you wouldn't be back in town until Friday."

"I'm driving over just for a few hours," Alice replied.

"Just to talk to me?" Icy pinpricks of fear attacked her skin. "Please, Dr. Baker, if there's something I should be worried about with Sadie . . ."

She let her words trail off. Of course there was. After last night, how could she *not* be worried?

Dr. Baker pretended Kris has said nothing.

"I can be at my office in an hour," she said. "I'll see you then."

There was a soft click, and the other end of the call went dead.

Each step up to Dr. Baker's door felt like the journey to a mountain's summit. When Kris finally reached the landing, she found that her hand refused to raise to knock.

Beside her, Sadie stepped up and pressed close to her mother's leg.

Taking a deep breath, Kris forced her body to connect with her mind. She balled her hand into a fist and rapped lightly on the frosted-glass window mounted into the top half of the office door.

A blurry form moved quickly up to the glass, and then the door swung open, revealing Dr. Baker dressed in her impeccable work attire: a cream blouse and slim pinstriped slacks. She smiled as she always did, but it lacked her usual warmth.

"Thank you so much for coming," she said as if there had been much of a choice. She glanced down at Sadie, who was peeking out from around her mother's leg. "Hi, Sadie. It's okay, you're not here for a session. I want to talk to your mommy for a minute, okay?"

Sadie looked from Dr. Baker to her mother and back again. She gave a small nod.

"Okay," Dr. Baker said, her fake smile growing wider. She checked the delicate antique watch fastened to her wrist with a braided silver strap. "This won't take more than a few minutes, I promise," she told Kris. "Would it be okay if Sadie waited out here on the landing? We can keep the door open a crack so we can see her."

Kris drew in a nervous breath.

Dr. Baker must have heard this, for she added, "She'll be all right. She'll be where we can still see her, I promise." Then, to Sadie, she said, "Just stay up here. Promise?"

Sadie looked to her mother, waiting for approval.

Kris gave a nod, and the little girl sat down on the landing, her feet resting on the top step.

Dr. Baker stepped aside to allow Kris to enter.

"Don't move," Kris told Sadie, and then she stepped into the office, pushing the door closed until only a crack of open air remained.

Dr. Baker was already crossing to her desk on the other side of the room.

"Please," Kris said, "why am I here?"

Without bothering to respond, Dr. Baker opened a folder on her desk. She picked up two pieces of paper, making sure to keep one side toward herself. The other side was blank.

Previously overlooked sounds in the room were suddenly all Kris could hear: the unwavering tick of a clock on a bookshelf; the faint buzz of a slender brass lamp in the corner; the muffled rumble of the occasional car passing, unseen, on the street below; Kris's own breaths, more frequent than she felt they should be, betraying her growing nervousness.

Finally Dr. Baker broke the silence.

"Do you remember why your father brought you to see me?"

The question was so unexpected, so out of left field, that it took a moment for Kris to make sense of it.

"He . . . he brought me to see you because my mom was sick. He wanted me to talk to you about her."

"About your mother."

"Yeah. Because she . . . she was dying. He was worried about me."

Dr. Baker made a sound in the back of her throat. She motioned to the leather couch that faced the chair—her chair—at the center of the room.

Kris did as she was asked and took a seat on the couch. Dr. Baker sat down in her chair, placing the pieces of paper atop each other on her lap. The blank sides were still up. Whatever was on the other side remained hidden.

"How has Sadie been since I last saw her?" Dr. Baker asked. Her tone had shifted to a higher register. It was the way she spoke to Sadie, the same way she had spoken to little Krissy Parker all those years ago. Kris assumed it was how she spoke to all troubled children.

Kris suddenly felt like an insect pinned to a Styrofoam backing, her limbs crooked and broken, her brittle wings spread wide in a forced simulation of flight.

She shifted nervously on the couch. "She's been . . ."

Her first instinct was to lie, to paint a picture of domestic bliss. But she knew this would do no good. She brought Sadie to see Dr. Baker because she needed outside help. That had not changed. In fact, Kris needed that help more than ever.

"She's worse," Kris admitted. "She doesn't seem happy anymore. But she's still spending all of her time alone. And last night . . ."

Dr. Baker waited patiently, giving Kris the time she needed to collect her thoughts.

"Last night she woke up screaming. She . . . she had pulled out a piece of her own hair."

A piece, her shadow voice scoffed. *That was a clump. You could have braided that motherfucker.*

Kris glanced up as if worried the doctor had overheard the voice in her head.

Dr. Baker's brow was furrowed, and she had leaned forward slightly in her seat.

"Pulled out her hair?"

"I think . . ." Kris searched for a rational explanation. "I think she had a nightmare. I think she did it in her sleep."

Dr. Baker's eyes flashed quickly over Kris's shoulder. Kris glanced back.

Through the crack in the door, she could see Sadie sitting on the landing, just as she had been instructed.

She's a good kid, Kris told herself, and the thought sent a pleasant surge of warmth through her chest.

"And how are you?"

The question drew Kris's gaze back to Dr. Baker.

"Are you sleeping?"

"Yes, I'm sleeping fine."

"Are you drinking? Alcohol, I mean?"

Kris stiffened. "A little wine now and then, but . . ."

"Are you self-medicating?"

Tell her to go to hell, her shadow voice commanded. The words were sleek daggers of whispered fury. *Tell her to mind her own goddamn business.*

Kris cleared her throat and forced herself to keep her composure. "My husband is dead and my daughter is pulling out her own hair, so yeah, I've probably been drinking more than usual. And I brought some Xanax from home. That a doctor prescribed."

Surprisingly, this answer appeared to satisfy Dr. Baker. She settled back into her chair, her expression relaxing. She kept her hands firmly on the papers in her lap.

"The last time Sadie was here, she mentioned her friend."

"From back home?"

Dr. Baker shook her head. "Here. In Pacington. You were right, Kris. She has been playing with an imaginary friend."

A painful spike shot through Kris's brain. It was brief, like a flash of lightning in a night sky.

"Yeah?" Kris heard herself say.

Again, Dr. Baker's eyes drifted over Kris's shoulder to Sadie out on the landing.

"I asked her if her friend had a name. She said it was Violet. Did you know that?"

"She, um . . ." Kris's mouth was suddenly bone dry. She could feel Dr. Baker's scrutinizing stare. It was like hot sunlight on burned flesh. "She may have said . . ." Kris went to stand and found that her legs had inexplicably gone weak. Gripping the edge of the cushion for support, she rose from the couch. "You know, I should probably . . . I should get Sadie—"

"It wasn't about your mother," Dr. Baker said suddenly.

Kris froze.

Dr. Baker had lifted the sheets of paper from her lap, but the other sides remained hidden from view.

"What?" Kris managed to ask.

"Your father. He didn't bring you here to talk about your mother," the doctor explained.

Don't listen, Kris's voice warned her.

She wanted to press her hands to her ears, to block out the sound of the doctor's voice.

"He was worried about you."

Don't listen to her.

"Not because you were sad."

Tell her to stop.

"Because you seemed so happy."

Shut her up.

"You acted like you didn't even know your mother was sick. You were playing and laughing. Your father was worried that you weren't accepting what was happening."

Kris felt as if she had forgotten how to breathe.

"You never even mentioned your mother to me," Dr. Baker told her. "You only wanted to talk about your friend. Your friend Violet."

The words no longer made sense. Dr. Baker may as well have been speaking a foreign language. Kris stared at her dumbly, unable to comprehend.

She watched, stunned, as Dr. Baker turned the pieces of paper over on her lap. She held them side by side.

On each sheet, a childish picture had been drawn with colored pencils. At the center of each was a little girl with a circle for a head, green dots for eyes, and red squiggles of curly hair. Behind her was a house with a peaked roof, square windows, and a single round window up in the right corner. Beyond this, a blue circle formed the water of a lake. Jagged red hills rose up over the lake.

There was another figure in the picture. Another girl, similar in size to the first. Except this girl had straight black hair down to her shoulders. Her eyes were black dots stabbed into the paper with the tip of a pencil. Her body was a triangle. A dress. And the inside of the dress had been colored purple.

Dr. Baker waited patiently for Kris to speak.

"Did . . ." Kris began. "Did Sadie draw those?"

With the index finger of her left hand, Dr. Baker tapped the first picture.

"Sadie drew this one during our last session."

With her other index finger, she tapped the picture held in place by her right hand.

"And you drew this one. Thirty years ago."

Kris looked back and forth between the two drawings. She saw now that the paper on the right was yellowed slightly with age. The red-haired girl on this page was smaller than in the other picture, the girl in the purple dress looming larger. And in this one, their hands were clasped. Other than that, the drawings were identical.

From behind her came the faint squeak of hinges.

Kris slowly turned around.

The office door had been pushed open an inch or two farther. Through the slim space between the door and the frame, she could see one of Sadie's green eyes, peering in.

CHAPTER FORTY

KRIS RUSHED OUT onto the landing and yanked Sadie to her feet, hurrying her down the stairs. Kris could hear Dr. Baker in the office doorway, pleading with her to stay. They needed to talk. There had to be an explanation. But Kris knew that they would not find the rational conclusion that Dr. Baker desired. A troubling concept was taking shape in Kris's mind, that a puzzle from her past was falling into place whether she liked it or not.

So Kris fled, driving Sadie home as quickly as she could. The second they were back in the driveway, Sadie climbed out of the Jeep and walked into the house, not with the unbridled excitement she had shown before but as if she were asleep, being called inside by a voice in a dream.

Kris hurried into the kitchen and threw the car keys onto the island. Behind her, the front door stood wide open, completely forgotten. She couldn't breathe. She tried desperately to pull air into her lungs. She needed air or she was going to pass out right there on the kitchen floor.

Storming across the great room, Kris threw open the French doors and rushed out onto the deck. She gripped the top plank of the wooden railing, digging her fingernails deeply into the old pulpy wood, and sucked in a breath.

She waited for the other voices to speak, for Timid Kris to blame her for their situation, for Shadow Kris to tell her that she was losing her mind, for Jonah to say that she was the problem—she was always the problem, this is why he never loved her, why he had to find someone else.

No other voices chimed in.

Kris was alone in her boiling, squirming mind.

Her eyes followed the small waves as they marched across the cove to the opposite shore.

The dark-haired woman was standing at the water's edge, staring back at Kris.

Kris dug her fingernails deeper into the soft wooden railing. The anger was back, but it was no longer the spark she had felt the night before with Sadie. It was a wildfire, whipped into a frenzy by a howling wind.

"What the hell do you think you're looking at?" she yelled.

The woman did not move. She was so close to the water that her image was reflected in its rippling surface.

"Mind your own fucking business!" she yelled. The words tore at her throat like broken glass.

The woman remained still. Staring.

"What do you want from me?!" Kris shrieked.

The day had become impossibly quiet. No leaves rustled. No insects buzzed.

She wanted to shatter that silence.

"What Do You Want?!"

For another moment, the woman did not move. And then she turned and slowly climbed the embankment toward her house.

The utter lack of fanfare only made Kris more furious.

She slammed a fist down on the top of the railing, and then she stormed off down the stairs toward the curved spine of the lakeshore.

Kris parted a curtain of cattails, and there before her was the cabin. She had been right: It was much smaller than hers, a one-story house with a short deck no more than ten feet deep jutting crookedly off the back. The posts beneath the deck were gnawed thin by termites. Overgrown oak trees thick with webworm nests shrouded the house, their tired branches resting on the crooked shingles of the roof. Heavy shadows draped the structure like a shroud. Had Kris not just seen the woman moments before, she would have assumed the house was abandoned.

A path of uneven gray flagstones led into the deeper shadows around the side of the house. Kris stepped from stone to stone, passing several small windows as she made her way to the front of the house. Despite the cooler weather, sweat had begun to pour down her face. It clung to the line of her jaw just as rainwater clings to the underside of a leaf. The back of her shirt was completely soaked through. She could feel it peeling away from her skin like a lizard's tongue every time she moved.

She raised her foot to take another step, but the path was suddenly gone. Unlike the clearing in which her lake house had been built, this place seemed to be encroaching on the forest's domain. Thorny vines curled up the side of the house, the chipping paint partially hidden by glossy, triangular leaves that lay flat against the wood siding. Tiny red bugs skittered across the surface of the leaves before disappearing into the darkness beneath them.

The cottage was tucked into the side of the slope so that its pointed roof extended up from the parched earth like a single tooth. There was one raised stair that served as the doorstep, flanked by two thin pillars growing thinner the closer they got to the overhang of the roof. The front door was an unfinished cedar. Once a deep tan, it was now aged and cracked, its color dulled to a ghostly pale.

Kris carefully grasped the thorny vines in both hands and parted them, just enough to slip up to the front door.

She knocked and waited.

There was no answer.

She knocked again.

Still, only silence.

A small animal—a lizard or a rat— skittered through the thick foliage that had wrapped itself around one of the columns just off to her right.

She slipped a sweaty hand around the doorknob and twisted it.

The door popped open.

"Hello?" she called through the tiny crack between the door and the doorjamb.

Nothing.

Silence.

She pushed the door open a few inches, then stopped, that scolding voice reminding her that there were still rules to obey.

You don't know when she'll be home. You weren't invited here.

Kris shook the voice away and took a step inside.

The door closed behind her with a soft click.

This was as far as Kris could go. It appeared that every inch of the cabin was filled with crumbling cardboard boxes, stacks of books, and yellowing newspapers. There was furniture under there somewhere. She glimpsed the corner of a sofa peeking out from under a blanket of open magazines, draped across the top of the sofa's arm like the spread wings of a dead bird. The dingy fabric of the sofa had peeled away in places, revealing the wooden bones beneath.

Even the air in this place seemed to be a physical barrier. It hung motionless around her, pressing against her face like hot, bristly fur. It felt too thick to even breath.

As Kris adjusted to the overwhelming sight of the room, she began to make out small passageways through the clutter. One trail led off to the left to a kitchenette buried under mountains of food-crusted dishes and filthy pots and pans. Another wound its way through a cityscape of stacked boxes to a narrow hallway running parallel to the main room. Behind the couch was a third path, wider than the other two, a direct shot to a sliding glass door that opened to the back deck. The glass itself was covered in layers upon layers of handprints, palms flat, fingers spread wide as if imploring anyone approaching to stop. Through this glass, the world outside was transformed into a swirl of blurred colors and shapes, an alien landscape too distant to make out. Even the sunlight seemed unable to penetrate the dirty glass, relinquishing the interior of the tiny cottage to the shadows.

Kris chose the second path. She moved in a sharp, zigzag line around the boxes, pausing to glance into a few that were partially open. Inside were random trinkets—small ceramic animals, a single bedroom slipper, a handful of pine cones—as well as stories clipped from newspapers and magazines and a few loose photographs.

Pulling back one of the lids, she picked up a photo. Written in crudely printed letters across the back were the words, "Melody—1st Grade." Kris turned the photograph over and found herself staring at the sweet, smiling face of a seven-year-old girl. One of her front teeth was missing, leaving a gaping black hole in her grin. Her hair was a pale yellow, like the first streams of sunlight that split the clouds after a summer rain. There was joy in that face. Hope. Innocence.

The girl reminded Kris of herself at that age.

There were more photographs in the box, some of the girl alone, others featuring adults who could have been anyone in the world. The girl was never older than eight or nine. There was one other school photo in the box. Scrawled on the back in the same crude handwriting was "Melody—2nd Grade." Beyond this, Melody did not appear to exist.

Kris carefully navigated the increasingly narrow path until she reached the entrance to the hall. Several stacks of books were lined up in the doorway, blocking her way. Most of the books were old paperbacks—romance novels and 1970s political thrillers whose covers were peeling away from their spines. But a few titles caught Kris's eye, seemingly at random, until one by one they began to fall into a strange but undeniable category.

Folklore of the Midwest.
North American Spirits and Monsters.
Stories of the Osage.
Kiowa Myths and Legends.
Kansas Ghost Stories.
Water Spirits and Lake Monsters.

Above her, something jingled lightly.

Kris glanced up. Copper nails had been driven halfway into the wooden beam at the top of the doorway. From each nail, a piece of twine had been tied in a double knot, and at the end of each length of twine, an empty aluminum soda can was suspended.

At first, Kris wondered how she could have missed seeing this the moment she entered the house. And then she remembered how overwhelmed she had been by the mountains of clutter, how she had looked down at the floor as she moved between the boxes, how the stacks of books had been the first thing she saw when she reached the hall entrance.

She tapped one of the cans softly with a fingernail and heard the sound of multiple hard objects jangling inside. Tipping the can slightly to let a bit of light in, she saw that the bottom was covered with old steel screws and hexagonal nuts. She gave the can a light shake, and the objects inside rattled harshly.

This isn't some bizarre decoration, Kris realized. *This is an alarm system.*

Between the stacks of books and suspended soda cans, there was just enough room to squeeze through into the hallway. Kris gripped the edges of the doorjamb and carefully leaned through.

The hall was just as gloomy as the rest of the house. Shadows swallowed one end, giving it the unnerving appearance of extending forever into darkness. At the other end, a bathroom door was open, allowing light to fall upon the closed door of a third room.

Another bedroom, Kris assumed.

She frowned, confused.

Two rusty safety hasps were mounted across the left side of the door, barring it from opening. It appeared to have been a rush job; the hasps were slanted at odd angles, the screws securing them driven in quickly and sloppily so that the heads were not flush with the tops of the metal strips. A hefty padlock hung from the loop of each hasp.

Two padlocks to keep a bedroom door from opening.

To keep people out.

Or something in.

"What the hell you think you're doing?" a sharp voice barked.

Kris leapt backward, her foot hitting a stack of books and toppling it. The back of her head knocked several of the cans and sent them swaying wildly, the contents inside sounding their alarm like a pit of baby rattlesnakes.

Standing in the front doorway was the dark-haired woman. Her eyes were slits as narrow and sharp as the edges of knives, her lips curled in a slight snarl to reveal crooked yellow teeth. Kris had never been this close to her, and she now realized that the woman's hair was not black as she had thought but a greasy brown, stringy and unwashed. Weathered, leathery skin marred by large patches of sunspots was stretched tightly over the sharp ridges of her bony face. She reminded Kris of the black-and-white photographs from the Dust Bowl era that she had seen in a museum—women on porches of clapboard houses, in the cabs of dingy pickup trucks, in the billowing tents of migrant camps, frail hands to their foreheads but their eyes looking up, battered but not beaten. This woman's hard stare let Kris know that she had dealt with tougher things than finding a stranger in her house.

"I knocked but no one answered," Kris said, as if this explained the intrusion. "I'm staying in the house across the lake from you—"

"I know who you are," the woman snapped, her Midwestern twang twisting her words like smoke from a campfire.

Of course, she knows, that shadow voice hissed from the depths of Kris's mind.

Suddenly Kris remembered why she had stormed over in the first place: the feeling of constantly being watched by this woman; the shock of finding her daughter watching from the woods; the terror of almost hitting the girl in the road. Kris was not the one at fault here. *She* was the one whose privacy was being invaded. *She* was the one who deserved answers.

"What do you want from me?" Kris asked. Both of her hands were clenched so tightly, she could feel her nails digging into her palms.

The woman gave a humorless snort. "I don't give two shits about you."

"Then why the hell do you find us so interesting?" Kris could feel her heartbeat beginning to thump in her temple. Her skin was hot and alive. "Why is it that every time I look out my goddamn window, you're staring back? Huh? What do you want?"

The woman opened her mouth to respond, but she was cut off by a third voice that seemed to materialize out of the thick, stagnant air.

"Mama?"

The woman's head jerked up.

"Mama," the voice called out again. "I wanna come out. I'm okay now. I promise, I won't run away."

In Kris's mind, pieces of a forgotten puzzle fell into place.

The barrier of books.

The hanging soda cans.

The padlocked door.

"Who's in that room?" she asked.

"You stay away from there!" the woman yelled. She lunged forward, grabbing Kris by the forearm. But Kris thrust her backward. The woman fell into a pile of old newspapers.

The girl in the room banged frantically on the bedroom door.

A thought sprang into Kris's mind, an image of the one person who had never been found.

Poppy, she thought, afraid to say the name out loud.

The scenario forced itself together: the dark-haired woman in the park the day Poppy went missing; dragging the frightened girl back to this cabin on the far side of the lake; locking Poppy away in a bedroom at the end of the hall; keeping her there until she forgot her own parents and began to call this insane person "Mama."

Kris cocked her head and stared at the woman with disgust. "Who is in that room?"

"Mama!" the voice behind the door shrieked. Fists pounded on the door.

"Who is it?"

"Mama!"

The woman cringed at the sound. She rose up from the pile of trash upon which she had fallen, and she yelled at the top of her lungs, "Melody! Stop!"

The sound of the name tore Kris's assumption to shreds.

Melody. She had seen it on the backs of photographs when she first entered. Melody. Sweet, smiling Melody.

"Is that . . . is that your *daughter*?" Kris asked. Somehow it would have been easier if it were Poppy. "Is your daughter locked in that room?"

The woman's cold strength drained away. She raised a hand out toward Kris, and Kris saw that it was shaking. "Please. You don't understand—"

"I want to come out, Mama," the phantom voice called from down the hall. "I'm sorry. I'll listen to you, I promise."

Kris turned back toward the hallway. She began to push one of the stacks of books aside with her foot as she made her way into the hall.

"Stop!" the woman yelled.

"I want to know why," Kris demanded. "Why you're watching us. Why your daughter is locked in that room. Why? Why?!"

The woman clenched her fists and pressed them to her eyes. "You won't believe me!"

"Tell me!" Kris yelled.

Run, her timid voice ordered. *She's crazy! She'll hurt you!*

But Kris's own voice screamed, *It's all here. Everything. The answers. They're here!*

She had to know. More than who was behind that door. She had to know how all of the secrets in this town fit together.

Staring down at the woman sprawled across a bed of old news-papers, Kris felt her anger subsiding. In its place was pity for this poor creature.

"What's your name?" Kris asked.

The mundane nature of the question seemed to throw the woman off. Her body quivered as she forced out the word, "Vicky."

"Okay, Vicky. Here's the deal. You're going to tell me exactly what the fuck is going on."

"Y'all gotta go," the woman whispered.

"Why? Why don't you want us here?"

"It's not me." She swallowed hard, wetting her dry throat. "There's something bad in that house. It's been there for years. I promise, I don't mean you or your daughter no harm. I just . . . I thought it was over . . . finally . . . and then you all showed up and my girl, my girl . . ."

Even in the dim light, the woman's eyes glistened with tears.

"She was doing better. She was. Until y'all showed up."

Kris leaned back on her heels, giving the woman some space. "What are you talking about?"

A strange little smile tugged at the corners of the woman's lips. "You mean to tell me you been staying in that place and you don't know?"

"I don't know what you—"

"You expect me to believe you ain't realized there's something wrong with that house?"

Kris did not move. She said nothing.

The woman's grin widened.

"You know, don't you? So does my Melody. She knows there's somethin' in that house. She's known since she was a little girl. We lost her once, in the middle of the night. Climbed right out her window, and when I went to check on her, all I found was an empty bed. You know how that feels? You know how goddamn scary that is, going to check on your baby girl and finding an empty bed?"

Sadie, Kris thought suddenly.

She was at home. Alone.

Kris needed to get back to the lake house. But her muscles would not respond. She was frozen in this spot, standing before this awk-wardly sprawled-out woman, hanging on her every word.

"We found her the next morning," Vicky continued. "She was in your house. And so we brought her back. Danny said it was a one-time thing, that she was just sleepwalkin' or somethin'. I knew in my heart that it wasn't true. There was somethin' off about that place. But Danny wouldn't listen. Even when Melody got out again. And again. And again. Always endin' up in the same place. Always in that house."

Please, go, her mind implored.

But Kris knew she could not go. She needed to hear this. She needed answers.

She tried to form a word but only a pathetic creak came out. She took a breath and tried again.

"Why? Why did she go there?"

"Violet," the woman said.

There was a moment where Kris was sure the ground was moving beneath her. The earth shifted beneath her bent knees, and she moved with it, turning in a slow circle as everything else stayed perfectly in place. The sensation made her queasy. She wanted to throw up. She needed to evacuate every solid thing from her body and then melt away, into the floorboards, deep down into the dark, forgotten soil beneath the house.

"How do you know that name?"

From down the hall, the unseen girl known as Melody began to sing in an octave too high for her meager voice:

"Blackbird singing in the dead of night . . ."

A vivid, inexplicable image filled Kris's mind: a star collapsing in on itself, like the weakened structure of a burning building, its fire growing intensely hot for one last time before its inevitable death.

She felt the hot air constricting around her, its serpentine muscles squeezing the breath from her lungs.

The woman's smile faded, replaced by a look of sad recognition.

We are united in this, her expression seemed to say. *We are bound by this horror.*

"We thought she would end up like the other girls, but we found her. Every time, we found her. Danny couldn't take it no more and the bastard left. But she's my only child. You know how that is. I had to do whatever it took to keep her safe."

The girl behind the door continued to sing off-key: "All your life . . . you were only waiting for this moment to arise."

"Why didn't you leave?" Kris asked.

The woman's leathery face wrinkled into an incredulous fist. "What the hell you think I could do? Sell this house and just go somewhere else? Ain't nobody wants to move to this shit town." She exhaled a breath through her nose, like an angry dog. "Besides, this is my home. I'm not leaving."

The singing from down the hall had become a scream. There was no music to the sound.

"But your daughter—" Kris began.

"Don't you pretend to give one shit about my daughter. She was fine until you and your girl showed up. She was getting *better*."

Without warning, the woman leapt up, her face inches from Kris's. Her mouth twisted into a snarl as if she meant to clamp her teeth onto Kris's lips and pull until they ripped free.

"I gotta keep her locked up or she'll end up dead, just like the rest."

A loud thud caused Kris's body to spasm, her joints locking painfully.

The girl at the end of the hall was banging on the bedroom door. She began to howl, a horrible, inhuman sound, as she pounded rhythmically on the door like the chiming of a giant clock.

"Dead!" the woman shouted.

No.

"Dead like the rest!"

From behind the bedroom door, the girl's howl reached an ungodly crescendo that jabbed ruthlessly into the soft flesh of Kris's joints, threatening to pry her bones apart.

The woman shrieked to match her daughter's insanity.

"Dead Like The Rest!"

No!

Kris did not remember leaving the house. She did not recall if she managed to navigate the narrow path through the cluttered room or if she simply barreled across the piles of trash in a desperate attempt to reach the front door. Her next memory was of running down the crooked stone path on the side of the house and into the dense black shadows of the forest.

There was a light ahead, the golden glow of a clearing, if only she could reach it.

Her entire body was a red-hot coal. Soon it would burn to ash, and she would blow away on the warm breeze, piece by miniscule piece, until she only existed as flakes of gray. Pieces of her being would fall upon the still surface of Lost Lake and dissolve. They would land on the flesh of passersby and be smeared into a charcoal streak as they were rubbed away. They would be whisked higher into the air and torn apart until there was nothing, no trace that Kris had ever existed, no evidence that this pale, dissipating cloud had once been a woman.

She heard wooden steps groaning under her feet as she hurried up onto the deck. She felt the smooth brass handle of the French door, still hot even in the fading sunlight. She caught a glimpse of her blurry reflection in the glass, like an accidental photograph of a passing stranger. But Kris was not aware of actually being there. She was not commanding her brain to do these things. Her body had taken over, while Kris scrambled further and further back into the darkness of her mind, toward the door where she kept the unpleasant things. She needed to know that it was shut. She wanted to press her back up against it and make sure that it could not open.

The lake house was quiet. Every now and then, she heard the thump of movement or a soft, distant giggle to ensure that Sadie was still there and okay, but otherwise a heavy silence had fallen over the house. It reminded Kris of those moments before a summer thunderstorm when the sky would become a sickly, eerie green and the air would hang perfectly still around her as if it were afraid to move. Because it knew something big was on its way. There was a beast stalking behind that wall of heavy, bruised clouds above.

The great room seemed impossibly deep, stretching off without end into shadow. Bright shafts of sunshine cut ruthlessly through the gloom like beams of a collapsed building jutting out of rubble. The stark contrast between light and dark made Kris think of a movie she had seen once when she was a little girl, a silent black-and-white horror film in another language, the subtitles flashing by too quickly for her young mind to comprehend. She remembered the odd angles of the streets and buildings and their clearly artificial appearance, as if the filmmaker wanted her to know that this was not the outside world but an illusion. It was all a trick—the street narrowing too quickly, the buildings becoming smaller and smaller to create a sense of false depth. She was being asked to believe in something and, at the same time, she was being shown all of the reasons to doubt its validity. She remembered the figure at the center of it all, a tall, slender man with flesh too pale to be that of the living, his wide eyes staring out from deep black circles as if at a world of madness only he could see.

Kris opened her mouth to call to her daughter, but her trembling lips refused to form the proper sounds. She knew if she tried to speak, the sound would come out as a horrible, animal-like moan.

Part of her was thankful that she could not speak, for she was afraid Sadie would rush into the room and see her there, eyes wide, skin drained of even its usual meek color, looking just like the demonic sleepwalker from that silent film, and Sadie would scream at the sight of her own mother.

You look dead, she thought.

Dead.

Dead like the rest.

The voice in her mind became that of the woman from across the lake, shrieking in her flat Midwestern twang:

Dead like the rest! Dead like the rest!

The rest.

The others.

The little lost girls, their bodies found in the hollowed-out tree, in the house in the lake, on the jagged rock that rose up from the forest floor like the teeth of a buried monster.

All the places Kris used to play when she was little.

Outside, the sun slipped out from behind a cloud, and the light shining in through the windows grew brighter. Kris winced, shielding her eyes.

Pieces of the great room began to glow as if illuminated by spotlights, and in this intense light, every imperfection was suddenly on display. The cracked stones of the fireplace. The warped boards of the hardwood floor. The paint peeling from the splintering walls.

High up where the top of the fireplace met the vaulted ceiling, a large dark stain had spread across the oak planks, the result of a years-old leak no one had bothered to fix. The wood, softened by dry rot, was flaking away, creating a crater like a necrotic wound in the wall. Near this, a vine had begun to twist its green fingers in through a crack in the ceiling, forcing its way into the lake house.

This was not the perfect lake house of her youth. This was a neglected structure being slowly torn apart by aggressive, heartless nature.

Like a cancer that eats away your mommy's brain.

Kris's body buzzed, electric, and she had the sudden, terrifying sense that she was a filament burning dangerously hot until—*pop!*—her light would go out forever.

She needed to calm down. She needed to get control of herself before the panic took over.

The pills.

Kris lurched quickly across the room, catching herself on the doorframe to the hallway. Her vision suddenly jumped, like a filmstrip that had hopped a sprocket, each frame quivering in the gate.

She pinched her eyes shut. She clumsily felt along the wall, her fingertips sliding over the rough, splintered wood until they hit the edge of another doorframe.

The bathroom.

Slipping a hand around the jam, she found the light switch and flicked it on.

Only then did she open her eyes.

The bathroom light flickered once, twice, then steadied, casting an orb of pale light over the discolored sink.

Reflected in the water-spotted mirror was a face not unlike the silent film monster Kris had envisioned: hair matted with sweat, flesh pale and greasy, a dark circle under each wild eye. Was this how she'd appeared this entire time? She tried to remember the last time she had looked—really looked—at her own reflection, but her mind was a pit of fiery, scurrying things, like an anthill kicked by a cruel child.

Kris gritted her teeth and tried to stay in her own body for a few more moments, just long enough to find the medication that would offer relief. She threw open the medicine cabinet, positive the plastic bottle would not be there, that it had been in her pocket the whole time, working its way out as she stormed around the lake to fall and be swallowed by the muddy shore.

But it was there, right where she had put it the night before.

She snatched the pill bottle from its shelf. Her hands were shaking badly, her sweaty palms making it nearly impossible to get a firm grip on the childproof cap. She felt the ridges of its side bite into her skin and she twisted.

The cap moved.

Thank fucking God, she thought.

There was a soft popping sound, like a cork freed from a bottle of flat champagne. In her excitement, Kris tipped the bottle quickly toward the open palm of her other hand, but the motion was too quick, too sharp, and a handful of pills arced out of the bottle, missing her hand entirely. They tumbled to the floor and across tiles once again caked with dirt and grime. Instinctively, she took a step back to see the mess she had made and felt a capsule crunch under her shoe.

Idiot! she scolded herself. She couldn't waste a single pill if she hoped to make them last until the next refill.

Carefully this time, she shook a single pill into her hand and slammed her palm to her open mouth. Its sticky body hit the back of her tongue. A bitterness immediately began to creep down her throat. Setting the plastic bottle on the edge of the sink, she gulped a mouthful of cool water straight from the faucet, swallowing it down and the pill with it. The water had an odd mineral taste she had never noticed, as if it had come from deep within the earth carrying thousands of years of sediment with it.

She waited for the medication—or at the very least, the placebo effect of taking the pill—to flood her body with that warm fuzziness she desperately needed.

No relief came.

Her entire body began to tremble. The insects seemed to have multiplied by the millions under her skin. They were digging beneath the twisted ropes of her muscles to scratch at her bones, their legs like needles as they attempted to bore to the very center of her.

Her hand flashed up to the edge of the sink, her action once again too abrupt. She knew she had made a mistake but there was nothing she could do. She could not stop in time. The back of her hand hit the lip of the sink and grazed the bottom of the pill bottle. And then it was falling forward, into the sink, the red-and-blue capsules tumbling into the rushing water and disappearing down the black mouth of the drain.

"No!" Kris shouted, "No, no, no!"

She twisted the handle hard to the right, shutting off the water, and slammed both hands down over the drain.

The pills were gone.

All of them.

"Goddammit!" Her heart was thundering in her chest. She stared dumbly at that black hole at the bottom of the sink as if at any moment it would regurgitate what it had swallowed.

You dumb, stupid shit, she thought. *Now what are you going to do?*

A flash of pain struck her head like a lightning strike. She pinched her eyes shut and clamped a hand on each temple, trying to keep her skull from splitting.

When she finally opened her eyes again, she was staring down at at least a dozen capsules lying on the bathroom floor.

Kris dropped to her knees so quickly, the hard tiles sent sharp reverberations up her legs into her hips. She barely noticed. She was already scooping up the pills like a child who had spilled her Halloween candy. One pill went into her mouth, then another, and another.

She swallowed them, hoping, praying that finally the medication would kick in and save her from the feeling of her body being torn apart from the inside.

Her desperate, shaking fingers found half of a capsule.

She must have stepped on it. Its two halves had come apart under her weight. The floor should have been covered in a powdery drug.

It wasn't. The tiles were clean.

Kris frowned, confused. She looked from the broken pill to the other capsules in her hand. She gripped the ends of one between her fingers and twisted until the capsule came apart at the center.

It was empty.

She let the other capsules roll from her open palm and picked them up from the floor, one by one, separating each like tiny Russian nesting dolls, expecting the next to be filled with medicine.

Every single pill was empty.

Allison, she thought. *She could tell something was wrong. She gave me a bottle of empty goddamn pills!*

A thought suddenly occurred to her, something so outrageous she immediately rejected it. But it took hold in the wild maelstrom of her feverish mind and would not let go.

Sadie did this.

"No," Kris said aloud, her voice echoing off the cold, hard surfaces of the bathroom.

You know it's true. Allison works for you. She did as she was told. Someone else emptied them and put them back together. And if it wasn't you . . .

Kris stood up, the sudden action throwing her off balance as her brain seemed to collide with the sides of her skull. Again, she closed her eyes in a desperate attempt to ward off the excruciating pain.

"Sadie!" she cried out.

The house answered her with silence.

"Sadie! Come here right now!"

Still no answer.

Holding on to the doorjamb for support, Kris stumbled out into the hallway.

"Sadie! Where are you?!"

Kris paused, listening.

From upstairs, she thought she could hear two voices. Low. Whispering.

One was Sadie's sweet high-pitched voice.

The other had a darker, commanding tone.

There was the click of a latch.

The tiny door to the room behind the wall, Kris realized.

Footsteps padded down the unseen staircase, and then Sadie was there, walking slowly, hesitantly toward her down the hall.

"What?" she asked.

The willful ignorance of the question infuriated Kris. Her entire being buzzed like a live wire.

"You know what!" Kris yelled. She had rarely taken this tone with her daughter, but she was beyond caring about tempering her emotions. She wanted Sadie to feel the panic she was feeling.

Sadie slowly shook her head. "Mommy, I don't—"

"The pills! You emptied the capsules!"

She expected Sadie to forcefully deny this accusation, but the little girl simply stood before her staring, her large green eyes shimmering even in the dim hallway.

"Did you do it?!" Kris cried.

Sadie nodded and said with an alarming lack of emotion, "Yes."

Kris felt as though the floor had opened beneath her and she were plummeting through open, endless air.

She forced out a single, breathless word: "Why?"

"Violet told me to."

Fury gripped Kris in a tight, burning fist.

"Stop lying!"

"I'm not lying! Violet told me to do it!"

"Sadie—"

"She said if you took the medicine, you wouldn't be able to see her!"

"Stop lying!"

"I'm not! I promise!" Sadie's freckled face scrunched up, her lips trembling, her eyes filling with tears.

Kris knelt down and grabbed Sadie roughly by the shoulders. "Tell me the truth!" she shouted in her daughter's startled face.

"I am! Violet told me to do it! She wants you to remember!"

No, Kris warned herself. *Don't listen to her.*

"She wants you to remember the day you met her!"

Shut her up! Make her stop!

Sadie was shrieking, "Remember the day you met her! Remember, Mommy!"

Make her stop!

"Remember!"

Make her—

The surface broke, and crystal clear waters flowed up from the depths. Little Krissy was ten years old. Her mother was not a beautiful fading flower but a living skeleton. The master bedroom smelled of shit and vomit despite the large vase of violets her daddy had placed on the nightstand. The lake house reverberated with her muffled howls of pain. Krissy stood outside the bedroom door, listening to the dying animal that had once been her smiling, joyful Mommy.

Make her stop, Krissy thought, her heart thudding like a cornered rabbit. *Someone please make her stop.*

Daddy had stopped crying. He seemed incapable of it, as if the well of tears had completely dried up. Krissy knew that he sat alone late at night in the great room. She saw the empty wine and beer bottles that filled the garbage can under the kitchen sink. She wondered if Mommy's screams scared Daddy as much as they scared her. She thought they did. He had deep purple shadows under his eyes, like he hadn't slept in a long, long time.

Sometimes Mommy just made noises, a ceaseless moaning that would build to shrieks. But other times she said words. It was worse when she said words. She would beg for her pills or curse them for their health or plead with God to let her go. That made Krissy the saddest, when Mommy begged to die.

Daddy said it was the cancer. The disease that had started in her liver and spread to something called a "limp note" was now in Mommy's brain. It was making her say things she didn't mean, like how someone who has had too much alcohol will yell or start fights. But she still loved them, Daddy promised. Somewhere inside, she was still Mommy.

They had been at the lake house for several weeks, and their plan to spend time with Mommy was beginning to feel like a big mistake to Krissy. She had envisioned sitting on the deck and looking out at the lake while Mommy, a warm blanket over her shoulders, told her stories about when she was a little girl, about growing up in a small Missouri town at the foot of the Ozark Mountains. She had come to Pacington with visions of being a big help to Daddy by taking care of Mommy—braiding her hair and feeding her spoonfuls of soup and snuggling with her when she was too weak to get out of bed.

But Mommy had gotten worse much faster than Krissy had expected. Daddy said sometimes people just get tired of fighting, and Mommy had been fighting her cancer for four long years. Once they give up, Daddy explained, there's no stopping the disease.

So Little Krissy stood outside the bedroom door and listened to her Mommy's awful howls. The sound had woken her before the sun was up. She had crept out of her room and tiptoed down the hallway, the floorboards creaking under her bare feet.

Daddy entered from the great room, pulling on the brown leather shoes he had kicked off before falling asleep on the couch the night before. He needed to go into town to get more medicine, but he would be back as quickly as possible. Krissy was to play in her room or upstairs or in the little storage room that she had turned into a makeshift clubhouse with a table and chairs and random items she had found around the house. But she was not to disturb Mommy, no matter how much Mommy begged.

Krissy said okay.

Daddy walked out the door.

She was alone with her mother in that sad, gloomy house on the shores of Lost Lake.

That's when the screaming stopped.

The house was suddenly, terrifyingly silent.

It's happened, Krissy thought to herself. *She's dead. My mommy is dead.*

She shuffled closer and pressed an ear against the bedroom door.

She could not hear a thing—not her mother's raspy breaths or the tired creak of the mattress as she attempted to shift out of its sagging center.

There was no sound.

All was still.

"Baby?" a voice cooed suddenly. "Baby, is that you?"

Krissy gasped, clapping a hand over her mouth for fear of being heard.

"Krissy, sweetie?"

She forced herself to reply, "It's me, Mommy."

"Come in," the soft voice beckoned.

Krissy took a step away from the door, unsure. "Daddy will be home soon and—"

"Come lie down with Mommy," the voice said. "Please, honey. I love you. I want to see you."

Slowly, Krissy reached out and grasped the doorknob. She turned it until she heard the latch click. She carefully pushed it open.

Her mother was nothing more than a lump under sweat-stained sheets. Krissy slipped into the room. The door clicked shut behind her.

The cooing voice came from beneath the sheets: "Lie beside me. I want to hold my baby."

Krissy took a step away from the door.

The shape under the sheets did not move.

She took another step, and another, until she was standing right beside the bed. Now she could hear her mother's labored breathing, slow and soft, as if she were trying to be as quiet as possible.

"Mommy?"

She waited for her mother to reply.

There was only the faint rasp of fluid-filled lungs attempting to draw breath.

Reaching out, Krissy took hold of the edge of the sheet. She steeled herself as she prepared to pull it away from her mother.

From under the sheet, a hand slipped out, its bony fingers wrapping themselves around Krissy's thin wrist. The flesh looked as if it had been cooked to the bone, the fat and muscle beneath melted away so that only the outer layer of yellow skin remained. The cuticles of each finger had receded so that the nails appeared abnormally long, their tips a sickly custard color, their edges brittle and cracked.

Krissy shrieked and tried to pull away, but the hand was surprisingly strong. She watched helplessly as her own hand was dragged beneath the sheet. She felt the heat of breath against her forearm. Cracked, blistered lips grazed her skin.

"Snuggle with Mommy," the voice implored. And then the thing under the sheet began to laugh, a harsh, wet cackle that devolved into a fit of wheezing coughing.

"Mommy, let go," Krissy cried. "Please! You're scaring me!"

The thing began to rise, the sheet falling away.

Krissy could not move, could not even blink, as she watched the thing that was once her mother come into view, piece by horrible piece.

Jaundiced skin stretched like a drying animal pelt over an oval stone, bald except for patches of thin, stringy hair.

Seemingly lidless eyes sunken back into deep, shadowed pits, the whites no longer white but a grayish green, like the yolk of an overcooked hardboiled egg.

Lips pulled taut over too-long teeth that were clenched tightly in a painful grin.

The sheet dropped to the mattress, revealing her mother's bony body draped in a T-shirt that had once fit her perfectly but now looked like a collapsed tent held pathetically up by broken poles.

Suddenly her mother's eyes bulged wider as every joint in her body locked. A high-pitched whine, like the first shrieks of a boiling tea kettle, forced its way through her clenched teeth. It was the sound of someone experiencing excruciating pain, and there was nothing Krissy could do to help.

"Make . . . it . . . stop," Mommy begged.

Krissy's screams became garbled as thick mucus clogged her throat. Tears spilled down her cheeks.

Her mommy lurched forward, that horrible corpse face inches from Krissy's.

"Make it stop!" she shrieked, her teeth clacking with each word. "I want to die! Why won't you let me die?"

Krissy leapt backward, but her mother did not release her grip. She watched as Mommy's frail body tumbled halfway off the bed. Her side slammed painfully into the nightstand, and the vase tipped over, falling to the floor. It shattered into jagged shards, scattering the violets across the wood floor.

Mommy lay draped over the edge of the mattress like a marionette whose strings had been cut. Her head twisted up on a neck that seemed ready to snap at any moment, and she glared accusingly at her little girl.

"Just let me die!"

Without warning, a strange wave worked its way through Mommy, her back arching sharply, her head thrown backward, her face wrinkling up as if she were about to burst into tears. She opened her mouth wider than any mouth should open and a geyser of pale yellow vomit sprayed out. It drenched Krissy's wrist, still held in her mother's skeletal fingers. Thick globs dripped to the floor and across the pale petals of the violets. The yellow was streaked with blood so dark, it appeared almost black.

A smell filled the room, a rotten stench that, even at ten years old, Krissy knew was the odor of death.

Behind her, the bedroom door flew open.

"Kris?" her father asked, shocked.

Krissy felt her mother's grip loosen. This was her chance. She yanked her vomit-covered hand free and ran, past her father, down the hall, across the great room, and out the French doors.

The morning was still cool. The sun had not yet crested the hilltops. Thick mist swirled above the surface of Lost Lake.

She raced barefoot over the deck. Splinters slipped painfully into the bottoms of her feet, but she did not slow down. She bounded down the steps and over the path leading to the dock.

The rowboat was there, tied to one of the wooden pilings.

Her only thought was to escape, to leave the horrors of that lake house behind.

She climbed down into the boat, the metal of the hull cool beneath her feet, and gave the rope a sharp tug. Thankfully the knot came loose easily, and the rope tumbled into the boat.

Gripping them by the handles, Krissy swung the red-and-white oars in their rowlocks, dipping the flat paddles down into the clear water of the lake. She leaned back and pulled hard. The boat began to move gracefully away from the dock and out into the pale fog floating above the lake. In her mind, she was on a cloud, skimming across the sky, thousands of feet above the earth, so far away from the shrieking thing that had once been her mother.

But she knew this was not true. She could only go so far until she reached the other side of the lake. And then what? She could not go back to the house. Not now. Maybe never. She was afraid that if she had to see the thing in the bedroom once more, to breathe in the rotten stench of death, her mind would snap and she would be forever changed.

She stopped rowing and lifted the paddles out of the water, letting the oars hang loosely in the rowlocks.

The boat slowly drifted to a stop.

The fog enveloped her, its misty fingers caressing her skin.

Krissy could not hold it in any longer. She began to cry. Her body shook with great, heaving sobs. She did not bother to make sense of her emotions. Her pain and loneliness, her fear and sadness poured down her cheeks, her tears falling to the water below and sending ever-widening circles rippling across the lake. She leaned over the side of the boat and moaned into its bottomless depths.

Reflected in the water was her face, and in it she saw a girl whose mother would soon be dead, whose father was disappearing within himself, a girl who was alone in a cruel world that did not care about her happiness.

I don't want to be alone, she thought. She began to chant the phrase in her mind like a mantra.

I don't want to be alone.

I don't want to be alone.

I don't want to be alone.

A falling tear sent ripples across her reflection, her image blurring. Then the water calmed, the ripples ceasing, and beneath her reflection, Krissy could see the face of another girl swimming up toward her from the cold, dark waters far below. She watched, stunned, as this face merged with hers until it broke through the surface, the eyes blinking away the water, the mouth opening wide to draw in a desperate gasp of air. Krissy reached down and took the girl's hand. With a loud grunt, she hoisted the girl out of the lake and into the boat.

She blinked and the girl was suddenly, impossibly dry. Her black hair blew gently about her shoulders. Her white skin was not marred by a single freckle or mole. Even here in the dense fog, her face shone like the glassy surface of a porcelain doll. She wore a short-sleeved, collared dress with three black buttons down the front and a small bow tied at the waist. It was the same color as the light purple flowers Mommy had planted in the garden outside Krissy's bedroom window. She tried to remember the name Mommy had called them, back when Mommy wanted to be alive.

"Violet," Krissy said aloud.

She's not real.

But she was.

She can't be.

But she is.

She is real.

Violet is real.

Kris shook her head. "No."

"She's real," Sadie was saying. "Violet is real."

"No!"

"Yes, Mommy. You know she is. You remember."

"She can't be real!" Kris shouted.

Sadie smiled. "Look," she said. She lifted a hand and pointed past Kris, to the end of the hallway.

Don't look, Kris's mind warned.

Sadie's smile widened, as if she had read Kris's thoughts. "You believe in her, Mommy. I know you do. Look at her."

An unspeakable fear gripped Kris. She began to tremble uncontrollably. "I don't want to."

Sadie leaned in close and whispered in her mother's ear, "Look."

Kris tried desperately to stay still, to force her muscles to lock in place, but no matter how much her mind screamed for her to stop, she was turning, her head twisting to see the thing that Sadie knew was there.

She had to look.

Because she did believe.

Because she *remembered*.

Kris looked down to the end of the hallway.

Peering around the corner with a single dark eye was Violet.

"You found me," she said, and half of a crooked smile spread like a smear of blood against her snow-white skin.

PART FIVE

THE KILLING MOON

CHAPTER FORTY-ONE

WHEN KRIS WAS very young, no more than five years old, her parents took her camping at a place called Fall River, just north of Blantonville. Massive boulders lined the riverbank, and Krissy spent most of the day scrambling around the giant rocks. To Krissy, they looked like petrified eggs, laid millions of years ago by lizards as tall as skyscrapers. She imagined that baby dinosaurs slept inside these stones, waiting for some great force—an earthquake, perhaps—to set them free. She told this story to Samantha, her favorite doll, who sat obediently atop a stack of smaller rocks. In fact, Krissy was so engrossed in her own story that she did not notice when a fat raindrop splatted down beside her. By the time her father called for her to come into the tent, the dark sky was rumbling with thunder and the rain was falling in sheets. Only when she heard the tent door zipping shut behind her did she realize she had left Samantha behind.

Krissy's father refused to look for the doll until the rain let up, but her mother, still not showing a single sign of the illness mutating within her, unzipped the flap and disappeared into the storm. Krissy saw the look on her father's face, and her childish mind confused it for frustration. Years later, she would see the same look on her husband's face when she asked him why he was spending so much time at the bar after hours. It was shame. It was the look of a man who knew he had failed at being good.

Krissy's mother finally emerged from the pounding rain, her clothes soaked through and sticking to the skin beneath. Her hands were empty, but Krissy hugged her all the same.

The next morning, as the sun dried the slate gray stones, the three of them searched every crevice, but Samantha was gone. She must have been washed off the rock by the rain, her father speculated. By then she would be miles down the river, easily in the next county.

Krissy cried all the way home, and then she found a new favorite toy, a stuffed zebra appropriately named Mr. Stripes. For a few weeks, she thought of Samantha when she pulled the covers up at night, but eventually she forgot about the doll entirely.

A year later to the day, they returned to Fall River. Krissy had not been playing on the boulders for more than five minutes before she stumbled upon the tiny, weathered figure of Samantha. The scorching summer sun had bleached her plastic flesh of all its color. The brutal winter wind had frayed her once-impeccable clothes. Beside her was a soda bottle, its label so faded, the logo was no longer visible.

She's no better than that bottle, Krissy had thought. *She's trash.*

Krissy did not want her doll anymore.

She wished she had never found her.

But you did.

You found her.

After all this time.

Kris stared in horror at the childlike thing at the end of the hallway. It was as if an electric current were passing through her body, welding her joints together. She was a statue—every bone, every muscle held in the grip of her short-circuiting mind. Her face was frozen in pure terror.

A single, coherent thought formed: *She's just like Samantha.*

Violet had been so beautiful, all those years ago. But now, long dark trails of dirt and dust streaked her purple dress. The hem was in tatters. Strands of ripped fabric hung down like the torn edges of a spider's web. Her white sneakers were grimy with dirt. One knee-high sock was pulled up to her scabby knee; the other drooped limply around her calf. Her once-sleek locks lay in ratty, frayed tendrils reaching her shoulders. Her uneven bangs were much too high on her forehead, as if they had been cut by a child. The glossy sheen her hair once held was gone.

Time had carved deep lines across Violet's forehead, beneath her eyes, around the sides of her lips, twisting what had once been a child's porcelain face into the pale visage of an old hag. Gone was the smooth perfection of her skin. Her flesh had turned the grayish white of eyes clouded by death, marred in places by dark, round sores—

Like Mommy's skin, when she was dying.

—and long, jagged cracks that broke the surface like canyons seen from high above the earth.

She was a forgotten doll.

Suddenly there was a click, and Kris's vision shifted. It was as if she were sitting behind a phoropter in an optometrist's office as new lenses slid into place before her eyes. For a moment, Violet became a perfect little ten-year-old girl again, just as she had been the summer Kris met her.

Made her, Kris's mind corrected. She tried to reject the thought. It was impossible. Violet had simply been a child's fantasy. She had *seemed* real when Kris was a kid, but she never really existed. It was all make-believe.

The image of Violet shifted once more, and she was little more than a blur. Her edges had softened so that they bled into the air around her. Her eyes were black holes, her lips a single red smear.

"She missed you, Mommy," Sadie said. Her voice sounded so far away, echoing to Kris from an incredible distance.

Violet's bloodred smile widened.

A low, helpless moan, like that of a dying animal, filled the hall, growing louder and louder until Kris realized with horror that the sound was coming from her.

"No . . . No, she's not there. She's not real."

The paralysis loosened its grip on Kris's body, and her limbs began to tremble uncontrollably as if she were freezing.

A small hand slipped around Kris's quivering fingers. Sadie peered up at her, eyes sparkling with excitement.

"Did you miss her, Mommy? Did you really, really miss her with your whole heart?"

The small, blurry figure stood perfectly still at the end of the hall, waiting for Kris to answer.

Sadie looked from Violet to her mother, and her brow furrowed in confusion.

"She's talking to you," Sadie said. "Why don't you answer her, Mommy?"

Because I can't hear her, Kris thought. *Because she's not really there!*

The child-thing cocked its head, black hair framing dark pools where eyes should be. They shimmered with a cold light.

Kris felt as if her mind were trying to release itself from her body. She took a step backward, and her numb legs threatened to buckle. She thrust out her hands, bracing herself against the wall on either side.

The hallway grew dimmer. At first she thought night must have fallen, despite the soft orange glow of evening sunlight arcing across the master bedroom door, half open at the end of the hall. A dark iris continued to narrow Kris's vision, closing in from all sides until all she could see was the fuzzy form of Violet. The little girl stood motionless, patiently waiting for Kris to accept her presence.

Icy terror sliced up Kris's spine. Her legs refused to support her. Her outstretched arms began to weaken. She gasped and stumbled to the side. Her shoulder collided with the wall beside Sadie's bedroom door. Quickly, she shifted so that her back was against the wall, its support the only thing keeping her on her feet.

Sadie was staring at her with growing concern. "Mommy?"

"This is not real," Kris whispered. Her voice vibrated against her shuddering breaths. "There's nothing there. There's nothing . . ."

She looked and saw that there was nothing at the end of the hall. There was only the swath of orange light falling across the master bedroom door and, across from this, the edge of the staircase leading up to the second floor.

"Mommy? Are you okay?" Sadie's voice called from across an impossible expanse.

Kris tried to speak, but her tongue was too large for her mouth. "I . . . I just . . ."

She felt herself sliding along the wall, toward the door. Felt the cool metal of the doorknob in her hand. Felt the door swing open, and the scrape of the jamb across her back as she moved into the bedroom.

Sadie stared at her.

"It's okay," Kris forced herself to say. "Mommy's okay. Mommy just needs to . . . to . . ." There was no way to finish the thought.

She pushed the door shut until the catch clicked into place.

Her legs gave out, her knees pounding onto the unforgiving wood floor. Her body shook uncontrollably. She shut her eyes and pressed her palms against them until stars exploded across the blackness.

She had gone crazy. The stress of everything—the house, the town, Jonah's death, the memories of her mother—had finally split an already fractured mind. Those voices she had heard for the majority of her life were warnings of a weakness in the foundation.

She could remember it now, the moment the door to her shadow voice creaked open. That day at the hospital, as she held her newborn daughter in her arms, when she looked up at Jonah and all she saw on his face was fear and doubt. *He's a runner*, the voice had purred. But she had pushed it away, convincing herself she was misreading his expression.

Her doubt had officially gained a voice years later. There was no single moment that announced its arrival. It began around the time Kris started picking up extra shifts to help Jonah open the bar. It told her that he should be able to pay for the venture himself, that she was killing herself working double shifts and weekends just so Jonah could spend more time away from his family. They were in their mid-thirties. Sadie was a handful, wandering around the house, getting into any-thing she could reach, squirming at the table whenever they attempted a night out. Kris told herself that Jonah could use the escape. He needed a job that he loved. *But is that really what he needs?* that timid voice had asked. *Do you truly believe that will make him happy?*

In the end, both voices had been right. She knew that now, just as she knew these voices had sprung from a chasm deeper than she could have imagined. They were the voices of her fear, her loss, her grief. They swam up from the black waters of a trench that had opened long before, during that summer when her mother was a howling skeleton wrapped in a sheet of vomit and piss. It was a lightless abyss where only blind things could survive. Perhaps the voices had come into being that day as well, but they needed a glimmer of illumination to guide them up. Perhaps every now and then they had seen such bursts of light—as her mother was lowered into the earth, as her father crawled deeper into a bottle. But it had been Jonah who finally lured them to her. He had burned like St. Elmo's fire on a moonless sea, drawing them close enough to whisper their warning through the darkness:

Everyone you love abandons you.

Kris mashed her palms harder against her closed eyes. "Not Sadie," she said aloud. She repeated it to herself over and over: "Not Sadie. Not Sadie. Not Sadie."

But she has, her shadow voice hissed. *For Violet.*

Violet is not real! she shot back.

She was. Back then. When you were sad and scared and you needed a friend. You played with her.

"No," Kris moaned. She had imagined she had a friend. It had been a game. A child's game.

But you're not a child anymore, Kris. And Violet's still here.

Kris tried to tap into her rational mind, her doctor mind, the one that took control when there was no one else guiding the ship, like the night Cap died. *I've snapped. It's some sort of psychotic break. The stress. The withdrawal. The guilt of thinking I've hurt Sadie by bringing her here. That thing in the hallway is a hallucination. It's not there.*

Then why can Sadie see her, too?

With her hands still pressed against her eyes, she lowered her forehead to the floor as if in prayer. "I have to get control," she whispered. "I have to get control. Get control. Get control."

And if you can't? her timid voice asked.

I can call Ben, she answered.

Great fucking idea, Shadow Kris chuckled. *Then he'll know you're crazy. He'll be obligated to protect Sadie. He'll send you to some hospital in another town for evaluation. And Sadie will have no mother, no father. She'll be all alone . . .*

Dr. Baker, she shot back.

Yes. She could call Dr. Baker. Dr. Baker wanted to help. She had said so.

Kris dug into her pocket and pulled out her phone. Her hands shook so badly, she could barely hold it. She tried to open her Contacts, but she accidentally tapped the Weather app.

"Dammit!" she growled.

She swiped the screen to close the app and the phone slipped from her sweaty, trembling hand. It tumbled to the floor, faceup.

Kris took a deep breath and exhaled slowly, but her body continued to quake. She began to whimper, and the sound of weakness infuriated her.

Get it together. You have to. For Sadie.

A solution forced its way through the squirming madness in her mind.

"Siri," she called out. "Call Dr. Baker."

A multicolored wave rippled across the bottom of the screen, and in an even tone, a robotic female voice announced: "Calling Dr. Baker."

Voicemail picked up on the third ring. The woman on the message sounded vaguely familiar. It was the receptionist Kris had spoken to when she scheduled Sadie's first appointment with Dr. Baker.

"You've reached the office of Dr. Alice Baker at Clearwater Counseling. Please leave a detailed message and Dr. Baker will return your call at her earliest convenience. If this is a medical emergency, please hang up and dial 9-1-1."

There was a loud beep, and Kris took another breath, hoping her voice would not reflect the panic tearing her psyche to shreds.

"Hi, Dr. Baker, it's Kris. Barlow. I . . . I really need to talk to you. I think . . . you were right. I need your help. I can't do this alone. Honestly, I'm—

The voices in her mind chimed in:

Going crazy.

Completely losing my shit.

A danger to myself and my daughter.

—kind of freaking out here," Kris said, doing her best to ignore them. She laughed and immediately wished she had suppressed it. It sounded unhinged, like the laugh of a lunatic.

Hold it together. Think it through.

"Please, call me as soon as you can. I—"

A sound from outside the door stopped her cold.

Kris held her breath, listening.

Someone was singing.

". . . in the dead of night, take these broken wings and learn to fly . . ."

It was not the cassette playing in the boombox. It was a child's voice, fluttering like a hummingbird through the air.

". . . all your life . . ."

The sound cut through the crashing waves inside Kris's mind like the hull of a ship. Regardless of what was happening in Kris's head, what she had or had not imagined, what others might think of her at that moment, Sadie was real. She was upstairs. And she needed her mother.

Kris focused on her daughter's voice. She felt her spasming muscles begin to relax. After a few seconds, she was able to push herself up from the floor and stand on wobbly legs. She opened the bedroom door.

The singing was louder, although it was still muffled. It was coming from somewhere farther down the hall, toward the staircase. But with the door open, she could hear that it was not one voice singing, but two. Two voices intertwining like lengths of braided string. Two children, singing together.

". . . you were only waiting for this moment to arise."

The song drew her into the hall. Sadie was gone, as was the thing she had convinced herself could not exist.

But the song *was* there. She was hearing it. There was no denying that.

An auditory hallucination, she told herself.

And yet she allowed it to guide her down to the end of the hall.

The song cascaded down the stairs like water over stone.

"Blackbird singing in the dead of night . . . take these sunken eyes and learn to see . . ."

One of the voices was clearly Sadie's. Kris had heard her perform at school and sing little songs while she got ready for bed back home in Colorado, but never like this: loud and confident, her voice pure joy.

The other voice seemed to be coming from another world. It faded in and out, growing in intensity one moment, falling back into little more than an echo the next. And yet it was clear that this voice was the leader. It set the pace. It never wavered.

Kris mounted the steps, her hand on the railing, pulling herself faster and faster toward the landing.

The rustic white entryway framed the upstairs room like a painting. Kris peered into the fading light, searching for any sign of her daughter among the furniture draped in sheets. Sadie was not there. Neither was the child-thing she had seen in the hall downstairs.

Thought you saw, her mind corrected.

Kris stepped into the room. The song was coming from all directions at once, acoustics that defied the simplicity of the rectangular room. It was like standing at the back of a music hall and hearing a performer's voice with perfect clarity.

It did not take long for Kris to discover the source of the singing.

The tiny door in the wall was wide open. A square of perfect blackness cut into the pale wood like a missing puzzle piece.

They're behind the wall, she realized.

They, her shadow voice mocked. *They. They. They.*

The more powerful voice, that of the thing which should not—which *did* not—exist, rose in volume, as if sensing Kris's presence.

"All your life, you were only waiting for this moment to arise."

The voices echoed about the room, and then the sound spun down the stairs like a fleeing spirit. The song was over.

Kris stared at the tiny doorway as silence settled over the house.

Then a voice spoke from within the darkness. Sadie's voice. Cheerful and sweet. The way she had spoken before Jonah's death had stripped away her joy.

"Come play with us, Mommy!"

Kris clenched and unclenched her fists. She let out a long, slow breath. She took a step forward. The floorboard creaked under her foot, and she whimpered at the sound.

Silence had once again fallen inside the impenetrable blackness beyond the doorway.

When she reached the far side of the room, Kris knelt down, one hand resting on the doorframe. She remembered being in that exact spot, when they'd first arrived at the lake house, when Sadie found the room behind the wall and claimed it as her own.

Kris wished she could go back to that day, take Sadie by the hand, and tell her that coming to the lake house had been a mistake. They didn't have to stay. There were too many memories. It was not a happy place. It was a tomb.

"Come in, Mommy," Sadie's voice called from behind the wall.

Kris Barlow could not turn back time. So instead, she crawled into the darkness.

She blinked as her eyes adjusted to the dim room. The first thing she saw were the mugs on the play table. They were the same ones Kris had used for their tea party. A third mug had been added, set atop a small plate that served as a makeshift saucer. A rusty metal watering can sat at the center of the table. Although she hadn't seen it since she was a child, Kris recognized it immediately. It had belonged to her mother.

Dying light filtered through the oval window and fell upon the sheet that hung above the play table like a canopy.

"Play with us," Sadie said. "We're having a tea party!" She tapped the table next to the third coffee mug. "We saved you a seat."

Kris slowly shook her head. "Sadie, please, come downstairs with me, okay, baby? We'll talk about this. We'll talk about everything."

Sadie glanced across the table to the other chair. It was empty, but she looked at it as if seeking permission.

She's not imagining it. She's seeing it.

A shared delusion. Was there such a thing? Had she somehow planted the idea of that . . . that *thing* in her daughter's mind? Maybe Dr. Baker had talked to her about Violet. That could be it. Dr. Baker had planted the idea, and Kris and Sadie's shared stress had created some sort of psychic link, like two people sharing one pair of binoculars, each looking through an eyepiece at the same object.

But Vicky knew, too, she realized. *Vicky said her name . . .*

There had to be a rational explanation. Something in the ground-water perhaps. Or mold. The house had been neglected for years. There could be mold somewhere in the walls. They had been breathing it in for almost three weeks. Toxic mold was known to cause psychosis. Yes. Yes, that could be it.

Sadie began to hum "Blackbird" again as she lifted the watering can from the table and pretended to pour its contents into the third mug. She turned to Kris and her smile widened.

"Hurry, Mommy, before it gets cold."

Whatever it was they were both experiencing, Kris sensed that grabbing Sadie by the wrist and dragging her out, kicking and screaming, would only make things worse. She needed to gain Sadie's trust and coax her out into the light.

Kris's heart thudded dully in her ears as she crawled into the white sheet that draped down from the ceiling. There was no chair for her to sit in, so she folded her knees beneath her and scooted up to the table. She clasped her hands in her lap, squeezing her fingers tightly together in a desperate effort to stop them from shaking.

For the first time, Kris saw that each mug rested on a plate similar to her own. Beneath the plate was a sheet of notebook paper that served as a placemat. Each was decorated with childish drawings of flowers and insects—ladybugs, butterflies, and odd, smiling beetles with black smudges on their backs. At the top of each sheet was the guest's name, written in a swirling script that mimicked cursive. "Mommy" for Kris.

Sadie's own name at the top of hers. Kris looked across the table to the placemat in front of the empty chair. It said "Violet."

At the center of the table was a mason jar. A wilted flower with rotted black petals sagged over its lip. A few other sheets of paper were scattered around, blank sides up. On top of these were the colored pencils that Dr. Baker had given Sadie.

Sadie sat up straight, her head held level in pretend elegance. "Now, who would like a cookie?" she asked. "Mommy?"

Kris tried to speak, but her throat had gone dry. She swallowed and forced out a weak, "Y-Yes, please."

From an imaginary serving tray, Sadie pretended to place a cookie on the edge of Kris's saucer. "They're peanut butter chocolate chip," she said with a giggle.

Kris watched as Sadie placed an invisible cookie on Violet's saucer. Then Sadie sat back in her chair. She turned to her mother, waiting.

"Are you going to try it?" she asked.

Kris could feel eyes on her, not just Sadie's but those of the thing across the table. She refused to look up. She did not want to stare into that shadow for fear that the darkness would melt away and she would see the awful face staring back at her.

Sadie shifted impatiently. "You're our guest, Mommy. You go first."

Reaching for her plate, Kris pretended to lift the cookie to her mouth. She mimed taking a bite, chewing, and swallowing. She had to force the mouthful of imaginary cookie down like bad medicine. She offered Sadie her best imitation of a smile.

"Mmm. They're good. They're really good."

If Sadie sensed Kris's fear, she did not show it. She picked up her own cookie and pretended to stuff it into her mouth. She puffed out her cheeks as she chomped.

"I think the tea is cool enough now." Sadie held her empty mug up to her lips and took a hesitant sip. She nodded. "Yep. Yep, it's good. It's *herbal*, Mommy. No caffeine, so we can have it." She shot a glance at the empty chair and giggled.

We, Kris thought. *She means them. She means her and Violet.*

Kris took a deep breath. "Is . . ." she began. She could not say the name aloud. "Is your friend here?"

Sadie nodded. "Uh-huh."

"Can you see her?"

"Of course, I can," Sadie said. "Can you?"

Kris glanced once more at the empty chair across the table. There was nothing there. She was sure of it.

She repeated it in her mind, *There's nothing there. There's nothing there.*

Ignoring Sadie's question, Kris asked, "What does your friend look like?"

Sadie turned to the chair and smiled warmly. "She's so, so pretty. She has pretty black hair, and pretty eyes that sparkle, and she has bright red lips—red like lipstick, but not crazy like the woman at the breakfast place. Mommy, why are you asking me? You can see her, can't you?"

"No one is there, Sadie," Kris said as she tried to calm her quavering voice.

Sadie shot Kris a playful look. "Yes, there is. Look, Mommy. Look at her."

Kris sat perfectly still, her eyes on Sadie.

"Look, Mommy."

Slowly, Kris turned and stared at the empty chair.

"Do you see her?" Sadie asked. "She's looking right at you. She's smiling at you, Mommy."

Invisible fingers crept up the back of Kris's neck. She flinched, her hand jerking away from her mug and saucer and knocking one of the loose sheets of paper off the table. The paper drifted to the floor, landing right side up beside her.

"She's trying to say something to you. Don't you hear her?"

Kris looked down at the loose piece of paper.

Drawn in a childish style with colored pencil were two little girls, one with red hair, one with black. They stood hand in hand at the edge of blue water.

Kris picked up the drawing. It was nearly identical to the picture Sadie had drawn at Dr. Baker's office.

"Try, Mommy," Sadie was saying. "You can hear her if you try."

But Kris was not listening. She reached for one of the other papers on the table and turned it over.

This one featured the same black-haired girl, but she stood at the top of what looked like a cliff. A different girl lay on the ground far below. Her eyes were closed. Red dashes flew away from her in great spurts.

Kris's heart thudded harder in her chest as she reached for a third sheet. The trunk of a large tree filled the page. At its center was a black oval, and inside this was the grinning face of another girl. Happy bugs crawled over her body. Nearby, the black-haired girl was smiling her bloodred smile. Musical notes floated around her head as if she were singing.

Her hand darted out and snatched up another page. She flipped it over on the table and found herself staring into the crudely drawn face of a little girl with Xs for eyes. Her mouth gaped open. Bees flew up from her throat and buzzed around her head.

The voice of Camilla Azuara drifted up from a recent memory: *Sarah Bell . . . they said the bees had gotten to her . . . they were starting to make a hive in her mouth.*

"Try, Mommy!" Sadie's voice had grown in intensity. "Try to hear her! Hear her talking to you!"

Kris held the pictures up and saw that her hand was shaking. "Sadie, how did you know . . . ?"

Because you were wrong, her shadow voice whispered. *It's not a delusion. Violet told her.*

Those phantom fingers returned, slipping beneath Kris's scalp, fingertips working their way under her skull. The sound of wind swirled in her ears, and suddenly Kris could hear a voice trying to push through like a radio station through a wall of static.

Krissy . . .

Kris jerked back from the table. Her hand shot out and grasped Sadie's forearm.

"Sadie. I want to go downstairs."

Sadie pulled back against her mother's grip.

"But we're not done playing!"

Kris struggled to keep an even tone, but her heart felt as though it were about to burst. "We can play downstairs. We can have a tea party down there—"

With unexpected force, Sadie yanked her arm free. She stumbled up from her seat, the chair tipping over and crashing to the floor.

"We're not done playing!" Sadie shrieked. There was fear in her voice. Panic. "Can't you hear her? Violet wants you to play with us!"

Kris reached out, but Sadie was beyond her grasp. "Sadie—"

Without warning, the room was filled with the sound of a thousand whispers crashing over each other like waves. Sadie's body instantly stiffened. Her head twisted like a doll's head as she turned to face the empty chair. She listened for a moment, finding meaning in the incomprehensible sounds whipping around them. She nodded, understanding.

Kris pushed herself up from her knees and lunged for her daughter.

"Sadie, we have to go!"

But Sadie moved faster, dodging her mother's grip. She snatched something off the table, a long, thin object that she clutched in a fist.

"Violet wants to play," Sadie hissed.

At first, Kris's mind refused to comprehend what she was seeing. But her body reacted, pulling away, her hands held up to show that she meant no harm.

Sadie was holding a colored pencil to her neck. Its purple tip was sharpened into a spearhead.

"Oh my God, Sadie!" Kris cried. "Stop! You'll hurt yourself!"

"Play with us, Mommy." Sadie gave a bright smile as if they were all just having fun. "Play with us."

Play. The word crawled into Kris's ear like a burrowing beetle.

Across the table, something shifted in the darkness. The gloom pulled back like a curtain, revealing deep red lips, nearly black in the dark. They wriggled like fat worms as they pulled into a grin. A sliver of light glinted off black eyes.

Plaaay with usss, the voice called from across a howling expanse.

Kris's tenuous connection to reality snapped like a frayed rope.

I see her, Kris thought. *She's real. Violet is real.*

Krisssy.

The voice no longer echoed from another place. It was so close, so clear, that it was as if Violet's lips were pressed against Kris's ear.

It doesn't matter what that thing is, she told herself. *If it even is. All that matters is Sadie.*

Kris spun back to her daughter. Against Sadie's neck, the pencil tip pulsed with the quick beat of her heart.

"Oh God, Sadie, *please* put that down!" Kris took a step forward.

In the same instant, Violet jerked her head upward.

As if responding to a command, Sadie tightened her grip and gave the pencil a sharp jab, just enough to drive the very tip into her skin. A bulbous spot of blood grew fat around its tip and then streaked down Sadie's pale neck.

"No!" Kris screamed. "No. No, please. Stop. Please, Sadie!"

"Violet wants to play a game," Sadie said. She appeared oblivious to the line of blood staining the neck of her T-shirt. "She said it's your favorite game in the whole world. But it's best when you play it at night. That's why you had to sneak out to play it. You had to be really quiet so your mommy and daddy wouldn't know you were up." A fresh bead of blood sprouted up around the pencil's tip. "Did you really do that, Mommy? Were you naughty like that?"

Sadie giggled at the thought. Violet's disembodied laughter joined in. Kris's skull seemed to reverberate with the sound. She slammed her hands over her ears, but the laughter was already in her head, twisting into her brain. She cried out as a jolt of pain ripped through her body—

She was slipping out of the pink bedroom, her bare feet padding down the hall as she prayed not to step on a squeaky board. Her mother moaned softly in the master bedroom, lost in the fog of a morphine drip. Her father was passed out on the couch in the great room, a collection of empty beer cans scattered across the coffee table.

Little Krissy just had to make it out of the French doors, and then she was free. Her friend was waiting there for her, at the bottom of the back steps, smiling that cherry-red smile, her porcelain skin glimmering in the moonlight. She couldn't wait to play.

"Ghost in the Graveyard," Kris heard herself say.

You remember how to play, don't you?

Yes, she remembered. It was just like hide-and-seek with a few minor alterations. The "ghost" would hide, and the other player would search for her. When she was found, the ghost would chase the other player, and if they were tagged, they became the ghost in the next game. Unless, of course, the other player made it back to Home Base.

Good, her friend said. *We're going to have so much fun . . .*

"Mommy?"

The sound of Sadie's voice pulled Kris the rest of the way out of the memory. She was back in the playroom behind the wall.

"You count to one hundred and we'll hide," Sadie said.

The corners of Kris's lips began to tremble. Tears blurred her vision.

"Put the pencil down, sweetie," she begged. "I'll play, okay? Just put it down."

Sadie gave a sly smile, like she suspected she was being tricked. "Not until you count to one hundred."

Kris lowered to her knees at the table. She nodded. "Okay. I'm going to start counting. We'll play one game. And then it's Mommy's turn to decide what we do, okay?"

Close your eyes, Violet's voice sang in her mind.

Kris did as she was told. She pinched her eyes shut, feeling the sting of the tears trapped beneath her eyelids. She began to count.

"One. Two. Three."

There was the shuffling of feet. The squeak of a chair being moved out of the way. Then there was nothing. Only the muffled sound of the breeze against the window, the creaking of tired beams overhead and her own quavering voice, counting aloud.

"Four. Five. Six."

Opening her eyes just a crack, Kris peered through the growing darkness.

Sadie and Violet stood side by side in front of the tiny square door, holding hands like very best friends. Sadie smiled with excitement, her other hand still gripping the pencil at her neck. Violet's too-wide grin stretched higher into her cheeks. There was madness in her eyes. In *both* of their eyes.

We're all mad here, Kris thought.

"No peeking!" Sadie scolded.

Kris snapped her eyes shut. Her body shuddered. Tears forced their way between her eyelids and flooded down her cheeks. She felt a mucus bubble pop between her trembling lips as she choked out, "Seven. Eight. Nine."

In the room behind the walls, Kris sobbed as she counted, slowly and steadily, never speeding up, never skipping a number. Those were the rules of the game.

At some point, the recitation of numbers became automatic. Kris's mind detached itself from the chore and began to wander.

She thought of the pictures Sadie had drawn. She imagined her daughter sprawled out on the floor of the upstairs room, colored pencil dancing across notebook paper, humming the song her friend had taught her as she drew a dead girl in a hollow tree.

Kris recalled Vicky's wild eyes staring up at her. Heard her voice cutting through the stagnant air of the cabin across the cove.

There's something bad in that house. It's been there for years.

She watched as the pages of Hitch's scrapbook flipped by. Those drawings of spirits and monsters had seemed so far-fetched. She had assumed Hitch was crazy.

A few minutes ago, you were sure you were crazy, she thought.

She heard herself counting, "Forty-six. Forty-seven. Forty-eight."

We thought she would end up like the other girls, Vicky had said. *I gotta keep her locked up or she'll end up dead, just like the rest.*

"Seventy-one. Seventy-two."

Dead like the rest.

"Seventy-nine. Eighty."

Vicky had looked at Kris, and she had grinned as she said, *You expect me to believe you ain't realized there's something wrong with that house?*

Kris could not deny it any longer. Something bad lived here. An entity beyond any rational explanation. And it was with Sadie. Kris's perfect little girl.

Dead like the rest!

She had to save her. She had to get Sadie away from that damned thing before she became another of the town's lost girls.

"One hundred."

Kris opened her eyes.

The small doorway was empty.

She sprang up too quickly, and her numb legs instantly gave out. Kris could do nothing but let her body fall forward. She crashed down on her shoulder, and pain shrieked up her neck to the base of her skull.

For a moment, she lay in a heap, her legs tingling with pinpricks as they woke. Fresh tears, born of fear and frustration, filled her eyes. She allowed them to course through the layer of sweat that covered her cheeks. Some of them reached her lips and slipped into her mouth. They were salty on her tongue.

She pushed herself up and crawled through the tiny door, back into the larger room.

The purple light of dusk covered the room in dark bruises.

A playful giggle flitted through the air.

Kris leapt to her feet and raced through the maze of draped objects. It was just furniture, she knew. Old chairs and hutches and a coat rack that had once been in the narrow foyer just inside the front door. Yet as she rounded each one, she looked quickly for any sign of movement. They could be under any one of these sheets. She could pull a sheet back and find the small form of that thing pretending to be a child, hugging her knees, staring up with a smile like a bloody wound.

Footsteps echoed up from the downstairs hall.

"Sadie!"

Kris shot through the archway to the landing. She was down the stairs in three bounds.

The hallway was empty.

"Sadie, where are you?" she cried out.

"Find us!"

Startled, Kris hopped to the side, wincing as her hip banged into the side of the newel post.

Sadie's voice had been right beside her. She was sure of it.

She threw open the door to the master bedroom, racing around the side of the bed and into the master bathroom. Nothing. She dropped to her knees and pressed her cheek to the floor as she checked under the bed. Only clumps of gray dust and the framed painting—her mother's favorite—that she had banished to the shadows.

From the opposite side of the house came the sound of two little girls giggling. More pounding footsteps.

Kris thundered down the hall and into the great room. Her eyes darted across every possible hiding place: the side of the stone fireplace, behind the couch and the chairs, under the coffee table.

In the kitchen, a cabinet door slammed shut.

Kris froze, listening.

Quietly, she crept into the kitchen. The cabinet doors still hung crookedly, a reminder of the many things she had failed to fix in the lake house. She no longer cared. The place could crumble to the ground. Let the weeds and vines reclaim it.

She only wanted Sadie, her baby girl.

Kris slipped around the island and crouched down in front of the first cabinet. Its door had refused to latch. It hung open an inch on loose hinges.

She rubbed her sweaty palms across the legs of her pants. She took hold of the knob and prepared to fling the cabinet door open.

An image flashed through her mind, so quickly it was almost subliminal: Violet, tucked back into the cabinet, her neck twisted at an unnatural angle, her dark eyes sparkling with the thrill of being caught.

Kris swung the cabinet door open.

It was empty save for a collection of clear baking dishes.

She let out a breath. Her entire body pulsed with her thudding heartbeat. She moved on to the next cabinet and the next, until the entire lower row stood open.

No Sadie. No Violet.

She peered up at the cabinets above the counter, which she knew were filled with shelves for plates and glasses. It would be physically impossible for anyone to hide in there.

Moving around the island, Kris was suddenly filled with an overwhelming sense of defeat. She slammed her fist down on the butcher block. Part of her longed for the eerie giggling that had filled the house only moments before. She hated the sound of the silent house. She felt so alone.

"Sadie!" she screamed. But the house devoured the name.

She's not in the house, she realized. *You know the game. You know where it's played.*

Kris stared through the archway into the great room. Her brain felt like an overheating engine. It wanted to shut down completely, to send her limp body collapsing to the kitchen tiles. She could not let that happen. She had to find Sadie.

Through the windows at the back of the great room, she could see the last line of sunlight fading behind the hills. Stars glistened in the mirrored surface of Lost Lake. A cluster of gray clouds hung in the distance, creeping closer across the purple sky.

She squinted, trying to make out an object she had previously overlooked. It was a thin shape hovering at the edge of the deck, a shard of darkness against the black of night.

As if in a dream, Kris felt herself being pulled out of the kitchen and across the great room. On the stone hearth, the boombox suddenly began to play. She recognized the song immediately. It was one of her mother's favorites. Echo and the Bunnymen. "The Killing Moon." The clean, reverberating notes of a twangy guitar filled the house. Ian McCulloch's swooning vocals echoed up into the rafters.

"Under a blue moon I saw you, so soon you'll take me . . ."

Kris twisted the latch, and the French doors swung open before her. She stepped out into the hot, stagnant air.

A little girl stood at the top of the back steps, staring out at the lake.

Kris opened her mouth to call out Sadie's name.

Her vision shifted, like a lens sharpening its focus. A warm breeze slipped through, tousling the girl's black hair and rippling the bottom of her tattered dress.

Kris stepped up behind her.

The little girl did not move.

"Violet?" Kris said softly.

In the distance, clouds lit up with a burst of lightning. But there was no thunder, no scent of rain on the humid air.

Violet remained motionless.

"Where is she?" Kris asked, her voice weak with desperation. She was suddenly exhausted, the shock and adrenaline draining from her body. Her weary muscles ached. "Please. I just want my daughter."

In the house, the song continued, the volume blasting so loudly through the boombox's small speakers that it seemed they would explode at any moment.

There was another puff of light in the clouds. Kris had seen this before, on a particularly hot summer night when she was five or six. Heat lightning. It silently exploded, illuminating the sky and the mountain of clouds drifting toward the lake, and then the world was plunged back into darkness.

"You know where she is," Violet said suddenly. Her voice, heard aloud for the first time, was both shocking and expected. It was the voice Kris had heard years before, as light and sweet as any child's, but there was an edge to it, a confidence that came with age. With survival.

Kris shook her head. "I don't. I swear. Just tell me, please."

Violet turned her head, just enough for one dark eye to peer back through a lank curtain of hair.

"You know," she whispered sharply.

A sound exploded from the sky, a terrible screech like the scream of incoming missiles.

Blackbirds. Hundreds of them, circling overhead. They spun like a cyclone beneath the dimpled bellies of storm clouds. One by one, they landed in the trees at the edge of the woods, perching on every branch until the forest was a wall of squawking beasts. They glared out with yellow eyes, their pointed black tongues flicking angrily inside their opened beaks. Their cries rose higher and louder until they sounded like children shrieking with laughter.

The woods, Kris realized. *Where we used to run and play.*

Violet held out her hand.

"Let's play," she said.

Kris had no choice but to take it.

CHAPTER FORTY-TWO

THE WOODS WERE alive. The last wisps of blue light slipped through the trees, and then it was night. Things stirred in the thick, twisted vines choking the forest floor. Things scurried through bushes and thickets. They scampered up the trunks of trees and along branches heavy with summer growth. Night creatures that slept deep within the earth pushed their way out into the open air to hunt. From time to time, their eyes would catch the light of the moon and shimmer like shallow pools of water. And then they would lower their heads and be gone, off to do things that could only be done in the dark.

Along the trail, two girls walked hand in hand as they had done so many times before when they were both children.

One of them, a dark-haired child of nine or ten, wore a large smile on her ghostly white face.

The other, a woman just past forty years old with brownish-red hair, tried to hurry the girl along, but she was held back by the child's leisurely pace.

As they walked, the little girl sang in a sweet, high voice, slightly off-key:

"Blackbird singing in the dead of night . . .
Take these sunken eyes and learn to see . . .
All your life . . .
You were only waiting for this moment to be free.
Blackbird, fly.
Blackbird, fly.
Into the light of a dark black night."

The Osage trees reached their arms out over the trail as if to bless them as they passed.

The fear that she had lost her mind was long gone. Kris found that she missed that fear. It meant that the hand she held could still be a fantasy. Or perhaps her daughter was next to her, safe and content, ignorant to the fact that her mother had lost her mind.

Out of the corner of her eye, Kris saw the dark hair and purple dress and knew that madness was no longer an option.

"Please tell me she's okay," Kris said. She could not look at the girl at her side. She could not bear the sight. It was enough to see the demon hovering at the corner of her vision.

"She's hiding. She's waiting." The voice did not seem to come from Violet. It was everywhere at once. In the trees. In the shadows along the trail. In the beams of moonlight.

Violet hummed the next verse of her tune, and then she fell silent.

Twigs crunched under Kris's feet. Kicked stones went skittering off into the darkness. Only her footsteps made sound. Violet seemed to move in perfect silence.

"I knew you would come back," Violet said as they neared the end of the tunnel of trees.

Kris said nothing.

"Friends don't leave each other," she continued. "Not forever. Not when you're best friends. Like us."

Violet began to hum her song again.

Kris felt Violet's hand in hers, but it was like a snake made of smoke. Violet was both there and not there. She seemed to have a physical body, and yet Kris got the sense that her corporeal state was tenuous. She was a walking dream, a thought made flesh, an inhuman spirit caught between two realms. She could not be injured as a regular person could. She could not be bludgeoned or shot or stabbed. The fingers that Kris felt entwined with hers would become puffs of mist if she were to squeeze them too tightly.

The trail seemed to stretch on infinitely. Sadie was out there, hiding somewhere in these woods, convinced she was playing a game. At least Kris could take some solace in knowing that Sadie believed they were all having fun.

"Promise me you won't hurt her," Kris said.

The thing at her side covered her mouth as she giggled. "Why would I hurt her? She's my friend."

There were moments when the moonlight caught Violet in such a way that Kris swore she could see straight through her. The streams of pale light, swirling with dust kicked up as they moved down the trail, would suddenly pass through her purple dress. And then, in the next instant, she would be whole again.

She's a ghost, Kris thought. But she knew this was not true. A ghost had once been a living person. Whatever Violet was, it had never lived.

You made her.

Perhaps. In her moment of profound grief, Kris could imagine a scenario in which a piece of her spirit split free to become this . . . this *thing*. A mutated cell. A cancer that had fed off the other girls, surviving on their grief until the day Kris returned.

There was a third option, but its callousness made it all the more horrifying. For it to be true, it meant that neither she nor Sadie nor Violet meant anything in the grand, fucked-up scheme of things.

Violet has always been here, Kris thought. *She's older than the first humans who settled this land, buried deep, deep below the earth, and you just happened to be there when she found her way to the surface.*

Kris did not want to even entertain this thought. Because then the little girl beside her was not a ghost or an extension of herself but something so alien, the human mind could barely make sense of it. It meant there were forces in the world that had been around for eons, trapped as plates shifted, as volcanoes erupted, as asteroids slammed into the earth and sent miles of dust billowing into the sky. It meant that there were things of which she could not make sense, for they simply *were*, as she was now, as something else may be once everyone was wiped from the planet. It meant that with those cool, pristine waters that erupted from below the muddy floor of the Verdigris River came something that should have remained buried.

They passed beneath the last of the Osage trees, and the trail became a path of flat, smooth stones breaking through the dirt. Soon they came to the edge of a sandstone cliff. Several trees growing too closely to the edge tilted over at odd angles, their roots pulled up from the ground as they desperately tried to keep their hold.

We played here that summer, Kris realized, the images flashing across her mind. *We played all through these woods. So I wouldn't have to be in the house with Mommy. Violet made me happy. She was my friend.*

"You remember," Violet purred.

Kris drew in a sharp breath.

How does she know?

Because she is you. And you are her.

As she neared the side of the cliff, Kris prepared herself for what she might see below. They were above the rocky canyon with its floor of jagged shark's teeth. Below was the path she had led Sadie through during their first few days at the lake house. They had put sticks between the canyon walls to keep from being eaten. She did not know then that the canyon had tasted blood and human flesh before, when Megan Adamson threw herself from the cliff top.

Kris peered over the edge.

The canyon was dark, but there was just enough moonlight filtering down through the branches to see that there was not a little girl splayed across the rocks.

Kris's legs buckled. She reached out, her fingers finding the rough bark of a crooked tree. She grasped it to keep herself from falling forward into the chasm. Carefully, she lowered herself down until she was sitting safely on the ground. She buried her face in her hands. Gone was the mad, scrambling heat inside her brain. Gone was the buzzing beneath her skull. Her mind felt clear for the first time in ages.

"We played here," Kris said.

There was the sound of Violet sucking air across her tongue as if she were tasting the words.

Kris closed her eyes and let herself remember . . . racing through the canyon with Violet . . . two young explorers out to claim a world as their own.

She could feel Violet staring at her.

"Tell me where she is," Kris begged.

You know, a voice boomed in Kris's mind. It had grown deeper. It sounded less like the voice of a child and more like something ancient pretending to be human.

In the darkness, the shadowy form gave a raspy chuckle.

She doesn't want Sadie, Kris realized with horrible clarity. *She wants me, all to herself. She wants Sadie gone so we can be together. Forever.*

"She's my daughter," Kris said, her voice shockingly weak.

Violet's dark eyes shimmered in the moonlight. "Don't worry, Krissy," she said. "Sadie won't be alone. She can play with the other ghosts."

Kris's guts twisted into a painful knot.

The other ghosts. Megan, on the rocks below. Ruby, in the old oak tree. Sarah, in her grave among the wildflowers. Poppy, who was never found. Melody, the girl who got away, the ghost that haunted the cabin across the cove.

"Why?" Kris managed to ask. "Why did you hurt those girls?"

The warm air misted as Violet exhaled an icy breath. "They wanted to be ghosts, so I helped them. I made them ghosts."

"You threw them away like . . . like old toys . . ."

Without a sound, Violet moved up next to Kris. She pressed her cold lips to Kris's ear and roared, "*You* threw *me* away!"

A pang of guilt rang like a bell in Kris's soul. After her mother's death, her father had quickly packed up their things and they left. The funeral was scheduled for three days later in Blantonville. He would return to properly shut down the lake house for the year, but in that moment, he just wanted to leave. He needed to escape. Little Krissy had been ushered into the back seat of the station wagon before she could even say good-bye to her friend. She remembered now, Daddy pulling the station wagon through the open gate and onto River Road, Little Krissy staring out the back window. She could see Violet in the house, staring out of the oval window in their secret playroom on the second floor. Watching with confused eyes as her friend—her only friend—left her. *I'll be back*, Krissy had thought. *I'll see her again. I'll explain everything.*

A fresh tear slipped down Kris's cheek.

"I'm sorry," she said softly.

A sudden, cool breeze whipped up, tossing the leaves high overhead. It swept down through the chasm and wrapped around Kris and Violet, pulling them closer like an invisible bow.

The dappled moonlight played across Violet's face, and Kris was surprised to find her features had softened slightly. The deep wrinkles had smoothed. Her lips were dry and sore around the edges, but they were no longer cracked. When Violet touched Kris's hand, her fingers felt almost solid.

She's becoming real, Kris thought.

From somewhere far off in the forest, a child's voice called out. "Mommy!"

The spell was instantly broken. Kris leapt up from the ground, pushed past Violet, and bounded off into the trees. She cried to the endless forest around her, "Sadie! Sadie, where are you?"

"Mommy!" Sadie called back.

Kris followed the sound, deeper into the woods to where a grove of ancient oaks stood like petrified giants.

CHAPTER FORTY-THREE

KRIS CAME TO a stop: it was a trick. It was not Sadie's voice but an imitation. It was luring Kris not to a tree but to a tear in the world through which she would fall into a vast nothingness. It had already taken Sadie. Once Kris was there, the thing that was Violet would have them as friends forever.

In the darkness, all of the massive oak trees looked the same. Kris raced between their gargantuan trunks, searching for the one with the giant split in its belly.

"Sadie!" she yelled into the night.

This time, there was only silence.

She broke the rules, Kris thought with dawning horror. *Sadie was supposed to hide until she was found . . .*

Her hands slipped around the side of a tree and fell into open space. The tree trunk opened wide like a hungry mouth.

The Wishing Tree!

"Sadie!" she yelled into the hollow of the trunk.

Silence.

Stretching her hands out before her, Kris walked straight into the dark, gaping maw. She felt blindly around the rough interior. The hollow was empty.

Kris spun back toward the opening in the bark.

A figure stood in her way. Violet's pale face floated above her purple dress like a grotesque balloon.

Suddenly it was daytime.

Little Krissy stood in the hollow of the tree, staring out at the beautiful, smiling face of her friend as she said, "Where should we go? Make a wish and we'll be there!"

Kris closed her eyes and thought, *I want to be back with Sadie.*

The tree. Why had she been so certain Sadie would be there? They had found Ruby Millan here, but of all the places in the forest, why would Sadie come back to this place or to the sandstone canyon where Megan Adamson had died? Sadie had no reason to be drawn to these places.

But Violet did. Because those were our favorite places to play.

Kris opened her eyes. Violet was no longer standing outside the tree. For the moment, she was gone.

She can only go to places where I took her when I was little, Kris realized. *The lake house. The swing set. The canyon. The hollow tree.*

Kris tried to return to that summer. In her mind, she attempted to see the forest from above, to map the landmarks of her friendship with Violet. The house. The canyon. The tree.

The meadow.

The place where they picked wildflowers and named bees as if they were pets. The meadow where Sarah Bell had dug her own grave, the meadow from which they could see the rooftop of that long-lost house on Old River Road rising up from the water.

We, she heard Sadie say. It was a recent memory, from their walk in the woods.

You said "we."

Kris suddenly remembered. It had been a slip of the tongue. *We used to pretend it was a mermaid's house,* she had told Sadie.

Who? Sadie had asked.

Violet, honey. I was with Violet.

The moonlight was fading. Kris sprinted toward it as its last beams were extinguished by a passing cloud. She flashed by the last of the oaks, and she was in the meadow, among the swaying heads of wildflowers.

"Sadie!" she cried out.

"Mommy!" There was hope in her voice, that she would be found.

Kris stomped through the wildflowers, snapping their stems as she made her way to the ridge overlooking the water. Before her was only blackness. The lake was gone. She was standing at the edge of a great abyss.

"Sadie!" she screamed into the void.

"Mommy!" a voice called back. "I'm here! I can see you!"

The voice was real. It had to be real.

From above came a pop of light, like a flare bursting into flame. The heat lightning, gone in an instant, lasted long enough for Kris to see the dark folds of the heavy black clouds hanging low over the lake.

She held her breath, waiting.

Another burst of light, brighter this time, rippled through the clouds like a series of silently detonating charges, lighting the still waters below. She scanned the surface, but before she could find the roof of the submerged house, the lake was gone again.

Kris peered out into the void, her hand tapping impatiently against her leg.

"Come on, come on, come on . . ."

Another burst of light.

There. The pitched roof rising up from the water. And on this, the small form of a child struggling to keep her balance on its slick, moss-covered shingles.

"Sadie!"

"Mommy!"

The lightning lived briefly in the clouds, and the world was once again covered in an impenetrable blackness.

"Stay there!" Kris called. "I'll swim to you! Don't move!"

Kris's foot slipped in the loose, dry dirt as she started down the slope.

Krisssy . . .

The voice came from everywhere and nowhere at once.

Kris's hand came down on the rocky ground as she tried to catch herself from falling. She peered up over the top of the slope.

There in the field of swaying wildflowers was Violet. Her pale skin seemed to be made of moonlight, and at the center were the bottomless black pits of her eyes. The breeze tossed her hair around her shoulders. It was no longer ratty and tangled but as smooth and sleek as it had been when Kris was a child.

Megan's head made the funniest noise when she hit the rocks. The voice invaded every corner of Kris's head.

She glanced back and saw Violet cup a hand over her mouth to stifle a giggle.

Like splat*! Like a pumpkin. She didn't even scream when she jumped.*

Overhead, the clouds lit up with multiple silent explosions.

Kris caught a glimpse of Sadie on the roof. She was standing perfectly still, her face staring straight at the shore. The heat lighting burned away, and she was gone once more.

I told Sarah to dig like a puppy dog, so she dug and dug and dug until her fingernails snapped. And she still didn't stop. Because she wanted to make me happy. That's what friends do.

Kris clenched her jaw, trying to fight off the sound of Violet's voice. She let her feet slide, the loose rock carrying her down to the bottom of the slope. She could no longer see Violet in the field, but she could hear her voice digging into her ear canal like a ravenous insect.

But Ruby was the funniest of all. I told her to hide in the oak tree and she stayed in there, curled up in a little ball with a silly smile on her face, like she couldn't wait to be found. She stayed in that tree for a long, long time. And even when she stopped moving, she still had that silly smile. Even when the bugs became her new friends, she was smiling, Krissy!

"What about Sadie? What did you tell Sadie to do?" Kris yelled through clenched teeth. She stared up the slope, waiting, but there was only silence. "What did you tell her to do?" Kris screamed.

A small figure stepped up to the ridge above. The wind tousled Violet's dress and swept her hair away from her face. Her dark eyes glistened with morbid glee. Her lips did not move, but Kris heard every word.

I told her to swim out to the mermaid's house until you found her. And then I said, If your mommy tries to come for you, I want you to dive into the water and swim down into that house and find the best hiding spot, where no one will ever find you.

Kris stood on the flat rocks leading out to the water's edge. She glanced out at the shape of the roof rising above the water, but she did not move.

She said, "Mommy says a mermaid lives there!" And I told her she could be a mermaid, too. She could live in the lake forever and ever and ever.

Kris began to weep, her hunched back hitching as a sadness she had held for most of her life spilled free.

"What do you want?" she asked weakly. *You know what she wants.* *You've known since Sadie put that damn pencil to her neck.*

Violet pointed into the void.

Heat lightning burst through the clouds.

Sadie was standing at the edge of the roof, her feet hidden below the water that rose up over its shingles. She was perfectly still, shoulders back, face forward, like a soldier awaiting instruction.

"Please, don't do this," Kris begged. "Please don't hurt her. Please. She's my little girl. Please. Please, I'll do anything you want."

"Stay with me," Violet said. The voice came from her, from the thing standing on the ridge above.

Kris watched as the sky behind Violet became a field of fire as the heat lightning appeared to reach the climax of its show. It was so strange to see the flashes of light but hear nothing. It was almost as if the phenomenon were glimpsed through a crack in the sky.

You have to stop her, she thought.

There was only one true choice.

"Let Sadie go. And I'll stay."

Violet's brow lifted as a grin spread across her pale face.

CHAPTER FORTY-FOUR

KRIS WAS THE first to emerge from the woods. A few seconds later, the small form of Violet slipped out of the trees and followed. There was no mistaking who was in charge. Kris walked with her head down and her eyes on the ground, while Violet had the tiniest hint of a spring in her step.

They passed the lake house. Several lights still burned inside, but there was no movement. It was an empty shell.

The rowboat was still floating on the dark water of the lake, the mooring rope tied to the last piling. Wooden planks squeaked softly as Kris and Violet made their way down to the end of the dock. An inch of water covered the bottom of the boat. Kris had not forgotten how she and Sadie had barely made it back to shore when the rusty hull began to crack. But this time, she would make sure to keep her weight at the edge of the boat. She was hopeful that the boat would hold long enough for them to cross the lake, get Sadie off the roof of the house and back to shore. Violet had promised Sadie would stay put until they could reach her.

Slipping the rope off the top of the wooden post, Kris threw the line into the boat before climbing carefully in. She held the boat against the dock as Violet stepped in beside her. As she had hoped, the bottom of the boat gave a bit, but no more water flooded in.

Kris pushed away from the dock and, one by one, placed the paddles into the oarlocks. She dipped the ends of the paddles below the water and slowly began to row out into the lake, careful not to put too much strain on the rusty hull.

She had lost all track of time. To the north, the stars and moon still shone brightly. But over the lake, the storm clouds were standing their ground. The heat lightning had become less frequent, although every now and then it would silently ignite the sky like a signal flare.

Mist was rising from the lake's surface. Spectral fingers reached up into the darkness, spinning away in lazy swirls as Kris pulled the boat through.

Violet sat on the rear seat, her hands clasped demurely in her lap. She hummed softly, the tune nearly impossible to discern. But Kris knew what it was: her mother's favorite. Violet had turned it into her siren song, the tune the girls had heard calling them to the woods, beckoning them to come play at the lake.

Her mother's favorite song, stolen by a thing Kris had never meant to create.

But you did. The other voices had fallen silent in her mind. There was only her own. *You created her. She is yours.*

So, Kris realized with terrible irony, she had given the song to Violet, because Violet belonged to her, just as the missing girls belonged to her, and the devastated parents whose lives would never be the same.

For thirty years, Kris lived away from Lost Lake while a piece of her remained to haunt the town of Pacington and feed on its children. Even if she could manage to get Sadie and escape, she would be leaving Violet behind, abandoned once again, her fury growing stronger, her tongue lapping the air like a snake, desperate for the bitter taste of grief. There would be more lost girls left in Kris's wake.

Kris lifted the paddles from the water and let the boat drift slowly to a stop. The mist settled around them. They were at the center of a cloud.

"It's my fault," Kris said suddenly. She turned the oars inward so that the paddles rested on the edge of the boat.

They floated in silence, the only sound that of the water lapping against the rusty hull. Overhead, a burst of white fire illuminated the sky.

Kris was hunched over, her head in her hands. For the first time since she was a child, everything made perfect sense. Her fractured mind was whole again. The pieces had all fallen into place, even the ones she had tried so hard to hide from herself. It was her puzzle, she realized. It had always been her puzzle. And it was her responsibility to put it back together, to see the picture it formed, no matter how much she wanted to look away. She had to accept her place in it.

When Kris finally raised her head, there were tears in her eyes.

"I thought I made you up," she said.

Violet's dark eyes glistened. Kris offered her a bittersweet smile. Violet smiled back. Her flesh did not crease. Her perfect, porcelain smoothness had returned.

"I believe in you, Violet," Kris said.

Violet smiled wider, her lips plump and healthy, pink gums curving around the tops of straight, white teeth.

That's her, Kris thought. *That's how I remember her. She's so beautiful. She's sweet and wonderful and she's mine. She's my friend.*

"I believe in you," Kris said again. She held out her hand.

The rusted metal groaned faintly beneath her as Violet rose from the rear seat. Carefully, she crossed the unsteady boat. Fresh water began to trickle in through an unseen crack in the hull, but it was not enough to alarm Kris. She kept her eyes on her friend, her hand stretched out and open.

Violet's fingers slipped across Kris's and then closed tightly around them.

She was solid. There was even a warmth to her touch.

"You're real," Kris said. The admission was like casting a spell.

Violet took a deep breath, and Kris realized that this was the first time she had seen the girl do so. Kris could no longer feel Violet's phantom fingers slipping into her mind. There was only the little girl before her. Her little girl. Her friend. Her Violet.

Kris pulled Violet down into her arms and held her close. Kris's mind tried to reject this cold, shuddering thing, to force her to push it away, but Kris held her even tighter. Violet pressed her cheek against Kris's chest. Her body hitched as she sucked in a sharp breath, and Kris was hit with the awful understanding that Violet was crying.

It was Kris's turn to whisper into Violet's ear. "You're real," she said, and she could see herself as a little girl, sitting at the end of the dock, sobbing as her mother's muffled howls drifted down the house. And Violet was there by her side, holding her, shushing her, taking her pain away. Kris said it over and over. "You're real, Violet. You're real. You're real."

She felt Violet's desperate grip tighten. She saw the boat tip slightly under the girl's weight. Violet was more real than she had ever been, more than back when Kris was a child and believed in things like magic forests and imaginary friends.

Kris was reminded of a time long ago when her father took her to Walmart and she got lost in the never-ending aisles. She had been so scared that even when an employee paged her dad, and he came rushing up to take Krissy in his arms, she had only cried harder. Somehow being reunited with him was even scarier. Because she was reminded of what had, for a few frightening minutes, been taken from her. She could feel it and hold it and fear its loss.

This was Violet, nothing more than a scared little child, clinging to the person she never wanted to lose again.

"I'm sorry," Kris whispered in her ear. "I'm sorry I left you. I'm sorry I let myself forget you."

Violet's tiny body shook as she sobbed harder. She clutched at the back of Kris's shirt.

"I just wanted to make you happy," Violet said. Her voice was squeaky and weak. It was no longer the voice of the ancient thing that had followed Kris through the forest with a smirk. She was what Kris had imagined all those years ago.

Kris breathed in, and she could smell the scent of flowers in the little girl's hair. "You did. You made me so happy. You let me forget all the pain and fear. But I tried to *keep* forgetting those things, even after you were gone. That's the problem, Violet. I didn't want to believe in them anymore. But they were there, just like you were here."

She felt Violet's grip loosen, but Kris continued to hold her tight, not willing to let her go. Not yet. Not yet.

"I believe in them now. Like I believe in you, Violet," Kris assured her. "I know you're real. And I can't run from that anymore. I have to face it. I have to do something about it."

Violet squirmed, slipping her hands between them until she was finally able to push away from Kris's chest. She peered up at Kris in confusion, blinking away tears. Her eyes were no longer black holes. Irises rimmed her pupils. They shimmered an icy blue, like the crystal waters of Lost Lake.

"What?" Violet asked.

The loop at the end of the mooring rope dropped down over Violet's head, and Kris pulled the slipknot tight around her neck. The prickly fibers of the rough, woven rope bit into the girl's soft, white flesh. She tore at it, trying to get her fingers beneath it, but the rope was fastened too tightly.

"What are you doing?" Violet choked out, confused.

Without a word, Kris lifted one of the oars from the oarlock and slammed the end down on the bottom of the hull. A large crack appeared in the rusty metal. Water began to gush around their feet.

Kris raised the oar again.

"No!" Violet cried. More than ever, she sounded like a child, scared and confused, unable to gasp why she could possibly deserve what was happening to her.

The oar came down, harder this time. A large chunk of the hull fell away. Water bubbled greedily up, desperate to fill the boat.

They were sinking. The stern was dropping quickly toward the surface of the lake. The water was over their shoes. It lapped at the one drooping sock around Violet's ankle.

Violet stared up at Kris with wide eyes, her fingers still prying helplessly at the rope around her neck.

"Why are you doing this?!" Her sweet face pinched into an awful, frightened mask. She began to cry again as panic overwhelmed her.

Water rushed over the back of the boat, filling the hull. Almost instantly, the rowboat tipped vertically. Kris and Violet tumbled into the lake. As Violet fell away, the rope went taut and yanked her violently back toward where it was tied around the boat's upturned bow. She lashed out, desperate to grasp anything to keep her from being pulled down with the boat. Her hands found Kris, and she dug her fingernails into Kris's shoulder, drawing blood.

Kris cried out in pain, struggling to keep her head above the water as Violet thrashed wildly. Cool lake water filled Kris's mouth. It tasted of minerals from the rocky floor far, far below. She gasped for breath, and water filled her lungs. She retched violently. She was going to drown. Violet was going to pull her down with her.

Beside them, the upended boat was quickly slipping below the surface. Soon the bow would be under, and with it the mooring rope. Violet would be next. And then Kris. They would all be pulled to the dark depths of Lost Lake.

A single thought filled Kris's mind:

Sadie.

She wrapped her hands around Violet's neck and squeezed. Violet's clear blue eyes bulged. There was still fight left in them. Her mouth opened and closed stupidly like a fish on dry land. She thrashed blindly. Nails scratched at her flesh, but Kris did not let go.

The bow of the rowboat disappeared, leaving a line of bubbles behind. The rope began to coil down into the water like a fleeing snake.

Kris pressed her mouth against Violet's ear and whispered, "Thank you, Violet." And then she pushed the little girl's head down into the water. Violet fought with every last ounce of strength, managing to get her mouth above the surface just long enough to suck in a desperate breath, but Kris put all of her weight on the girl, forcing her back down.

The mooring rope snapped taut around Violet's neck, the slip-knot pulling tighter. Violet's face was turning purple, her eyes bulging so far out of their sockets that they looked as though they would pop out. She stared up at Kris through the rippling water as the weight of the boat began to drag her down.

A lock of hair curled around Kris's wrist.

Kris could look no longer. She closed her eyes, her hands still around Violet's neck as she felt the girl's body pull away from her. The little girl's attacks weakened. Her frail body shivered one last time, then went still.

Kris replayed it in her mind: one final flash of lightning illuminated hair that was not black but red. It spread across the surface of the water like blood. She saw the green eyes, hollow, devoid of life, peering up at her with one last pleading question: *Why, Mommy?*

It was Sadie.

Kris gasped, loosening her grip. But she refused to open her eyes. She did not want to see the unblinking face staring up from beneath the water.

The thought had slipped out of the darkness, like the moon sliding out from behind a cloud. It infected her mind with a terrible certainty.

Violet isn't real. She never was.

Panic gripped Kris.

"No," she said, water splashing into her mouth as she struggled to stay afloat.

"No!"

Kris felt the girl's body slip away from her fingers. She tried to regain her hold, but the weight of the sinking boat pulled the girl down faster. Kris opened her eyes and peered down into the water, but the waves obscured her view. She could barely see the small form of a child drifting farther into the depths. Her skin was fair and familiar. Her arms dangled out before her, and Kris thought, *Those hands, I've held those hands, I was the first to touch those fingers when she was born!*

"Sadie!" Kris shrieked. She stared into the water and caught sight of a strand of hair as it spiraled down into the dark. It was red, she was sure of it. She had been blinded by her own madness.

She plunged beneath the surface, hands digging into the water, legs kicking wildly as she tried to catch up with the rapidly sinking body. Her fingertips grazed soft flesh. Kris took the girl's face in her hands and turned it up toward her.

A barrage of images slammed into Kris's mind like a blast of frigid, winter air. Her brain seized in their icy grip. Kris cried out in pain as the memories took hold, her scream muffled by the water around her, precious air slipping from her mouth and bubbling up toward the surface above. She clenched her eyes shut, but there was nothing she could do. She was held in this strange, brutal power, her every sense under its control.

She felt the knowledge pass over her like the sudden chill of a shadow.

The loneliness of Sarah Bell, bullied by a boy at school for no other reason than the fact that he was weak and she was strong. And so he tore that strength down, day by day, until Sarah believed the things he said. That she was ugly. That she was stupid. That his own unhappiness was somehow because of her simply existing. She cried at night, alone in her bedroom, beneath a field of purple stars cast across her ceiling from the shell of a plastic turtle, until the moment she heard the song. She followed it to a friend who promised to take her sadness away. Even as she dug at the dry earth with her bloody fingers, the flesh peeling away to expose the tips of white bone, Sarah did so because her friend promised it was part of the game, and winning the game meant finding peace.

Kris felt the girl lie down in the cool earth, and the darkness enveloped her as she—

Huddled into the hollow of the oak tree, waiting to be found. Ruby had felt safe in that tree. It was a wishing tree, her friend told her, and if she thought long and hard enough about where she wanted to go, she could leave this world behind. She would no longer feel the fear slip like a splinter beneath her skin every time Daddy began to yell in his slurred, howling voice from the living room. Sometimes he shoved her against the wall or held her facedown to the floor so hard that she thought her head would smoosh like one of the squishy toys Mommy bought her in the toy aisle at Safeway. But he never hit her. He said he would never hit her, because then people in this town would talk, and he didn't need those sons of bitches spreading rumors behind his back. Ruby had often dreamed of running away, and then she heard the song, and she knew it was time. Her friend made her laugh. Her friend showed her the magical tree where she could wish away her fear. But if she left, the spell would be broken. So she stayed, even when she got thirsty, even when her stomach ached for food. She stayed and wished—

That someone could know the sadness she felt. Megan Adamson knew there was no reason for it. Her parents and teachers had told her as much. She had a good life. Her grandparents even said she was "spoiled" and "ungrateful." But no matter how much she tried to ignore the sadness, it was always there, like a black cloud hanging low in a blue sky. It seemed to hover over her and no one else. But when she played with Violet, the cloud went away. She felt the warmth of the sunshine. She never, ever once wanted to cry, even when she stood at the edge of the canyon, above the jagged rocks of the chasm known as Blanton's Pass. Megan felt a lightness within her, like she could float up into the air. Her friend had given her that. She could trust her friend, because her friend believed her. So when her friend said "Jump," Megan jumped—

And Kris was falling through the open air, plunging down toward the rocks that jutted up out of the ground like teeth. But she wanted to be there, falling free, she wanted—

To be with her good ol' dog Speck again, because Speck loved her more than anything in the world. Poppy heard her parents fighting, even though they thought they were being quiet enough to keep from waking her. It helped to ride Cap in the field beside her parents' garage, but Poppy knew that the garage place was part of the problem. Buying it had been a mistake. There was not enough work in Pacington, which meant there was not enough money to pay the bills. So Mommy and Daddy argued and said nasty things that they wished they could take back. Poppy knew she was part of the problem. The food she ate and the clothes she wore and the supplies she needed for school each year, these things "cost money," her parents said. And there was never enough money. But Violet made Poppy feel just as happy as Speck had. Violet never got angry, just like her good old dog. Violet even said there was a game they could play that would fix things with Mommy and Daddy, because Poppy would no longer be a burden. They would never have to buy food or clothes or school supplies for her again. She could even see Speck, if she promised not to break the rules. But Poppy was sneaky. She found the best hiding place of all, where no one would ever look—

In the bedroom where Melody was locked away, scratching at the walls with fingers long scabbed over, hearing the song that promised to take her pain away, to silence the whispers of the folks in town who called her family "mud bums" and "lake trash." The words made her hate herself because she *believed* them. If only she could get to her friend . . . they could play, forever and ever, and the world that wanted to crush Melody like a moth would fade away . . .

Kris had a vague sense of cool water around her and of the child's face clutched in her hands, but she was paralyzed. She floated, motionless, as the memories unfolded faster, overpowering her senses with a profound intensity. She felt a terrible energy flowing into her as she lived Sadie's grief through her daughter's eyes—the pain of losing her father, the fear that something could happen to her mother and she would be alone in the world, the insidious realization that her parents were not perfect people and that fate was neither nurturing nor cruel but *random*.

Kris's body spasmed as her own grief returned to her, held by Violet for so many years. It had been seeping back into Kris since the day she returned to the lake house.

And then she was no longer herself. She was a different little girl, one who had known only darkness until she had heard a voice calling to her from above. She had pulled herself up through frigid waters, toward the shimmering promise of light, until she broke the surface. She was staring up at the freckled face of a ten-year-old girl, her cheeks streaked with tears. She took a breath and an intense bitterness assaulted her tongue. At the same time, the girl in the boat smiled, as if a bit of her weight had been lifted.

Kris watched through Violet's eyes as they ran through the woods together, laughing and singing. She peered through the oval window on the second floor with dawning horror as Krissy rode away in the back of her father's car. She knew the emptiness of being alone in the lake house as she waited for Krissy to return, and the strange, untethered sensation as time became meaningless. She tasted the flood of bitterness in her mouth as she woke after days or weeks or years. She knew Violet's excitement as she sang the song that would bring Krissy to her, the confusion as she realized the girl with whom she was playing was a stranger, the fury of realizing she had been abandoned, the perverse joy as she began to crave the taste of that bitterness.

All of it belonged to Kris.

The temperature of the water dropped suddenly as she sank deeper. It's shocking coldness snapped Kris out of her trance. She looked to the upturned face still clasped in her hands.

Her fear had mislead her. In that last burst of lightning, the dark hair had captured a glint of red that did not exist. This was not Sadie.

Violet's wide, dead eyes stared back.

There was a sharp tug as the rowboat suddenly dropped faster, and Violet was yanked violently out of Kris's grasp. The memories also released their hold. Kris blinked as if waking from a dream. She was still underwater. Her lungs ached as they cried out for air. But Kris remained for one last moment, long enough to see Violet sinking down, her black hair billowing around her pale face, dark eyes wide and staring, arms reaching up as if to embrace her long-lost friend.

Then the darkness of the lake swallowed her, and Violet was gone.

Kris broke the surface and sucked in a desperate breath. She bobbed in the water, gasping until her pulse began to steady and the pain in her lungs subsided.

The sounds of the lake faded in around her. The drone of the bullfrogs. The chirp of crickets. The rustling of leaves as a breeze blew through the dark forest along the shore.

Kris was treading water, glancing around, trying to get her bearings in the thick, white fog. The wall of mist momentarily broke apart, and Kris realized that she was staring down into the mouth of their own cove. Her lake house was somewhere in the blackness at the far end. Across from this, a light flickered like a candle. A shape moved in front of the light. Kris squinted and could barely make out the shape of a person staring back at her.

She saw, Kris thought. *Vicky saw.*

The mist rolled back into itself, obscuring her view.

From somewhere on the opposite side of the lake, a voice called out, "Mommy!"

Kris splashed frantically around, trying to locate the direction of the sound.

"Sadie!"

"Mommy!"

The mist was too thick. She would never find her.

Kris began to swim, kicking madly against the weight of her wet shoes as she propelled herself across the lake.

"Mommy!" Sadie called again. She was closer.

Her arms ached, but Kris gripped the water and pulled harder. The muscles in her legs burned, but she kicked faster.

She was going the right way. She knew it. She had to believe—

Her fingertips collided painfully with the side of a wooden structure. Her hand found an edge and she pulled herself up onto what felt like sandpaper covered in slick green moss.

Shingles.

The roof! She was on the roof of the house. She flopped farther onto it, the rough shingles scraping across her bare stomach as her shirt rode up. She scrambled to her knees and felt the grit take off a layer of skin.

Little hands grabbed her. A child's face was pressed against hers.

"Mommy!" Sadie cried. "I'm sorry! I'm sorry, Mommy!"

"Oh God, baby."

Kris pulled her daughter so tight, she feared she would squeeze the breath from her. But Sadie did not struggle. She held her mother twice as tight.

CHAPTER FORTY-FIVE

KRIS HELPED HER daughter to shore, their arms around each other's waists. Only when their feet were back on the slick rocks did they let go of each other. Kris held Sadie's hand to make sure she did not fall as they made their way up the slope to the meadow of wildflowers. Their wet clothes hung heavily on their bodies. Lake water dripped from their fingertips and fell to the parched ground.

Kris turned and looked out at the swirling white cloud that was Lost Lake. It seemed smaller, as if what she had seen before was nothing but the exaggeration of a memory. The storm clouds had blown off to the southeast, headed toward Cherryvale and then Blantonville. The heat lighting gave a few weak pops. Soon it would burn out.

"Where is she?"

Sadie was standing beside a cluster of sunflowers, their yellow-and-brown heads bobbing on long green stems. Her clothes were soaked through, but her hair was already drying in the warm night air. She blinked as if fighting the confusion of being startled awake from a deep sleep.

"Gone," Kris told her.

Sadie nodded, but her brow furrowed, eyes searching the open space before her as if she had forgotten something important.

They walked hand in hand as Kris guided Sadie along the ridge to where the forest collided once more with the lakeshore. They moved through the trees, blazing their own trail. She could not stand the thought of taking the old route through the oak grove and past the sandstone chasm. She never wanted to walk that path again.

For twenty minutes, they trudged through thick bushes and low branches, always keeping the water within view at their side. When they finally broke through, they found themselves down on the mud and rock of their cove. The dock was up ahead, stretching out over the star-speckled water. Sadie glanced over at it. If she wondered where the rowboat was, she did not bother to ask.

They were halfway up the stone steps set into the slope leading to the lake house when Kris came to a sudden stop.

Sadie looked up at her, confused. "What's wrong?"

"Nothing," Kris assured her. "I just . . ."

She had no way of finishing the thought. Sadie had already been through enough. This was not her burden to carry.

Kris crouched down so she could look Sadie straight in the eyes. "Are you okay?"

Sadie nodded as if her head had become too heavy for her neck.

"Okay. Well, I need you to do me a favor." From her pocket, Kris pulled out her car keys. She hoped the key fob would still work after being submerged in the lake. She folded the keys into Sadie's hand.

"I want you to go around to the front of the house, get in the Jeep, and wait for me. Can you do that?"

"Why?" Sadie's voice quavered.

Kris gave her arm a light squeeze. "There's something I need to do."

"But—"

"Sadie, please." Kris heard the frustration in her voice, and she paused, letting it pass. Sadie had every reason to be frightened. Kris could not blame her for that. She started again, being sure to keep her tone soft and even. "I know you're scared. We need to talk about . . . well, everything. I can't promise that I can explain it all. But right now, I need to do something and I can't have you with me. It won't take long. I'll be around soon. Just wait in the car for me."

Sadie took a breath and gave her mother a confident nod.

She's trying to be brave, Kris thought.

She gave the hand holding the keys a soft pat. "Go on. Honk the horn twice when you get there."

Sadie forced her tired legs up the rest of the steps. Kris followed. She reached the top of the slope just in time to see Sadie disappearing around the side of the house, toward the front yard. There was a long moment of silence, then a quick double-tap of the car horn.

Kris sighed and turned to face the lake house.

Within her mind were Violet's memories of this world. That had been her final gift to Kris. Violet had held her grief for over three decades. It was time for Kris to own it once more.

But reclaiming her grief had come at a price. She could still feel the pain and sorrow of those lost girls, Hitch's angels, the innocent children who had heard the siren song of a lonely soul calling to them from the lakeside. They had all been found. All but one.

Poppy had chosen the best hiding spot of all. A place no one would think to look.

Kris thought back to the game she and Violet had played—Ghost in the Graveyard. The sneakiest trick any ghost could pull was to hide at Home Base, the one place where the searchers felt safe. If the ghost were found there, the others would have nowhere to run.

Kris had forgotten all about this trick, but there were no more secrets, not even from herself.

One last memory played out before her eyes, the night becoming a bright summer afternoon as a red-haired girl raced out of the forest, laughing and squealing. Her friend was close behind, a girl around the same age with straight black hair and fair skin. She wore a purple dress with knee-high socks and white sneakers. Violet chased Krissy toward the lake house, but she would never catch her in time. Krissy was already leaping up the stairs to Home Base.

The memory folded before her, and night fell once more.

Crossing through the tallgrass, Kris stepped up to the back of the deck and wrapped her fingers through the holes of wooden latticework that skirted its lower half. For once, the rotted wood and rusty nails worked to her advantage. She gave the lattice a hard tug, and a square section pulled free.

She crouched down and peered into the gloom beneath the deck.

A few thin lines of moonlight filtered in through the skirting, but it was too dark to make out anything in detail. This was not a job she wanted to do by grasping blindly with her hands. She needed a flashlight.

Hurrying up the back steps, Kris rushed into the house and down the hall. The cell phone was right where she had left it, on the floor of Sadie's bedroom. She snatched it up, and the screen illuminated. In the corner, the battery symbol had turned red. An alert on the screen warned her that there was only twenty percent left. But it was enough to do what she needed to do and, if she were right, to make the one necessary call after.

Going back down the deck steps felt like willfully walking into a nightmare. Her mind screamed for her to join Sadie in the car and let someone else deal with this. But Kris knew it had to be her. It was her responsibility.

She tapped the Flashlight button on the phone, and a brilliant LED beam exploded from its front corner. Holding the phone out in front of her, Kris crouched down and crawled under the deck.

The flashlight beam cut across countless spiderwebs in her path. Carefully, she maneuvered around them. One snagged her ear, and she felt a strand of sticky silk drift down across her hair. She swiped at it until she was sure the web—and any spider with it—was gone.

Sitting on her knees, her back hunched over so that the top of her head wouldn't graze the planks above her, Kris slowly swept the beam through the darkness like a searchlight. Her heart pounded with each passing second.

Please let me be wrong.

The light fell upon a heap leaning against the foundation of the house, and Kris knew she had been right.

She crawled a few feet deeper under the deck, then stopped. This was as close as she wanted to get. She could smell the faint odor of decay, that sickening smell that had hit her when she first opened the front door. She had known it couldn't have only been the dead bird. Her gut had told her there had to be more.

She held the phone out as far as her arm would reach. Shadows shifted across the heap as the harsh light brought out details previously—mercifully—hidden. Poppy was a bundle of bones held together with the last vestiges of ligaments. Dried, weathered flesh clung to her arms and legs, but the rest had been stripped away by insects and rodents. Several large beetles crawled across her limbs and back, their pale yellow thoraxes dotted with an irregular black smudge. Thankfully, her head was lowered so that all Kris could see were the last few strands of brown hair clinging to what was left of her scalp. Her face was tucked down into her arms as if she had become tired of waiting and decided to take a nap. But she never would have left her hiding place. She had to remain here until she was found. Those were the rules.

Kris's phone buzzed in her hand. She turned it over to check the screen, and the corpse of Poppy Azuara was reclaimed by the darkness.

A new alert was waiting for her, letting her know that the battery was at ten percent.

She pressed the Flashlight button with her thumb, and the LED beam clicked off. But she did not move.

Kris crouched in the dry earth below the deck and wept.

The game was over.

EPILOGUE

INTO THE LIGHT OF THE DARK BLACK NIGHT

STROBING LIGHTS PAINTED the lake house with splashes of red and blue. There were four vehicles parked in the front yard, not including the Jeep: two Dodge Chargers from the Greenwood County Sheriff's Office, a Kansas Highway Patrol Police Interceptor, and a windowless white van from the Medical Examiner's Office in Eureka. All had their light bars flashing, but all were empty. Their owners were around back where orange extension cords had been strung to power several twin-head work lights.

Through the Jeep's windshield, Kris could see the long shadows of the investigators stretching out into the darkness. A white glow hovered around the side of the house, illuminating a large pile of latticework that had been stripped from the back deck.

Ben Montgomery had been the only call she made and the first person on the scene. She had quickly concocted a story about dropping her cell phone between a gap in the deck planks, even though no such gap existed. She told him that she had gone down to retrieve the phone. That's when she saw the body. She didn't say that it was Poppy. She didn't have to. There had been a shift in Ben's tone when he heard that it appeared to be the corpse of a young girl. He had simply told Kris to sit tight. He was on his way.

That had been over an hour ago. In that time, Sadie had only asked once why the police were coming. Kris told her that she had found something underneath their deck that had to do with a missing girl. Sadie had nodded but said nothing. She had shown a surprising lack of interest in the events of the past few hours. She apologized for swimming in the lake without telling her mother first, and then she had said nothing more about it.

Kris remembered everything though. The longer she sat with her thoughts, the more numb her body became. She kept seeing Violet's face, over and over, her eyes staring up as her tiny body drifted down into a lake many claimed was bottomless.

It was close to one in the morning when Ben came trudging up from the back of the house. He motioned for Kris to join him outside, away from Sadie. Kris turned to Sadie in the passenger seat. Their clothes were nearly dry, although they still held the scent of lake water. Sadie's eyes drooped. She could barely keep them open.

"Why don't you climb in the back seat and lie down? I'll wake you when we're ready to go." She helped Sadie climb between the seats and stretch out on the second row, then she opened the glove compartment and took out the iPad. She powered it up and saw that it had just enough battery left to entertain Sadie until she fell asleep. She handed it to Sadie. The glow of the device lit her exhausted face with a soft white light as Kris started the engine, rolled up the windows, and cranked the air conditioning. She stepped out into the thick weeds.

Ben was waiting for her at the side of the front porch. His brown hair was slick with sweat. He wore blue rubber gloves, which he picked at like dead skin. The knees of his tan pants were covered in dirt. She walked over to him.

For a long moment, neither spoke. Insects droned from their hiding places in the overgrown yard. Finally, Ben nodded as if answering a question and said, "It's her. She still had some scraps of clothing on her that matched what she was wearing when she . . ."

Kris wanted to tell him what she knew, that Poppy had simply sat down against the house and remained there until dehydration or the heat did her in. But even if her foggy brain had been able to put these facts into coherent thoughts, she could not be sure that Ben would believe them.

"What about Camilla?" Kris managed to ask.

Ben gave his beard a hard tug. "Haven't called her or Jesse yet. Figured they could sleep for a bit longer."

Kris saw that his eyes were wet with the threat of tears.

From around the back of the house came the sound of stern voices barking orders.

Kris ran a hand over the back of her neck and felt the grit of sweat and dirt beneath her hair. She opened her mouth to speak, then paused, realizing that nothing she could say would make things better.

Ben's chest heaved suddenly, and Kris was shocked to see tears slipping down his cheeks. They disappeared into the thicket of his beard. "She looked like she was taking a nap down there. Just pulled her knees up to her chest and laid her head down and took a nap until someone came looking for her." He swiped at the tears, his sadness overtaken by a seething anger he had carried with him long before this night. "She was there for over four years. Four years. Waiting for someone to find her."

Kris did not mind waking Darryl Hargrove in the middle of the night. He had said to call him for "anything," and so she did, requesting a different house, just as so many other renters of River's End had done before her.

She met him one block north of Center Street, on Maple. The house was a single-story ranch, built in the 1960s but still in relatively good shape by Pacington standards. The owners had moved to Overland Park to be closer to their son, who was attending the University of Kansas, but the house had been on the market for over a year. There was not much threat of the place selling before Kris and Sadie left town.

Kris had asked Ben if someone could gather up their clothes and toiletries from the lake house and drop them off at the new place, and he volunteered to do the job himself. She hated to add one more thing to his plate, but she couldn't stomach the thought of entering that house at night. She thought of the Prozac capsules she had left scattered on the bathroom floor and what scenarios might run through Ben's mind when he saw them, but in the end, she decided she just didn't care.

As it turned out, Ben wasn't the one to drop off their things anyway. A deputy whose name tag read J. Williams rapped on the front door at a quarter past three in the morning. Kris felt the muscles in her neck tighten as she stared at the uniformed officer on the doorstep. The last time she had spoken to the police at such an ungodly hour, they had called to tell her that her husband was dead. She took a breath and let the moment pass, then thanked Deputy Williams as he carried in their duffel bags.

The new house had three bedrooms, but Kris and Sadie chose to sleep on the pullout couch in the living room. Kris turned on the TV as soon as they crawled into bed. She found the first mindless program she could among the 800-plus channels: a marathon of *Diners, Drive-Ins and Dives* on the Food Network. They fell asleep just as Guy Fieri was explaining the history of Vietnamese cuisine while cheeseburger banh mi dribbled down his bleached goatee. Kris took one last look at her daughter, snuggled up to the crooked-eyed frog she called Bounce, and then closed her eyes. When they woke, it was almost noon, and a sous chef from Fort Wayne, Indiana, had just found out he had been Chopped.

For the next two days, the TV stayed on nonstop. All rules went out the window as Kris let Sadie watch as many shows as she wanted. They curled up on the thin mattress, avoiding the support bar that bit through at the center, and zoned out to everything from *House Hunters* to *Bubble Guppies*. Sadie drifted in and out of sleep, sometimes using the iPad, freed from the car's glove compartment, to play Angry Birds or Crossy Road. They ate from the two restaurants in town that delivered: Mama Mia's Pizza and a Chinese restaurant that may as well have been called Overcooked Noodles and Dry Rice. There was something liberating in their self-imposed confinement. It was the sensation of being in control of their own destiny. There were no chores to drag them out of bed, no cleaning, no home-improvement projects—only this temporary home with its dated shag carpet and cheap furniture that had been easily assembled with a single Allen wrench. There were no fingers under their skulls or whispers in their ears to force them down a predetermined path.

Sadie was back to communicating mostly through nods and shrugs, just as she had when they first left Colorado. But this behavior no longer concerned Kris. She would give her daughter the time she needed to process her emotions. Sadie's silence had become a comfort rather than a concern.

But as Sadie became more and more placid, Kris found her mind working to make sense of the events that had occurred. She had never truly considered herself a religious person. She had to admit that she had tried on numerous occasions to sense the presence of her dead parents, but she also knew that these had been moments of weakness, seeking an otherworldly connection to dull the loss.

Violet had been something entirely different. She was born not from a biblical prophecy but from a dark power deep within the earth. There was a fissure below Lost Lake that bled into a world no human had thought to name. Kris could not be sure if it was good or bad or indifferent. But she knew that it existed. There was no doubt in her mind. And its existence kept her up at night, staring at the popcorn ceiling while Sadie lay beside her, snuggled into a musty pillow. She thought about what was down there, shifting, searching once more for a way into the light.

Three days later, Poppy Azuara was committed to the ground. So many people crammed into the tiny chapel at Hope Church that two old stereo speakers were run out into the yard so that the overflow crowd could hear the services.

Camilla and Jesse saved two spaces in the third pew for Kris and Sadie, while they took their designated places in the front row. There were no words exchanged before the funeral began, only a moment where Camilla's eyes met Kris's and the two mothers nodded as if to say, *This is the pact we made, the beautiful, terrible responsibility of bringing a life into the world.*

The weather had thankfully decided to cooperate that day. A cool breeze blew in over the lake, twisting its way through the woods along the highway and through the church grounds. A few people fanned themselves with the programs they had been handed when they entered. On the cover was a color photo of Poppy in the field beside the Auto Barn. Cap rested his head against her shoulder. In her lap was a large white bird dog with brown and black spots. The dog was clearly too big for the little girl to hold, but she wouldn't have had it any other way. She hugged him around his neck and peered up over his back, a huge smile on her face. She was missing both lateral incisors, and her top front teeth tucked over her bottom lip in a way that made her look like a grinning bunny.

The same photo had been blown up and displayed on an easel at the front of the chapel. Numerous potted flowers and plants left little room for movement on the chancel. Kris spotted a cluster of purple violets and her stomach turned.

Pastor Charles Murphy (simply "Pastor Charles" to the people of Pacington) stepped up to the pulpit and cleared his throat. A heavy silence fell over the room. Kris glanced around and, for the first time since entering the chapel, saw just how many faces had become familiar to her in this town. There was Hitch in a pinstripe suit and black tie, his eyewear toned down to a chunky black frame. There was Dr. Baker, elegant as always in an understated black dress. Her perfect posture radiated a soothing calm, but her eyes were puffy and bloodshot from crying. There was Doris, her makeup even heavier than usual, wearing a lace flower dress, a gaudy turtle broach clipped to her breast. There was Ricky Redfern with his silver hair pulled back into a ponytail, his best denim shirt tucked into a stiff pair of Wranglers. There was Darryl Hargrove, already dabbing at his sweaty forehead with a mono-grammed handkerchief. She even spotted the beady-eyed girl from the Dairy Godmother sitting with the Safeway checkout boy. Their hands were barely clasped in a strange loose hold, as if they were mimicking something they had seen in movies.

At the back of the sanctuary, Ben stood by the open chapel doors, dressed in his uniform. His beard was recently trimmed and his hair was parted neatly on one side. He gave Kris a sad smile. She recalled something he had said to her on the night she found Poppy, that recovering her body was the best outcome he had ever hoped for. He knew in his gut that she would never be found alive. "This is the best of the worst," he had said.

The best of the worst.

Kris glanced over the tear-streaked faces in the crowd. The town had come together to say good-bye to their lost girl. They would cry their tears and hold each other close and feel themselves bound by a much-needed sense of closure. But burying Poppy Azuara would not bring their small town back to life. It would go on dying, forgotten in a river basin just a little too far off the main highway. There would be more reasons in the future for them to come together as a community, but it would only serve to distract them from the fact that they were living a tragedy.

And Ben Montgomery would be there to stand with them.

A breath thumped the microphone as Pastor Charles began to speak. "On behalf of the Azuara family, I want to thank you all for coming today as we pay our last respects to our beloved Poppy."

A chorus of sniffles and soft moans rose up from the congregation.

"She was an angel in life, so it is no surprise that God our Lord has called her back to be an angel at his side in heaven."

Not by God, she thought.

Soon Pastor Charles was deep in an anecdote about fishing for trout at Roscoe Lake, followed by a clunky transition into the Bible verse that formed the core of his sermon:

"Revelation. Chapter 21. Verse 4." He paused dramatically, glancing down at the open Bible before him, and then in a booming voice, he read: "And God shall wipe away all tears from their eyes; and there shall be no more death, neither sorrow, nor crying, neither shall there be any more pain: for the former things are passed away. And he that sat upon the throne said, Behold, I make all things new. And he said unto me, Write: for these words are true and faithful. And he said unto me, It is done. I am Alpha and Omega, the beginning and the end. I will give unto him that is athirst of the fountain of the water of life freely. He that overcometh shall inherit all things; and I will be his God, and he shall be my son."

Kris knew the rest of this story, the part that Pastor Charles conveniently left out. Seven angels had broken seven seals, and when they sounded their trumpets, death and destruction rained down on earth. Kris couldn't help but make the connection: years ago a seal had been broken in Pacington. Something had rushed up from the depths. And in all that time, during all the pain and suffering, heaven was silent.

Up a short path from Hope Church was Fairview Cemetery. From the state of the oldest headstones, their edges chipped and crumbling, this had been the main resting place for the town's residents since its founding. A surprising amount of land was tucked back in a stretch of lowlands not visible from the road. Gravel paths cut seemingly at random through sections of graves.

Kris held Sadie's hand as they followed the progression lead by Jesse, Ben, and four more pallbearers carrying a much-too-small coffin.

"We don't have to stay for this," Kris told Sadie.

She shrugged and murmured, "I want to." Then, as if she'd completely forgotten why they were there in the first place, she asked, "What was her name again?"

"Poppy."

"Was she a little kid?"

"Yes."

"Like me?"

Kris took a sharp breath. "Yes," she admitted.

"Can kids die?" She asked the question not out of concern but simple curiosity.

"Everybody can die," Kris said.

The group reached a small patch of grass near the swaying arms of a willow tree. Green fabric had been laid down to cover the bare dirt of the recently dug grave. Straps of poly webbing were stretched across the hole to support the casket until it was time to lower it down.

Kris watched as Jesse, Ben, and the pallbearers carefully set Poppy's coffin down on the straps. Jesse stepped back beside Camilla. Their faces were completely slack, as if they had cried all they could in the past three days. Behind them, an elderly man in a well-worn suit reached up and put a hand on Jesse's shoulder. He looked familiar to Kris, and it took a moment of intense searching to remember where she had seen him. It was Albert Bell, the man who made it his duty to keep downtown free of weeds. Sarah Bell's grandfather. Kris glanced over the faces of the others gathered around Albert and a terrible understanding fell over her.

It's the families. Of the other lost girls. Sarah and Ruby and Megan. They're here to welcome Jesse and Camilla to the club.

She hated herself for the crudeness of the thought, but that's what it was: a club none of them had ever wished to join.

Sadie tightened her grip on Kris's hand. Kris looked down at her daughter, green eyes peering out of her sweet freckled face, and she was suddenly struck by an intense sense of guilt. Her daughter was alive.

She waited for the other voices in her mind to speak up, for the shadow voice to mock her—to say *all of this, this is your fault*—and the timid voice to judge her—*maybe if you hadn't abandoned her, they would still be alive*—but they held their tongues.

The rest of the ceremony was a blur. Soon the pallbearers were lowering the casket down into the ground. Hitch stepped forward with a small stack of chapter books, which he handed to Camilla. If she had thought she had shed every last tear, she was wrong. At the sight of the books, Camilla began to sob. They must have been some of Poppy's favorites, Kris assumed, perhaps the books the little girl had read when her parents took her to the Book Nook.

If Poppy had lived, she would have been around fourteen years old. Just starting high school. Experiencing the astounding awkwardness of first crushes, the pain of first heartbreak, the strength that came as wounds healed and turned to scars. Kris wondered: What if someone else had been on the lake in Kris's place? Could the power that rose from the depths have become an angel instead of a demon?

Violet wasn't a demon, Kris thought. *Not at first. She was a child. This world turned her into something else.*

Kris did not see Jesse until he was almost past them. He seemed to spot Sadie out of the corner of his eye and stopped suddenly, kneeling down to speak to her in a hushed tone. For the first time, Kris realized that there was something clutched in his hand: a plush Beanie Boo dog with large blue eyes and brown spots across its back.

"This was my daughter's," he told Sadie. He turned the animal over in his hand, then held it out for Sadie to take. "Can you love him as much as she did?" he asked.

Sadie took the dog and clutched it to her chest.

"I'll try," she said.

That's all you can do, Kris thought as she watched Jesse walk away.

Kris had just slammed the back hatch shut and was coming around to the driver's side when she saw Dr. Baker. The doctor stood, tall and strong, at the corner of Maple and Center, waiting for one of the few streetlights to change despite the lack of traffic. She met Kris's gaze.

"Hi there," Kris called out as she forced a smile.

Dr. Baker walked the half block down to where Kris's car was parked in the new house's short driveway. She pursed her lips, as if unsure what to say. Finally she offered an innocuous, "Leaving town?"

Kris gave a sharp laugh.

Is there any other option?

"Yeah," she said. "Heading back to Colorado."

Dr. Baker nodded, considering this. "I really wish we could have talked more while you were here, but . . ." Her words trailed off. There was no way to finish that sentence.

"Maybe next time," Kris said.

A wry smile spread across Dr. Baker's face. "You're never coming back, are you?"

Kris shook her head. "Not a chance."

Dr. Baker leaned over and looked through the windshield at Sadie in the passenger seat. She gave an exaggerated wave, and Sadie waved back.

"Well," Dr. Baker said, but she made no effort to leave.

"What?" Kris asked. She knew there was nothing Dr. Baker could say that would shock her. Not anymore.

Dr. Baker sighed. "The other night, the night that . . ."

Kris nodded, understanding.

"You left me a message," Dr. Baker continued. "You were upset."

"I was," Kris said.

"You needed to talk."

"I did."

"But something distracted you. You didn't finish the message. But it kept recording." She clenched and released her fists. She did not want to admit what she was about to say. "I heard it, Kris. Someone singing. Two girls singing. Children. There in the house with you."

Kris kept her gaze steady, unwavering. She knew what she believed. She needed to hear it from the doctor.

"I need you to tell me who that was," Dr. Baker said finally.

In the Jeep, Sadie impatiently shifted in her seat.

"It was Violet," Kris said suddenly.

Dr. Baker's brow furrowed and she took a step back as if attempting to physically reject the statement.

"You'll never get over your loss if you don't accept the reality of what happened," she told Kris.

Kris smiled, but there was no humor in it.

"Thank you," she said. "For everything you do."

On their way out of town, Kris stopped by the lake house. They drove in silence under a blazing sun in a cloudless blue sky. The heat was back, but not quite as bad as in days past. Kris rolled the window down and let the lake air whip through their hair and down the backs of their shirts.

The house was neither as rundown nor as romanticized as Kris remembered. It simply *was*. With its crooked shingles, flaking paint, and a yard overrun by native plants, it was downright quaint. Even the headless stone bird perched atop the birdbath seemed to add character to the place.

Kris told Sadie that it was okay if she wanted to stay in the car and play on the iPad, but Sadie was out of the Jeep before Kris could reach for the door handle.

"Can I play on the swings?" Sadie asked.

A pang of fear hit Kris in the chest. She turned and looked at Sadie's wide, hopeful eyes.

"Sure," she said. "Just stay on the swings. Promise?"

"Promise," Sadie replied.

Kris waited until Sadie had disappeared around the side of the house, and then she trudged up the brick path to the front porch. She slipped the key into the lock and opened the door.

There was no foul odor of rot and decay, only the musty scent of a house in need of airing. She stepped through the narrow foyer and into the kitchen. Despite a layer of fresh dust, the floors gleamed in the bright sunlight.

Kris's footsteps echoed as she walked through the great room. She paused at the far windows to check on Sadie. The girl was where she had promised to be, rising higher and higher on the swing, her legs pumping as if she meant to reach the sky.

In the hallway, Kris paused and glanced in the bathroom. The pills were no longer on the floor. Someone, probably Ben, had picked up each one and disposed of them. She smiled. He was one of the good ones.

The door to the master bedroom was still ajar, and Kris pushed it the rest of the way open. She peered in at the unmade bed and could see the edge of a wooden frame peeking out from underneath it. She entered the room, crouched down beside the bed, and slid the frame out into the light. At the center of the painting, the little girl stood at the end of the dock, one eye peering out through wind-blown hair. She no longer seemed to be looking past Kris but straight at her.

Kris paused, considered taking the picture with her, then shoved it back into the shadows under the bed. It could stay there forever, where no one would see it again. She had no intention of ever returning to the lake house, nor did she plan on letting Hargrove try to rent it out. The massive summer crowds drawn to the cool waters of Lost Lake were a thing of the past. The town was dying. The house could die with it.

Let it rot, she thought, and she imagined she could smell sawdust and liquor on the air.

The walk up the stairs was more difficult than she had expected. Each step felt heavier than the last. When she reached the second-floor landing, she paused to catch her breath as if she had just hiked to the summit of a mountain. She stared across the room at the small square door in the wall. Its door was open just a crack.

Kris moved through the gallery of ghosts covered in sheets on either side. She bent down beside the small door and took hold of its handle. She paused. What did she expect to happen when she opened it? To feel a rush of power and know that Violet was still there? To sense the touch of her mother's hand on her shoulder? To hear the howls of those who had gone missing because of the thing she wished into existence?

She opened the door and heard nothing.

Silence.

She felt nothing.

It was the best feeling in ages.

The creak of chains greeted Kris as she stepped out onto the back deck. Sadie was still on the swings, although she had slowed to a leisurely rhythm that paired well with their view of the lake. The second swing—the empty swing—jostled slightly, but its movement was caused only by the tug of the chain on the swing set's crooked frame.

"Just a couple more minutes," Kris called to her.

"Okay," Sadie said. She pumped her legs harder in an effort to milk every last second.

Kris looked out at the sparkling waters of Lost Lake. She had to admit, it was beautiful. She knew that at either end, the brownish-green current of the Verdigris River collided with this unintended body of water, but here, nestled against the red hills, the water was as clear as a diamond. She could not explain it. Perhaps being trapped below the earth for eons had filtered out its imperfections. Perhaps it was the fact that, at its center, the floor of the lake was mostly stone. Or perhaps it was because the water came from another place, a crack in the world. Perhaps its coldness was the price they paid for its clarity.

Sudden movement pulled Kris out of her thoughts.

There was someone across the cove, between the swaying vines of two weeping willow trees. A dark-haired woman standing on the deck behind a rustic cabin. At her side was a younger woman in her early twenties. Their arms were around each other as they took in the effortless glory of the lake.

The dark-haired woman looked up, and even from that great distance, Kris could see her lips stretch into a smile.

She waved. And Kris waved back, good-bye.

They drove away from River's End just as they had arrived, with the lake sparkling through the trees at their side and puffs of cottonwood blooms drifting through the air. Sadie sat in her booster behind the passenger seat, Bounce on her lap, his head bobbing gently on his limp neck.

As they reached the highway out of town, Kris recognized an approaching car and flashed her lights, signaling for it to pull over.

Deputy Montgomery obliged, turning his cruiser onto the shoulder so that Kris could idle up next to the driver's-side window.

"I'm usually the one pulling people over," he said, smirking. Then he asked, "You off?"

Kris nodded. "Yeah. Just stopped by the lake house to . . ."

"Yeah," he said, completing a thought that required no explanation.

"Thanks," Kris told him. "For everything."

Ben shrugged. It was all part of his job, even the things he could not quite explain.

"You know," she said, "with that beard, you'd do pretty well in Colorado."

Ben smiled. "Might have to head out that way some time. But my job's here."

Kris nodded, understanding. She eased off the brake, preparing to pull out onto the highway.

432   SCOTT THOMAS

"You're a good man, Charlie Brown," she told him. And then she was gone.

They passed through the red gypsum hills, and the town of Pacington fell away behind them. The rocky slopes on either side grew wider as the hills sloped down to meet the Kansas prairie.

She thought of home. She thought of the life that would be waiting for them there. She thought of the days to come. She wondered if she would ever love again. She cringed at the thought of online dating profiles. Life in Black Ridge would not be easy for Sadie. The kids would know her as the girl with the dead dad. But Kris was sure that Sadie could hold her own. They would face the ghosts of the past and their fears of the future together. They would know that any earthly challenge would pale in comparison to what they had been through.

From the back seat came the sound of a child giggling.

Kris glanced in the rearview mirror. "What's so funny?"

"Nothing," Sadie replied. She looked out the window, her face reflected in the glass, eyes checking to see if her mother was still watching.

The whir of the car's wheels was hypnotic. Kris reached out and punched the stereo's power button. The digital tuner began to roll through fields of static, searching for a station.

She checked the rearview mirror again, and saw that Sadie's left hand was resting between the seats, her palm up and open, as if she were waiting for another hand to take it.

On the stereo, a voice tried to break through the static, then was left behind as the tuner continued its quest. She glanced quickly over her shoulder. Sadie's hands were clasped in her lap around Bounce. She was leaning forward, a smile playing at her lips as she peered through the windshield.

Stop, Kris thought. *It's over.*

Up ahead was the old railroad bridge they had passed under on their way into town. Vines crept over its rusted metal. Through the tangle of leaves, Kris spotted the graffiti that had caught Sadie's eye.

Kris had said they were names painted on the side of the bridge. She had been right, although only now did the names have meaning.

Ruby.

Megan.

Sarah.

Poppy.

The names of the lost.

In bright neon colors, someone had memorialized a small town's grief.

You're part of the club, too, she realized. It took her a moment to understand her own thought. True, she had not lost Sadie, but there was another little girl who went missing one summer, over thirty years ago. Little Krissy, who had loved her mother with all her heart. Little Krissy, who watched a ruthless disease devour the woman who had given her life. Little Krissy, who accidentally created a monster and paid the price with her childhood.

She was the first and last of the lost girls.

ACKNOWLEDGMENTS

WRITING A BOOK can be a very solitary experience. The long nights. The many hours living in your own head. The moments when you realize you've been speaking all the dialogue out loud. Even when you're not at the computer, your mind constantly returns to where you left off. In a way, the book is your imaginary friend. You hope that you bottle enough magic to transform it into a real thing, and that you don't lose your mind in the process. Of course, the truth is, I was never really alone in the process. I was fortunate to have the support and encouragement of many amazing people as I plunged into the cold waters of *Violet*. To them, I would like to express my profound thanks.

To Adam Gomolin at Inkshares for his superhuman ability to challenge me as a writer and remind me to come up for air every now and then. There isn't an editor in the business who is more committed or who works harder than Adam. He is a force of nature.

To Pam McElroy for her swift and masterful copyediting. As she did on *Kill Creek*, she took the book to the next level and made me look like I knew the difference between "gray" and "grey" and "farther" and "further."

To Avalon Radys and everyone at Inkshares for their hard work and dedication. This company is amazing. If it weren't for all of you, my ideas would never make it out of my head and onto bookshelves.

To Marjorie Deluca, J-F. Dubeau, Christopher Huang, Chase Pletts, Noah Broyles, Becky Lake, Erin Evans, John Grillz, Emma Mann-Meginniss, Sara Nivala, Phil Sciranka, and Elle Welch—the incredibly talented and insightful readers who volunteered their time to pore over every word, question every detail, and offer invaluable notes, all in the name of making this book as strong as possible. I owe you one.

To Lauren Harms for her breathtaking cover design. I mean seriously, close this book and check out that cover again. Isn't that freakin' beautiful? She killed it. I am so lucky that she shared her talents with us.

To my mom, my brothers, and my sisters-in-law for always cheering me on. Your support means the world to me.

To my dad, who read the things I wrote unprompted. Cancer destroyed him, but his life defined him. He set the bar for us all. We spend every day making sure we rise to those heights.

To Jed Elinoff, Jim Martin, Rick Williams, Molly Haldeman, Camilla Rubis, Anthony Hill, Danielle Calvert, and Brittany Assaly for being amazing writers and even better friends and for listening to me ramble in a sleep-deprived daze about all of the messed-up things dancing through my brain.

To all of the incredible people online who help spread the word about the books they love. It's been amazing to get to know many of you. Your posts keep the fires burning in the dead of night.

To my girls, Aubrey and Cleo, who continue to amaze and inspire me. I could write for a thousand years and never string together a sentence that comes close to their perfection. They also sometimes do creepy things, which helps when you're writing a book like this.

And finally to Kim—my love, my partner, my rock. I'm sure that being married to a writer is often like having a cranky ghost in the house, one who incessantly rattles keyboard keys and moans about deadlines. Yet somehow you are always able to lift me up, even when you are carrying more than your share of the weight. You are the hero of our story.

I would also like to tell the little girl who lived at the end of my street when I was a kid: You said his name was Charlie and that he was real. One day I thought I saw his shadow on the wall. I've always told myself that I imagined it. But now I wonder . . .

INKSHARES

INKSHARES is a reader-driven publisher and producer based in Oakland, California. Our books are selected not by a group of editors, but by readers worldwide.

While we've published books by established writers like *Big Fish* author Daniel Wallace and *Star Wars: Rogue One* scribe Gary Whitta, our aim remains surfacing and developing the new author voices of tomorrow.

Previously unknown Inkshares authors have received starred reviews and been featured in the *New York Times*. Their books are on the front tables of Barnes & Noble and hundreds of independents nationwide, and many have been licensed by publishers in other major markets. They are also being adapted by Oscar-winning screenwriters at the biggest studios and networks.

Interested in making your own story a reality? Visit Inkshares.com to start your own project or find other great books.